THE LAST PARTY

Clare Mackintosh is the multi-award winning author of five *Sunday Times* bestselling novels. Translated into forty languages, her books have sold more than two million copies worldwide, have been *New York Times* and international bestsellers and have spent a combined total of sixty-four weeks in the *Sunday Times* bestseller chart. Clare lives in North Wales with her husband and their three children.

For more information visit Clare's website www.claremackintosh. com or find her at www.facebook.com/ClareMackWrites or on Twitter @ClareMackint0sh

Clare Mackintosh

THE LAST PARTY

SPHERE

SPHERE

First published in Great Britain in 2022 by Sphere

1 3 5 7 9 10 8 6 4 2

A CIP catalogue record for this book is available from the British Library.

Hardback ISBN 978-0-7515-7710-5
Trade Paperback ISBN 978-0-7515-7711-2

Typeset in Sabon by Palimpsest Book Production Limited, Falkirk, Stirlingshire
Printed and bound in Great Britain by Clays Ltd, Elcograf S.p.A.

Papers used by Sphere are from well-managed forests
and other responsible sources.

Sphere
An imprint of
Little, Brown Book Group
Carmelite House
50 Victoria Embankment
London EC4Y 0DZ

An Hachette UK Company
www.hachette.co.uk

www.littlebrown.co.uk

For my book club crew – the best bunch of readers around.

And now the whole wide lake in deep repose
Is hush'd, and like a burnish'd mirror glows.

William Wordsworth

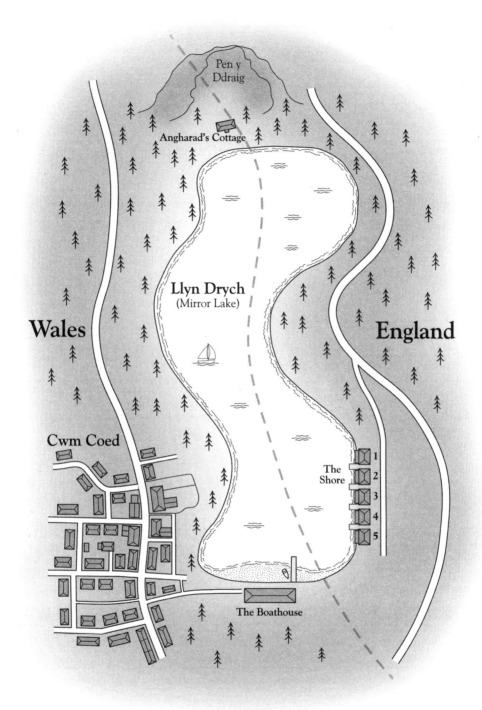

Pen y Ddraig

Angharad's Cottage

Llyn Drych
(Mirror Lake)

Wales

England

Cwm Coed

The Shore

1
2
3
4
5

The Boathouse

Cwm Coed village

Y Llew Coch public house
Glynis Lloyd's hardware shop
Elen, Ffion & Seren Morgan
Huw Ellis
Mia Williams
Ceri Jones

The Shore lakeside resort

1 Jonty & Blythe Charlton, Woody & Hester
2 Dee Huxley
3 Bobby & Ashleigh Stafford
4 Clemmie Northcote, Caleb
5 Rhys & Yasmin Lloyd, Tabby & Felicia

NEW YEAR'S DAY

No one in Cwm Coed can remember what year the swim began, but they know they wouldn't welcome the new year in any other way. They don't remember which year it was that Dafydd Lewis went in wearing nothing but a Santa hat, or when the rugby lads bombed off the jetty and drenched poor Mrs Williams.

But everyone will remember today's swim.

There's been snow on the peaks since before Christmas, and, even with the protection from the mountains, the temperature in the town hasn't climbed above seven degrees. The lake itself is even colder. Four degrees! people gasp, at once gleeful and incredulous. We must be mad!

As if rebelling against the clear skies, wisps of mist curl above the surface of the water, their reflection giving the disorientating impression that the sky's been tipped upside down. Above the mist, the air is vivid blue, an echo of last night's moon suspended above the forest.

From the very top of Pen y Ddraig mountain, Llyn Drych seems more river than lake. It's long and serpent-shaped, each bend a flick of the dragon's tail it's said to represent. 'Drych' means 'mirror', and, when the wind drops and the water lies still, the surface shimmers like silver. The reflection of the mountain stretches into the centre of the lake, so solid you feel you could step on to it, no hint of the black and fathomless depths beneath.

Along the path that winds its way up the south side of the mountain – from the dragon's back to its head – ramblers stoop to pick a pebble from the path. They straighten, feel the weight of it in their hands, then look around sheepishly, before hurling the stone towards the water. Legend has it that Llyn Drych's dragon rises up if its tail is hit – few ramblers can resist the myth.

Around the edge of the lake, pine trees stand sentry, their shoulders so close that, if one were felled, you could imagine them all toppling, one after another. The trees steal the view from the village of Cwm Coed, but they take the worst of the weather too, which feels like a fair exchange to the people who live there.

On the far side of the water – less than a mile from where the crowd is now gathering – a line of buildings squats in the foothills. The trees directly in front of them have been ripped from the ground, the wood used to clad the lodges and make the vast carved sign that stands at the end of the long private drive – each letter as tall as a man.

The Shore.

There are five of them, so far. Two-storey rectangular boxes, with timber-clad roofs and decks thrusting forward, extending out above the lake on stilts rising from the mist. Metal ladders glint in the winter sun, the pontoons bereft of the boats that tug at their ropes in summer.

Luxury lakeside lodges, *the glossy brochure calls them.*

Carafanau ffansi, *Ffion's mam says. Fancy caravans. Airs and graces.*

A bloody eyesore, most of the villagers agree. And at that price!

For a place you can't even live in all year round. Owners are not permitted to make The Shore their primary residence, says the website. As if North Wales needs any more weekenders.

Soon, there'll be another row behind this first. Another, behind that. A spa, a gym, shops, an outdoor swimming pool.

'God knows why they can't swim in the lake.' *Perched in the boot of her car, Ceri Jones pulls off her tracksuit bottoms, goose-fleshed thighs white against the dirty bumper.*

'Because it's bloody freezing, that's why.'

The laughter comes fast and high – fuelled by last night's New Year's Eve party, by too much wine and too little sleep, by cold which forces its way through towelling robes and lodges itself into bones.

'Good night, though.'

There are murmurs of agreement.

'Chwarae teg.' *Fair play. That lot at The Shore know how to throw a party. More importantly, they know to invite the locals. Curiosity wins over grudges, every time.*

Splinters of ice cluster in the shallow puddles on the lakeshore, cracked by toes freed from fur-lined boots.

'There are still ten minutes to go. You'll get frostbite.'

'Can't even feel it. I think I'm still pissed.'

'This better sort out my hangover – I've got the in-laws coming for lunch, and they give me a headache as it is.'

'Kill or cure.'

'I'll take either.'

The first of two klaxons rings through the crisp air, and a cheer goes up.

'Ready?'

'As I'll ever be!'

Coats and robes are cast aside, towels draped over waiting arms and hot water bottles readied for the return. There's a rush for the shore – a tangle of white limbs and bathing suits, brave bikinis and judicious woolly hats – and excited chatter so loud they wonder if they might miss the second klaxon. But when it sounds there's no mistaking it, and they let out a whoop and a 'Blwyddyn Newydd Dda!' *as they run towards the lake, screaming as they reach the icy water.*

When they're deep enough, they plunge. Mind over matter, through the low-lying mist. Cold clamps a vice around their chests, mouths opening in shock as their breath is wrenched away. 'Keep moving, keep moving!' *cry the veterans, dopamine pumping smiles to their faces. Ripples become waves, the movement of people this way and that, as the wind picks up and sends shivers across shoulders.*

As the mist begins to clear, a woman cries out.

It stands out among the screams of excitement, sending shivers of a different kind down the backs of those waiting on the shore. Those still in their depth stand on tiptoes, straining to see what's happening, who's hurt. The rescue boat dips its oars into the water. In and out, in and out, making its way towards the commotion.

Out of the mist floats a man.

Face down, and quite unmistakably dead.

PART ONE

ONE

NEW YEAR'S DAY | FFION

Ffion Morgan scans the prone figure beside her for signs of life. The man is tall, with broad shoulders, and black hair cropped close to his skull. On the back of his neck, where a shirt collar might lie, is a small tattooed name. *Harris.*

Ffion clears her throat, testing the silence with a tiny, tentative noise, as though about to make a speech she isn't sure how to start. The man doesn't stir. That makes things easier.

There is, however, the small matter of the arm.

The arm is big. It has smooth dark brown skin, stretched across the sort of bicep Ffion always wants to bite, although clearly now is not the time. It lies diagonally across Ffion's stomach, its hand hanging loosely by her hip. Habit makes her check the man's fourth finger and she's relieved to find it bare. She looks at his watch. Eight a.m. Time to split.

She shifts her legs first, shuffling them sideways a millimetre at a time, before bending her knees to drop her feet to the floor, all the time keeping her torso still, like a contortionist folding herself into a box. She waits a moment, then presses her upper half into the mattress as she slides slowly towards the edge of the bed. The manoeuvre is practised, honed over the past year, thanks to whatever misplaced gene it is which makes men cast out a proprietorial arm in their sleep.

The owner of this morning's arm gives a grunt. Ffion counts to fifty. If he wakes, he'll suggest breakfast – or coffee, at least – despite neither of them wanting it. Not with each other, anyway. Ffion blames Generation Z. All those *feelings*. There was a time when men showed you the door before they'd even tied a knot in the johnny, but now they're all *woke*. It does her head in.

She tries to recall who the arm belongs to. *Harris* doesn't ring a bell. It begins with M, she's sure. Mike? Max? She fishes for pieces among the murky depths of the previous evening's drinking, reeling in a memory of straight white teeth, a shy smile, a desire to please which she found as attractive as it was unusual.

Mark?

She tears a piece of skin from the inside of her top lip. Fuck fuck fuckitty fuck. She hates it when she can't remember their names. It feels . . . slutty.

Marcus!

Ffion grins at the ceiling, relief making her giddy. Rule number one: always know who you're spending the night with.

Marcus.

Recalling his name unlocks the rest, New Year's Eve unfolding in all its drunken, glorious splendour. Marcus Something-or-other (surnames don't count): a sky-diving instructor (*I'll sort you and your mates out with freebies*) who matched her shot for shot and slipped a hand around her waist when he leaned forward to make himself heard above the noise of the bar. *Shall we head somewhere quieter? We could go to mine . . .*

Ffion closes her eyes and indulges in the memory of the tingle of Marcus's thumb on her bare skin; so full of promise. For a second she thinks about rolling over and waking him up and—

No second helpings. Rule number two.

Marcus's bedroom has the sparse, anonymous feel of a rental. Magnolia walls and vertical blinds; a scratchy carpet bristling with static. Ffion sweeps her right foot across it and finds her pants. Her left foot yields a sock, and, as the breathing beside her steadies, she slides out from under Marcus's arm and on to the floor with all the grace of a sea lion.

The blue top she was wearing the previous evening is by the wardrobe, her jeans a few steps behind it. The classic clothes trail: Ffion is nothing if not predictable. With luck, she'll find her shoes kicked off in the hall, her jumper in a puddle by the front door.

She dresses swiftly, stuffing her socks into her jeans pocket for speed, and hunts fruitlessly for her bra, before chalking it up as a loss. A quick wee, and a peek in the bathroom cabinet (a box of condoms; a half-squeezed tube of haemorrhoid cream), then she checks for her car keys and skedaddles. The pavements are frosty, and she zips up her coat. It's khaki green and covers her from chin to ankle, its warmth and practicality the trade-off for looking like a sleeping bag with feet. As she retraces her steps to her car, she does the traditional alcohol-units-into-hours calculation and concludes she can just about get away with it.

It's after nine when she gets home, and Mam's making porridge. Two swimming costumes hang on the radiator.

'You've never missed a New Year's Day swim before.'

Elen Morgan's voice is neutral, but Ffion has thirty years' experience interpreting her mam's stirring techniques, and the way she's snatching at the wooden spoon right now doesn't bode well.

Sixteen-year-old Seren bounces out of a pile of blankets on the big chair by the window. 'They found a—'

'Let your sister have some breakfast before we get into that.' Mam's sharp voice cuts across Seren.

Ffion looks at Seren. 'They found a what?'

Seren looks at Mam's back and rolls her eyes.

'I saw that.'

'God, you're good, Mam.' Ffion lifts the kettle from the Aga, sloshing it to check how much water's in it before moving it on to the hot plate. 'Did you ever think of joining the Secret Service? I imagine "eyes in the back of your head" are right up there with jiu jitsu and fluent Russian.' She plugs in her phone, dead since the previous evening. 'How was the swim, anyway?'

'It wasn't.' Seren shoots a defiant look at Mam. 'I was only in up to my knees when they made us all get out.'

'How come?'

'Well, if you'd been there, you'd know,' Mam says tightly.

'I overslept.'

'At Mia's?'

Ffion gives a non-committal *mmm*. Seren – sharp as a tack – looks between Mam and Ffion, instantly alert to the possibility of drama.

'Because I'm told she was at the party till late.'

Mia Williams. Two years ahead of Ffion at school: the sort of age gap which gives you nothing in common in your teens, and everything in common a decade later. They are friends by default, rather than choice, Ffion always thinks; who else would they drink with, if not each other?

'Mam, I'm a grown—'

'And Ceri left early and saw your car heading out of the village.'

Ceri Jones, the postwoman. Is it any wonder, Ffion thinks, that she prefers to do her socialising away from the town? You can't fart in Cwm Coed without it making the front page.

'I had an errand to run.' The kettle whistles, harsh and insistent, as though challenging Ffion's lie. She finds a clean mug and drops in a tea bag.

'On New Year's Eve?'

'Mam, stop being—'

'I worry about you. Is that a crime?'

'I'm perfectly safe.'

'That's not what I mean.' Elen turns to look at her eldest daughter, voice low; expression loaded. 'It can't make you happy, Ffi.'

Ffion holds her gaze. 'It does, actually.'

Mam settled down too young, that was the trouble. Elen was seventeen when she'd met Ffion's dad, nineteen when they married. She'd never slept around, never even dated anyone else. How could she possibly understand how good no-strings sex could be? How *liberating*?

'Anywaaay . . .' Ffion changes the subject with a single, drawn-out word, turning to Seren for sibling solidarity. 'Why weren't you allowed to swim?'

'Because someone only bloody died!' The gossip bursts out of the girl like water from a dam.

Mam cracks the tea towel at Seren. 'Watch your language.'

'Ow!'

'I'd be keeping my head down if I were you, young lady. You know full well you weren't to go to that bloody party.'

Ffion looks at Seren. 'You were at The Shore last night?'

The girl's chin juts out defensively. 'Everyone was there.'

'I don't give a monkey's if the Queen of Sheba was there – I told you to stay away from that place!' Mam's voice rises, and Seren looks as if she might cry.

'Someone drowned?' Ffion says quickly.

Mam drags her attention away from Seren and gives a curt nod of confirmation.

'God. Who?'

Elen dishes up the porridge, mixed with stewed apple and with a swirl of cream on top. 'A man, that's all we know. Face-down, so . . .'

Ffion's phone chirrups into life, the screen flooding with texts and missed calls. She scrolls past the *Happy New Year* messages, until she reaches that morning's.

Did you hear about the body in the lake?
Do you know who it is?
Where were you last night???

She presses the blinking icon to listen to her voicemail. At any other time of year she'd put money on it being a visitor who drowned. Someone not used to the cold, or to swimming outdoors; someone who didn't grow up around water. Cwm Coed sees them every year, pouring out of the campsites and on to the lakeshore as though it's Bournemouth beach, throwing themselves off the jetty and letting their kids loose on cheap inflatables.

But the New Year's Day swim is strictly for locals. No one wants incomers, driving an hour or more in anticipation of the smug status update they can post on Facebook afterwards. There's no advert, no T-shirts, no sponsorship. No official organiser.

No safety measures, Ffion thinks grimly. She knows there's a faction of the community who will say they've been proved right by today's tragedy; people who refuse to attend the swim because it's dangerous. *All that running and laughing and falling over; the water so cold it'll freeze your lungs. And all with drink inside from the night before. It's only a matter of time before someone drowns.*

Ffion's phone is full of drunken voicemails from Mia and Ceri, shouted over a backdrop of fireworks, and one from Mam that morning – *We're leaving for the swim – lle wyt ti?*

'I heard it was old Dilwyn Jones,' Seren says.

'In a tuxedo?' Mam says. 'In forty years, I've never seen that man out of a cardigan.' She lowers her voice as she turns towards Ffion. 'They moved everyone away from the body as soon as they could. He was—' She breaks off. 'He was in a bad way.'

'Someone said his face was all smashed in.' Seren rises, eyes wide, deliberately ghoulish. Her hair is even redder than Ffion's, with the same frizzy curls you can't do a thing with. Ffion mostly fights hers into a messy bun, while Seren leaves hers loose, to settle on her shoulders like a big ginger cloud. She's pale, smudges of last night's make-up around her eyes.

'Stop your gossip, Seren, and eat your porridge. Your bones'll be cold till lunchtime.'

'I only got in as far as my knees.'

'You've bones in your legs, haven't you?'

'Someone will have been reported missing, though, surely . . .' Ffion starts to say, but then she reaches the final message in her voicemail and her pulse quickens. She unplugs her phone. 'I have to go.'

'You just got home!'

'I know, but . . .' Ffion jumps up to pull a clean top off the airer, wondering if she can swipe a bra without Mam seeing. Half a dozen socks fall off the rack, one landing neatly in the porridge pot.

'Ffion Morgan!'

Thirty years old, with a marriage and a mortgage behind her,

13

yet Mam's tea towel is still a force to be reckoned with. For the second time in as many hours, Ffion beats a hasty retreat.

As she pulls away, the car's exhaust coughing in protest, she dials one-handed, balancing her phone on the passenger seat. Leaving the village, she pulls out in front of a car: a Sunday-best couple on their way to visit family, three bored kids in the back. The driver leans on the horn, staying on Ffion's tail, making a point.

'Mia?' Ffion says, when the voicemail kicks in. She puts her foot flat on the accelerator. 'It's Ffi.' Her pulse buzzes in her temples. 'If Mam asks you where I was last night, tell her I was with you.'

TWO

NEW YEAR'S DAY | LEO

'Keep your coat on!'

The shout comes as Leo Brady reaches his desk at Cheshire Major Crime Unit, at precisely nine a.m. Reluctantly he buttons his heavy wool overcoat back up and heads to the boss's office, where Detective Inspector Simon Crouch is standing by his chair. Leo has only walked from the car park to the police station – a few hundred metres at most – but his feet are like ice cubes. He wiggles his toes inside his brogues. *Too cold to snow*, people keep saying, which has never made sense to Leo.

'I need you to get your fat arse over to Mirror Lake – they've had a body wash up.'

Leo isn't fat. He is, in fact, in far better shape than Crouch, whose pale flesh looks as though it's been moulded from lumps of Play-Doh, but this doesn't stop Crouch asserting his authority through the medium of playground insults.

'Isn't that in Wales?'

'I didn't ask for a geography lesson.' Crouch shares his iPad screen to the smart board on the wall, and for a split-second Leo is treated to the first two lines of everything in Crouch's inbox. In among the burglary overviews and the violent crime statistics, Leo sees a message from a Joanne Crouch entitled *Your mother AGAIN,* and an *urgent*-flagged email from Professional Standards, before Google Maps fills the screen.

Leo takes a moment to get his bearings. In the centre is a thin, meandering lake marked *Llyn Drych*, through which runs the border between England and Wales. Mirror Lake, Leo knows, although he has never had a job take him that far towards the boundaries of Cheshire Constabulary. A mountain range stands on the northern tip of the lake, and on the west side, just into Wales, is the small village of Cwm Coed. Between the town and the water is a band of green, running around the lake.

Crouch points at a patch of green on the eastern side, at the far end of their area. 'Just before you got in, we had a MisPer report from here.' He taps his screen, and the map changes to a satellite view. The green is woodland, not grass, Leo realises: trees packed tightly around the water's edge. Crouch draws a wonky circle and taps it meaningfully. 'This picture's a couple of years out of date.' He closes the map and swipes through his apps to find Safari. Mail, Weather, Sky News – is that *Tinder*? 'This is what's there now.'

A website appears on the large screen, a film playing soundlessly in the banner image. *It's a Shore thing . . .* reads the caption. Sun sparkles on the surface of Mirror Lake, as the camera swoops closer to a row of wooden cabins at the edge of the water. A laughing child, frozen in mid-air, swings on a rope above a deck more suited to the Maldives than North Wales. It isn't a film, Leo now sees, but a computer-generated animation: an artist's impression of what is clearly a high-end development.

'This is The Shore,' Crouch says. 'And don't get any ideas, because the chances of you affording a place there are on a par with you ever progressing beyond the rank of constable. One of them's owned by that ex-boxer actor. The one who's married to her with the massive tits.'

'Who's the MisPer?'

'The resort's owner, Rhys Lloyd. A *male opera singer*.' Crouch slots the words alongside each other as though the combination were experimental. He refers to himself as *a traditionalist*, which Leo has found, during the course of his own thirty-six years, is often synonymous with *bigoted arsehole*. 'Very well known, I'm told,' Crouch goes on. 'If you like that sort of thing.'

'I take it you don't like that sort of thing?'

'Tights and nancy boys? Do you?'

Leo opens his notebook with the attention one might give a portal into another world. 'Who reported him missing?'

'His daughter. Rang in on the nines. The wife confirms he didn't come to bed last night, but apparently that wasn't unexpected. She thought he was partying, or sleeping it off somewhere else. Or *having* it off, maybe.' Crouch snorts.

'Do you want me to speak to the family?'

'Take a gander at the body first. Make sure the Welsh haven't fucked it up. Local enquiries, last known movements – the usual. North Wales has sent a DC – he'll meet you at the mortuary.'

'No problem.'

'If it's an accidental drowning, bat it back to Wales.' Crouch clears his screen. 'He washed up on their side.'

'And if it's murder?'

'Depends. If it's going nowhere—'

'Bat it back to Wales?'

'Not as thick as you look, are you?' Crouch waits expectantly. Leo isn't sure how to answer. 'But if there's a suspect, keep the job, and we'll get it squared away soon as. First murder of the year, done and dusted in a day, boom.'

Boom? Crouch often bemoans the fact that he is never drafted in to give statements to the press, standing on the steps of the court, or next to the fluttering tape of a murder scene. Based on what Leo has seen of his boss, this is a wise decision on the part of the comms team.

It's more than an hour from Major Crime's offices to the force boundary. The sky is bright blue, the streets full of people chasing away hangovers and the excesses of Christmas. A walk in the fresh air. Perhaps a pint, or a Bloody Mary. *New year, new you.*

Leo listens to a phone-in on 5 Live and feels a crushing sense of despair at the passing of another year with nothing to show for it. He's still living in a shitty flat with a neighbour who burns herbs in a tin by her door to ward off evil spirits. He's still working for a boss who belittles and bullies him on a daily basis. And he's still doing nothing about it.

Leo taps the screen on his phone and listens to the ringtone fill the car's speakers.

'What is it?'

'Happy new year to you, too.' Leo hears the tiny exhalation which means his ex-wife is rolling her eyes. 'Can I speak to him?'

'He's out with Dominic.'

'Can I ring later?'

'We've got some friends coming over for drinks.'

'Tomorrow, then?'

'You can't expect me to drop everything and—'

'I just want to wish a happy new year to my son!'

Allie leaves a silence so long Leo thinks she's hung up. 'I write it down, you know,' she says finally, her tone clipped. 'Every time you lose your temper.'

'For God's sake, I don't—' He stops himself, clenching a fist and driving it through the air, stopping just short of the steering wheel. How can he ever win, when the very existence of the allegation provokes him into proving it right? 'This isn't fair, Allie.'

'You should have thought of that before . . .'

'How many times do I have to say I'm sorry?' Leo's voice rises again. Over and over again, the same narrative, the same guilt-trip.

'You're lucky I let you see him at all, after what you did.'

Leo counts to ten. 'When would be a convenient time for me to call again?'

'I'll text you.' The line goes dead.

She won't. Leo will have to ask again, and, by the time he gets to speak to his son, *happy new year* will feel like an afterthought.

As Leo drives, the distances between the villages grow, and even the sky seems to open up, until he can look in every direction and see nothing but emptiness. Bleakness.

One day, when his lad is a teenager, Leo will be able to simply pick up the phone and call him. They'll make their own arrangements to meet after school, or to go to a football match, without Allie as a self-appointed gatekeeper. Without her constantly reminding Leo of what he'd done. *You're lucky I didn't call the police*, she's fond of saying. *Or Social Services. I still could, you know.* It hangs over him, shadowing every conversation, every brief contact she allows him to have.

I still could.

God, it's miserable in Wales. It isn't raining, which is a blessing – not to mention a rarity – but clouds are rolling in from the north, and wind bends the trees sideways. What do the police *do* all day, out here? There must be *some* crime, Leo supposes – sheep theft, the odd burglary – but he doubts CID is a hotbed of activity. Today's drowning will be the highlight of their year.

The mortuary is in Brynafon, and Leo's glad of the SatNav as he winds his way around the mountain roads, before dropping back down into what passes for civilisation. A light drizzle hangs in the air, settling on the town's slate roofs. Leo follows the hospital signs to a small car park, empty except for a silver Volvo XC90 and a brown Triumph Stag held together with rust. The mortuary itself is a low boxy building. Leo presses the buzzer.

'Push the door,' comes the tinny response. 'There's no one on reception today, but I'll be through in a sec.'

Leo does as he's told, finding himself in a small L-shaped waiting room. The clock on the wall reads ten thirty-five. Sensing he isn't alone, he turns, and his mouth drops open. Standing in the corner of the room, her face flushed and uncertain, is a woman.

Harriet.

'What are you doing here? Did you . . .' Leo can barely find the words. 'Did you *follow* me here?'

The woman gives a bark of laughter. 'I was here first! If anything, you must have followed me.'

Holy crap. Harriet. Harriet Jones, or Johnson or something. A primary school teacher from Bangor, a detail Leo only remembers because he did indeed bang her.

He's about to interrogate her further when a door opens on the far side of the room, and a woman in a white lab coat brings with her the unmistakable smell of death and Dettol.

'Leo Brady, I presume? I'm Izzy Weaver, the pathologist handling your man. Shouldn't be here, to be perfectly frank, but my mortuary technician's gone AWOL. He's on borrowed time, that one. I've already told your SIOs I can't do the PM till the day after tomorrow, but if we can get an ID on him, that'd be great.'

'*Leo?*' Harriet says loudly.

There's a brief pause, as the pathologist looks keenly at Leo, then at Harriet. Leo coughs. Okay, so this is awkward. But Leo isn't the first man to give a fake name to a girl he's met in a bar, and he won't be the last. In the three years he's been divorced, Leo has found dating an uncomfortable experience. Eighteen months ago, he had enjoyed what he'd understood to be a mutually agreeable one-night stand, only to find himself stalked – no, *hounded* – for several months afterwards. He hasn't used his real name since.

But this still doesn't explain what Harriet Jones – or Johnson, or whatever – is doing at the mortuary.

'I take it you haven't met,' the pathologist says. Leo and Harriet look at each other.

'Well—' says Leo.

'No,' says Harriet, firmly.

The pathologist looks baffled. As well she might: Leo is struggling to understand, himself. Has Harriet been following him? Intercepting his messages? For one wild moment Leo imagines her bugging Crouch's office, keeping meticulous notes on Leo's movements.

'Harriet . . .' Leo says warily. He'll be firm with her, but not *too* firm. She's quite probably mentally unwell – this is not the action of a sane woman.

'Harriet?' says the pathologist.

'Um . . .' says Harriet. There's a long pause.

'Shall we crack on?' There's a note of frustration in Izzy Weaver's voice. She waves a hand in Leo's direction. 'Detective Constable Leo Brady, of Cheshire Constabulary.' Then waves the other in the opposite direction, towards Harriet. 'Detective Constable Ffion Morgan, from North Wales Police.'

Leo raises an eyebrow. 'Ffion?'

'Ffion,' Harriet says, quietly. Or rather, Ffion says. Leo's head

21

spins. At the same time, quite unexpectedly, his groin recalls the previous night. It's an unsettling combination, helped little by the waft of disinfectant.

Harriet – *Ffion!* – Christ – had taken forever to leave this morning. Leo had been desperate to pee, and instead he'd had to lie there, pretending to be asleep while she fidgeted next to him, clearly waiting to be taken for breakfast. Leo never knows what to say the morning after, and staying asleep is infinitely easier than negotiating a conversation. She'd thumped out of bed eventually, crashing about in the bathroom in the hope he might wake up, before giving up and going home.

Detective Constable Ffion Morgan. She doesn't look like a Ffion. Harriet suits her better. Perhaps it's a middle name, and she only uses Ffion for work. So, by introducing herself last night as Harriet, she wasn't giving a fake name, exactly, just—

'Not Marcus, then?' Ffion raises an eyebrow.

'Who the hell is Marcus?' the pathologist says. 'I was told there were only two of you coming – it's a morgue, not a séance.'

'Sorry,' Leo says, on behalf of both of them, although Ffion doesn't look remotely sorry. Her expression is amused – a little quizzical – as though waiting for Leo to expand.

As Izzy Weaver ushers them into the depths of the mortuary, Leo feels a sense of misgiving come over him. He hopes to hell this turns out to be an accidental drowning, because Ffion Morgan looks like trouble.

THREE

NEW YEAR'S DAY | FFION

Well, this is awkward. In the twelve months since walking out on her marriage, Ffion has successfully avoided bumping into a one-night stand after the event. It's one of the reasons she spends her social life away from Cwm Coed; that, and the fact that, when you live and work in the village in which you grew up, you remain forever a child in the eyes of everyone who knows you. Look at Sion Ifan Williams: sixty-five if he's a day, yet known by everyone as Sion *Sos Coch*, on account of a schoolboy enthusiasm for tomato ketchup.

Ffion herself has tried, and failed, to shake off the moniker of Ffion *Wyllt*.

Wild Ffion.

'It's only because of your hair,' Mam used to say firmly, wrestling Ffion's frizzy mane into a plait; refusing to acknowledge that an entire community considered her young daughter untameable. Elen Morgan had grown up thirty miles from Cwm Coed, and, despite a long marriage and two children through the village school, there are many who still consider her an outsider. A place like Cwm Coed needs four generations in the graveyard before you can call yourself local.

At first, Ffion went along with her *Wyllt* moniker. If the hat

23

fits, she thought, impressing friends with booze stolen from her parents' drink cabinet, and inventing ever more outlandish 'truths' at the inevitable games of Truth or Dare. It was funny, living up to her name.

Until it wasn't.

Sometimes, when she and Mia have a pint at Y Llew Coch, they look around at the faces that haven't changed in twenty years.

'Still would,' Mia would say of Hari Roberts, who fitted bathrooms and volunteered as a firefighter.

'Definitely wouldn't,' they'd say in unison of Gruffydd Lewis, who now teaches in the same school that once gave him detention for sliding a mirror under the door to the girls' changing room.

Ffion steals a glance at Leo Brady, as they don shoe coverings and remove their coats in an anteroom outside the morgue. Would she? Hypothetically, of course, because: rule two. But would she? He's good-looking, no doubt about that, although perhaps not quite as good-looking as when seen through a filter of vodka and dry white wine.

Still would, she concludes. Probably.

'After you, *Ffion.*' The English detective emphasises her name, as Izzy Weaver opens the door to the morgue. The faux chivalry irritates Ffion. How has this even happened? The look of horror on Leo's face when he saw her told Ffion all she needs to know. They can't possibly work together, although Ffion hasn't yet worked out how she's going to get out of it. *Sorry, boss, I accidentally shagged the DC you've assigned me to work with – any chance of a swap?*

'Thank you, *Leo.*' Ffion mirrors his tone with a guileless smile. The pathologist raises an eyebrow at her, but Ffion ignores the unspoken question. 'Any idea of cause of death?' she says instead.

'I'm reserving judgement. What's the name of your MisPer?'

'Rhys Lloyd,' Leo says, before Ffion can. She looks at him, her head still reeling. This is all so weird. So *awful*. 'He's a singer,' Leo continues. 'Originally from Cwm Coed.' He pronounces it *cum co-ed*. Ffion wants to correct him. *It's coom coyd, actually.* She wants to say lots of things, but she's transfixed on the long drawer Izzy is sliding out from the fridge.

'I wasn't sure how long you'd be, and I didn't want him thawing out. All I need now is for your guvnors to agree who I'm invoicing.'

Leo turns to Ffion. 'The body was found on your side.'

'He went missing from yours.' With Cwm Coed in such proximity to England, cross-border working is inevitable: Ffion has experienced Cheshire's Teflon-coated handovers on several occasions.

'Lloyd owns a holiday resort on the English side of the lake,' Leo explains to Izzy. 'Last seen at a party there yesterday evening.'

'The Shore,' Ffion says, although neither of them is listening. 'It's been subject to a planning dispute for years.'

Izzy pulls off the sheet and the three of them stare at the corpse. 'He's not in great shape,' Izzy says. She swallows what sounds like a belch, pressing her fingers to her lips and closing her eyes, remaining perfectly still for several seconds. 'Excuse me.' She opens her eyes just as Ffion is wondering if she's alright. 'I was up till three playing Cards Against Humanity, and that last glass of port was perhaps a mistake. Anyway – let's see if this is your singer.'

The corpse is naked. Broad-chested, with a six-pack which shows even in this sorry state, and tan lines hinting at holidays Ffion could never afford. A deep gash splits his face in two. Ffion takes slow, even breaths.

25

'I bagged and tagged him at the scene, fingernail scrapings, swabs, yadah yadah.' Izzy waves a hand towards the bench table that runs the length of the room. 'Property and clothes are over there, if you want a gander. Bloody nice suit. Don't get a lot of Savile Row in here, I can tell you.'

Ffion walks towards the sealed bags, glad of the excuse to look somewhere other than the corpse. The tuxedo is draped across a folding rack, the stench of lake and death steaming from the fabric. Ffion catches a flash of gold cufflinks and moves on, her stomach reminding her that vodka and wine don't mix.

Behind her, Leo opens a portfolio, the zip loud within the unforgiving acoustics of the morgue. He pulls out a sheet of paper. 'Lloyd's wife has given a description. Six foot one, dark hair, brown eyes . . .'

After each attribute, Leo and Izzy check off the relevant characteristic on the body between them, a macabre game of pairs which turns Ffion's stomach.

On the narrow stainless-steel table are two smaller bags, one containing a gold signet ring, the other Lloyd's smartwatch.

'I'll get the tech team to pull the data from his Apple account.' Ffion walks back to the others and makes herself look at the body. 'It should give us his movements, and, if he has the health app installed, we can see what time his heart stopped.'

'You'll make me redundant,' Izzy says.

Leo runs a finger down to the next item on his list. 'Appendix scar.'

'Snap,' Izzy says, indicating the diagonal line above the man's right hipbone.

Ffion feels suddenly hot.

'Mole underneath his left nipple?' Leo says.

'Check.'

26

'Scar on his—'

'Right thigh,' Ffion cuts in abruptly. 'Can we quit playing Operation now? It's pretty obvious we've got a positive ID, isn't it? This is Rhys Lloyd. End of.' Without looking at the body again, Ffion turns and leaves the room.

Outside, she lights a cigarette and draws the smoke hard into her lungs. Then she calls her boss, keeping her voice breezy. As though it doesn't matter.

'I'm not going to be able to work this job, sir – conflict of interests.'

'How come?' DI Malik sounds distracted. He's been Ffion's boss for a little over a year, but the topography of their patch means she's met him just a handful of times.

'I know the victim.'

'Ffion, you know everyone in Cwm Coed. Six months ago, you gave evidence against your own aunt.'

Ffion stares at the tip of her cigarette, the glowing tip consuming the paper.

'She got six months for fraud.'

Ffion won't win this one. Aunty Jane isn't a close relative – a twice-removed, second cousin's mother sort of thing – but she and Ffion do indeed share a family tree.

'Yes, but—'

'Is the victim in your immediate family?'

'No, but—'

'Then you're keeping the job.' DI Malik ends the call, and Ffion takes a final, angry drag on her cigarette, before stubbing it out on the wall and chucking it into the bushes. Fucksake. She stares at her phone. Nothing from Mia.

Ffion slides into the driver's seat of the Triumph Stag. The car is older than she is, a constant source of arguments during her short-lived marriage. It breaks down regularly, struggles on hills and leaks like Julian Assange; and boasts a hole in the footwell which blows wind up the driver's skirt. But then, Ffion never wears skirts. She bought the Triumph with the money her dad left her, and she was damned if she was going to swap it for something more practical, just to please her husband.

'We can't drive kids around in that,' he'd said. 'It's not safe.'

'I don't want kids,' Ffion had replied, and that was beginning of the end. He'd tried to persuade her, and then he'd tried to accept it, but eighteen months later Ffion was stuffing her clothes into the back of the Triumph and moving back in with Mam.

Wind rattles the windows, whistling through the cracks around the doors. Ffion rests her forehead on the leather steering wheel and lets out a long, slow breath. It's true, then: Rhys Lloyd is dead. He's really dead.

Thank God for that.

FOUR

NEW YEAR'S EVE | 11.25 P.M. | RHYS

Rhys Lloyd has the worst hangover ever. His head is pounding, and his skin crawls with something which feels like the flu. Vomit lingers in his throat. He blinks in the darkness.

What time is it?

In the distance, he hears the strains of the party – music, laughter. He remembers now: he left early, in search of his bed.

Only he isn't in bed.

There's no soft pillow beneath his head, and something hard digs into his back.

Where is he?

There's a sharp pain between his eyes, and something sticky and wet trickles down his nose. He feels a cold wind on his face, then something even colder.

Rhys is outside.

Did he go on to the balcony of the bedroom, to get some air, but fall asleep?

He can hear the lake. It's reassuring at first – he's become accustomed to the sound, as they eat on the deck, or drift off to sleep with the windows ajar. But this isn't the gentle breaking of waves on the shore, heard from the balcony, or through a window.

The lake is right here, all around him. It moves rhythmically, insistently. It sprays across his face.

What is he doing here?

Did he sleepwalk?

He hears a voice, and he wants to call out, in case its owner doesn't realise he's here, surrounded by water, but his body won't comply. The pain is swallowing him whole and the water is all around him, and as he manages a pathetic jerk of his body he realises he is too weak to move.

And that's when Rhys knows he's about to die.

FIVE

NEW YEAR'S DAY | LEO

Leo scrolls through Wikipedia as he walks from the mortuary towards his car. Rhys Lloyd had been well respected in the music business. He hadn't charted in a while – the top ten seemingly a constant stream of manufactured bands and 'fresh talent' – but a few years back the guy could do no wrong. Awards left, right and centre, and charity work, too: playing for laughs in a spoof version of *The Pirates of Penzance* for Children in Need. Lloyd was working class – which everybody loves nowadays – and even though he'd apparently lost his accent, he spoke glowingly in interviews about his 'idyllic' upbringing in north Wales.

Lloyd was a rags-to-riches poster boy, plucked from obscurity when Lesley Garrett's agent was on holiday in Llangollen, and had popped into the Eisteddfod arts festival to find a loo. In the years that followed, Lloyd had released numerous albums, including a Christmas hit with Leona Lewis, crossing the bridge from light opera and musical theatre into something Leo is more likely to listen to. In fact, Leo realises, as he scans the list of tracks, he *has* listened to some of these. Liked them, even.

The brown rust-bucket Leo saw when he arrived belongs to Ffion. She's sitting in the driver's seat, staring into space. Leo raps on the glass and Ffion spends a few seconds trying to wind down the window, before giving up and getting out.

'Feeling any better?'

Ffion frowns at him.

'Some people put Vicks VapoRub around their nostrils,' Leo says. 'For the smell.'

'Thanks, Columbo, but this isn't my first rodeo.'

'I thought maybe . . . I mean . . .' Leo thrusts his hands into his pockets. Why is Ffion being like this? She'd been fun last night, they'd had a laugh. 'I guess you don't get a lot of crime out here, that's all.'

Ffion is nodding sagely. 'Yup, it's all pretty low-key in north Wales. Mostly sheep, as you'd expect. If we're not shagging them, ha ha, we're rustling them!'

'You're taking the piss.'

'No, *you're* taking the piss, mate, resorting to lazy stereotypes. For your information, I was here last week for a PM on a woman who'd shot herself in the face. The rest of the week I was in court with an armed robbery. So enough of the big I am, yeah?'

Leo has a sudden thought. Is this because he didn't message her? He'd asked for her number after they had drunkenly agreed that going to Alton Towers together would be *oh my God so funny!* and she'd punched it into his phone. This morning, after Ffion left his flat and driven home, she had no doubt expected a text from him. *Sorry I was asleep when you left . . . had a great time . . . when are you free again?* That sort of thing.

Leo takes a deep breath. 'Look, I think we need to clear the air. Last night was . . .' He stops. The right word is important. Not dismissive, but not meaningful, either. 'Fun,' he settles on. The corner of Ffion's mouth lifts in a half-smile. Shit, is 'fun' *too* meaningful? He doesn't want to lead her on.

'Yeah, it was.'

Ffion's spikiness softens and, despite himself, Leo feels the same heat he experienced when he first saw her on the dance floor last night. There'd been a sort of electricity about her, as though your hair might stand on end if you got too close. Ffion hadn't played games, either; just returned his gaze with a cool, even stare, then stopped dancing and walked right up to him. 'Hot, isn't it?'

'Very,' Leo had replied. 'Fancy some air?'

'The thing is,' he says now, 'I mean, it's not that you're not – it's just that . . .' Leo falters. Ffion's face has gone all crooked. Is she going to cry? Fuck. 'I'm not really looking for a relationship.' He finishes too quickly, the words gaining volume, so he practically shouts the last few.

'Me neither.' Ffion gives a brusque nod, as though concluding a business meeting. 'That's that sorted, then.' She gestures to the mortuary. 'Any hints on cause of death?'

Leo doesn't know whether Ffion's genuinely okay with this, or just sparing his feelings, but either way he's grateful to be back on more comfortable territory. 'You know what pathologists are like,' he says. 'There could be a knife sticking out of the bloke's back and they'd still hedge their bets till the inquest.'

Ffion gives the ghost of a smile. 'I'll go and see the wife on my way home. Yasmin Lloyd's down as next-of-kin, right?'

'Yes, but . . .' Leo hesitates. 'Well, she's at The Shore.'

'So?'

'So, that's technically England. My patch,' he adds, when Ffion doesn't say anything.

'*Technically*, yes, but Rhys is from Cwm Coed. His mam, Glynis, still lives there. And it's literally on my doorstep. So I'll—'

'We'll do it together,' Leo says, with uncharacteristic decisiveness.

If this turns out to be a juicy job and Leo gives it away, Crouch will never let him forget it.

There's a long pause as they lock eyes, before Ffion breaks away with a sigh presumably intended to suggest she doesn't give a shit either way. 'Fine. Follow me. Call me if you get lost – I'll give you my number.'

'I've got it, remember?' Leo takes out his phone. 'I'll call you now, then you've got mine too.' He scrolls through his contacts to find *HARRIET NYE*, and dials.

Instantly, Ffion's cheeks colour. Leo could kick himself. Now neither of them can pretend he doesn't have her number and that's the reason he hasn't texted her—

Why isn't her phone ringing?

Leo lifts his own to his ear, to check it's working.

'Thank you for calling the showroom. Our offices are closed over the holidays, but if you'd like to book a test drive, please leave your name and number and we'll get back to you as soon as we reopen.'

A long and uncomfortable silence falls between Leo and Ffion, before he can bring himself to look away from his phone. Ffion smiles sheepishly. 'It really was fun. And it's not that you're not – I mean, it's just that . . .' Her eyes glint, as she mimics his own efforts at letting her down gently.

Leo winces. Ffion keeps a level gaze on him, then grins. 'Let's start over, shall we?'

Leo nods forcefully. 'Good plan.'

'We'll forget last night ever happened, and crack on with the job, yeah?' She winks. 'Forget we've seen each other naked.'

It's impossible, Leo thinks, as he follows the little Triumph out of the car park, to not think of the thing you're supposed to forget, when you have literally just been reminded of it.

*   *   *

34

Ffion drives as though she's making on blues and twos to a burglary in progress. She throws the Triumph around corners, hurtling over potholes with such vigour that Leo flinches on behalf of the suspension. No wonder the poor car looks as if it's falling apart. Leo follows more sedately as the Triumph bounces over a humpback bridge – a foot of sky between tyres and tarmac – before taking a sharp left to climb the track which leads to Cwm Coed.

The narrow, winding road is hewn from the mountainside, with passing places at regular intervals. Sheep appear suddenly at the sides of the road, or wander carelessly from one side to the other, and Leo slows to a crawl. There was no snow earlier, but, here, a dusting lines the roads and collects in the crevices of the rocky sides. As the incline grows steeper, Ffion's car drops to a walking pace, and Leo falls further back. He glances at his hands-free, thinking he might try Allie again, but of course there's no service.

How do people live in places like this? In fact, *why* do they live in places like this? Where you can't get anywhere except by car, and you have to walk down a mountain to get a phone signal? Leo had found the move from Liverpool to Chester painful enough, struggling to adjust to an area with more fields than factories, but Allie had wanted to be closer to her parents when Harris was born.

Career-wise, transferring to Cheshire had felt like a shrewd move. Bigger fish, smaller pond. Leo was on CID within six months, successfully applied to Major Crime the following year, and hoped for promotion within the department. He hadn't reckoned on DI Crouch, who had taken an instant dislike to him. *Calm down, calm down,* Crouch is fond of saying whenever Leo opens his mouth in a meeting, paddling the air with his flat palms in a poor imitation of Harry Enfield's TV Scouse character. Do the rest of the team laugh because it's funny, or because they're licking the boss's arse? Either way, Leo's jaw always tightens, unwillingly justifying Crouch's stupid impression.

He considered moving back, after the divorce. He thought longingly of the familiarity of his old force, of slotting back into drinks on Friday night and five-a-side on Sundays.

'So go back to Liverpool,' Allie had said, when Leo mentioned it.

'I'd never get to see Harris.'

Allie had shrugged, as though he'd made his own bed, when Leo wasn't even allowed to sleep in it any more. Allie was the one who made the choices. Choices like where they lived, where and when they went out. Choices like fucking her friend's husband, then ending her marriage to Leo.

'I might as well be in Liverpool,' Leo mutters now, pulling over as a trailer full of hay bales clatters perilously close to the low barrier between the road and the sheer drop on the other side. He'd envisaged having Harris every other weekend, and maybe one night in the week. But, after Dominic moved in, Allie decided it was *disruptive* for Harris to sleep anywhere but home. Leo had to pick him up at nine, waiting by the front door of a house he had once paid the mortgage on, and have him back by six. If Leo was rostered to work the weekend, he lost that Saturday with Harris: it was *disruptive* to switch weekends around, apparently. How Allie loves that word. Slowly, it became *disruptive* to collect Harris before eleven, or to return him after two. Leo finally understands why there are so many single dads in McDonald's on a Saturday lunchtime. Where else do you go when you're only allowed three hours with your kid, every other weekend?

36

Then, of course, Leo had fucked up. Lost his mind, just once, just for a moment. And Allie won't ever let him forget it.

Having climbed steadily – and slowly – for the previous ten miles, the road begins to fall away in front of them, and the Triumph picks up pace, racing down the winding path at a speed Leo isn't inclined to follow. He drags his mind away from Allie and Harris, and back to Rhys Lloyd, and the message he's about to deliver to the man's family. There was little online about them. The twin daughters are fifteen; Lloyd's wife, Yasmin, is forty-six, the same age as her husband. She's a *space consultant*, whatever that is. Something to do with NASA?

The road bends sharply to the left, before dropping steeply away. As the view opens up, Leo finds his mouth dropping open. The lake is a lazy letter 'S' in the bottom of the valley, its border of forest dense and dark. Around it, woodland covers steep hills, making it look as though the trees in the distance are a hundred feet tall, towering over the lake.

Mirror Lake itself is a shimmer of silver beneath the day's thin sunlight. At the far end looms a vast mountain, snow-capped peaks half-hidden in a swirl of cloud. The English–Welsh border runs directly through the middle of the lake, and it feels odd that it should be so invisible; that the water bears no sign of where one country ends and another begins.

Leo's ears pop as the road descends still further, until he can't see the lake any more, only the trees closing in either side of him. Ffion brakes hard, taking a left-hand fork so fast that the Triumph skids on to the opposite side of the road. Leo follows. This is the English side of the lake, an unmarked road which gradually narrows to become a single track. Every now and then the trees thin around shallow coves, the lake glinting in the winter sun.

It would make a nice walk on a sunny day, Leo supposes. If you liked that sort of thing. Maybe by next summer Allie might have forgiven him; might let him take Harris for a whole day – for a weekend, even. They could paddle, or buy one of those fishing nets on sticks and see what they could catch.

Leo is brought up short by a wide turning, flanked by enormous pillars. Vast wooden letters are positioned along the first twenty metres of the driveway.

THE SHORE.

Leo takes his foot off the accelerator. You can't see the resort from the main road, and a sign to Leo's left makes it clear the site is private property. Clipped hedging runs either side of the drive, and every few metres rustic posts suspend discreet bulbs to light up the route when dusk falls. This is more like it, thinks Leo, as he follows Ffion's Triumph into the complex. Stylish, luxurious, and not a sheep in sight.

As he nears the end of the drive, the space widens into parking. On the right, nestled into the trees, are several visitor bays, and Leo pulls in next to Ffion.

'Hideous, isn't it?' Ffion says, as he gets out. Leo is too busy staring at the lodges to answer. They're built directly on the lake-shore, each with a narrow path leading from the front door to a private parking space marked by more discreet lighting. The lodges are clad in wood, the grain left to weather naturally, and with the pine trees as a backdrop Leo thinks they could be in Switzerland, not north Wales. It feels a few degrees colder here than in Chester, and Leo pulls up the collar of his overcoat.

'Until the seventies, this was all Wales,' Ffion says. 'Then they messed around with the county boundaries and shifted the border. This bit' – she waves an arm, outlining the strip of land where the lodges lie – 'belonged to Rhys Lloyd's dad, Jac Lloyd.

There was a fishing shack here, round about where we're standing, called Tŷ'r Lan. Shore House,' she translates, seeing the question on Leo's lips.

Behind them, more trees have been felled, presumably to make way for the other lodges Leo saw on the resort's website.

'They've done a good job,' he says.

'You know what's under that wood?' Ffion walks towards the end of the row. 'Breeze blocks. It's all pretend, like a film set. A Hollywood director's idea of what lakeside living should look like.'

'It's pretty cool, though.' It's an understatement: the place is incredible. A covered storage rack contains half a dozen immaculate mountain bikes in forest-green, with off-white lettering on the frames proclaiming *It's a Shore thing!* The front doors to the lodges are painted in the same dark green.

Ffion walks up the path to number five, even as Leo is checking his paperwork to see which lodge is owned by the Lloyds. 'It got a lot of backs up,' she says, still filling him in on the history. 'The locals set up a petition to at least keep the original Tŷ'r Lan name, but apparently Welsh names are too hard for English people to say.' Ffion's voice is scathing.

'They can be a bit—'

'Manage alright with Cholmondeley, do you?' There's a beat. 'Well, then.' Ffion looks around. 'It's fancy enough on the surface, but it's all been done on the cheap. The developers promised to use local employment, then bussed in a load of zero-hours contractors. The whole place is fake as a four-pound note.'

Leo pictures his shitty flat and wonders if fake is such a bad thing. He follows Ffion up the path, only for her to stand aside as they reach the door. 'Your patch, I believe, DC Brady.'

Leo has no sooner lifted his hand to ring the bell than the door is wrenched open by a teenager with such hope in her eyes, Leo almost can't bear it. A second girl, identical to the first, comes running to the door, stopping short when she sees Leo.

'It's not him,' the first girl says. She starts crying, and her sister – these are presumably the Lloyd twins – wraps her arms around her. They walk back into the lodge, still clutching each other.

Leo glances at Ffion, then follows the girls inside.

Aside from the small hall, the ground floor of the lodge is open-plan. The front of the space, nearest the hall, is taken up with a white leather corner sofa, positioned around a wood-burning stove, and what looks like a projector. In the corner of the kitchen stands a large Christmas tree, its lights switched off, and parallel to the stretch of bifold doors leading on to the deck is a zinc table, artfully scuffed and surrounded by eight metal chairs in different colours.

'Have you found him?' A grey-haired woman stands by an open cupboard, a tea towel screwed up next to her. Outside, the sky is darkening, shadow clouds scudding across the deck.

'Is it him?' A second woman – younger, with olive skin and long, straight hair – sits at the table, a mobile phone clutched in one hand. She's wearing pyjamas, a silk dressing gown trailing to the floor.

'Mrs Lloyd?' Leo says. Both women nod and Leo is momentarily confused, before realising the older woman must be the dead man's mother, Glynis Lloyd. She moves to sit next to her daughter-in-law, trembling as she pulls out a chair.

'I'm Detective Constable Leo Brady, Cheshire Major Crime. This is Detective Constable Ffion Morgan, North Wales CID.'

The crying girl bursts into even louder sobs.

'Tabby, please . . .' Yasmin Lloyd's voice is broken. She stares bleakly at Leo. 'It's him, isn't it?' she says quietly.

40

Ffion puts a hand on a chair opposite the two women. 'May I?' She sits, making eye-contact with the older woman, who nods in recognition. They exchange a few words in Welsh, and Leo hears his own name repeated. It's warm in the lodge – stuffy – and, despite the cold outside, he wishes someone would pull open the big doors and let in some air. Tabby is wailing, a high-pitched, mournful note which makes the hairs on the back of Leo's neck stand up.

'It's all over Twitter,' Yasmin says. 'They found a body in the lake.' She takes a slow breath. 'Is it Rhys?'

Leo holds her gaze. 'We think so. I'm so sorry.'

Yasmin closes her eyes, gripping the edge of the table until her knuckles turn white. Tabby collapses into a chair, sobbing so hard she has to fight for breath. Her twin sister stands rooted to the spot, shaking her head over and over.

'We'll need someone to formally identify the body,' Ffion says.

Glynis Lloyd is trembling, her chair rocking against the tiled floor. The blood has drained from her face and Leo keeps a watchful eye in case she goes into shock. She's perhaps in her late sixties – not old, but no parent expects to bury a child.

'I . . .' Yasmin starts, before her voice fails. She pulls herself together and tries again. 'I should do that.'

'I'll take you,' Leo says. 'We need to speak to your neighbours, so please, take your time. I know what a shock this must be.'

'He was right here,' Yasmin says, half to herself.

Tabby's twin starts crying. 'I don't believe it.'

'Felicia, *cariad.*' Glynis holds out her arms to the teenager, but the young girl doesn't move. Her grandmother speaks to Ffion in Welsh.

Ffion answers in English, a concession to Leo and Yasmin, Leo assumes. 'We won't know that until after the post-mortem,

I'm afraid.' She turns to Yasmin. 'When did you last see your husband?'

Yasmin is ashen. 'Last night. Ten, maybe? I—'

'You should have called the police when he didn't come to bed!' Tabby says suddenly, angry tears blotching her face. 'But you didn't care, did you? Even this morning, when I said Dad was missing, you said *He'll turn up*, and now . . .' She collapses again, burying her face in her arms.

'Mrs Lloyd,' Leo says, 'was your husband fit and well when you last saw him?'

'Yes.' Yasmin glances at her mother-in-law. 'Although, not *well*, exactly.'

'He was ill?' Leo flips open his notebook. The pathologist will want to know about signs of illness. Perhaps Lloyd died from natural causes. *Bat it back to Wales*, Crouch said, but Leo can't do that, if Rhys died at The Shore.

'You could say that. It was . . .' Yasmin closes her eyes for a second '. . . self-inflicted. He was very drunk. But it was New Year's Eve,' she adds, a little defensively.

'I'm sorry to ask this,' Leo says, 'but what was Rhys's state of mind yesterday evening?'

Yasmin looks up sharply. 'Are you suggesting he committed suicide?'

There's a stifled gasp from Glynis.

'Dad wasn't depressed.' Tabby sniffs hard. 'Why would he kill himself?'

'Maybe something upset him.' Felicia speaks quietly, a hard undercurrent threading her words. She's staring at her mother, who seems unaware of her daughter's sudden change in mood.

'Like what?' Leo directs his question to Felicia, but it's Yasmin who answers.

'Rhys was fine. Drunk, that's all. As I said: it was a party.'

'Did he have any medical conditions?' Leo asks.

Yasmin shakes her head. 'He was very healthy. He had to be – people don't realise how fit you have to be to sing at a professional level.'

'Did he take drugs?' Ffion says. The briefest of glances passes between Tabby and Felicia.

'Absolutely not.' Yasmin's response is too fast. Leo makes a note to request a rush job on the toxicology.

'Had he fallen out with anyone?' Ffion asks.

'Everyone loved Dad.' Tabby's words are punctuated by juddering breaths. 'He was the nicest man you could ever meet.' Felicia puts her arms around her sister, but Leo thinks he sees a dart of anger in her eyes, before both girls' faces are lost to the embrace.

It could be something or nothing, thinks Leo. There's always a reluctance from family to admit to an argument, even a trivial one – *especially* a trivial one – when a loved one has been found dead. The deceased is always a *loving spouse* or *parent*; their relationships always unsullied by petty spats. So many victims able to *light up a room* before their lives are snuffed out, it's a wonder it hasn't put the National Grid out of business.

Yasmin chokes back a sob. 'I just can't believe he's gone.'

'I'm so sorry,' Leo says.

'Sorry?' It explodes from Tabby with such vigour that Leo instinctively tenses, the way he does if something's about to kick off. But although the girl's fists are clenched, and her eyes blazing, her lip wobbles, and tears stream down her face. 'You're sorry? Even though Dad told you he had a stalker, and you did nothing about it? But now you're sorry?'

'A stalker?' Ffion looks at the girl.

'Darling, I don't think—'

'They fobbed you off, Mum. And now Dad's dead!' Violent hiccups swallow what might have come next, and she runs upstairs, the lodge shaking with the force of her feet on the stairs. Her sister follows, and for a second there's silence.

Leo makes another note. 'Your husband had a stalker?'

'It's being dealt with by the Metropolitan Police. They never found out who was responsible. It was never anything serious, though, just online stuff. Internet trolls, you know? It comes with the territory.'

'That's not what Rhys said.' The older Mrs Lloyd speaks hesitantly, glancing at Yasmin, who continues to stare straight ahead as though the other woman hasn't spoken. There's an uneasy silence, broken by Ffion speaking the older woman's mother tongue.

'*Beth ddywedodd*—'

'Enough with the bloody Welsh!' Yasmin cuts herself off, squeezing her eyes shut and shaking her head. 'Sorry. I'm sorry. Sore point.' She glances at her mother-in-law. 'Glynis was desperate for us to bring the girls up bilingually.'

'It's part of their heritage, is all.' Glynis Lloyd keeps her eyes fixed on the table.

'Perhaps if Rhys had been hands-on from the start . . .'

'He was touring,' Glynis says quietly. 'He could hardly change nappies from Italy, could he?'

Leo intercepts. 'What did Rhys tell you about his stalker, Glynis?'

'He said someone was obsessed with him. That they'd made threats.'

Ffion turns to Yasmin. 'Is this true?'

Yasmin hesitates, then nods. 'Keyboard warriors. We didn't take them seriously.'

'We'll look at it again,' Leo says. 'In case . . .' He leaves the sentence unfinished. There's something in Yasmin's face he can't read. From upstairs, the sound of the twins sobbing pulsates through the ceiling.

'I'll go.' Glynis Lloyd pushes back her chair, the metal legs screeching against the tiled floor. She waits for a second, as though she can't quite remember why she stood, before crossing the room with tears streaming down her cheeks.

'This'll break her,' Yasmin says, when her mother-in-law has gone. 'She hasn't been the same since Rhys's dad died, and now this—' She breaks off, shaking her head fiercely, as though something's trapped. 'I'm sorry. It just – it doesn't seem real.'

'If you don't feel up to identifying your husband—' Leo starts, but Yasmin shakes her head fiercely.

'No no, I want to see him. I have to see him. I'll just . . .' She gestures to her dressing gown.

'Of course. Take your time, Mrs Lloyd.'

Tears brim over Yasmin's lower lashes. 'Thank you.'

'Have you met them before?' Leo asks Ffion, when the door to the lodge closes. From upstairs, they can still hear the twins – or perhaps Rhys's mother – sobbing.

'The Shore only opened last summer.'

'Is that a no?'

'Yup.'

Leo looks at her, exasperated. He's had more intel from a no-comment interview. 'How about Glynis Lloyd?'

'She owns the hardware store in the village. Lives above the shop.'

'So you know her?'

Ffion shrugs, as though the answer was obvious. 'She's local.' She lifts both hands, fingers pointing in opposite directions. 'Do you want lodges three and four or one and two?'

45

Leo is torn between relief that Ffion doesn't want to team up, and apprehension about setting her bluntness loose on The Shore. This is technically his police area, after all. 'Three and—'

Ffion is already striding off.

At number three, Leo pokes a hand gingerly through the centre of a door wreath to find the knocker. Inside, a woman is shouting. The words are indistinct, but the sentiment behind them is clear – Leo's been on the receiving end of similar ones enough times. He raps loudly, earning himself a holly scratch in the process, and the shouting stops. Leo hears footsteps.

'Hi.'

Leo takes a moment to centre himself. He grew up watching Bobby Stafford fight, and, although Leo's not into the soaps, Stafford's instantly recognisable as the ne'er-do-well bare-knuckle boxer in the long-running show *Carlton Sands*.

'Um, hi.' Leo produces his warrant card, and Stafford raises an eyebrow.

A woman joins them at the door, slipping an arm around Stafford. 'Who is it, babe?' Ashleigh Stafford is one of those celebrities famous for being famous, segueing from one reality TV show to another, until no one is quite sure how she started. Although she looks a little flushed, there's nothing to indicate Ashleigh was screaming her head off a minute earlier. She leans a head on her husband's shoulder. She's several inches taller than Bobby, and the stance looks awkward.

'It's the police,' Stafford says.

Ashleigh's eyes widen. 'Have you found Rhys?'

'Do you mind if I come in?'

* * *

46

The Staffords' lodge is identical to the Lloyds'. Same kitchen, same layout, same furniture. Same view. Leo finds himself walking towards the sliding doors, drawn to the vast expanse of water. Did Lloyd go into the lake willingly, or was he forced in? Did he thrash in the water, shouting for help? The trees on the opposite shore are reflected upside down, blurring the line between lake and land. Leo imagines Lloyd slipping from one to the other, fighting to surface, each breath more frantic than the last.

'Coffee?' Bobby Stafford says. The vast, gleaming coffee machine would be more at home in a Starbucks.

'Thanks, but I won't keep you. A body was retrieved from the lake earlier this morning.'

It's evident from the Staffords' expressions that this isn't news.

'A formal identification hasn't yet taken place, but we believe it to be Rhys Lloyd.'

Ashleigh's hands fly to her face. 'Oh, my God.'

'Fucking hell,' Bobby adds.

It seems this *is* news. Although Leo reminds himself that Bobby is an actor, and Ashleigh is . . . what *is* Ashleigh? An *influencer*, Wikipedia says, which is still performing for the cameras, isn't it?

'When did you last see Rhys?' Leo asks.

'He was proper hammered last night.' Ashleigh takes the coffee Bobby hands her, cradling it in two hands. 'I saw him chucking up in the bushes.'

'What time was that?'

'Ten? Eleven?' Ashleigh says, with little conviction.

Leo looks at Bobby, but the former boxer shrugs. 'Don't ask me, mate – I didn't see him.'

'At all?'

'There were a lot of people partying last night. I was talking. Drinking. Having a good time.'

Leo catches a note of defensiveness in Bobby Stafford's tone, and the briefest glimpse of resentment in the glance his wife shoots him. He remembers the argument he interrupted. 'Were the two of you together at the party?'

'No,' Bobby says, just as Ashleigh says, 'Yes.' Leo waits. 'Bit of both,' Bobby adds.

There's something going on here that Leo can't work out. 'How did Rhys get on with the other residents of The Shore?'

'Alright, I guess.' Again, that guarded reaction from Bobby.

'You didn't like him, did you, babe?' Ashleigh's looking away, but Leo catches a flicker at the corners of her lips. Bobby shoots his wife a look.

'Is that right, Mr Stafford?'

Bobby holds Leo's gaze. 'I didn't have much to do with him.'

'But you didn't like him?'

'For fuck's sake! Does it matter?'

Leo waits long enough for Stafford to feel uncomfortable. 'A man is dead, Mr Stafford. Possibly murdered. I think establishing who disliked him is quite important, don't you?'

'Murdered?' Ashleigh breathes out, her eyes wide in apparent shock, and Leo mentally kicks himself. The official stance on any dead body, until a forensic pathologist confirms otherwise, is 'unexplained'. Leo will be in deep shit with Crouch if Ashleigh Stafford starts gossiping.

'My colleagues and I will be taking statements from everyone who attended the party or saw the deceased immediately prior to his death.' Leo hands Bobby a card. 'If you think of anything in the meantime, please let me know.'

'Do you have a suspect?' Ashleigh follows Leo to the door.

'I'm sure I don't need to remind you, Mrs Stafford, not to make any observations online in relation to the police investigation.'

'I've got two million followers on Instagram. I have a responsibility to keep them updated.'

What did she think she was: a war correspondent? 'I imagine it will be tricky to update your social media status when you're serving two years for contempt of court.'

Ashleigh's mouth drops open, and Leo heads for the lodge next door.

Clemence Northcote, at number four, has short hair streaked with pink and purple. She wears a dress which forms a triangle, like the Ladies' sign on a loo door.

'Do you need to speak to us both? Only, Caleb – that's my son – is still in bed.' She gives Leo a conspiratorial grimace. 'Teenagers! I managed to stay awake to see in the new year, but that's still early when you're sixteen, isn't it? No idea what time he got to bed. I was dead to the world.' As she realises what she's said, a look of horror passes over her face. 'Ouch. Sorry.'

'We'll speak to him tomorrow, if that's alright? Sounds like it was quite the party.'

'It was wonderful.' She winces again. 'God. Awful to say that, after what happened to Rhys, but of course we didn't know he was missing until this morning, let alone . . .' She shudders. 'Do you think there's any risk to the rest of us? Is it okay for us to stay here? Only—' Clemence cuts herself off, taking a steadying breath. 'Sorry. I'm all over the place. It's all such a shock.'

'We'd prefer you to stay at least until you've given a statement, please, Mrs Northcote.'

'Please, call me Clemmie. Of course. Gosh, it's just awful, isn't it?' She moves to the hob and stirs the contents of a large pot. 'Soup. For Yasmin and the girls.'

In place of the long metal table Leo had seen in the Lloyds' and the Staffords' lodges, Clemence Northcote has a small wooden one with two folding chairs. Against the wall, Leo recognises an Ikea bookshelf he has in his own flat. On the other side of the glass doors is a clothes horse with a wetsuit dripping gently on to the deck.

'It must have been cold,' Leo says, nodding towards the wetsuit.

'Sorry, what?' Clemmie is opening and closing drawers with dizzying inefficiency.

'The New Year's Day swim. A village tradition, I hear.'

'Oh, that. Yes. I'm used to it, though – I swim all year round.'

'Were you there when the body was found?'

Clemmie presses her hands either side of her face. 'I left right away. Came back to The Shore. It seemed intrusive. And . . .' She seems reluctant to finish. Leo waits. 'The locals are a bit funny about us,' Clemmie says eventually.

'About The Shore?'

Clemmie nods. 'I've tried – believe me, I've tried. I organised a litter-pick, volunteered to help at the library . . . People are polite enough, but it's . . .' She sighs. 'It's very *them and us*, you know? Did you see the massive letters at the bottom of the drive?'

'You can't miss them.'

'Well, quite. Before The Shore opened, someone spray-painted letters on the o and the r, so it read *The Shite*. They had to sandblast them to get it off.'

Leo laughs. 'The locals aren't keen on the development, then?'

'They're not keen on *us*. There's an assumption that we're all rolling in it; that we're *up ourselves*, as my son would say, just because we've bought lodges.'

'I imagine a place here isn't cheap.' Leo speaks neutrally. He's already checked out The Shore's website, where a three-bedroomed lodge starts at £550,000. In tiny font, at the bottom of the page, the annual maintenance fee is listed at an eye-watering ten grand a year.

'It is a lot of money, I know, but . . .' Clemmie stretches an arm towards the lake '. . . look at it.'

Leo can think of better things to spend half a million quid on than a view.

'The trouble is, they think we're all living in mansions the rest of the year.'

'You mean you're not?'

'Some of the others are.' Clemmie sighs. 'Well, all of them, I suppose. The Staffords have staff and a swimming pool, and the Charltons live in Kensington and have a place in the Cotswolds. And of course the Lloyds' family home is beautiful.'

'You've seen it?'

'In magazines.'

'So where do you and your son live?'

'London.' Clemmie colours. 'A one-bedroom flat in Zone Five, where I sleep on the sofa and have the bad back to prove it.'

'But how . . .' Leo breaks off, not wanting to be rude.

'How did I afford this?' Clemmie flushes again. 'It's on a private repayment plan. Although the others don't know I didn't buy it outright, so I'd be grateful if you'd keep that to yourself.'

'Of course.' Leo glances around the room. 'I assumed the lodges were all decorated the same.'

'You pay extra for furnished. Quite a lot extra. They really push you into it – I suppose they want a certain *look* in photos, I do understand how it works – but it wasn't an option for us.'

'Rhys Lloyd owned the resort, I understand?'

'That's right.'

'What was he like?'

Clemmie looks at her soup with more concentration than

it requires. 'He was a wonderful singer. I remember hearing him at—'

'As a person.' Leo keeps his eyes on Clemmie.

There's a long silence before she speaks. 'He was very different from the way he'd been portrayed in the press.'

'In what way?'

'The interviews always show him as down-to-earth. They talk about how he walked to school with newspaper in his shoes because they leaked, and how he spent his first West End pay cheque on a holiday for his mum.'

'And he wasn't like that?'

'He looked down on us,' Clemmie says. 'Me and Caleb. Because I don't wear the right clothes, or drink the right wine. I didn't fit with his vision of The Shore.' She speaks calmly, but there's a hint of bitterness beneath her words.

'That must have been hard to take,' Leo says neutrally.

'Not so hard that it would give me a motive for murder, if that's what you're suggesting?'

'This isn't a murder enquiry,' Leo says. *Yet*, he adds, silently.

Clemmie gives a half-laugh. 'If it were, I think you'd have your hands full.'

'Why's that?'

Clemmie looks at him, her expression unguarded and resigned. 'Because I've been at The Shore for six months, and I've yet to meet a single person who liked him.'

As Leo leaves Clemence Northcote's lodge, he feels the familiar fizz of adrenaline. He looks at the lodges, thinking of the breeze block walls under the wooden cladding; of the secrets they house. Leo doesn't know how Rhys Lloyd died, but he knows this: beneath the glossy surface of The Shore is another story entirely.

SIX

NEW YEAR'S DAY | FFION

Judging by the look on Leo's face, he'd obviously expected to pair up for the house-to-house, but Ffion prefers to fly solo. Besides, regardless of what she'd said to Leo about forgetting last night's escapade, it was easier said than done. *Never dip your pen in company ink*, a sergeant once told her. Patriarchal, but nevertheless sound, advice. Ffion finds herself distracted by flashbacks entirely inappropriate for a potential murder enquiry.

Deirdre Huxley, the owner of lodge two, is of indeterminable age, with sharp eyes that are at odds with the wrinkles around them. She wears a pale pink cardigan with mother-of-pearl buttons, and straight-cut trousers with a sharp crease down the centre. On her feet, velvet slippers are topped with tassels and a swirl of gold embroidery. Her hair is more silver than grey, expertly coiffed into a smooth shoulder-length bob. *Well-preserved*, Ffion's mam would call her.

Mrs Huxley examines Ffion's warrant card through tortoise-shell glasses strung on a chain around her neck. 'You don't look like a burglar, but one never knows, does one?'

'I'm not a burglar,' Ffion promises.

'Then come in and warm up, and you can tell me I might want to sit down because the body that washed up on the other side of the lake earlier today is almost certainly Rhys Lloyd.' She turns, leaving Ffion standing in the open doorway with her mouth open. Talk about getting straight to the point.

Ffion steps inside and closes the door, before following Mrs Huxley into the lodge. The older woman walks with a stick, a beautiful-looking dark-wood affair with a polished metal handle the size of a small fist. She leans it against the sofa and sinks into the cushions with a contented sigh.

'You're quite the detective.' Ffion joins her on the sofa. The lodge has the same furniture she saw at the Lloyds', but configured differently, so the long table is at the back of the open-plan space, and the corner sofa by the sliding doors on to the deck.

'One missing man. One body in the lake. We hardly need Miss Marple, do we?'

'You'll be telling me how he got there next.'

'I imagine he was murdered. Would you like a slice of fruit cake?'

Ffion looks up, startled. 'What makes you say that?'

'I always have one about this time.'

'No, I mean, why do you think Rhys Lloyd was murdered?'

'Wasn't he?' Mrs Huxley pushes herself upright and makes her way to the kitchen.

'Mrs Huxley, if you have information relating to the investi-gation, I need to—'

'I think I have some fondant fancies, if you'd rather?'

'No cake,' Ffion says firmly. 'How well did you know Rhys?'

'I'm not sure any of us really know anyone, do we? The chair of my local WI embezzled thousands of pounds every year, and no one suspected a thing, until she turned up to the AGM in a pair of Jimmy Choos. Now: Earl Grey or Lapsang Souchong?'

Ffion gives in. 'Earl Grey.' Her stomach rumbles. 'And maybe just a small slice of cake. Were you at the party last night?'

'Oh, yes, dear. I retired before midnight and listened to the bongs with a cup of tea in bed, which is by far the best way to see in the New Year, don't you think?'

Ffion briefly allows herself to remember snogging Leo outside the club as one year ended and a new one began. 'Sounds great. When did you last see Rhys?'

'I don't wear a watch.' Mrs Huxley places a tray in front of Ffion, and begins setting out cups. 'My late husband gave me a beautiful Cartier wristwatch when we married, and when he died, it stopped. It was as if it knew. Do you think watches have souls, DC Morgan?'

'Was he still at the party when you left?'

'I took it to several places to be mended, and no one could fathom it out.'

'Extraordinary. Were you aware of Rhys arguing with anyone at the party? Anyone with a grudge against him, perhaps?'

'People bear grudges over the silliest things, don't they?' Mrs Huxley cuts two generous slices of fruit cake and pushes one towards Ffion. 'A friend of mine refused to talk to her brother for years, because he'd said something disparaging about one of her children. Are you sure you wouldn't prefer a fondant fancy?'

Ffion should have sent Leo here. He strikes her as the sort who gets on well with old ladies.

'Can't you just look at the cameras to see what time Rhys left the party, dear?'

Ffion puts down her cup. 'There's CCTV at The Shore?' She's been so preoccupied, it hadn't even occurred to her there might be evidence on camera. Rookie error.

'Isn't there everywhere? Jonty Charlton has the key. He's at number one. Did you know, the lodges were supposed to be named after Welsh mountains?'

Ffion does know – it made the local paper. The names were 'unpronounceable', according to a focus group commissioned by The Shore's investors, who had proposed English versions in their place. *Dragon's Head. Red Ridge.* 'Over my dead body,' Ffion's mam had said, when the petition came around. The local Plaid Cymru councillor took it to Westminster, and the lodge names were quietly replaced with numbers.

By the time Ffion manages to extricate herself from Deirdre Huxley's lodge, her head is spinning. She scans her surroundings for cameras. They're well hidden, nestled in the trees lining the drive. Ffion rolls a cigarette and walks down towards the edge of the lake to smoke it in private. It's astonishing how many people feel it's their God-given right to lecture a complete stranger on their health.

'Every cigarette takes ten minutes off your life, you know,' Leo says, walking up behind her.

'Eleven, actually. Want one?'

'Go on, then.'

Ffion passes the tin to Leo, who rolls the loose cigarillo of a social smoker.

'How were your two?'

'I haven't done the Charltons yet, and Mrs Huxley is batty. Good tea stop, though.'

'I'm all done,' Leo says. 'No one remembers seeing Lloyd at midnight, but Ashleigh Stafford saw him barfing into a bush at some point before that.'

'Classy.' Ffion looks out at the water. The dark clouds that had met them on their arrival have cleared, and the snow tips of Pen y Ddraig are stark against the blue winter sky.

'Clemence Northcote says there was a group pissing about by the water, late in the evening – daring each other to go in, that sort of thing – but she can't be certain if Lloyd was with them.' Leo turns towards the lodges. Between each deck, ladders run down to floating pontoons, shared by the lodges on either side. 'If he went in the water there, would the current take him across to the other side?'

'Do I look like the Little Mermaid?'

Leo picks up a stone and throws it into the lake, sending a tern flapping into the air.

'Hey!' Ffion glares at Leo. 'I've dragged kids home by their ears for doing that.'

'I didn't hit it.'

'I'd have bloody hit *you* if you had.' She stares out at the lake. Beside her, Leo starts fidgeting. God, it's worse than taking a kid out.

'Doesn't it drive you insane?' Leo says. 'All this.' He waves an arm at the expanse of water, the harsh rock face of Pen y Ddraig mountain looming over it.

'Yup.'

'You should put in for a transfer. South Wales, maybe?'

'Yeah, I can't do that.'

'Why not?'

Ffion makes the same gesture Leo did. 'Because of all this.'

She walks away from him, her leather boots darkening as water splashes across the toes. Leo follows, a few feet further from the water's edge. Heaven forbid he should get those brogues wet.

'The lake gets under your skin,' she says. 'It's just always there, you know? When I was growing up, the lake was where we hung out. It's where our mams dragged us for special photos; where we had to wash our rugby boots when they were too filthy for the sink.'

'You played rugby?'

'Play,' Ffion corrects. 'Fly-half.'

'Have you ever tried to move away?'

She laughs. 'It's not *Little House on the Prairie* – some big homestead folk can't leave because Mama's apron strings are too darn tight.' She puts on an American drawl, and Leo looks sheepish. 'I did move, actually. I went to university in Cardiff, and then I lived in London for a bit. But my boyfriend was here, and . . . other stuff, so I came home,' she finishes lamely.

The boyfriend bit isn't true. They saw each other on and off during university holidays, but they were never exclusive. No question of him trekking down to Cardiff or meeting her friends. It was only afterwards that they had become a proper couple, when Ffion came back home.

Mam had been forty-four when Seren (not an accident, she told people firmly, a *surprise*) arrived, the pregnancy having been overshadowed by Dad's illness. He'd missed the birth by two weeks.

Seren was four when Ffion finished school. 'If I apply to Manchester,' Ffion told Mam, 'I could carry on living here. Drive in for lectures.'

'Don't stay home for us.'

'But I should be here to help out—'

'I'll be just fine.' Elen had encouraged Ffion to spread her wings. 'There's a big world outside Cwm Coed, *cariad*.'

It wasn't the lake that had brought Ffion back home, it was guilt. Guilt that Elen was home alone with a small child; guilt that Dad would have thought badly of Ffion for leaving. One day she had seen a job advert, and it was as though it were calling to her.

'I'm going to join the police,' she'd announced. Seren was seven by then, still small enough to squeeze on Ffion's lap. She thought Ffion the coolest sister ever; Ffion found Seren endearing and exasperating in equal measure.

Mam was quiet. 'Who'd have thought,' she said. 'Ffion *Wyllt*, a police officer.'

'Is it a terrible idea, Mam?'

Elen smiled, clasping her hands around Ffion's cheeks. 'Your dad would have been proud of you.' They'd both cried, then, and Seren had cried too, even though – or perhaps because – she had no memory of him.

The ping of a text message brings Ffion back to the moment, she and Leo reaching for their phones at the same time. 'Yours,' she says, seeing her blank screen.

Leo stares at his phone. 'I have to make a call.' He moves away, standing beneath the trees, and Ffion walks to the edge of the lake, giving Leo the illusion of privacy.

'But you said to call now—'

Ffion tries not to listen.

'Well, it's only just come through. That's hardly my fault!'

Ah, who's she kidding? Ffion skims a stone and tries not to make it obvious.

'Can I speak to him? Please, Allie.' There's a long silence. Ffion checks her emails and sends a quick update to DI Malik.

'Hey, little man!' Leo says. 'How's it going? Happy New Year!'

His tone is so different, it's all Ffion can do to stop herself turning around and double-checking it's the same guy. She falls into the spaces between Leo's words – *He did? And what did you do? No way!* – and the past grips Ffion's heart and squeezes it hard. She imagines being on the phone to her own dad, and she picks up another stone, a bigger one this time, and hurls it far into the water.

'You've got a kid,' Ffion says, when Leo's finished. She looks along the lakeside, to where the resort squats in the break of the trees. A vast marquee covers one of the decks, fairy lights criss-crossing the windows. 'Harris,' she remembers.

'How did – oh, yeah, right.' Leo puts a hand to the back of his neck, the small tattoo now hidden beneath his collar. He stoops and picks up a stone; throws it hard into the water, scattering the terns. Ffion lets it go. 'He's four. You got any?'

'God no.'

Leo glances at his watch. 'The DI wants us in the office to brief him on the job, as soon as Yasmin confirms ID.'

'You can do that. I don't do DIs.'

'I wasn't aware they were optional.'

'They are when you cover two hundred square kilometres and your DI works two towns away.'

Leo opens his mouth to say something, then gives up, shaking his head. He points across the lake to a large single-storey structure. 'What's that?' The building is surrounded by boats, some listing to the side, others sitting in huge cradles, their hulls naked and exposed.

'The boathouse. Steffan Edwards owns it. He fixes boats; rents out paddleboards and dinghies in the summer.'

'Would he know about the currents?'

'Probably.' Ffion begins walking back towards the lodges.

'Meet me there in the morning?'

'A third date, already? You're a fast operator, Mr Brady.'

60

'What happened to "Let's forget last night ever happened?"'

'I forgot.'

The woman who answers the door at number one has the sort of frame which looks as though it might blow away in a light breeze. Her blonde hair is fine, the skin across her cheekbones so tight it's almost translucent. She wears yoga pants, and a loose top that hangs from shoulders thin as a coathanger, with huge scrunched-down legwarmers pulled over her feet, making her look like a child borrowing her father's socks.

'Come in, come in. It's all so awful! Darling, there's a detective here to see us.'

Ffion is ushered into a large open-plan room, and two children, a boy and a girl, are shooed out. The same zinc table as in the other lodges dominates the space nearest the bifold doors, but, where the others were bright and airy, this place is gloomy, the marquee on the deck stealing both the light and the view.

Jonty Charlton – at least, Ffion assumes this is Jonty – sits on the short end of an L-shaped sofa in the other half of the space, where a log burner pushes out suffocating heat. An open bottle of red wine stands on the table next to him.

Jonty rubs his hand across his brow. 'What a mess, eh? Can I get you something? A glass of wine, perhaps. Blythe, could you find another glass?'

The kitchen surfaces are covered with drying glasses and stacked foil platters. Ffion spots a streamer hanging limply from the curtain pole, and a single shoe abandoned in a corner.

'I'm fine, thank you. You've heard the news?'

'Ashleigh Stafford put it on the residents' WhatsApp group,' Blythe says. 'I just can't believe it. He was just *here*.'

61

'How long have you known the Lloyds?'

Blythe puts her hand in the air, like a schoolkid. 'Yasmin came to one of my yoga classes about five years ago. It's amazing really. I wasn't going to teach on a Tuesday – everyone's chakra's always a bit *off* on a Tuesday – but I did, and she did, and the rest is history.'

'The girls became friendly,' Jonty says. 'Blythe told me Yasmin's husband had inherited a patch of land and needed investors for a development.'

'And you saw an opportunity?' Ffion says.

'It's what I do.' Jonty takes a slug of wine. 'Match projects to investors. It's rare for me to invest personally, but I find it hard to say no to my wife.'

'North Wales is on the cusp of regeneration,' Blythe says. Ffion suppresses a snort. Wait till the lake floods and it pisses down solidly for three weeks. 'And the energy here is extraordinary – you can really feel it pass through you.'

The only thing Ffion has felt pass through her in Cwm Coed is a dodgy kebab. Maybe the *chakra* had been off. 'Is it a good investment?'

Jonty makes a weighing motion with his hands. 'Property's like the stock market. To make real money you have to hold your nerve. Play the long game. Once the whole development's been rolled out, this place'll be a goldmine.'

'I'd like to take a look at the CCTV, if I may?'

There's a moment's hesitation. 'Of course! Anything to help. Hang on, I'll get the key.'

Ffion follows Jonty across the drive to a stone building. Inside, a vast circuitboard lists every external light, and a generator stands in silent anticipation in the corner.

'In case of power cuts,' Jonty explains. 'It's quite the selling point. Heaven forbid our owners should be without Netflix.' He shows Ffion a computer in the corner, logging on in a blur of keystrokes. 'I'd have had cameras at the back too, if I'd had my way – would have brought the insurance down no end – but apparently it's an invasion of privacy?' He adds a question mark, the thought preposterous. 'Anyway, there's a camera on the main entrance . . .' he presses a key '. . . *here*, and two others covering the driveway: *here* and *here*.'

'Nothing pointing directly at the lodges?'

'Just the drive and the parking bays, I'm afraid.'

'Great. You can leave me to it, if you like. It'll take me a while to work through it.'

'I'd better stay. It's an expensive piece of kit.'

Ffion smiles. 'Honestly, I'll be ages.'

Jonty glances towards the lodge, the bottle of red and the warmth of the wood burner calling to him.

'Hand on heart,' she says, placing her palm flat on her chest and looking up at Jonty through her eyelashes. 'I promise I won't break your fancy generator.' Jesus. She'll have to hand in her membership of the North Wales Feminists' Action Group at this rate.

Just kidding. There is no North Wales Feminists' Action Group.

'Okay, then. Give me a shout if you need anything.'

Ffion locks the door behind him. The last thing she needs is the victim's business partner breathing down her neck while she's trying to do her job.

There's no chair in the office, but under the desk she finds two empty crates of champagne – how the other half live – and she balances one on top of the other and perches gingerly on top. She scrolls through the dates until she finds New Year's Eve, then spins the digital clock forward. Midday, one p.m., two p.m., three . . .

There.

Ffion glances over her shoulder at the locked door, blood singing in her ears. Drifting through the dusk from the Lloyds' lodge comes the sound of Rhys singing. Ffion imagines Yasmin – or the girls – torturing themselves over his recordings. She stares at the screen, her fingers poised above the keyboard.

Then she presses delete.

SEVEN

NEW YEAR'S EVE | 10 P.M. | RHYS

Rhys wants the party to be over. The room is swaying, his vision blurred. He feels a hiss in his ear.

'If I were you, I'd be checking over my shoulder.'

Rhys lurches away, hot and unsteady. He feels sick. In his mouth his tongue feels twice the size, no longer capable of speech. He makes his way unsteadily through the room, a strained smile bolted to his face. His shirt pulls at the back of his neck as he moves, sweat soaking into the collar, and he feels the burn of brandy move dangerously up his throat. He swallows it back down.

'Amazing place, Rhys!'

'Great party.'

'Oops – easy there!' A steadying hand catches Rhys before he falls, good-natured laughter rippling around the room. 'You've peaked too soon, old man – it's not midnight yet.'

Rhys manages a laugh, as is expected, but his forehead prickles with sweat, and his skin feels clammy and cold. The marquee is empty and the party has retreated inside. There are too many people, standing too close to each other, and Rhys feels crowded. Trapped. He hates this place. He should never have built it, never have come back to the lake. Nothing has turned out the way he intended.

Rhys's vision for The Shore had been a place for artists. A place for singers, actors, creatives. He'd imagined a fusion of English and Welsh culture.

'Slight problem with that, old man,' Jonty had said, when Rhys had finished his impassioned pitch. 'Creatives don't have money.'

The windows of the lodge have steamed up, the dark expanse of the lake filtered by fogged glass. Out on the deck, the inside of the marquee runs with condensation, Blythe's disco ball sending silent fireworks across the swathes of draped fabric that make up the walls and ceiling. The noise has reached fever pitch, and Rhys feels it vibrate through the floor, through his bones, as he moves towards the front door. All around him, people are dancing in tight knots, alcohol giving them loose limbs and lazy gazes. Faces appear in blurry snapshots, like photographs floating in developing fluid. He stares at the faces as they swim in and out. *Yasmin. Ashleigh. Jonty. Dee. Huw. Seren.*

He can't stay here. He pushes on, pushes past. He knows most but not all of the people at the party, but in this alcohol-glazed fug they could all be strangers. He feels disconnected from them, from himself, as though he's viewing the party through thick glass. So many people. They were curious to see inside The Shore; to see what Rhys had made of himself, since he'd left Cwm Coed. Or perhaps they simply wanted more fuel for the fire that had started the day the planning application went in.

A shout rings out. 'Give us a song, Rhys!'

The request prompts a chorus of pleas from around the piano, but Rhys waves them away, pointing vaguely across the room as though he is on his way to see someone, to do something. A

66

pianist begins thumping out 'Yellow Submarine', and Rhys stumbles towards the door. He thinks it's likely he will throw up, and he would prefer to do so outside. In fact, he'd prefer to do it in his own bathroom. Suddenly, he wants nothing more than to be in his own lodge, slipping between cool sheets, within dashing distance of the en suite. His heart's racing, and he wishes he could stop the images in his head; memories he thought he'd forgotten.

It isn't too late to be a better person, he tells himself.

As he reaches the front door, he hears the opening bars of 'Don't Cry for Me, Argentina', and he's grateful he didn't stay. Outside, the icy air brings a moment's relief, but the clarity is short-lived. His stomach heaves and he lurches from the path, vomiting violently into the bushes. He thinks of his cool sheets, of the bottled water in the bedroom minibar.

The driveway is pooled with lights from the lodges. Despite the cold, there are shapes huddled in the trees – teenagers, perhaps, skulking out of sight with the cider they think they stole unseen.

As he staggers towards his own lodge, Rhys sees movement upstairs in Dee's place; at number three, the Staffords' door is wide open. He stumbles on, past Clemmie's lodge, to number five. He's glad to find the front door unlocked – he can't remember where his keys are – and he pauses only to throw up again, beside the ornamental grasses.

He doesn't take off his shoes. He doesn't turn on the light. He grips the banister and grits his teeth as his guts churn. He reminds himself he is seconds away from privacy, a clean loo, crisp white sheets. Seconds away from the oblivion he craves, and tomorrow will be a new start, a chance to make good the mistakes he's made. When he wakes up, everything will feel better. He will *be* better.

EIGHT

JANUARY 2ND | FFION

'Did he kill himself, then?'

Ffion looks at her watch. She's going to be late to meet Leo. 'Mam, you know I can't talk about the case.'

'Not even to your mother?' Elen's folding laundry, a mug of tea going cold on the side. Elen isn't built to sit down. Occasionally Seren makes her watch something on Netflix, but after twenty minutes Elen starts twitching, looking for a job to do.

'Especially not to my mother. Everyone knows I'm job, and they'll all be asking you what you know.' Ffion balances her toast on her hand, spreading marmalade awkwardly with the other.

'*Plât*, Ffion!'

'Saves washing up.' Ffion eats the toast in four bites and brushes the crumbs into the sink.

'I'd tell them I didn't know anything.'

Ffion snorts. 'You're a terrible liar, Mam. Your ears go pink.'

'You'd be surprised what I know and haven't told you.' Elen folds the last piece of washing and picks up the basket. 'People are saying he had a stalker. From London.'

Ffion puts on her coat. 'People can say what they want.'

'So that means you're not looking for someone round here, doesn't it? If it was the stalker who killed him?'

'Bye, Mam.' Ffion closes the door firmly. God, she has to find somewhere else to live. She could have rented somewhere when she walked out on her marriage, only it had been so easy to go back home, and the couple of weeks she planned to stay have somehow turned into a year. It is, she's ashamed to admit, nice to be looked after, but . . . well, turns out you can have too much of a good thing.

Ffion has arranged to meet Leo at the lake, so she leaves the Triumph parked outside the house. She's barely out of the gate when Elen hollers after her. She turns to see her mam in her slippers, legging it down the path. Either side of her, the husks of verbena lean like skeletons, last summer's colour long since faded. *Rewilding*, Elen calls her approach to gardening.

'Mam, really. I can't tell—'

'Glynis just rang. She's got reporters asking questions.'

'So?' Ffion winces at her instinctive response. What is she, fourteen? She'll be whining for a Juicy Couture tracksuit next, and refusing to tidy her room. 'Tell her I'll get uniform to send someone round.'

'They're banging on the door, Ffi. She's really scared.'

Ffion sighs. 'Okay, I'll go now.'

'*Diolch, cariad.*'

This is the trouble with living on your patch: you're the go-to police officer for everything from lost property to murder. Not that the latter's too common, so no wonder the press are sniffing about. And Rhys is – was – the golden boy, of course. Yesterday, his name trended on Twitter, fans sharing stories of when they saw him live.

@BigCSurvivor: #RhysLloyd sent this signed sheet music for our charity auction.

69

If only they knew.

Ffion has read every tweet Rhys has received for the last two years. The tech team are all over this, she knows, but she wanted to see them for herself. She checks Twitter now, as she walks down the high street to Glynis's hardware shop, scrolling back to the last abusive tweet Rhys received, on the morning of New Year's Eve. It's short and to the point.

@RhysLloyd5000: I WISH YOU WERE DEAD.

The location of Glynis's shop would have been obvious, even if Ffion didn't know it as well as her own home; even if she hadn't spent most weekends dragging her heels on one of her dad's missions to fix the lawnmower or fit a washing machine. She hasn't been inside for years and as she draws nearer, her feet slow of their own accord.

Two men stand outside the shop, one in a three-quarter-length black wool coat and a striped scarf, the other wearing a thick fleece under a bodywarmer with pockets stuffed to bursting. The latter carries a camera on one shoulder, and a furry mic on a long pole.

'We just want to ask a few questions, Mrs Lloyd.' Striped Scarf is rapping on the door. 'We're very sorry for your loss,' he shouts, as an afterthought.

'Let's do the headteacher,' the cameraman says. 'Come back later.'

Ffion crosses the road and points at the sign saying *ar gau*. 'Shop's closed today. As a mark of respect,' she adds pointedly.

'Did you know Rhys Lloyd?' The reporter gets straight to the point, his colleague setting a readying hand on his camera.

'Is that why you're here?' Ffion furrows her brow. 'I'd have thought you'd be at the vigil.'

'What vigil?'

'Up Pen y Ddraig mountain. There's a path leading up from the lake and, halfway up, there's a little stone hut where Rhys used to sing, before he was discovered. Someone lit a candle in his memory and now there are hundreds there. They're having a sort of service for him this morning so the children can sing in his memory.' Ffion closes her eyes briefly, one hand flat against her heart. 'It's going to be so beautiful.'

For two men who don't look in peak condition, they can't half shift.

Ffion retraces her steps and heads back towards the lake, where Leo's waiting for her. 'Sorry, manic morning.'

'Late night?'

Ffion spent last night watching re-runs of *Call the Midwife*, while Seren skulked in her room on YouTube and Mam did the accounts for the holiday cottages, but she finds herself giving Leo a lop-sided smile; the sort of smile which says *wouldn't you like to know?* It's habit, this playing to type; the Ffion *Wyllt* of long ago. The comparison makes her feel cold.

'Are you alright? You look as if you're having a stroke.' Leo nods towards the boathouse. 'What's the skinny on Steffan Edwards?'

'The business has been here forever. Busy in the summer, dead in the winter, like most places around here. Steff took over from his dad a few years ago.'

'Reliable?'

Ffion starts walking towards the boathouse. 'Completely.' She stoops to pick up an empty bottle of vodka from outside the workshop door. 'Unless he's had a drink.'

When Steffan Edwards senior died, young Steff went on a bender that lasted five days. The locals were largely sympathetic, but when he threw up in the font at Emyr Williams' christening, enough was enough. An intervention was staged, and whatever was said was enough to make Steffan Edwards pack in the drink for good.

Until now.

'How're you doing, Steff?' Ffion says. The man's eyes are blood-shot, and, although he doesn't seem drunk, he certainly isn't sober.

'Investigating Rhys Lloyd's death, are you? No comment.'

'We wanted your advice, actually.' Flattery gets you everywhere. 'No one knows the lake better than you.'

Steff stops work, but his fist is tight around the wrench.

'The victim washed up by the jetty yesterday morning,' Leo says. 'We think he'd been in the water for less than ten hours. If he went in by The Shore, could—'

'Victim? That man's a victim of nothing!'

'Could the water have carried him to the jetty?'

Steffan doesn't answer.

'This is a police enquiry, Mr Edwards,' Leo says.

The boatman looks away, then shrugs. 'There's a current. Runs past The Shore. If he'd gone in from there, he'd have ended up down the bottom, not across by the jetty.'

Leo brings up a satellite view of Llyn Drych on his iPad, and takes a digital pen from his pocket. 'Can you show me how the current flows? Where would the vict—' He stops. 'Where would the deceased have to have been, in order to end up *here*?' He marks the jetty with a red cross, then hands Steffan the pen.

Steffan leans over the map, in a waft of stale booze and sweat, and draws a series of curved lines across the screen. 'He'd have been higher up. Here. Or here.'

'Can you point out the access points?' Leo says. 'Anywhere you can get a vehicle to?'

Steffan adds half a dozen crosses around the edges of the lake, pinching the image and moving it to find the coves he wants. He draws a huge cross in the middle of the lake. 'More likely he went in here.'

'From a boat?' Leo says.

Ffion raises an eyebrow. Check out Einstein. 'Got any out on hire?' she asks Steff, but she knows the answer already. It's winter: the boathouse is only open for repairs. If Rhys was killed on a boat, it didn't come from here.

'Is there any way of knowing which boats were on the lake on New Year's Eve?' Leo asks. Ffion wanders across the room, to where a workbench serves as a desk, and picks up a blue A4 book. Steffan either doesn't see, or doesn't care.

'I'm not the keeper of the lake. There's not many want to sail this time of year, but Llyn Drych doesn't close. There are always a few boats out on a good day.'

Each entry in the blue book covers two pages: the date and name of the owner on the far left, followed by a summary of the problem, and Steffan's solution. On the far right are columns for the cost of repairs, and the date of collection. Ffion flicks to the end of December. She sees a few names she recognises and several with addresses further afield, owners of boats moored locally. It's a meticulous – if old-fashioned – record of work, but all it tells Ffion is what boats *weren't* on the lake, not which were. She takes a photo of the two pages covering the period between Christmas and New Year, then replaces the book.

'Thanks for your time.'

'If I'd found him, I'd have pushed him back and let the fish have him.' Steffan stumbles against the boat, the wrench falling on to the concrete with a clatter. 'Rhys Lloyd's no loss to Cwm Coed.'

'Should he be working on boats, in that state?' Leo says, as they leave. 'Surely he's breaking some sort of law?'

'Probably.'

They take Leo's car to The Shore. There's a child's car seat on the back seat, but none of the detritus Ffion expects from kids. When Seren had been little, Mam's car was a repository for clothes, squashed raisins, broken breadsticks and toys. Leo keeps his car the way he keeps his flat: strictly functional.

'Your son doesn't live with you, then?'

'I was looking into Lloyd's career.' Leo sidesteps the question. 'He's not done much recently, has he?'

'I wouldn't know.'

'He was massive ten, fifteen years ago, but then everything tailed off. He hadn't had a West End role for five years. His website talks about "TV work" but all I can find is a couple of adverts.'

'What's your point?'

Leo shrugs. 'Maybe he was depressed, or worried about money.'

'Suicide?'

'Maybe.'

Ffion pushes her hands deep into the pockets of her coat. Suicide would have been too good for Rhys Lloyd.

* * *

74

Outside number three, The Shore, the reporter Ffion chased away from Glynis's shop is talking to Ashleigh Stafford, who wears a floor-length dress more suited to the red carpet than Llyn Drych.

'We will all miss him so very, very much.' Ashleigh wipes away a tear.

Striped Scarf turns to face the camera. 'And that concludes our special report into the death of musician Rhys Lloyd. I've been speaking with Ashleigh Stafford, whose latest reality TV show, *Stuff with the Staffords*, airs later this year.' He holds a rictus smile for three seconds, then mimes a swift cut across his throat. The cameraman swings the heavy camera from his shoulder.

'And that'll be on tonight?' Ashleigh's make-up and hair are immaculate.

'Should be.'

'Great!' She turns to Bobby. 'Isn't that brilliant, babes? Such perfect timing.' She pulls her husband back into the house, but not before Ffion sees the embarrassment on his face. She gets the impression Bobby Stafford is a nice guy. What does he see in someone like Ashleigh?

Stupid question, she thinks, as the woman's perfectly peach-shaped behind disappears.

Leo walks towards the reporter. 'This is private property.'

Striped Scarf stares past him, to Ffion. 'You! Thanks for the wild goose chase. My shoes are wrecked, and Gav's pulled a hamstring.'

'Is that Gav?' Ffion looks at the cameraman, whose forehead is glistening with the effort of packing away his kit. 'He doesn't look as though he could pull a cracker, never mind a hamstring. Now, as my colleague said, this is private property.'

'Yeah? Call the police, then.'

'Nee nah nee nah.' Ffion pulls out her warrant card. 'How's that for a response time?'

They walk around to the rear of The Shore. Each lodge has its own deck, stretching the full width of the property. A near-invisible glass balustrade runs along the edges of each deck. Beneath it, the water is shallow, jagged rocks just visible beneath the surface.

A narrow balcony on the first floor of each lodge provides shelter on the deck below, the first few feet screened on either side to give privacy from the neighbours. Several of the owners have dining sets in these undercover areas, the rest of the deck dedicated to sun loungers and more sociable seating arrangements.

There are no curtains on any of the windows. The glass is tinted, and reflections of the lake ripple across each set of sliding doors. In return, the lodges shimmer in the water below, the resulting loop unsettling to Ffion. Each deck is separated by a gap of around four feet, ladders leading down to floating pontoons shared between neighbouring lodges.

There are two men in the marquee at number one, un-fastening the swathes of material. Ffion pushes her way inside. 'Stop right there.'

'Please!' Leo has followed her in. Ffion shoots him a look, then turns to the men. They're in navy work trousers and polo shirts; a company logo embroidered on their chests. *Markham Events.*

'DC Morgan, North Wales CID,' Ffion says, snapping open her warrant card. 'This resort is subject to an active police investigation and could well be a crime scene. That marquee's going nowhere.'

'Can I help you?' Jonty Charlton opens the doors on to his deck. He frowns at Ffion. 'Oh, it's you. What can I do for you, PC Morton?'

'DC Morgan. I'm just telling the lads we'll be needing the marquee *in situ* for a while longer. Just in case.'

'At seventy quid a day?' Jonty says. 'I don't think so.' He jerks his head towards the navy-clad men, who glance nervously at Ffion.

'It's that or you get nicked for interfering with a crime scene.' Ffion smiles at him. 'Would you like to decide now, or phone a friend?'

'We'll, uh . . .' One of the men gestures vaguely towards the road. 'Let the office know when it's okay to come back, yeah?'

When they've gone, Jonty Charlton folds his arms across his chest and glares at Ffion. 'I assume North Wales Police will be compensating me for the additional cost.'

'I suppose it depends on what we find,' Ffion says cheerfully. 'This is my colleague, DC Brady, from Cheshire Major Crime.'

'Major Crime? Good grief. Is that really necessary?'

'Jonty, darling, close the door, it's freezing in— Oh, hello!' Blythe appears behind her husband, shivering dramatically. 'Come in, come in!' She ushers Ffion and Leo inside. 'Is there any news?'

'Yes,' Jonty says drily. 'Your bloody marquee is going to bankrupt us.'

Blythe lets out an outraged squeak. '*My* marquee? You were the one who didn't want riff-raff traipsing through the house.'

'And look how that turned out,' Jonty says. 'The world and his wife rocked up.' He turns to Leo, ignoring Ffion. 'Have you found out what happened to Rhys?'

'The investigation is still ongoing,' Leo says. He's like one of those spokespeople you see on the news, Ffion thinks, giving an update without actually saying anything new. Men are especially good at it, she's noticed; it must be all that practice talking bollocks.

She glances towards the lake, although the water can barely be seen through the marquee. 'Where are the boats?'

'Boats?' Jonty says, as though he's surprised to find himself near water at all.

'There were several here in the summer.' Ffion saw them, tugging at their moorings. A small sailing dinghy, two rowing boats.

'We store them at the boathouse over winter. They'd get damaged in bad weather, otherwise. Too close to the rocks.'

'*Blythe Spirit* is ours.' Blythe beams. 'I was named after the play – by Noël Coward, you know? Only my name's with a "y", so—'

'PC Morton doesn't want to hear all that, darling.'

'DC Morgan,' Ffion mutters. He's doing it deliberately, she'd swear it.

'Here she is.' Jonty walks over to a small desk, where there's a framed picture of a small sailing boat. Jonty's at the helm, his son and daughter in bright red lifejackets, nestled under their mother's arms. 'One of Rhys's girls took that – she's quite the photographer.'

'And the other boats?' Leo says.

'They're just rowing boats,' Jonty says dismissively. 'I don't think I've even seen Dee Huxley out on hers – the Northcotes hogged it all summer, from what I could see.'

'That's Clemence and her son Caleb?' Leo clarifies. 'Number four?'

'Correct. Then of course Rhys has the green boat on the end. *Had*. Christ. Sorry. The guy from the boathouse – what's his name?'

'Steffan Edwards,' Ffion says.

'Correct,' Jonty says, as though she'd passed his test. 'He did it up as a present for Rhys's girls in the summer hols.'

Ffion frowns. It seems a curious thing for Steffan to have done, given his animosity towards Rhys now.

'When was the last time you used your boat?' Leo asks.

'Not since half-term. It's hardly the weather for sailing.'

'Not New Year's Eve?' Ffion says.

'I spent the entire day getting ready for the party, PC Morton.' Ffion bites her tongue.

'My beloved wife took it upon herself to create a lake-themed *indoor-outdoor room*.' Jonty waggles his fingers around the term. 'I'm only relieved I managed to talk her out of the two tonnes of beach sand she wanted brought in from Abersoch.'

'It would have looked incredible,' Blythe sighs.

'It was bloody hard work as it was.'

'Did the other owners not help?' Leo asks. 'I got the impression it was a joint effort.'

'Yasmin was here all day,' Blythe says. 'Rhys conveniently disappeared the second there was work to be done. We were all done by around five o'clock, and everyone went off to get ready.'

'What time did the party start?' Ffion says, although she knows the answer. The invite had been a proper thick-card affair, with black embossed lettering and a dedicated email address for replies.

> The residents of The Shore warmly invite the neighbours for drinks and canapés.
> RSVP: happynewyear@theshore.com

'It was supposed to be half-seven,' Blythe says. 'But a few people drifted in before then.' She looks at her husband. 'The Lloyds got here just as you were putting the children to bed, do you remember? What time was that?'

'Six-thirty?' Jonty says. 'Seven?'

Blythe sighs. 'He's a marvel with them. Bedtime used to be my job, but they were absolute horrors for me. Jonty has the magic touch, don't you, darling?'

'And how did Rhys seem, when he arrived?' Leo says. It's too hot in the lodge, and Ffion has an overwhelming urge to throw open the doors and let in the cold lake air.

'Absolutely fine,' Jonty says.

'Oh, darling, he wasn't! He was behaving most oddly.'

'In what way?' Leo asks. Ffion's pulse thrums.

'Well, he was having a stupid argument with Yasmin, for one thing,' Blythe says.

Jonty sighs. 'He was drunk. From the get-go. And considering the whole point of the party was to chat up the locals—'

'It was not!' Blythe pouts. Ffion half expects her to stamp her foot. 'The party was for us; for The Shore owners to have a good time. Only Jonty and Rhys tried to turn it into an olive branch.'

'I don't follow,' Leo says.

'Let's just say the natives haven't warmed to us.' Jonty gives a lopsided grin. Ffion's fingernails press into her palms. 'We thought a few bottles of bubbly and a snoop at how the other half live might do the trick.'

'And it did!' Blythe claps her hands. 'Everyone got on famously. They'll be talking about it for months,' she adds guilelessly. Even Jonty has the grace to wince.

'When did you last see Rhys Lloyd alive?' Ffion says bluntly.

'He was here at midnight,' Jonty says. 'Wasn't he?'

Blythe raises her palms skywards. 'I think so, but it was all a bit crazy.'

'Come to think of it,' Jonty says, 'I don't know when I last saw the chap. People were coming and going all the time – you

80

know what it's like. Champagne flowing . . . just your average party.'

'"Just your average party",' Leo says, when he and Ffion are back outside. 'Just a dead body and thirty-odd potential witnesses, all drunk.'

'Forensics'll be a nightmare.'

'Pinning down the guest list will be a nightmare. They basically don't have a clue who was there, and it's not as though they all came up the drive – at least half of them walked through the woods.' Leo's phone rings and he glances at the screen. 'It's the boss.'

Ffion stares at the lake. Several guests had come by boat, Jonty told them. At one stage there'd been a line of motorboats, making a bridge from one pontoon to the next.

'Yes, sir,' Leo says. 'I'll tell her, sir.' He covers the end of his phone. 'The DI wants you at the five p.m. briefing.'

'Why?'

Leo's mouth works silently for a moment, before he addresses his boss. 'Um, in terms of added value, sir, what are you hoping she'll bring to the . . . er . . . table?' Ffion raises an eyebrow. 'Right. Yup. I'll tell her. Thanks, sir.' He ends the call. 'He says—' He catches himself. 'Actually, never mind what he said. You have to be there.'

'No, I don't.' Ffion rolls a cigarette. 'Your DI, your briefing. I'll see you at the PM.'

Leo stares at her. 'You're something else, you know?'

'I'll take that as a compliment.'

'It wasn't meant as one.'

Ffion follows the shoreline back towards the village. She can just about keep her shit together when only Leo's involved. But a DI and a packed incident room? She simply can't risk it.

NINE

JANUARY 3RD | LEO

Once Yasmin Lloyd had formally identified her husband's body yesterday afternoon, and the newly appointed Family Liaison Officer had driven her home, Leo had reported to Crouch, as per his instructions. He was there for under five minutes before Crouch dismissed him. *Come back when you've got something useful to share.*

Ffion had made the right call. Leo thinks enviously of the freedom she seems to have. On paper their jobs are practically the same, but in practice they couldn't be more different. Ffion appears to work her patch entirely unsupervised, while Leo reports for duty at the start and end of every day, as though he's a schoolkid, not a murder detective.

Yesterday, after the briefing, he had felt suddenly emboldened. 'The post-mortem's at midday tomorrow,' he told Crouch. 'Is it okay if I work from home in the morning?'

'They did a survey about people who work from home,' Crouch said. 'Thirty-nine per cent said they masturbate during the working day.'

Leo bitterly regretted asking.

'Work from home? More like *wank* from home.' Crouch guffawed with such ferocity that he went puce.

Not for the first time, Leo considered how much easier it would be to deal with Crouch if Leo were a woman. A female officer making a complaint about inappropriate language from a male boss would surely be robustly dealt with, in the current age. Did the fact that Leo was a man make this sort of thing okay? Allie frequently accused him of being a snowflake.

'Is that alright, then?' Leo said. 'To go straight to the mortuary from home?' he added quickly, before Crouch could repeat his earlier witticism. The DI reluctantly agreed.

As a result, Leo has achieved more in half an hour this morning than he would have done in an entire morning in the busy open-plan office, with Crouch ripping the piss at every opportunity. He has read all the open-source material available on Rhys Lloyd, slowly building a picture of him and his family, as well as the history of The Shore. The ill feeling from the Cwm Coed community is well-documented in the local papers, but ignored by the glossy magazines, which tout The Shore as *the luxury resort Wales has been waiting for. Hello!* magazine gave over three pages to interior shots of the Lloyds' lodge, and Leo studies the photo of Rhys at his desk, a shelf of awards on the wall above him proof of his early success.

Had Lloyd's stalker been an obsessive fan? A jealous rival? Leo had requested details of Lloyd's harassment complaint from the Metropolitan Police, and the file came through first thing this morning. Rhys Lloyd had been receiving abusive messages on social media for almost a year before he'd reported it to police, some six months before he died. Was there a connection? Leo reads the statement, handwritten by an officer attending an incident at the Lloyds' house in Highgate, London.

My Twitter address is @RhysLloydSings. I use the account to let fans know about tours and album releases, but otherwise am not active on the platform. Mostly the tweets directed at me are enthusiastic, but occasionally I receive negative comments about my appearance, voice or politics. These generally amount to one or two tweets, which I ignore. Around twelve months ago I noticed I was receiving frequent messages from an account called @RhysLloyd1000, and also from @RhysLloyd2000. Later, accounts were set up with the suffixes 3000 and 4000. The messages began as relatively harmless, criticising my dress sense or my decision to take a particular role. They escalated to (unfounded) accusations of nepotism and deception, and began to take on a threatening tone. I did not make a report of harassment at this stage, as I was not concerned by the messages and considered it an unfortunate side-effect of being in the public eye.

On the evening of 28th April this year I was having a drink at my club in Soho. I returned home to find my wife, Yasmin, in a state of distress, having received a visit from a stranger she described as a 'madwoman'. The woman had referred to our children, Tabitha and Felicia, by name, and made threats which gave Yasmin – and therefore me – grave concerns for our safety.

The door buzzer sounds. Leo ignores it. It'll be another package for the people in the flat upstairs, who go away for weeks at a time then act as though it's a terrible inconvenience when Leo schlepps up with whatever they've had delivered in their absence.

He opens Yasmin's statement.

The woman was white, with blonde hair in a ponytail. She was around five foot six, and wore black jeans, a brown leather jacket and a baseball cap with writing on the front. She was very threatening and the whole experience left me shaken and terrified.

Did Lloyd's London stalker follow him to The Shore to kill him? Or had she hoped for some kind of reconciliation, and instead ended up in a confrontation which led to Lloyd's death?

The buzzer rings again, more insistently this time. Reluctantly, Leo crosses the room and presses the intercom. 'Hello?'

'We need to talk.'

Leo used to find it endearing, the way Allie skipped conversational preambles and got straight to the main event. *I was thinking about next summer*, she'd announce when she met him for dinner, before launching into an idea for a holiday. Her enthusiasm had been infectious.

But then, so is smallpox, Leo thinks, as he presses the door-release button. He glances around, trying to see the flat through his ex-wife's eyes. The narrow hallway has a bathroom immediately opposite the front door, and two doorways on either side. On the right are the lounge and kitchen; on the left his own room, and what he had naïvely imagined would be Harris's, but which has instead become a dumping ground for boxes, Leo's weights, and anything else that doesn't fit in the tiny hallway cupboard. The walls are cream; the carpet a beige fleck which hides the dirt. It's the sort of flat which manages to be perfectly inoffensive yet completely awful all at the same time.

'Allie?' The stairwell is quiet. Grabbing his keys, Leo runs down the stairs. He needs to leave for the post-mortem soon – he doesn't have time for another of her dramas.

His ex-wife is pacing the path, her breath clouding in the cold air.

'Why didn't you come up?'

Allie points to the car, parked in the disabled bay adjacent to the block of flats. 'Unlike *some people*, I take responsibility for my son.'

'You could have brought him up.' Leo takes a step towards the car, a grin spreading across his face as Harris smooshes his own smile across the window.

Allie puts out a hand, firm against Leo's chest. 'I don't want him hearing this.'

Leo sighs. 'What have I done this time?' He isn't sure how much more of this he can take. A few months ago, he'd nipped to Tesco for a sandwich, only to be served three days later with a notice knocked up by Allie's solicitor friend, threatening legal action if Leo 'continues to harass our client or her partner'. Leo hadn't even *seen* Dominic in the supermarket, let alone given him the 'threatening look' referred to in the letter, but Allie always did take a liberal approach to the facts.

Before she can answer, the car door opens, and Harris barrels out. 'Daddy!'

Leo crouches as Harris flies into his arms, then stands and spins around, Harris's arms tight around his neck. 'Hey, little man! How's it hanging?'

'I told you to stay in the car,' Allie snaps.

Leo's chest is tight. He got to be a dad for a single year. One year of bedtimes and bathtimes, of getting Harris dressed and deciding what to do with their weekends. Now he's doled out dad-time in the same practical, unemotional manner he's allocated shifts at work. It feels like a bereavement.

'Can I have a snack?'

'Back in the car, Harris. I need to talk to your dad.' Allie pulls him from Leo, who has to resist the urge to pull back. Parenting isn't a tug of war.

'Go on, chief.' Leo kisses his son fiercely on the forehead and lets Allie strap him back into his seat.

'We're moving,' she says, when she returns.

'Where to?'

'Australia.'

Leo blinks. A car drove past, just as Allie spoke, and for a second he thought she'd said . . .

'We're sick of England.' Allie fiddles with her car keys. 'Brexit, house prices, the bloody rain . . . Dominic's got a job offer, great prospects, and we've found a house with an annexe. Mum and Dad are going to spend half the year with us, half back home.'

'You can't.'

It's as simple as that, surely? Legally, Leo has joint parental responsibility. Allie can't take their son to another country.

'It's an incredible opportunity for Harris to experience a completely different lifestyle.'

'But I won't be able to see him.'

'You can use the annexe, when my parents aren't there. And when Harris is old enough he can fly on his own.'

'Are you actually insane? "Use the annexe"? What, for those six months of annual leave I get? Even if I save all my holiday allowance, even if I spend a month every year in Australia – bloody Australia! – that's eleven months of the year when I don't get to see my son.'

'There's Zoom.'

'Jesus, Allie.' Leo sweeps a hand across his face. 'How can I have a relationship with my—'

'Relationship?' Allie's shouting now, and Leo glances towards the car. 'You hardly even see him now!'

'Because you don't let me!' Leo makes himself calm down – the last thing he wants is for Harris to hear them arguing. He speaks quietly. 'I'll take you to court over this.'

'I'm sure they'll be very interested to hear what a *devoted father* you are.' Allie swipes purposefully at her phone and Leo turns away. He knows what's coming, and he doesn't want to hear it. The communal door slams behind him, but not before Allie's pressed play on the voice note, and Leo has been forced once again to hear the soundtrack of his nightmares.

'Daddy left me. I'm all on my own and it's really dark. I'm scared, Mummy, please come and get me. I'm so scared . . .'

Leo doesn't need the sound file to hear his son's cries. He hears them all the time. He hears them at night, when he can't sleep; at work, when he looks at the photo of Harris on his desk.

He hears them now, as he drives towards Wales, his knuckles white on the steering wheel. He has two options. Either he lets Allie take Harris to Australia, or she finally drops the sword she's dangled over him for the last year. Either way, he's going to lose his son.

Izzy Weaver has already started the post-mortem when Leo arrives. 'I'm still standing,' she announces, inexplicably.

'Morning,' Leo offers in return.

'Afternoon,' Ffion says pointedly. The clock on the wall reads 12.01 p.m. Izzy continues her careful examination of Rhys Lloyd's body, while the radio plays quietly in the background.

'Which country does iconic pop trio A-ha come from?'

'Norway,' says Izzy.

Ah, Leo realises: that's where 'I'm Still Standing' had come from. Elton John, obviously. 1983, if there's a bonus point on offer.

'What time did you finish up at The Shore yesterday?' he asks Ffion.

'What are you, my mam?'

'I was only asking.' Talk about prickly. Ffion's scowling now, as though Leo was checking up on her, instead of simply making conversation. 'Any cause of death yet?' he says to Izzy.

'Patience, grasshopper.' Izzy examines the pulpy mess that was once Rhys Lloyd's face. For a few minutes, the only sound in the room is the tinny noise of the radio quiz. 'Dissection scissors,' Izzy says, and Leo is just thinking *I've never heard of them – who's the lead singer?* when the mortuary technician crosses the room and hands them to her.

Izzy hands them straight back. 'Dissection scissors, Elijah!' He ambles across to the trolley to find the right ones and Izzy rolls her eyes. 'See what I have to deal with?'

'Sorry,' Elijah says, not sounding it. 'Miles away.'

'If only.' Izzy looks at Leo. 'Last week he sent the wrong bloods to the lab, and a sixty-six-year-old man with multiple organ failure came back pregnant.'

She circles her scalpel around Lloyd's face.

'These injuries were sustained prior to death.'

Ffion comes closer, to look. 'Did they kill him? There are rocks in the lake beneath the decks – could he have fallen on to them?'

'I'll know more once I take a look at the brain, but there are no facial fractures, and if it were rocks, as you suggest, I'd expect more diffuse abrasions. What we've got here are more localised lacerations – more consistent with a sharp object.'

'A weapon?'

'Frankie Goes to Hollywood,' Izzy says, to the radio. She bends

89

over Lloyd's face, poking at his injuries with a pair of long, narrow tweezers. 'Interesting.' She snaps her fingers and Elijah passes her a sterile pot from a stack on the trolley next to her. Leo wonders if working for Izzy Weaver is better or worse than working for Crouch.

'What is it?' he asks.

Izzy screws on the lid, then hands Leo the pot, at the bottom of which is a tiny, blood-covered dot. 'A fragment of whatever was used to give your man his new look. I'll clean it up and take a closer look at it when I'm done here.'

Leo holds up the pot to show Ffion. Beneath the blood, something metallic glints.

'And if that isn't enough to upgrade your unexplained death to suspicious,' Izzy says, 'take a look at this.' She walks around the slab to where Lloyd's waxy feet fall at ten to two, and points to the outside of each ankle. A faint indentation runs horizontally above the ankle bone.

Leo is beginning to form a picture. 'Lloyd was restrained. Someone hit him over the head, bound his feet and then dumped him in the lake.'

'A fair assumption. Although I don't see the same marks around his wrists, which is interesting.'

'Because the rope wasn't to tie him up,' Ffion says slowly. 'It was to weigh him down. To drown him. Only the rope broke, or came untied, or whatever, and he floated back up.' She looks at Izzy. 'Any fibres?'

'After a night in the lake? Come on, DC Morgan, this isn't Netflix. The best I can offer you is a pattern match if you bring me the rope. Now, let's open him up, shall we?'

Leo will never get used to the casual brutality with which a body is opened up. The clean letter 'Y' sliced through skin and muscle; the briskness of the saw as it makes short work of the ribcage. He keeps his eyes on the clock on the wall, until Izzy starts talking again.

'Well, he didn't drown.'

Leo peers into Lloyd's chest cavity. 'How can you tell?'

'Five years at medical school, several years in histopathology, and twenty years as a forensic pathologist.' Izzy says drily. Ffion snorts. 'If you take in water, it reacts with the protein lining your airwaves and produces froth. See the trachea, here?' Izzy points. 'And the bronchi? Clear.'

'So he was dead when he went into the water?'

'Correct. The lake was merely a method of disposal.'

Leo looks at Rhys Lloyd's mutilated body. The man had a squeaky-clean image. He'd gone to London to seek his fortune, then returned with a stunning wife and two beautiful daughters. He had given his time to charity concerts, had hundreds of thousands of fans. Yet someone had hated him enough to kill him.

'What now?' Ffion says. They're standing in the mortuary car park, both having a cigarette. Leo has washed his hands and divested himself of his PPE, but the stench of death still clings to him, and tobacco feels like the lesser of two evils.

'Crime scene.' Leo blows a smoke ring. 'Scenes.' He ticks them off on his fingers. 'The location of the assault to the head, the boat – assuming he was in a boat – and wherever it entered the water. And potentially at least one other, given we don't actually know what killed him.'

Izzy Weaver refuses to commit on the precise cause of death – toxicology and tissue samples will tell them more – but she has made the most important call. Rhys Lloyd did not die of natural causes. Crouch can press Go on the incident room.

Leo's phone rings. 'Guess who?' He shows Ffion the screen.

Ffion shrugs. 'Don't answer it.'

'He'll keep ringing.'

'I'm not going to the fucking briefing, alright? They bore the shit out of me.'

'They bore the shit out of everyone. We still have to go.'

'I work better alone.' Ffion grinds out her roll-up. 'I do my own thing and I get results.' The ringing stops as Leo's voicemail cuts in. Seconds later, it starts again, Crouch's name flashing on the screen. 'This whole *team* stuff – it's not me. I'm like . . .' Ffion fishes for the thought, then snaps her fingers. 'The Lone Ranger.'

'Right.'

'Just tell him I'm not coming. I'll tell him myself, if you're not man enough.'

The phone rings again. This time, Leo answers it, speaking before Crouch can get a word in. 'Boss, I'm just finishing something up, but DC Morgan's right here, I'll pass you over.' He hands the phone to Ffion, who glares at him.

'Hi.'

Leo doesn't know what Crouch is saying, but a deep crimson flush creeps across Ffion's face.

'Yes, sir. Five o'clock? No problem. I'll see you there.'

Leo takes back his phone and grins. 'Shall I saddle up your horse?'

TEN

NEW YEAR'S EVE | 9 P.M. | JONTY

'Darling, *please* do something about that awful drunk man – he's just poured red wine all over the sofa.'

Jonty is perched on the arm of the sofa, from where he has an excellent view of Ashleigh Stafford's cleavage. Reluctantly, he tears himself away from it to speak to his wife.

'It's a party, Blythe. Everyone's drunk.' Everyone except for Jonty. Jonty drinks a lot, but he rarely gets drunk. He enjoys the power that accompanies being the only one to precisely remember the events of an evening.

'Jonty, he's ranting at Dee. She's seventy-two, it isn't right.'

'Okay, okay!' Jonty gives a last, lingering look at Ashleigh. 'Don't go anywhere. I'll be back in a jiffy.'

'I'll hold you to that, babe.'

Jonty is prepared to overlook Ashleigh's Essex accent, given what else is on offer. They had been about to retreat to somewhere a little more private when Blythe rudely interrupted them. He half-wonders if his wife did it intentionally.

'Which awful drunk man?' he asks her. The room is full of drunk people. Ceri the postwoman is limbo-dancing under a broom held at either end by Clemmie Northcote and some woman who arrived with four cans of Stella and a bottle of Lambrini.

93

You shouldn't have, Blythe had responded smoothly, swifting them away and passing champagne around. Jonty wouldn't have wasted Bolly on the chavs, but Blythe is big on *aesthetics*, and having cans of lager knocking about the place offends her.

'That one.' Blythe points to a man gesticulating wildly at Dee Huxley. 'The boat man.'

Unlike the residents of The Shore, who have at least tried to make an effort with the dress code, *the boat man* is wearing jeans, a fleece jacket and a beanie hat. Jonty sighs and makes his way across the room.

'Jonty, dear, have you met Steffan Edwards?' Dee says. 'Steffan, this is Jonty Charlton, investor of The Shore, and our host tonight.' A solid introduction – Jonty's grudgingly flattered. He doesn't understand what Rhys has against Dee. She's batty, of course, but harmless with it.

'You invested in this place?' Steffan stretches his mouth into something approximating a smile. It shows every one of his red-wine-stained teeth, and Jonty recoils slightly.

'Yes, I'm Rhys's financial partner.'

'Well, you can fuck off, then. And once you've fucked off, you can fuck off some more. And then you can—'

'Okaaaaay . . .' Jonty grips Steffan by the underside of a bicep which would be intimidatingly large were the man not too pissed to use it, and propels him towards the exit. 'Time to go home, mate.'

'I'm not your fucking mate.'

Jonty pushes onwards, the packed room parting like the Red Sea and Steffan shouting his mouth off to anyone who will listen. 'What have I got left, eh? Fucking nothing.'

Jonty smiles apologetically as they press towards the front door. 'So sorry about this. Yes, a little too much of the old vino, ha ha!'

'I'm fucking ruined!'

'Just needs to sleep it off, I expect.'

'If they find me hanging, it's on you – you hear me?'

'Yes, I'll make sure he gets home safely.'

Outside, the crisp air seems to sober Steffan up. He stands upright, shakes Jonty off and jabs a finger towards him. 'You've fucked me up, you and Rhys.'

Away from his guests, Jonty no longer needs to play *mine host*. He pushes Steffan hard in the chest, and the man stumbles backwards, tripping over his own feet and smashing on to the path. 'Fuck off, you piece of shit.'

'Tell Rhys Lloyd this isn't over!'

'I'm not interested.'

'It isn't over!'

It is beyond over, Jonty thinks. Now, where was he?

Back in the lodge, Ashleigh hasn't moved. When she sees him, she stands and adjusts her dress, which has ridden up high enough to show a flash of panties. She follows him into the hall, and Jonty glances around to make sure no one is watching them, before they slide into the loo and lock the door.

'Finally,' Jonty says.

'You're really keen, in't ya?'

'We'd better get a move on, otherwise someone'll want to get in.' Jonty isn't here for the conversation.

Ashleigh pulls up her dress. 'Alright, alright!' She rummages in her underwear and emerges with a clear plastic bag filled with white powder. 'Nice to have company for once.'

'Bobby not up for it?'

'He's a right bore. Says he did all that shit years ago, after he left the ring. Wouldn't touch it with a bargepole now, he says. It's all bloody kale smoothies now.' Ashleigh cuts two lines, kneels on the loo and snorts the first cleanly off the cistern. Jonty takes a moment to appreciate her backside, then does the same.

'I'd usually buy from my bloke in Essex,' Ashleigh says. 'But I got this here – it's alright, I reckon. What do you think?'

'I think it's bloody marvellous.'

Ashleigh's a dark horse, Jonty thinks. The Shore's only been open for six months, and she's already found herself a dealer. He unlocks the bathroom door, and the pair of them exit with significantly less caution than they entered.

'Let me know when you want another bump, yeah?' She plants a kiss on his lips.

As Jonty weaves through the party, his renewed good humour is only marginally dented by finding Mia once again standing around talking. 'I'm paying you to waitress, not socialise,' he chastises.

'Technically, you're paying me to hand canapés around,' Mia says. 'And they're all gone, so . . .'

She turns away from him, talking to Rhys's assistant. Jonty almost doesn't recognise the girl. He's only ever seen her in casual, mostly scruffy clothes. Now, she's in a dress almost as short as Ashleigh's. The neck is high, and the sleeves are long, and the contrast between the modest top and the crotch-hugging hem is . . .

'Ding dong,' Jonty mutters to himself, as he makes for the kitchen, where Rhys is taking what he presumably thinks is a covert swig of brandy from the cupboard. Jonty slaps him on the back, sending Rhys into an uncontrollable coughing fit. 'Have you seen your admin girl, old man? Ding bloody dong, that's all I can say.'

'That's out of order.'

'Honestly, she's . . .' Jonty gives a chef's kiss.

'She's off limits. Just a kid.' Rhys is slurring his words. *Jusht a kid*. He puts a hand on the kitchen counter for balance.

'You know what they say.' Jonty nudges him. 'If there's grass on the wicket, time to play cricket.' He opens his mouth, a guffaw at the ready, but Rhys looks so revolted it takes the wind out of Jonty's sails. 'Joke!' he says, both palms out, in self-defence. This is what happens when people get drunk – they lose their sense of proportion. It was just a bloody joke.

Rhys looks as though he's about to say something else, and Jonty is relieved to be interrupted by Tabby and Felicia, the former thrusting a sandwich at Rhys. 'Mum says you have to eat this.'

'Not hungry.'

'She says we're not to leave you alone till you've eaten it.' Tabby rolls her eyes dramatically.

'Might be a good idea to get something down you, old man,' Jonty says. 'Line the stomach, and all that.'

'Can you just eat it, please, Dad? Like, we've got better things to do with our time than pass messages from Mum.'

'Eat,' Felicia says, sharper than her sister. 'You're lucky she still cares enough about you to make you something. You're lucky *we* care enough.' She gives her father a loaded look, then flounces off, Felicia close behind.

'Fallen out with the famalam, have you, old man?' Jonty claps a hand on Rhys's shoulder, then swiftly removes it when the other man glares at him. Rhys mumbles something unintelligible through his sandwich. Jonty makes out . . . *all your fault*. His cocaine-fuelled good mood is being severely tested. 'Now, come on, I hardly think—'

'. . . should never have helped you out,' Rhys mumbles.

Jonty has had enough. How dare Rhys try to take the moral high ground, after everything he's done?

'Look here, that's simply not fair. Yasmin would never have found out, if you hadn't told her. And, frankly, she's not the only one pissed off with you – I'm pretty fucked off with you myself, truth be known.'

Rhys is staring at Jonty, but his eyes are wild, unfocused. Jonty can't even be sure Rhys can see him, hear him, even. The man is utterly wasted. He won't remember any of this in the morning, and Jonty can't resist the opportunity to twist the knife.

'I'm not going to bail you out, you know. I had to fend off that chap you owe, earlier, and if you think I'm going to do it again, you can think again.' Jonty leans closer, hissing in Rhys's ear. 'If I were you, I'd be checking over my shoulder.'

ELEVEN

JANUARY 3RD | LEO

'Your boss is a dick.' Ffion sits on Leo's desk, the heel of one boot resting on the handle of the bottom drawer. A crescent of dried mud has fallen on the floor, and Leo itches to pick it up. 'I wouldn't put up with it.'

Crouch had greeted them with a loud aside to Ffion to tell her to *let me know if he doesn't pull his weight – he's a lazy fucker.*

Leo doesn't want to put up with it. He even started writing an email to HR once, but when he'd looked at the list of Crouch's petty taunts it had seemed so pathetic that he'd deleted it. Moaning about someone calling you *fatty bumbum* is the sort of behaviour you were supposed to leave behind in primary school. It's just banter, isn't it? What lads do. He hears Allie's voice in his head. *Snowflake.*

'Is he like that to everyone?' Ffion says.

'Yes.' Leo's response is automatic, then he thinks for a moment. 'Actually, no. Just me.'

'Racist, then.'

'No, he's never said anything racist. He wouldn't dare.'

Ffion yawns. 'Exactly. He targets you for no apparent reason, and the only difference between you and the rest of the office is . . .'

99

She looks around the room, where every officer has one thing in common. They're white.

An email pings into Leo's inbox, relieving him of the need to continue the conversation. Out on the streets or in an interview room, resolving conflict comes naturally to him, but his personal life is another matter. Leo once switched gyms rather than tell the personal trainer he'd been allocated that he hated the cross-trainer.

'Tech team update.'

Ffion jumps off the desk to see over his shoulder, resting a hand on the back of Leo's chair. It brushes against him for a second, before she leans forward to read out the email. 'Lloyd's Apple Watch stopped recording a heartbeat at 11.38 p.m., which is consistent with the pathologist's report.'

'But look at his heart rate.' Leo points to the reading, which averages sixty beats per minute for the first half of New Year's Eve, then shoots into the eighties from mid-afternoon onwards, before it finally slows and then stops completely. 'Something made it spike. Or some*one*,' Leo says.

Ffion's bent over the data, and for a second he thinks she looks guarded. 'Maybe he had an argument,' he says.

'For seven hours?'

'He could have been shagging.'

'I refer my learned friend to my earlier rebuttal.'

'Drugs, then,' Leo says. 'Yasmin said he wouldn't touch them because they mess with the vocal cords, but she wouldn't be the first wife not to have a clue what her husband was up to. Or maybe someone slipped something into his drink.'

'In that case,' Ffion says, 'we're wasting our time looking at the locals – the party started hours after the data shows a heart-rate spike.'

'Plenty of suspects at The Shore, though. Not to mention plenty of opportunity: I doubt that lot waited till seven-thirty to open the champagne. Did you see their recycling bins? They must have it on their cornflakes.'

'Granola,' Ffion says. 'They wouldn't have anything as common as cornflakes.'

'Have they all given elims?' Uniformed officers have been tasked with requesting elimination fingerprints from all the owners who consented, a process which will also need to be undertaken with every guest identified as being at the party.

Ffion opens the file. 'Clemence Northcote refused permission for her son.'

'Refused?'

'She says Caleb spent the evening hanging out with the Lloyd twins in the Northcote lodge, a story which is backed up by the twins themselves.'

Leo looks over Ffion's shoulder. 'I see Caleb's got previous.'

'Cut his teeth at eleven with shoplifting, then graduated to theft from person. He's currently on a tag – three-month curfew – and a two-year supervision order, after he and a mate robbed a petrol station.'

'Charming. How about the others?'

'Bobby Stafford's got a bit of historic stuff – all before he got famous, and mostly breach-of-the-peace stuff. Everyone else is clear. Jonty Charlton – no previous – refused elims. Doesn't trust us to destroy them, blah blah blah. One of those who rants about CCTV and ID cards but hands over all his personal data to Waitrose. He won't give a voluntary interview either. '"Either I'm a suspect or I'm not",' Ffion mimics. '"And if I'm not a suspect, why should I be interrogated?"'

'I hate people like that.'

'Me too.'

'I hope he did it.'

'Me too.'

They grin at each other, and Leo thinks what a shame it is, that after this job they'll go their separate ways. Leo hasn't clicked like this with a colleague for a long time.

With anyone, come to think of it.

A name on the elim list catches his eye and he points at the screen. *Seren Morgan*. 'Any relation?'

Ffion closes the file. 'My sister.'

'Your sister was at the party?'

'To be fair, I'm related to at least half the people on this list, so . . .'

'It says she refused to give elims.' Around them, people start standing, and picking up notebooks, and Leo looks at his watch.

'You know what teenagers are like,' Ffion says. 'It's all *hashtag defund the police*, and *where are my civil liberties?* Nightmare. Come on, we're going to be late.'

They follow the trickle of people down a narrow corridor lined with framed certificates. Ffion takes them in as they pass, and Leo hopes she'll lose interest before they get to—

'It's you!' She stops abruptly, reading the commendation out loud. '"For his brave and selfless actions while off-duty, resulting in the apprehension of a violent offender".'

Short of pushing past her, Leo has nowhere to go, so he nods shortly and stares at the wall.

'Wow. *Da iawn*, mate. Closest I've ever come to a commendation is a letter from a councillor saying I was a great help in addressing the dog-fouling problem around the village hall.' She grins. 'Shit, right?'

'Yeah, well.' Leo nods towards the briefing room. 'We should . . .'

They gave him his own framed copy. Leo wanted to smash it,

but he isn't the dramatic type, so instead it's in a box in what should be Harris's room.

Brave and selfless? That's not what Allie called him.

'Are you coming in or what?' Crouch shouts. Leo and Ffion join the others around the long, wide table. 'Hey . . .' The DI nods towards Leo, as he addresses the rest of the room. 'How do you make a Scouser run faster? Stick a DVD player under his arm!'

There's a ripple of good-natured laughter around the room, and what else can Leo do but laugh too? He feels Ffion's eyes on him.

'And this must be our Welsh representative.'

'DC Ffion Morgan, sir.'

'Sorry you've ended up working with Lard Arse.'

Leo can't bring himself to laugh, this time. He shouldn't care what Ffion thinks of him, but it seems he does.

'Don't put yourself down, sir.' Ffion smiles sweetly. 'I'm sure you're just big-boned.'

Leo thinks he can actually hear his boss's double-take. Silence stretches across the room like a rubber band, and Leo braces himself for the twang, but it doesn't come.

Crouch narrows his eyes at Ffion, then looks away. 'Down to business, then.' He taps his iPad authoritatively, and the screen on the wall behind him comes to life with a bullet-pointed summary of the post-mortem. 'Cause of death still unclear, but the pathologist is leaning towards heart failure, brought on by assault from an unknown weapon. We're still waiting for a full toxicology report, but initial bloods show very low levels of alcohol.'

'That doesn't make sense, boss,' DC Parry says. 'The witness statements all say Lloyd was hammered.'

'Science doesn't lie, DC Parry.' Crouch holds up a printed report – the lab results, Leo assumes. He thinks of Izzy Weaver's disparaging tirade about the unfortunate Elijah – *last week he sent the wrong bloods to the lab* – and hopes Izzy double-checked the submissions.

'The post-mortem also revealed extensive superficial injuries to the victim's face,' Crouch continues, 'delivered pre-mortem. There was a fine linear cut on his tongue and one on his chin, a couple of days old, likely to be a shaving cut – and marks around both ankles, consistent with some kind of rope. It's likely he was tied to something designed to keep him at the bottom of the lake.'

'Well, that's a fail,' DC Clements says. 'Any chance the rope might wash up?'

'Tac Support are doing a fingertip search of the shore. As it stands, the implement used to inflict the facial injuries is unknown, so if they come across anything which looks likely they'll bag and tag it. Traces of some kind of varnish or paint were found in the victim's facial wounds, but it's not clear what they're from.'

'Could it have been a hit and run?' DC Thorngate looks around the room, testing the idea. 'Someone panicked – chucked the body into the lake? Might be worth checking the sample against the national paint database.'

Ffion nods. 'The injuries aren't consistent with blunt trauma, but it's worth a shot.'

'We're still waiting for the call history from Lloyd's mobile.' Crouch says. 'But apps in use include Tinder and Plenty More Fish. The analysts are digging into both, to establish who Lloyd was in contact with, in case we're looking at a rejected lover or a jealous husband.'

'Which might also account for the stalker.' The suggestion comes from DC Walton, making notes on her pad with the keenness of someone new in post.

Next to her, Thorngate spins a pen through her fingers. 'Would he have reported it, though, if it was someone he'd had an affair with?'

'He didn't have much choice,' Ffion says. 'The woman turned up on their doorstep.' She looks at her notes. 'White, blonde hair, black jeans, brown leather jacket, baseball cap.'

'That's pretty detailed.' DC Thorngate's pen skitters on to the desk. 'Any cameras about?'

Ffion shakes her head. 'The woman tried to force her way into the house, demanding to see Rhys. When Yasmin refused, the woman made threats towards her and their teenage daughters.'

'Did she call on the nines?' Crouch asks.

'No,' Leo says. 'Her husband phoned it in, when he got home. He said Yasmin had been in shock and hadn't been thinking straight. Obviously, there was no sign of the offender by the time police got there.'

Crouch draws on his iPad, and a question mark appears on the smart screen behind him; a caption reading *Stalker*. 'There's our first suspect. DC Thorngate, I want you to be the liaison between the Met and our analysts – see if there's any crossover between women Lloyd was seeing on Tinder and our mystery stalker.'

'Yes, boss.'

'Who's on boats?' Crouch looks around the room.

'Sailors, sir,' comes a response from the back. There's a collective burst of laughter.

'I am, boss.' DC Thirkell waves a hand. 'I've got the list of everyone with a permit and I'm working my way through it, and the team on CCTV are looking out for trailers on the roads coming into the area.'

'Can we get the underwater search team out?' DC Thorngate asks. 'We might still be able to get something from the weapon.'

'Maybe if we had another body outstanding,' Crouch says. 'Not on the off-chance of finding something which *might* yield some prints.'

Ffion raises an arm. 'I've got a contact for an underwater drone operator. Would you like me to—'

'Great idea, thanks.'

When did Crouch ever say *thank you* to Leo? Ever acknowledge he'd done a good job?

'Any CCTV at The Shore?' the DI continues.

'I'll look into it right away, sir,' Ffion says quickly. Leo feels a flicker of resentment. Talk about sucking up to the boss.

'Great. And do a sweep for other cameras. Shops, front doors, dashboard cams, et cetera.'

'Sir.'

'Eight a.m. tomorrow, then, people.' As always, Crouch is first out of the door.

Leo contemplates his evening – the empty flat and the funny smell from next door – and turns to Ffion. 'I don't suppose you fancy grabbing something to eat, do you?'

The second he's said it, he regrets it. Ffion's face carries that look: the one which says *how can I let him down gently?*

'I want to go through the hashtag on Instagram,' Leo adds quickly. 'Be quicker with two of us.'

Ffion shrugs. 'Sure.'

They settle on a Chinese restaurant called Wok this Way, sliding into a narrow booth by the door. 'King prawn chow mein?' Leo says, scanning the list of dishes.

'Whatever you want.'

'Lemon chicken?'

'Why are you asking me? Oh, God.' Ffion puts down her menu. 'You're one of those.'

'One of who?'

'A sharer. Look, I don't mean to be funny, but if I order crispy duck, it's because I want crispy duck, not because I want half a crispy duck.'

'Technically, it actually *is* half a—'

'You order what you want. I'll order what I want. That's how restaurants work.'

They work as they eat, each scrolling through Instagram on their respective phones. A woman at the next table gives them a pitying glance, whispering to her boyfriend. She thinks he and Ffion are a couple, Leo supposes, out on date night with nothing to say to each other.

'This was posted at eleven p.m.,' Leo says, looking at a photo of Lloyd in the Charltons' kitchen. His face was red and shiny, sweat sticking his hair to his brow.

'It could have been taken earlier, though. Some of the guests will have waited till they got home to post. The reception's rubbish on that side of the lake, and I can't imagine Jonty Charlton handing out his wifi password.' Ffion shows Leo a series of images. 'Loads of them are in a weird order. Clemence Northcote hadn't finished drying her hair when the party started – look – but this photo wasn't posted till the end of the night. And see this one of the Charltons? There's an almost identical one from a different angle, but posted two hours later. We'll have to get Tech to check the time-stamp on them all.'

Ffion stops. She flips her phone around. 'This is interesting.'

The image is heavily filtered, but Leo can make out Bobby Stafford, talking to a woman with a nose ring. 'Who's that?'

'Eira Hughes. Primary school teacher. But that's not the interesting bit.'

Eira is laughing, perhaps at something Bobby was saying – he has a smile on his face. Next to them is another knot of people. The image is cut off, but you can see the back view of a woman in black leather leggings, standing with her back to Stafford.

'Look at his hand,' Ffion says.

Leo looks. Bobby's fingers are entwined with the woman's behind him. 'Ashleigh?'

Ffion shakes her head. She takes back her phone and scrolls to a different Instagram post. 'This is what Ashleigh was wearing.' Bobby's wife is in a red dress, clingy and short. Ffion taps back, her thumb swiping images across the screen. She stops, and Leo catches a glimpse of a woman in black.

'Is that her? Do you recognise her?' Leo squints to view the photo Ffion's staring at.

'Nope.' Ffion swipes away quickly. A little too quickly.

'Not local, then?'

'What?'

'If you don't know her' – Leo finds himself leaning across the table, his head low, in an effort to get Ffion's attention – 'she's probably from out of town. Right?'

Finally, Ffion looks up. 'Sorry. Yes.'

'So if the Tech team pull the metadata on all these posts we can cross-reference them with the data from Rhys's Apple Watch, to see what he was doing when his heart-rate went loopy.'

'Hoping to see Professor Plum in the drawing room with the candlestick?'

'You never know.'

Leo scrolls through the Instagram feed on his own phone, looking for more pictures of the mystery woman in black. There are a couple of Yasmin and Rhys Lloyd on their own deck, presumably taken before the party – Lloyd looks significantly less dishevelled. Behind them, the lake is a dark mass, the outline of black clouds heavy overhead. Perhaps it's only because Leo knows that by the end of the evening Rhys will be in the water behind him that even the twinkly lights strung along the balustrade seem full of foreboding.

Rhys's twin daughters are both on Instagram, their grids carefully curated and heavily edited. Tabby Lloyd's most recent post is a poignant photo of her father's empty study, his chair at an angle as though he's just left the room for a moment. Leo stares at the image, remembering the glossy photographs he looked at this morning and trying to pinpoint what looks different. He wishes he hadn't left the magazine at home. 'Are there any photos of Lloyd's office from before he died?'

'Yasmin showcased the whole place on her grid, back in the summer. Hang on.' Ffion scrolls through the images, and the Lloyds' life spools backwards, in tiny filtered squares. New Year's Eve, then Christmas, then London life. Half-term holiday at The Shore, then London again, then summer at The Shore. Ffion stops. 'Here.'

Leo holds his phone next to Ffion's, and they bend over the near-identical images of Rhys Lloyd's study. The room is small – essentially a wide landing between the master bedroom overlooking the lake, and the two smaller rooms at the front of the lodge. In addition to the desk – tidier in Yasmin's photo than in her daughter's – there's a small armchair, a music stand and a potted plant. Above the desk is a shelf on which stand a number of trophies and awards.

Leo counts the awards visible in Yasmin's photograph, then does the same for Tabby's. He looks at Ffion, and the first piece of the puzzle falls neatly into place.

'There's one missing.'

TWELVE

NEW YEAR'S EVE | 7 P.M. | MIA

Mia walks back to The Shore, barely an hour after she left. She's been there all day, setting out canapés and being bossed about by Blythe. Who has a project plan for a party, for fuck's sake? A few bowls of crisps, some banging tunes, bring your own booze, and job's a good 'un.

Not at The Shore. At The Shore, it's trays of sushi and tiny Yorkshire puddings hiding a curl of rare roast beef. It's row after row of foil-topped bottles, and one of those pyramids of glasses Mia's only ever seen in films. It's a marquee – the sort you find at posh hotel weddings – with deckchairs and parasols and a sand-coloured carpet because Jonty drew the line at actual sand. Crazy money. Crazy people.

Mostly.

Mia didn't take the job as cleaner (and now, apparently, waitress) because of a man, but that's why she's stayed. That's why she's put up with the condescension and the casual insults, and the feeling that she's invisible unless she's done something wrong. And she knows how insane it is, and what people would say, and God, doesn't she know how wildly unsuitable he is . . .

But.

Her heart soars as she picks her way over the rocks in trainers she'll change out of before she reaches The Shore. In her hand she swings a pair of six-inch heels and okay, they're not the Loubo-whatsits Blythe bangs on about, but they make Mia's legs look as though they go on forever. The cheek of that woman, suggesting Mia might wear a waitress uniform! Mia has spent six months wearing a cleaning tabard for stolen trysts with her lover, and tonight she intends to wow him. They managed the briefest of encounters earlier today, and she's hopeful that tonight, when everyone is distracted by the party, they will be able to sneak off.

He's not everyone's cup of tea, she knows that. A bit full of himself maybe; a bit flash. But underneath all that, away from his *set*, he's lovely. Mia smiles to herself. After the party, he's going to leave. He's promised her. He's going to walk away from all these trappings of success, and be with her. 'Who needs money, when you've got love?' he always says, and Mia knows he means it.

Why would he lie?

There's an atmosphere in Jonty and Blythe's lodge – an undertow to the conversation – and Mia immediately thinks (as she always does, when she gets to work and discovers something is *off*) that people *know*. It's self-centred of her, of course, but people in love are often self-centred.

'. . . sneaking around, up to no good,' Blythe is saying. Mia freezes in the doorway, her heart pounding.

'They're just kids,' Jonty says. 'Didn't you sneak around when you were a teenager?'

Mia relaxes. Sashays into the room with as much poise as she can muster in vertiginous heels, pretending she doesn't know the effect she's having.

'Ding dong!'

Blythe glares at her husband. 'I do wish you wouldn't say that

111

all the time. It's so disgusting.' She bears down on Mia with her bloody spreadsheet, and Mia grits her teeth. It'll all be worth it, in the end.

The local guests aren't due for another half-hour, but Rhys and Yasmin are here, talking to Bobby and Ashleigh. Mia tops up their champagne, and there it is again – that weird atmosphere, like something tugging beneath the surface.

'. . . said I was a natural, didn't they, babe?' Ashleigh is saying. 'Even though Bobby's the actor.'

'Can we call someone an "actor", when they're essentially just playing themselves?' Rhys says. He grins, as if it's a joke, but his eyes are stony, and although Bobby laughs there's a hardness to it.

'Can we call someone a "singer",' he says, 'when they're essentially just an arsehole with a microphone?'

The two men turn to face one another, and it looks like the start of every pub brawl Mia has ever seen. Yasmin looks almost gleeful, as though her husband being beaten up by an actual champion boxer is the best thing ever. Whatever Rhys has done, it's given Yasmin the right hump.

Ashleigh, of course, is oblivious. 'You should get them to make a reality TV show about you, Rhys. It's dead easy: they just follow you around for a few months, get shots of you at home with the kids, going to rehearsals, and that.'

'That would assume he had some rehearsals to go to,' Yasmin says, acidly.

Something is seriously up with that lot. Mia's glad when Clemmie and Dee arrive. Clemmie's wearing a dress which, as she tells anyone who will listen, is made from recycled plastic bottles, complete with flattened bottle tops as buttons.

'Amazing,' Mia says, which isn't exactly a lie. 'And you look fabulous, Mrs Huxley.'

Dee is wearing black velvet trousers and a white blouse with frills down the front. On her feet are shiny black dress shoes. 'Fallen arches, dear,' she tells Mia, when she sees her looking. 'Besides, men's shoes are so much more comfortable.'

Mia is supposed to hand food around, but none of the posh lot wants to eat, and the beautiful platters stay untouched until the locals arrive.

'Holy crap,' Eira says, when she walks in. 'This place . . .'

'I know, right?' Mia feels a weird sense of pride, as though she lives here. For a second she imagines what it would be like if she did. If all this money, all this *stuff* were hers. Maybe it will be, one day.

It's awkward, to begin with. Most of the locals don't know anyone here, and so they stand in clusters, talking to each other and looking around. On the other side of the lodge, the Shore owners talk too loudly and laugh too hard, and it reminds Mia of school discos: boys on one side, girls on the other. Only Clemmie and Dee make an effort to welcome their guests, and slowly the two groups begin to mix.

'. . . the same layout, yes, but really they're quite different,' Yasmin says, to a couple Mia knows full well don't give a shit about interiors. 'I'll give you a tour, if you like?'

'That would be great,' the pair say, desperate for a poke around.

It's the start of an endless stream of people traipsing from one end of The Shore to the other. Mia's feet hurt, and she'd like to take off her shoes, but she knows he's watching her. Just now, she offered him a top-up and he whispered in her ear as she leaned forward. 'I want you.'

He'll find time for her later, she's sure. She just has to be patient.

Someone has turned down the lights and turned up the music. The lodge throbs with heat and noise, bodies pressed against

113

bodies. There's an icy draught, as the bifold doors are yanked open, the side of the marquee left flapping. A load of lads from the pub stroll in, giving it the big I am and heading straight for the drinks table.

'Who are these people?' Blythe says anxiously to Mia. 'Were they invited?'

Mia can see a folded invite in one of the men's back pockets. 'I guess so,' she says. 'That one's Gruffydd.' Mia points. 'And that's Hari Roberts, Sion Williams . . .' But Blythe doesn't care about their names. She doesn't really mean *who are they?* – she means *what are they?* What do they do, what kind of people are they?

'They drink in Y Llew Coch,' Mia adds. Blythe blinks rapidly, looking visibly pained as the group takes over a corner of the sitting room. There are eight of them, all in jeans and scuffed work boots, jackets thrown carelessly in a heap. The coats are shiny with spray and Mia realises they must have come in boats, almost certainly straight from the pub.

Caleb is trying to sneak unseen through the party. In the kitchen, he opens a cupboard, Mia intercepting him with his fingers on the bottle of brandy stashed behind the tins. 'I wouldn't, if I were you.'

Caleb jumps. 'Fucking hell, Mia, you shouldn't sneak up on people like that.'

Mia takes the brandy out of his hand. 'There's a coolbox by the side of the lodge, with a load of lager in it. They won't miss a few cans.'

He grins. 'Cheers.' And then he's gone, off to wherever the rest of the teenagers are hanging out tonight. Mia follows, to make sure he hasn't lifted the whole coolbox, and the night air is a relief on her hot, aching limbs. She walks around the outside of

114

the marquee, hidden from view, and slips off her shoes. She presses her bare feet into the freezing grooves of the decking.

'I'm sorry!' she hears a man yell. 'There, I've said it. Happy now?'

Mia blinks in the darkness. Dark clouds move slowly across the moon, disorientating her.

'I'm not the one you should be apologising to.' Dee Huxley's voice is unmistakable, and Mia realises the voices are coming from the deck next door. But who is Dee talking to? 'What you did to that woman . . .'

Dee leaves the sentence hanging, and Mia holds her breath. Inside the marquee, the doors to the lodge open, a burst of noise breaking over the quiet voices from next door.

What woman?

There's a roar from the water – the throaty pull of a motor-boat – and when the engine is cut a moment later the silence is deafening. Young Seren Morgan appears at the top of the ladder, disappearing into the party before Mia can say a word. She wonders if Elen's gone soft, or if Seren's spun her mam a tale.

Mia walks to the edge of the deck, just as Huw Ellis is pulling himself up the ladder from the pontoon.

'Alright, Mia?'

'Should you be here?' Mia likes Huw, but the whole village knows what he thinks about this place.

'Where is he?'

'Who?'

'Lloyd.' He doesn't wait for an answer and Mia follows him inside, watching him scan the room, then walk through to the hall and open the front door. People are dancing, now, the furniture pushed to the walls to make more room. She stops to speak to Seren, who holds her glass behind her back, as though that's enough to hide the fact that she's drinking, even though her eyes are wild.

'Amazing party, right?' Mia says.

Seren shrugs. 'It's okay.' She's all done up – bodycon dress and heels almost as high as Mia's. Hair teased into ringlets and eyes ringed with black. She looks dangerously sexy, and Mia wonders if Elen saw her leave the house like this.

'Is your mam here?' Mia asks.

'Mam, at The Shore?'

Yasmin squeezes into a space beside them. 'Seren! Have you seen Tabby and Felicia? I've been looking everywhere for them.'

'I think they're watching Netflix at Caleb's.'

'Tell them I need them to make their father eat something.'

'Um. Okay.'

'He won't listen to me. I put a sandwich under clingfilm in the fridge; they can give him that.' Yasmin looks at Mia. 'He's completely off his face, it's mortifying.'

He's not the only one, Mia thinks. There are now more empty bottles under the table than full ones on it, and even Clemmie has two bright spots on her cheek, as she demonstrates what might be some kind of Irish dancing. Steffan Edwards is knocking back red wine, which isn't going to end well.

Maybe she'll join him, Mia thinks. She has been relatively abstemious so far – taking swigs of champagne between canapé rounds – but she's done with this lot. She looks across the room. Jonty is practically drooling down Ashleigh Stafford's cleavage, and she feels a sudden burst of anger at being the waitress, the cleaner, the bit on the side. Ashleigh pouts and preens, and flicks her expensive hair extensions with her expensive nails.

Mia hates her more than she's ever hated anyone before.

116

THIRTEEN

JANUARY 4TH | FFION

Ffion has had a restless night, eventually dropping off in the early hours and then sleeping through her alarm. She hasn't showered, and her hair is a frizzy mess. As she turns into The Shore, she stops to show her warrant card to the uniformed officer stationed at the bottom of the drive. He's talking to two men, and Ffion recognises them instantly: Striped Scarf reporter and his camera-man sidekick, Gav. Early-morning mist envelopes the trees and a light drizzle hangs in the air, settling in silver beads on Striped Scarf's jacket.

'These guys have been hanging around for a few days,' Ffion says to the uniform. 'They've been warned, but—'

Instantly Gav's camera is on his shoulder, the reporter thrusting a hand-held mic towards Ffion. 'Now that this is a murder enquiry – do the police have any suspects?'

'You'll have to speak to the press office.' Ffion shuts the car door, reminding herself for the umpteenth time to fix the window.

'It's DC Morgan, isn't it?' the reporter shouts. 'North Wales Police? Are you working with the Cheshire team because the victim is Welsh, or because the suspect is?' As Ffion moves off, he walks with her, yelling his questions. 'A source has reported historic tension between The Shore and the local community –

117

can you comment on that? What's the relationship like between you and your English colleagues?'

Ffion puts her foot down. 'Fucking hell.' For once she's grateful for The Shore's rarefied enclave, tucked away from prying eyes. Outside the Lloyds' lodge, blue and white tape flutters in the breeze, and white-suited CSIs move back and forth between the lodge and the van outside. Behind the lodges, the lake lies beneath a blanket of fog.

Ffion sees Mia's pink tabard coming out of Dee Huxley's lodge and calls out. 'You owe me a text!'

Mia hesitates, before walking over to Ffion. '*Ti'n iawn?*'

'Not bad. Busy.' Ffion gestures to the crime scene tape. 'Did you get my voicemail on New Year's Day? About saying I spent the night at yours, if Mam asks?'

'I did. What's the big deal, though? How come you need an alibi?'

'Personal stuff.' Ffion shrugs. 'No drama, just don't want the whole world knowing my business.'

'You're a crap mate, you know. You only ever message me when you need something.' Mia says it lightly, but her words have an undercurrent which is hard to ignore.

'That's not true.'

'Whatever.' Mia walks away.

'I haven't told anyone, by the way,' Ffion calls after her. 'About what you've been up to.' Mia stops, but doesn't turn around, and a second later she's heading for her car. Ffion chews the inside of her cheek. She's not a crap mate. A crap mate wouldn't keep a secret, would they? Especially in the middle of a murder investigation.

Ffion speaks to the uniform outside the Lloyds' lodge. 'Is DC Leo Brady in there?'

The officer checks her clipboard, on which everyone's movements are neatly marked. 'Just arrived.'

Ffion gives her shoulder number for the list, then ducks under the blue and white tape and pulls on PPE from the box by the front door.

Upstairs, Leo is speaking to the lead CSI.

'Sorry I'm late,' Ffion says.

'Tough commute?' Leo's voice is muffled by his mask, and Ffion can't tell what kind of mood he's in. 'The lads have seized a bunch of medication from Lloyd's bedside cabinet.'

'Mostly over-the-counter,' the CSI says. 'Some prescription. We'll get them submitted to the lab.'

'Any evidence of a crime scene?' Ffion says.

'Blood-spatters. Here, by the desk.' The CSI indicates. 'It's been cleaned up pretty well, but there's also blood and fibres which suggest the victim was dragged from the study through the master bedroom.'

Ffion and Leo follow her across the stepping plates positioned to protect evidence. There are more plates on the balcony, and the metal railing bears the telltale traces of fingerprint dusting.

The CSI bends down and points to the bottom of the glass barrier, which stops around thirty centimetres above the deck of the balcony. 'There's blood on the underside of this glass. It looks as though the victim was pushed underneath it.'

On the main deck, a yellow cone marks a spot around which a further white-suited officer is swabbing. Leo looks down. 'And that's where he landed?'

'Ten out of ten,' the CSI says. 'We'll push on in here, but it's going to be a real needle-in-a-haystack job: there are prints every-where. The awards shelf isn't so bad, but I'm not sure that's much

119

help – the offender wouldn't need to touch the shelf itself to take an award.'

'Maybe it wasn't personal,' Leo says, as they make their way back outside. 'Maybe someone came to burgle the place – the awards are plastered all over Instagram, after all – and Rhys got in the way.'

'So why not take the other trophies?'

'No time?'

'They had time to drag his body on to the balcony, push it on to the deck and then the pontoon, get it on a boat and dump it in the middle of the lake, but they didn't have time to bung a few awards in a bag?'

Leo grins. 'I admit, it's not my best theory. We'll see if the CCTV yields anything.'

Ffion feels hot. 'That's on my list. I'll go and seize it.'

'Already done. I got the keys while I was waiting for you this morning.'

'I said I'd do it!'

The force of Ffion's response makes Leo hold up his hands in surrender. 'Easy. I thought I'd lighten your load, that's all.'

'I don't need your help.'

Leo shakes his head. 'You're hard work, you know? You don't do briefings, you don't do teamwork . . .' He blows out his cheeks, letting out the contents in a slow, noisy stream. Ffion says nothing. 'Anyway, I seized the hard drive and downloaded twenty-four hours from nine a.m. on New Year's Eve. There's a glitch in the afternoon, around three p.m., where the footage skips forward an hour.'

'Rhys Lloyd was alive for several hours after that.'

'Exactly, and it seems fine from then on, so we can cross-reference people arriving at the party with the guests already on

120

our list. See who's missing. The cameras are trained on the drive, rather than the footpaths – but it's a start.'

Ffion's phone buzzes in her pocket, and she glances at the screen before answering, glad of the distraction. 'Alright, boss?'

'Good news,' DI Malik says. 'Now the crime scene's been identified as being on the English side of the lake, they've got no justification for keeping you. I've spoken to DI Crouch and I've persuaded him to let you go.' There's an edge to this last, suggesting Crouch's reluctance was short-lived. Ffion's backchat clearly went down like a shit sandwich, but if the man can't take it, he shouldn't dish it out to Leo.

The thought of Leo makes her remember the CCTV, and her stomach hollows. If she isn't working on the case, she'll have no way of knowing what's been uncovered. How close they are to the truth. She walks away from Leo.

'The thing is, boss, I think I should stick with it.'

'Ffion, you begged me to take you off!'

'There are a lot of local enquiries to do on our side of the border. A number of witnesses who prefer to be dealt with in Welsh.' She knows just how to play this one. 'And I think it's good experience for me. You know, working in a team. It's an area for, um, personal development.'

There's a long – and somewhat surprised – pause. 'I can't argue with that.' Malik sighs. 'Fine. Stay. But next time you ask me for a favour I want a cooling-off period.'

Yasmin and the twins have temporarily moved in with Rhys's mother. Ffion hears music through the ceiling, as she and Leo sit on Glynis's Dralon sofa, Yasmin opposite them in a narrow, high-backed chair. Glynis fusses around, making a pot of tea, and finding a plate for biscuits no one wants to eat.

'*Dach chi isio rwbath*—' Glynis breaks off, glancing at Yasmin and switching to English. 'Would you like something more substantial? A sandwich, maybe?'

'We're fine, really,' Leo says.

'When can we go home?' Yasmin's pale and thin, her long legs drawn into her chest, like a child.

'The Crime Scene Investigation unit will be there for another couple of days, I'm afraid,' Ffion says. 'But if there's anything you need, we can arrange—'

'Not The Shore! I'd be happy if I never set foot there again. I want to take the girls home, back to London.'

'Yasmin, *cariad*,' Glynis says, 'don't take the twins away – they're the only family I've got left now.' She pulls a handkerchief from her sleeve and rubs at her nose.

'We'd prefer it if you'd stay local,' Ffion says. 'Just while the investigation is ongoing.' From the window, she can see down into Glynis's back garden, which is almost entirely taken up with a wooden summer house.

'You've already been targeted once at your London address,' Leo adds. 'We still haven't ruled out a link between your husband's stalker and his murder.' He takes out his phone and brings up the image from Yasmin's Instagram grid of Rhys's trophy shelf, zooming into the award they suspect is now at the bottom of the lake. 'We believe this is what caused your husband's facial injuries. What can you tell us about it?'

Glynis looks at the image over Yasmin's shoulder and sobs again. She starts rifling through the drawers of a large oak dresser.

'That's the Rising Star Award,' Yasmin says flatly. '2010. Awarded to a musical theatre actor deemed to have delivered the best performance of the year. Rhys won it for Judas, in *Jesus*

Christ Superstar. Last decent job he had.' She glances at her mother-in-law, but Glynis doesn't react.

'I imagine it's a tough industry,' Leo says.

'Everyone wants the next big thing.' Yasmin picks at a loose thread on the arm of the armchair. 'Every agent wants a breakout hit, and, when they've got that, they move on to fresh talent. Rhys's agent had him doing commercials for car insurance, for fuck's sake.'

'And fair play, he was brilliant at them,' Glynis says. She hands Ffion a glossy photograph. In it, Rhys Lloyd wears a black tux; Ffion wonders if it's the same one he died in. Yasmin's in a full-length gown with plunging neckline, glittering diamonds around her throat. They stand on a red carpet, in front of a backdrop peppered with sponsors' logos. One of Rhys's hands rests loosely on his wife's waist; the other grips the neck of a huge award.

'Very impressive,' Leo says.

Yasmin works the loose thread free, winding it around her fingers. 'It's hideous.'

Ffion looks at the photo. 'What's it made of?'

'The base is marble; the rest is metal. The whole thing's covered with gold leaf.'

Above Rhys's hand is a starburst of metal spikes. Ffion shivers. 'When was the last time you saw it in his office?'

'New Year's Eve, I suppose.'

'You actually saw it then?' Leo says.

'Well, no. I mean . . . you don't *see* things you know are there, do you? You just assume they are.'

Leo opens his notebook. 'Can you give me a list of people who have been in that room, please? We need to cross-check it against the elimination prints we've taken.'

'I'm sorry, that's impossible.' Yasmin blinks. 'I've taken everyone up there. I'm an interior designer – The Shore is a very important part of my portfolio.'

'When you say *everyone* . . .' Leo says.

'Jonty and Blythe, obviously. Clemmie, Dee, the Staffords – Ashleigh wanted my advice on lighting, although can you believe it, they've put spotlights in the—'

'Who else?' Leo interrupts.

'The builder, Huw Ellis. There have been a few snags, and he has a set of keys. He's been in all the lodges. Same goes for Mia, the cleaner. And then, of course, I did tours at the party.'

'You did tours?' Ffion imagines giving tours of Mam's place. *This is the bathroom, where you have to whack the pipe with a hammer to make the shower come on. This is my bedroom, which still has a poster of the Backstreet Boys on the wall . . .*

'People were curious.' Upstairs, the sound of music grows louder, and Ffion realises it's Rhys singing. She pictures the twins up there, listening to their father's voice, and she swallows hard. She hands a sheet of paper to Yasmin.

'This is a list of medication found in your husband's bedside drawers. Do you know which of them he was taking?'

Yasmin scans the list of tablets. 'He took ibuprofen for a bad back sometimes. These are multivitamins – I take the same ones. Oh, and these sleeping tablets were for jet-lag.' She hands back the list. Upstairs, the girls' music goes up another few decibels, Rhys's soaring voice making the hairs on the back of Ffion's neck stand up.

Yasmin stands. 'I can't bear it.'

'Let them be,' Glynis says, but Yasmin's already leaving the room. Convenient, Ffion thinks. She isn't interested in what Yasmin said about the drugs – all run-of-the-mill stuff – but she *is* interested in the way the woman's hand shook as she read the list, and in the intentionally offhand manner with which she rattled through her explanations. Something on that list is significant. Ffion looks at Leo and knows he's thinking the same.

Upstairs, Rhys's voice cuts off, mid-note.

'I keep forgetting,' Glynis says quietly. 'Then it all comes back and . . .' Tears brim over her eyelashes.

'It must be very difficult for you,' Leo says. 'I'm sorry if we're making it harder, asking all these questions. We just want to find out what happened to your son. Did he ever talk to you about his harassment case?'

'Yes, I was very worried for Yasmin and the girls.'

'Not for your son?'

'I'm sorry?'

'You said "Yasmin and the girls". Were you worried about Rhys?'

'Of course I was worried about him!'

'He received a number of abusive messages online,' Ffion says. 'Do you have any idea who could have been sending them?'

'None at all.'

'Had Rhys fallen out with anyone?'

Glynis's hands are shaking. She looks nervously at the ceiling. There's no sign of Yasmin.

'Mrs Lloyd?' Leo prompts.

'People locally were very upset when The Shore was built,' she says, eventually. 'With Rhys, and with me, too. There's been a lot of ill feeling.'

'You've been stuck in the middle,' Ffion says. It's a statement, not a question, but Glynis answers it anyway.

'Yes. It's been very unpleasant.' Her voice cracks.

'So why do it?' Leo says. 'Why let Rhys develop the land, if there was so much resistance to it, locally?'

'The land was passed to Rhys in my husband's will.' Glynis

shrugs helplessly, then drops her eyes to her lap. 'And besides, my son could be very persuasive.'

Ffion looks out of the window. They've been forecasting snow for days, and a tiny flake tests the waters, drifting down on to the high street.

'I brought it on myself,' Glynis says. She follows Ffion's gaze, staring out of the window, talking more to herself than to Ffion and Leo. 'I spoiled him. I'd have loved a big family, but it didn't happen, and so I poured everything I had into Rhys. He got used to getting his own way.'

Leo leans towards Glynis. 'Did your son ever hurt anyone? Did he ever hurt you?'

'No! He would never . . .' She shakes her head, over and over.

'But he intimidated you? He was a bully?'

'No! Stop it! He wasn't – I mean, at school, maybe, as a child, but . . .' Glynis starts crying again, tears streaking her cheeks.

'I'm sorry,' Leo says.

Ffion feels a rush of anger. Why does Leo have to be so pathetic? He's doing his job; he shouldn't apologise for it. 'What do you mean, he was a bully at school?'

She doesn't think Glynis is going to answer, but the woman stands and walks to the window.

'It's a store room now,' Glynis says, looking down at the summer house. 'But for years it was Rhys's music room, and where he spent time with his friends. Teenagers don't want to be around their parents, do they?'

Ffion doesn't answer. She looks around the room, at the photos of Rhys as a boy, then as a man, and then she pictures his corpse on Izzy Weaver's slab.

'I should have been a better mother,' Glynis says. She's still staring out of the window, and it's as though she's forgotten Leo

126

and Ffion are there. 'Checked in on them, made a nuisance of myself.'

'Mrs Lloyd.' Leo's frowning. 'Did your son do something when he was at school? Something bad?'

Glynis gives a little shake, turning away from the window. She glances at Ffion. 'There was some unpleasantness with a local girl. Ceri. I feel terrible about it, looking back, but—'

Ffion interrupts. 'Ceri Jones?'

'She was very troubled, the school said. Rhys teased her, but I'm sure he wasn't the only one – some children are picked on more than others, aren't they?'

Ffion doesn't trust herself to answer.

'What happened?' Leo says, but Glynis is shaking her head, bustling around the table, clearing away the tea and plates of biscuits.

'I really don't remember. It was a long time ago. You know what children are like.'

There's a creak from upstairs, the strains of Yasmin's voice just audible. Leo glances towards the sound. 'What was your son's marriage like?'

'They seemed happy.'

'Was he a good father?'

'Rhys doted on those girls.' Glynis's voice breaks. 'They never wanted for anything, and nor did Yasmin. He gave her a generous monthly allowance.'

'What will she do now?' Leo asks.

Glynis folds her handkerchief into a neat square and presses it between her palms before she answers. 'Yasmin's the sole beneficiary of Rhys's life assurance policy.' She tucks the handkerchief up her sleeve then meets Leo's gaze directly. 'She'll be better off now than when he was alive.'

FOURTEEN

JANUARY 4TH | LEO

'Who's Ceri Jones?' Leo looks at the shops as they walk down the high street. They haven't yet reopened after Christmas, their windows dark and tills empty.

'The postwoman.' Ffion is striding ahead, her body tense with fury. 'They always said – and all the time Rhys—'

'Ffion, you're not making any sense.'

Ffion stops. She pushes her hands deep into her pockets. 'Ceri has lived here forever. She's in her early forties, I guess. She'd left secondary school by the time I got there, anyway, but people were still talking about her.'

'What did she do?'

'Took an overdose in the stationery cupboard. The caretaker found her and took her to hospital. She was supposed to be going to art college, but she dropped out. Now she's the postie.'

'Because of Rhys Lloyd?'

'That's the first I've heard of that. I only know about the overdose because Mam sat me down and told me it was okay to be gay, straight whatever – because *that's* not an awkward conversation to have when you're twelve – and that if anyone at school ever gave me grief, I was to tell her right away.'

'Your mum sounds cool.'

'She has her moments.' Ffion starts walking again. 'The official line on Ceri was that she was "struggling to come to terms with her sexuality".'

There's a pause before Leo speaks. 'She was at the party.'

Ffion looks at him. 'Ceri isn't a murderer.'

'She might be.'

'Because she was bullied – what – thirty years ago? That's not a motive for murder. Not like money is.'

'You think Yasmin did it?' Leo says.

'Did you see how jittery she got over the drugs list? I'd put a tenner on the toxicology showing high levels of sleeping pills. I reckon Yasmin liked being married to a rising star. Once he was burned out, she bumped him off for the cash.'

'Why now, though? She'd inherit more once the rest of The Shore was built.'

'Only if she's the beneficiary there. Jonty Charlton's the financial partner, remember.'

'I'm sure he'll be delighted to talk to us again.'

Jonty Charlton is not delighted. He looks at Leo and Ffion as though they've been dredged from the bottom of the lake. 'Are you harassing the other residents of The Shore, or is that pleasure reserved for me and my wife?'

'We don't discriminate,' Ffion says cheerfully, taking a step into the lodge, so Jonty has no choice but to move back.

'This really is getting rather tiresome, you know. I thought incompetence was a quality particular to the Metropolitan Police, but clearly it's endemic.'

'You told me this place would be a goldmine when it was finished,' Ffion says. 'Who gets that goldmine, now Rhys is dead?'

Jonty looks a little taken aback. 'Ah . . . Yasmin will inherit almost all of Rhys's shares.'

'Almost?' Leo says.

'He owned fifty-one per cent of the business. I have forty-nine per cent. Our agreement was that, in the event of Rhys's death, two per cent of the business would be passed to me.'

'Making you the controlling partner?' Ffion says.

Jonty waves a hand, as though her point were moot. 'It simply means that whoever Rhys chose to pass his shares to, the integrity of The Shore would be maintained.'

'Why did Rhys have the controlling shares, if you put up all the money?'

'Running a business is a little more complicated than issuing a parking ticket, officer.' Jonty laughs. 'I had the money, but Rhys had the land. Most of the plot was owned by an English farmer. There was no planning permission and no likelihood of getting it, so Rhys bought it for a song.'

'But the land he inherited from his father already had a building on it,' Ffion says slowly. 'So there was a precedent.'

'Not just a pretty face, eh?' Jonty says. Ffion stares at him, unsmiling. 'You're spot on. A small, scrubby bit of land, but arguably priceless. It was still a battle, but there was already a structure of sorts on the foreshore, and eventually we were able to make authorities see sense.'

'Was the business going well?' Leo thinks it's possible Ffion might actually implode.

'The lodges were harder to sell than anticipated. We had to drop the price and, even then, they didn't shift. We don't offer payment plans or accept mortgages – we're strictly top-end – and it was tricky to find the right place in the market. In the end, we employed a PR firm to create a campaign around The Shore. Paid influencers, tweeting about how incredible it was, when the place was still a building site – that sort of thing.'

'It sounds highly unethical,' Leo says.

'Everybody does it. And it worked – that's how we got Ashleigh Stafford. We implied there was a waiting list, that applicants were being vetted . . .' Jonty looks smug. 'The truth was, Rhys and I had taken a lodge each in lieu of shares, and the other three were standing empty. Ashleigh was just what we needed – there's genuine word-of-mouth now. Once the rest of the lodges are built, we'll be able to sell them three times over.'

'Did you and Rhys always see eye to eye on business matters?' Ffion says.

'Pretty much.' Jonty blinks several times in quick succession.

'Are you sure about that?'

He blows out his cheeks. 'Look, I was a bit pissed off with him before he died, alright? Someone's bound to tell you, so there you go – I'm telling you now. We had a bit of a cashflow problem last year and had to let the builders go. Rhys hired a local chap, Huw Ellis, to finish the job, and I bankrolled the thirty-grand bill. Only, Rhys spent the money, and the builder still needs paying.'

'And you're still owed thirty grand?' Leo says.

'Well, yes. Not a fortune, I know. But with a builder on the warpath as well, you can see why I'd be a bit pissed off.'

'I'd imagine Huw Ellis is pretty pissed off, too.' Ffion's voice is cold. Leo doesn't blame her. After almost ten years in the police, his take-home pay is a fraction under thirty grand a year. It might not be a fortune to Jonty Charlton, but it is to most people.

'He had a go at me, at the party,' Jonty says. 'Didn't get any-where with Rhys, so came after me, the—' He stops himself. 'It all seems rather irrelevant now, doesn't it? Now that poor old Rhys has gone.'

On the contrary, Leo thinks, it seems very relevant indeed.

Outside, he's about to suggest to Ffion they compare notes over a coffee when she announces she has to go.

'But we're in the middle of a job.'

'I've got stuff to do.' She zips up her capacious coat and flashes an unconvincing smile. 'Lone Ranger, remember?'

'Lone Shirker, more like,' mutters Leo. He'll still grab a coffee, he decides, and he begins walking towards the village. The investigation is a tangle of weeds in his head, and he pulls at each strand, trying to make sense of it. Both Jonty Charlton and Yasmin Lloyd gain financially from Rhys Lloyd's death. They both had a motive, but did they have the opportunity? Both feature in Instagram images posted throughout the evening, giving the impression they hardly left the party. The tech team hasn't yet retrieved the metadata that might enable them to pull together a more reliable timeline, and Leo wonders if it will show that either Jonty or Yasmin were absent for long enough to kill Rhys and dispose of his body.

As Leo reaches the high street, a teenager with a mass of red curls is walking towards him. There's no mistaking that hair, nor the stubborn set of her jaw. Leo stops.

'It's Seren, isn't it? Ffion's sister?' The girl looks at him suspiciously. 'Leo Brady.' He shows his warrant card. 'I'm working with Ffion on the murder case at The Shore.'

'Lucky you.'

'I wondered if you might reconsider giving elimination prints.' Seren looks at him blankly.

'It *is* voluntary,' Leo says. 'You were quite within your rights to say no – only it's incredibly helpful to be able to rule people out.'

'Fingerprints? What happens to them afterwards?'

'They're deleted. They can't be used for anything except this case – Ffion must have explained all this to you?'

'Nope. But I don't mind doing it. It's quite cool, actually. I've never been involved in a murder investigation.'

'Thanks for changing your mind. I appreciate it.'

Seren shrugs. 'No one asked me in the first place, but whatever. Can I . . .' She gestures vaguely up the street.

'What? Oh, yes, of course. Thanks.' Leo watches her go, his mind working overdrive. Seren Morgan was on the elimination list as a refusal, and there's only one explanation for the discrepancy.

Ffion lied.

FIFTEEN

NEW YEAR'S EVE | MIDDAY | YASMIN

Yasmin Lloyd can't wait to be divorced. If she's completely honest (which she rarely is) she hasn't wanted to be married for a long time, but things have now come to a head. She has been utterly betrayed by her husband, and, although she appreciates the irony of that, she simply can't stay with him another minute.

Except she has to. Yasmin isn't a monster, and it will hit Tabby and Felicia hard when she and Rhys separate. The least she can do is let them enjoy the party tonight. As the girls are fond of pointing out, there's nothing else to do around here, and it would be cruel to ruin the festivities by announcing on New Year's Eve that their parents are splitting up.

Yasmin gazes out from the bedroom balcony. A lone boat tacks lazily across the water, and a flock of birds are diving for fish. On the opposite shore, someone is perched on a stool, painting or drawing. Yasmin sighs. She no longer sees the beauty in the lake, or in the sharp outlines of the surrounding mountains. She no longer cares for the reflection of the trees; or the lodges, mirrored in the silvery water. The novelty of The Shore wore off when the nights drew in, and the decks were no longer sun-kissed. She thinks wistfully of Tuscan villas and Caribbean beaches.

Yasmin steps back inside and closes the door, walking through Rhys's study towards the stairs. On his desk is a stack of mail ready to be posted to fans all over the world. Yasmin shuffles the post into a neat pile, straightens the chair, and picks up a throw which is supposed to be draped artfully over one arm, but which Rhys insists on sitting on and creasing. She steps back and eyes the room critically. She's very proud of her design work at The Shore, and is looking forward to showing it off to tonight's party guests. If only it were possible to pick up the lodge and put it somewhere more interesting. There must be lakes in the Home Counties, surely?

She tweaks the curtains for symmetry. Outside on the drive, her husband is talking to Dee, and Yasmin can tell from his stance that he wants to get away. She could rescue him, she supposes, as she makes her way downstairs, but why should she, after what he's done? She makes a few adjustments to the cushions in the sitting room and turns the table arrangement to face the door. It's funny how all the lodges are the same, and yet look so different. Take the Charltons' place: Blythe talks a lot about aesthetics, but the woman has no eye for colour.

Yasmin takes a bottle of brandy from the kitchen. Rhys's agent sends him an extraordinarily expensive one every Christmas, which Rhys opens on New Year's Eve to bring him luck for the forthcoming year. Yasmin always joins him. Rhys's career needs more than a glass of superstition, but it happens to be excellent brandy.

By the time Yasmin gets outside, Rhys is marching towards the lake with his phone clamped to his ear, and Dee is nowhere to be seen. Yasmin can imagine how the conversation went.

So sorry, Dee, I have to call my agent back.

Oh, of course, dear, don't let me stop you.

Rhys is forever getting out of dull social situations by fabricating urgent calls with Fleur. She can see him now, through the trees, pacing the little cove and talking furiously into his mobile. Doesn't he realise Dee has gone back inside, and his little act is being wasted?

'Yasmin, where's that naughty husband of yours?' Blythe says, the moment Yasmin joins the others in the Charltons' lodge. 'Jonty needs help putting more lights up.'

'We're not joined at the hip,' Yasmin says tartly. She resumes the balloon-blowing she'd half-hoped someone might have finished in her absence. Privately she thinks balloons are terribly naff, but Blythe has had a hundred delivered, in The Shore's signature green and off-white, putting Yasmin in charge of creating an arch.

'That marquee's a bloody eyesore,' Jonty mutters. Yasmin couldn't agree more.

'It frames the lake,' Blythe says.

Jonty stomps through the bifolds with a box of lights. 'It blocks the bloody lake!'

The local girl is on canapés. They arrived in a Fortnum & Mason van half an hour ago, and Mia's transferring them from their boxes on to platters. Blythe has issued strict instructions to all the lodge-owners to clear their fridges to allow for storage – it truly is a military operation.

'Imagine if nobody comes!' Yasmin says. She laughs to show it's just a joke, but it's too late for the flash of panic that crosses Blythe's face at the prospect of such social embarrassment.

'Course they'll come.' Bobby is moving drinks around with a marked lack of haste. He's probably avoiding Ashleigh, who has been conspicuously absent during the party preparations. 'They'll all want a nosy at the poshos.'

'No one will be troubling you, then,' Jonty murmurs. He's fired up the log-burner, but every five minutes Mia takes more food out, or Jonty comes in for more lights, and an icy blast blows through the lodge. Above the lake, thick clouds hold the promise of snow.

Where is Rhys? Yasmin is torn between not wanting to be anywhere near her husband, and resenting the fact that she's blowing up bloody balloons while he skives off for pretend phone calls. He'll have skulked back to his study, no doubt, messing it up so she'll have to tidy up again before people arrive. After the divorce, she'll repurpose his office at home. Perhaps she'll take up art: it would make a stunning studio, and Yasmin could source one of those antique easels as a centrepiece.

Rhys will try to take the house, of course, but Yasmin will be ready for him. He won't want his shameful behaviour splashed across the papers. As soon as the holidays are over, Yasmin will lawyer up. If Rhys thinks he's coming out of this better than Yasmin, he's got another think coming.

Clemmie is at the drinks table, taking the bottles Bobby and Caleb dump on the kitchen counter and arranging them into neat rows. Yasmin swoops up Rhys's brandy just as Clemmie spots it. 'Sorry, this one's personal use only.' Yasmin smiles, then turns to Blythe. 'Darling, can I stash this somewhere?'

'Here, I'll hide it behind the cans.' Blythe puts the brandy in a cupboard. 'I can't imagine anyone will be rootling through the chickpeas at a party.'

'I wouldn't bet on it,' Jonty says. 'Some of them probably aren't even housetrained.' He laughs raucously and Yasmin notices Mia's eyes on him from the other side of the room. She notices something else too. She waits for Jonty to look in her direction, then discreetly gestures to her own neck, nodding towards Jonty's collar. Jonty frowns, then looks down and clamps a hand over the smear of lipstick on his shirt, before slinking gratefully out of the room. Such a cliché. Yasmin wonders if Blythe has noticed. Maybe she doesn't care – you never know what people's marriages are like beneath the surface.

It takes Yasmin three hours to inflate all the balloons and arrange them to Blythe's satisfaction, her progress hindered by demands to carry this and move that, and *would you mind popping to get some more cheese?* She smiles tightly at this last – surely the cleaner could do that? – but slips on her shoes and finds her coat.

As she reaches the hall, she hears a car engine, revving angrily. By the time she's opened the Charltons' front door the car's disappearing around the corner, a black cloud of exhaust smoke in its wake. As if that wasn't extraordinary enough – this is The Shore, not some sink estate – her husband is on his knees in the middle of the drive.

For a second she forgets what he's done, and that she hates him for it. She forgets that she's restless, that she's frustrated by his lack of success. She forgets that she wants a divorce. She runs to him, panic making her stumble. 'What's happened?' He looks at her wordlessly. Is he having a heart attack? 'Who was in that car?'

The question seems to galvanise Rhys. He gets shakily to his feet, but he still doesn't answer, and now Yasmin is annoyed. He clearly isn't having a heart attack; she almost twisted her ankle for no good reason.

'No one. It's nothing.'

It's the final straw. *No one* doesn't drive away in a cloud of exhaust smoke, and *nothing* doesn't push a grown man to his knees. Yasmin didn't want to upset the girls on New Year's Eve, but she simply cannot maintain this charade a moment longer.

'We're finished,' she says. 'You're pathetic, Rhys.'

Yasmin walks away without looking back. She doesn't care, now, what people think. She doesn't even care what – or who – has prompted this extreme reaction from Rhys. She only cares – as she has for most of her life – about herself.

SIXTEEN

JANUARY 4TH | FFION

'I'm guessing this isn't a social call.' Huw Ellis leans over the scaffolding, a hi-vis tabard stretched over so many layers he looks twice the size. He's small but wiry – the sort of man you might underestimate in a pub fight.

'I need a word with you – can you come down?'

Ffion had driven around town until she'd found Huw's white van parked in a cul-de-sac. He's working on a two-storey extension with three other guys, one of whom gave a wolf-whistle he turned into a cough when he realised who the gaffer's visitor was.

'You want me, you come up.'

'Stop playing games, you tosser. This is a serious—' A hard hat drops at her feet. Ffion sighs and squashes it over her hair, before clambering up the ladder with neither speed nor grace.

At the top, Huw props one foot against a stack of slate tiles. 'Haven't seen you for a while.'

'Been busy,' Ffion says, looking out across the rooftops. Llyn Drych is spectacular from up here. The water sparkles in the winter sun, clouds scudding towards the village as though hurrying from the mountainous dragon looming above it. At the far end of the lake, smoke curls from the tiny cottage in which Angharad Evans lives with her rescue animals. All Ffion's life is here, laid out in a patchwork of forest green and grey slate, and the silvery-mirror blue of Llyn Drych.

'The murder investigation, is it?' Huw seeks out Ffion's gaze. 'How are you keeping?'

'You were at the New Year's Eve party at The Shore.'

'Me and half of Cwm Coed. You're looking well.'

'Why did you go?'

Huw puts a hand on the scaffolding. His skin is tanned and rough, his fingers scarred by years of work. He never wears gloves at work, even in the depths of winter. 'Come home, Ffi,' he says softly. 'I miss you.'

'You hate that sort of party.' Ffion blinks hard. The cold is making her eyes water. 'Small talk and champagne. Poncey canapés. Why did you go?'

'Don't be like this.'

'Did you go to try and get back the thirty grand Rhys owed you?' Ffion examines her husband's face for signs she's hit the mark, but he's looking at her with such intensity she has to turn away.

'Ffi.'

'We've been through this.'

'I love you,' Huw says, quietly but forcefully, and Ffion stares at the lake and wishes she were out on the water, racing the wind. 'I'd do anything for things to be back the way they were.'

'Please don't make this any harder than it is already.' Ffion doesn't mean to sound angry, but her words come out clipped and hard. 'I only came because it looks bad for you. Thirty grand, Huw! Why didn't you tell me?'

'Bit hard to do that, when you've gone out of your way to avoid bumping into me.'

Ffion flushes. She didn't realise it had been so obvious. 'You should know that we're processing the prints from the crime scene. If yours are found in Rhys's office—'

'Of course they'll be there!' Huw laughs. 'Ffi, I worked there. Fitted windows, finished the flooring. I dealt with the snags after they'd all moved in. I've still got keys to the place.'

'Should you still have keys, if you're not working at The Shore?'

'They can have them back when I'm paid my thirty grand. And, since I hear Yasmin Lloyd's due a bit of a windfall, that shouldn't be a problem now.'

'Where did you hear that?'

Huw, the one person in Cwm Coed who can match Ffion for stubbornness, taps the side of his nose. They stare at each other, and for once it's Ffion who looks away first.

'I'd better go.'

'I've been thinking.'

'You're supposed to check with a doctor before taking up new activities.'

'We could have a drink some time. Like before we got married. No pressure, no baby talk, just a drink. See how things go.'

The wind whips Ffion's hair across her eyes and Huw reaches up to push it back, a gesture which a year ago Ffion would hardly have noticed. She steps back hurriedly, forgetting where they are, and sees the alarm in his face as she clutches at the scaffolding.

'Jesus, Ffi. Am I that much of a bastard?'

'You're not a bastard.' She's the one at fault, the one who finished things. She pushes her hands in her pockets to stop herself from reaching for him. She's promised herself she won't hurt him any more than she already has, but he still loves her, and so much about that is tempting.

142

'That drink, then? I'm out with the mountain rescue lads tonight, but—'

Ffion takes off the hard hat and hands it to him. 'Maybe once this job's out of the way.'

She has five missed calls from Leo. She deletes the notifications and switches her phone to silent, then sits in her car and scrolls through her emails. The crime analysts have dug into the applications downloaded on Rhys's phone, and Ffion opens the attachment. Most of the apps are familiar to her – a fitness tracker, social media, various shopping platforms – and there are several music apps listed, including instrument tuners and a vocal warm-up. It's strange to see someone's life listed in this way, their priorities and privileges categorised into folders and shortcuts. Ffion imagines her own digital footprint on display: photo editing and pizza vouchers, wind speeds and stargazing apps.

DC Thorngate, from Crouch's team, has been tasked with looking into the various dating apps Rhys used – some of which were deleted from his phone several weeks prior to his death – but Ffion's curious about the other apps. *Number 36* is listed as a membership club.

I was having a drink at my club in Soho, Rhys said in his statement, about the evening the unknown woman visited his home, threatening Yasmin.

Is Number 36 the Soho club? A limited amount of data has been retrieved from the app and is recorded beneath the listing. Rhys made reservations there most weeks, until June last year, when his membership ended. Lack of money? Perhaps Rhys was starting to feel the pinch, without work coming in.

Ffion googles the club. Number 36 doesn't appear anywhere, and there's nothing on social media. The investigating officer in

Rhys's harassment case is listed on the scanned statement Leo shared with her, and Ffion fires off a quick email, asking what he knows about Rhys's club. It feels dodgy to Ffion. Even if Number 36 is stuck in the dark ages, nowadays every business has *some* kind of online presence, doesn't it?

Unless it doesn't want to be found.

SEVENTEEN

JANUARY 5TH | LEO

Leo is running a personal errand on job time. This is such an unprecedented occurrence that he can feel his pulse quickening, and he wonders if Ffion 'Lone Ranger' Morgan operates in a constant state of stress, fuelled by adrenaline and caffeine, and whether it bothers her. He suspects not.

He's standing on the doorstep of what used to be his house, a three-bedroomed semi on a respectable estate in Chester. Allie – or, more likely, Dominic – has painted the front door a glossy black, and a for sale sign skewers the front lawn. After their divorce, Allie had bought Leo out, leaving him with not quite enough to start over – not once you factored in the monthly direct debit Allie insisted on.

'I gave up my career to look after Harris.'

'Oh, come on,' Leo had said. 'It was hardly a *career*.' He'd regretted it as soon as he'd said it, knowing it would find its way into Allie's little black book of Leo's wrongdoings. Before Allie fell pregnant, she had been office manager at a removal firm. They'd offered her part-time hours, but she had declined, putting Harris into full-time nursery when he was six months old and spending the day doing fitness classes.

She's in her gym wear now, answering the door in burgundy

leggings and a matching top, a tight Lycra band around her hair. 'What do you want?'

'Can I come in? It's freezing out here.'

Allie hesitates, then sighs and walks inside. Leo follows her into the kitchen. A pile of cream invitations sits on one side of the table; matching envelopes on the other. In the centre is a printed spreadsheet, on which Allie has ticked some of the names.

'Wedding invitations,' Allie says. She sits and pulls one off the pile, checking her list and writing a name across the invite, before sliding it into an envelope and licking the seal.

Leo's heart has long since stopped hurting, so he ignores his ex-wife's lack of tact, and sits opposite her. 'Please don't take my son away.' He's been awake most of the night, having this conversation in his head.

'I'm not "taking him away".' Allie waggles her fingers in the air. 'I'm giving him opportunities. This country's a shithole.'

'Somewhere closer, then.' A note of desperation creeps into Leo's voice. 'France. Spain.' He doesn't want his son to go anywhere at all, but at least if he's in Europe Leo will be able to visit more often.

Allie wrinkles her nose. 'Nobody speaks English there.' She licks another envelope, then winces, running her tongue around the inside of her mouth. 'Why do paper cuts hurt so much? Anyway, it's all arranged. Dominic's going to be departmental head at a great secondary school, and there's a primary school on site, so he can take Harris with him.'

'Like fuck he can.' Leo promised himself he wouldn't lose his temper today, but it's that or give in to the sobs welling up in his chest, and he won't give Allie the satisfaction of seeing him cry.

'You see? This is what I mean. Time and time again I give you another chance, only for you to go off on one. It's not acceptable,

146

Leo. To be honest I think Harris would be better without you in his life. You're a bad influence.'

'I love him.'

'You put him in danger!' There it is. Allie's trump card. 'He was terrified, Leo! God knows what mental scars it will have left. When I think of his little voice on the end of the phone . . .' She puts a hand to her mouth, crocodile tears squeezing from her closed eyes. Leo says nothing. What can he say, that he hasn't already tried?

He had been taking Harris back to Allie when it happened. Along with most of his colleagues, he'd spent much of the week looking for Kieron Tackley, a sixty-five-year-old paedophile with enough of the right contacts for his prison van to be intercepted. Instead of facing trial, Tackley was now roaming the city, and every day that passed put another child at risk.

'Who let the dogs out?' Leo was singing along to the radio.

'Who, who, who, who, who?' came the response from the back seat. Never mind "Wind the Bobbin Up", Baha Men had Harris throwing shapes like nobody's business.

Kieron Tackley was standing by a bus stop. Head down, hood up, but definitely Tackley. Leo switched off the music, pulled in behind a parked car and reached for his police radio.

'You put the job before your own son,' Allie says now. 'It's quite obvious where your priorities lie, and they're not with Harris.'

Leo walks out. What's the point?

'Wait!'

He turns, and Allie thrusts an envelope at him. 'Here you go. Saves me a stamp.'

Ffion's getting out of her car when Leo pulls into Brynafon mortuary. She doesn't wait for him, and by the time he catches up she's with Izzy Weaver. Leo has the distinct impression Ffion is avoiding being alone with him. He wonders if Seren's told her about their exchange on Cwm Coed high street.

'I gather you've got a tenner on the wife offing him with his own sleeping tablets?' Izzy says, as he joins them in the morgue. The technician, Elijah, is tidying up from a previous autopsy.

'It's just a hunch,' Ffion says. 'She was definitely weird when we showed her the list of medication.'

'Well, I can't comment on the wife, but toxicology showed no trace of the tablets, I'm afraid, so DC Brady's quids in.'

'Are you sure?'

Izzy gives Ffion a withering look. 'No drugs at all, in fact. Your man was relatively healthy.'

'Then why did he die?'

'Much as we pathologists like to think we're God, post-mortems are often more about elimination than diagnosis: narrowing down the clinical signs until they point to one thing.' Izzy takes off her glasses and hooks them on to the top of her gown. 'In this case, the assault itself appears severe but in fact it's relatively superficial. There are no cerebral contusions, no subarachnoid or subdural haemorrhage. Not enough to kill him, but enough to bring on the heart attack that proved fatal.'

'Witnesses say he was completely out of it at the party,' Ffion says. 'Everyone assumed he was drunk.'

'That would fit with the early stages of heart failure, especially in otherwise healthy patients. We know from the health app on his watch that his pulse was erratic for most of the afternoon, becoming dangerously slow in the evening. That drop in blood pressure alone would have triggered symptoms of confusion.'

'And vomiting?' Leo asked. 'A witness saw him throw up outside.'

148

'It's not uncommon.'

'Ask if they had mushroom canapés at their party,' the technician says. 'And who made them.' Like Izzy, Elijah is in a disposable gown, with blue plastic bags over his shoes. He wears small round glasses, his long hair pulled into a high bun. 'Even a small amount of death cap will make you feel sick in a matter of hours.'

'Elijah is midway through a toxicology degree,' Izzy says. 'Which apparently makes him an expert.'

'The symptoms would fit,' Elijah says mildly, ignoring the barb.

'But death cap mushroom poisoning would also cause kidney and liver failure, neither of which I found in our chap.' Izzy turns to Ffion and Leo, effectively dismissing Elijah. 'Practically all poisons leave their mark. Corrosives burn the digestive tract, paracetamol shows as jaundice in the whites of the eyes, arsenic gives the stomach lining a velvety texture.'

Leo feels a bit queasy. He feels sorry for Elijah, who has gone back to his tidying, and he wonders if the technician really doesn't mind Izzy's rudeness, or if he's quietly plotting her downfall. Sometimes, when Crouch is being particularly unpleasant, Leo imagines his boss falling from a great height, or afflicted by uncontrollable diarrhoea.

'Izzy Weaver's a bit much, isn't she?' he says, once they've left the mortuary and are safely out of earshot.

Ffion leans against her car. 'I like her.'

Leo checks his emails. Twitter has finally released the IP addresses attached to some of the threatening tweets Lloyd received, and Leo is expecting results on the trace. Had Lloyd's stalker travelled from somewhere else to confront Yasmin at the family home, or did she live in London? If she murdered Lloyd, how did she get to The Shore? The mystery stalker is still their

149

prime suspect, and the sooner they identify her, the better. They might even find her prints at the crime scene. The thought reminds him of Seren Morgan.

'I bumped into your sister—' he starts, but Ffion talks over him.

'The Met's been looking into Rhys's club. Number 36. They've had low-level intel on it over a number of years, and guess what?' Ffion takes a drag of her cigarette. 'It's a brothel.' She blows a slow plume of smoke. 'A high-end one – whatever that is – but nevertheless a brothel. They're pulling an operation together as we speak.'

'Do you think Yasmin knows?'

Ffion grinds the butt of her roll-up beneath the heel of her boot. 'That her husband was a cunt?'

Leo isn't quite sure what to say. He refreshes his inbox and reads the incoming email with a slow smile. He looks at Ffion. 'I think we've just found Lloyd's stalker.' Leo taps the number at the bottom of the email and puts the call on to loudspeaker.

'I thought it wouldn't take you long to get back to me.' Gwen, from Major Crime's tech team, sounds pleased with herself.

'I've got Ffion Morgan with me,' Leo says. 'Talk us through what you've got.'

'In October last year, someone sent an abusive tweet to the victim's account, and get this: the IP address is a café on Cwm Coed high street.'

Leo and Ffion look at each other. Lloyd's stalker is local.

'That in itself doesn't tell us anything – the mobile's untraceable – but most criminals carry their own phones with them as well as a burner, so I looked to see how many other devices were logged by the wifi network at the same time.' Gwen pauses for what can only be effect.

'And?' Ffion prompts.

'Just one. Another mobile phone, but a contract one, this time.'

Leo's pulse picks up. 'Registered to whom?'

Gwen's triumph is audible. 'Yasmin Lloyd.'

EIGHTEEN

DECEMBER 27TH | CERI

The Shore is the last stop on Ceri's postal route. She leaves the engine running, the midday news on the radio, and opens the rear doors of the van. There are more clothes for Ashleigh Stafford, who frowns at the parcels when Ceri hands them over.

'There should be one from ASOS.'

'That's all I've got.' Ceri wonders if Ashleigh does anything with her time at The Shore except online shopping. In the summer, when the couple spent the whole of August here, Ceri delivered packages every single day. Ashleigh never once said thank you, but once, when Ceri had staggered up the path with a pile of boxes, Bobby Stafford had pressed a twenty-pound note into her hand.

Jonty and Blythe Charlton, at number one, rarely have post.

'Everything goes to the main house,' Blythe explained in the summer. Ceri hadn't long turned forty, celebrating by completing on a two-bedroomed house with a mortgage she'll still be paying into her seventies. How the other half live.

She has a stack of post for number four. Ceri's curious about Clemence Northcote and her son. She delivered all their Christmas cards, and a number of bills, and today she has a brown envelope from the DVLA, which seems an odd thing to have delivered to your holiday home. A fat package is too big to fit through the door, so she rings the bell. Caleb answers, yawning so widely Ceri can see his tonsils. He scratches the band of midriff between his pyjama bottoms and a faded hoodie featuring a band Ceri has never heard of.

'Alright,' he says. It isn't really a question.

Ceri hands him the mail. The boy smells of cannabis and sleep, but he's still preferable to Call-me-Clemmie, whose insistence on limping through a conversation in Welsh has made Ceri late to clock off on more than one occasion. She wonders if Clemmie knows that her son smokes weed, or that he's been seen on the hillside, gathering the psychedelic mushrooms that have grown there ever since Ceri was at school.

There's only a postcard for number two. Ceri could pop it through the letterbox, but she has a soft spot for Dee Huxley, and likes to check in on her.

'Ceri, dear, it's minus one.' As always, Mrs Huxley is in her slippers, with several layers beneath her cardigan. Ceri looks down at her bare knees and grins. They have a variation on this exchange most mornings, but it'll take more than the threat of snow to get Ceri out of her shorts.

'How are you, Mrs Huxley?'

'Still alive, which is a good starting point for any day, I always think.'

'I thought I told you to use this?' Ceri rattles the door chain, which hangs uselessly on the frame. 'I might be someone after your money.'

'I'd give you short shrift if you tried.' She lifts her stick and bangs it on the floor, then laughs at Ceri's expression.

At number five, Ceri takes out the package marked for the Lloyds. She'd leave it on the doorstep, if she could, but the big padded envelope marked with his agency address has to be signed for. Signed for! A bunch of stamped addressed envelopes, waiting for Rhys's autograph. Ceri's never known anything so ridiculous.

Hopefully one of the twins will open the door. Or Yasmin. Ceri doesn't much like Yasmin, but she's undoubtedly the lesser of two evils. The Lloyds have one of those doorbells with a camera attached, so if they're lazing on the deck they can see if whoever is at the door is worth getting up for. Early last summer, Ceri had rung the bell and been greeted by Rhys's disembodied voice.

'Parcel for you.'

'Could you stick it upstairs in the office? Door's open. It's a surprise for Yasmin – I don't want her to see it.'

'Fucksake,' Ceri had muttered, pushing open the front door. 'What did your last servant die of?' She'd noted the shoes by the mat and kept her own on, wishing they were muddier. The stairs turned halfway up, and she saw the office at the top. All the bedroom doors were open, the heat stifling. A pile of sheet music, pinned to the desk by an empty mug, wafted in the breeze coming from the balcony in the main bedroom. Ceri put the parcel on the armchair, covering it with a throw so soft it was all she could do not to hold it to her face. She ran a hand over the polished mahogany desk and thought of the crappy furniture in her own house. On the wall, generic framed prints hung in a perfect quartet. Ceri took it all in, moving silently around the small space, her fingers trailing lightly over artfully placed ornaments.

She glanced into the master bedroom, thinking how incredible it would be to wake up to that view – how she would sit and paint on the balcony all day – then she caught sight of the full-length mirror on the wall and screamed.

Rhys was lying in bed, the sheets pushed to one side and one hand resting idly by his naked thigh. 'That you, Ceri?' he'd called as she ran down the stairs, as though he hadn't been watching her, hadn't just made eye contact with her, hadn't smiled as if to say *You can't resist me, can you?*

Afterwards, Ceri had complained to her boss.

'You should never have gone in his house,' he'd said. 'You went *upstairs*, Ceri. What did you think was going to happen?'

'Morning,' Rhys says now, as he opens the door.

Ceri doesn't look at him. She hands him the envelope full of fan mail, and stares at her machine while he signs his name with a flourish too big for the screen. She thinks about the names he called her, when she was twelve, and he was old enough to know better. She thinks about the constant drip drip drip of abuse whenever she saw him, the obscene graffiti on her locker. She thinks about turning up full of nerves, to meet the girl she fancied, only to find Rhys and his mates, pissing themselves laughing. *All water under the bridge*, Ceri always says, if anyone from school ever mentions it.

'I've got something for you, actually.' Rhys coughs. He's never mentioned that day she saw him on the bed. Never even referred to it. Ceri wonders if Rhys is one of those *all mouth and no trousers* type, too scared of humiliation to try anything he can't explain away as an accident. 'I'll go and get it.'

Ceri waits on the doorstep, thinking it might be a tip, although Yasmin already gave her a Christmas card with a gift card for Primark.

Rhys comes back with a pile of creamy cards. 'We're having a New Year's Eve party. Thought we'd invite some people from the village.' He clears his throat again.

'Are you . . .' Ceri is incredulous. 'Are you inviting me to your party?'

155

Rhys colours slightly. 'Well, if you like. But actually, we wondered . . . I mean . . . I've written a list. Of people who might like to come.' He hands her a printed list of around twenty people.

The penny drops. Ceri's the postwoman, so she can deliver their mail. For free. Rhys Lloyd has got a bloody nerve. She stares at the invites and she wants to tell him where to stick them, only inside she's still the fourteen-year-old girl who once threw herself into stinging nettles to avoid Rhys's cruelty; still the teenager made to hate herself so much, she swallowed every paracetamol she could get her hands on.

Ceri takes the invitations.

After she's dropped the van at work, she walks through the village towards her house. Glynis is cleaning the shop windows. She asks how Ceri is, as she always does, in an intense, insistent way as though checking on Ceri's welfare now negates what her son did back then.

'They're having a party at The Shore.' Ceri holds up the creamy invitations.

'It's nice they're asking people from the village,' Glynis says, with a touch of defensiveness.

'It is indeed.' Water under the bridge, Ceri thinks, as she moves on. She looks at the list of people Rhys and his friends consider worthy of an invitation. Business owners, Rotary members, the vicar and his wife. A local historian; a television presenter with a family home nearby. Does Rhys even like these people, or is it all just for show? Ceri flicks the invites with her thumb, mentally working out a route to deliver them.

What is she doing?

Ceri feels a surge of anger that she's once again allowed Rhys Lloyd to fill her time and her head. She pushes open the door of

Y Llew Coch. The lunchtime regulars sit in the window seat – old boys with pints of ale and years of memories – and a couple of walkers tuck into sausage and chips. At the bar, Huw Ellis is talking to Steffan Edwards.

Ceri nods to the men. '*Iawn?*'

'Alright, Ceri?' Huw says. Out of habit, Ceri glances at Steffan's drink, but – like Huw's – it's just a coffee. Steffan doesn't notice, he's intent on his conversation with Huw, and Ceri slaps the pile of invitations on the bar.

'Can I nab a bit of paper?' she asks Alun, behind the bar.

He picks up an invitation and reads it. 'They don't seriously expect anyone from round here to go, do they?'

'Glynis Lloyd's going.' Ceri scribbles a note on the piece of paper Alun gives her.

'With instructors,' Steffan is saying to Huw, beside her.

Alun is shaking his head. 'Shame on her. When she knows full well Jac wanted Tŷ'r Lan left alone. Even put it in his will. The man must be turning in his grave.'

'Why didn't he say anything?' Steff is saying, but Ceri has had enough of The Shore, enough of broken-record locals and blokes in pubs. She walks out of the pub, leaving the invitations on the bar, topped with her note.

Open invitation, it reads. *Free bar.*

Ceri tells people it's all water under the bridge.

It couldn't be further from the truth.

NINETEEN

JANUARY 5TH | FFION

Just as Ffion and Leo arrive at The Shore, Bobby Stafford jogs towards them.

'I've downloaded the footage from my door-cam,' he says, as he reaches them. 'I don't know if it's useful, but Rhys passed our place around half-ten on New Year's Eve.'

'Thanks.' Leo takes the USB stick.

Ffion's already walking away, her attention caught by a movement in the trees. She walks towards it, Leo a few paces behind, and finds Caleb Northcote lurking by the water's edge, a hoodie pulled over his face. He throws a cigarette into the undergrowth behind him.

Ffion eyes him suspiciously. 'What are you doing skulking about here?'

'I'm not skulking. I thought you were going to nick Bobby.'

'Should we?' Leo says.

'He's alright, he is. He's teaching me to fight.' Caleb shifts his weight, his eyes looking around, as though searching for the emergency exit. His face is pinched and anxious.

Ffion thinks of the glance that had passed between Felicia and Tabby, when they'd heard Rhys was dead. 'You hang out with the Lloyd twins a lot, right?'

'I guess.'

'How did they get on with their dad?'

'Dunno.' It's automatic, but then: 'They had a row.'

'The twins?'

'Rhys and Yasmin. Felicia and Tabby heard them arguing on Christmas Eve – Tabby said it was really bad.'

'Over what?'

Caleb shrugs. 'Ask them.' He's too savvy to talk, Ffion thinks, but too well-brought-up to walk away.

'So, where's home?' Leo asks.

'Here.'

'Before here.'

'London.'

'Like it?'

Caleb shrugs. Then, after a moment: 'Mum doesn't.'

'How come?'

'She doesn't like my mates.'

Leo nods. 'It's kind of a given, to be honest. Mums aren't supposed to like our friends. My lad's only just started school, and a few of his classmates are well dodgy.'

Caleb laughs, a sound which seems to surprise even him. He looks at Leo. 'I don't like them much, either.' He picks up a stone and throws it from one hand to the other.

'Troublemakers?' Leo says. The boy nods.

'You're not exactly squeaky clean yourself,' Ffion says. She'd like to warn him off – Seren's dropped him into conversation too often for there to be nothing in it – but she knows better than to add fuel to something that might still burn itself out. Telling a teenager not to do something is a sure-fire way to make it happen.

'I know you won't believe me, but they made me do all that stuff.' Caleb scuffs his trainers on the ground. 'I'm not trying to make excuses – like, I know I could have said no, I know I did it. I did the crime, I gotta do the time, blah blah blah.'

'As you get older, it'll get easier to stand up for yourself,' Leo says.

'That's why Mum got this place.' Caleb nods towards The Shore. 'She saw it online and got, like, obsessed with it. No one around to be a bad influence.' Caleb perfectly mimics Clemmie Northcote's voice.

'Expensive way to make a fresh start.'

Caleb shrugs. His phone pings with a message. 'Gotta go.'

'Fresh start, my arse,' Ffion says, once he's gone. 'My sister reckons he's supplying cannabis to half of Year Eleven.' She yawns. 'I should really do something about that, I suppose.'

'I think he's a good kid. Underneath.' Leo gives a half grin. 'He reminds me of the way I was, at that age.'

Ffion snorts. 'He reminds me of the way you are now. You learn to stick up for yourself as you get older, do you? I didn't see much evidence of that when your DI was ripping the piss.'

Leo starts walking back towards the lodges. 'Will you do the full character assassination now, or are we actually going to nick Yasmin Lloyd?'

'Now that you mention it, you've got a terrible habit of—' Ffion cuts off, as Leo stops dead and glares at her. She grins. 'Oh, alright. We'll nick Yasmin Lloyd.'

In the Lloyds' lodge, Tabby picks out mournful tunes on the piano, while Felicia kneels at the glass coffee table, surrounded by photographs of her father.

Yasmin sighs. 'I told her not to. It's only going to make her feel worse.'

'I have to,' Felicia cries, as she works through her father's mail.

'Dad's fans are devastated – he'd want us to reply.' In every reply, Felicia is including a printed statement. Ffion picks one up.

We are grief-stricken by the loss of Rhys Lloyd, a loving husband and father.

Felicia slips a signed photograph into an envelope along with the statement, and licks the envelope. A fat tear falls on to the address as she adds it to the pile to be posted.

'We need to speak to you,' Leo says. 'Is there somewhere the girls could—'

'Whatever you've got to say to me, you can say it here,' Yasmin snaps. 'It can't be any worse than being told their father's dead.'

Ffion shrugs. 'Yasmin Lloyd, I'm arresting you on suspicion of the stalking and harassment of Rhys Lloyd.' As Ffion recites the caution, Felicia bursts into fresh tears. Yasmin says nothing.

Tabby lets the lid of the piano slam, the sound echoing through the lodge. 'You can't arrest her, it's against her civil liberties. I'm calling Daddy's legal team.'

Rhys's legal team – comprising several contract lawyers and an intellectual property expert – turn out to be about as much use to Yasmin as a waterproof teabag. She's allocated the duty solicitor, who listens to Ffion's brief disclosure without expression, then withdraws to consult with his client.

'Don't you think it's a bit macabre?' Leo says. 'Getting a signed photo from Rhys Lloyd a week after he's been murdered?' They're waiting in the corridor outside custody, eating the contents of the vending machine.

'People are weird.' Ffion tips her bag of crisps up, catching the broken bits in her mouth. 'I've never understood the point of autographs anyway.'

'Some of them are worth a lot of money.'

'Not when you're punting them out to anyone who wants one.' She folds the packet into a triangle. 'There must have been fifty in that pile alone, and Ceri reckons she delivers a batch every week. That's a fuck of a lot of signed photos.' She looks at Leo. 'What? That's your *I've had an idea* face.'

'No, I've just put two and two together, that's all. Lloyd had a cut on his tongue, remember? It was on the post-mortem report, with a shaving nick, and the injuries to his face.'

'So?'

'I was at my ex-wife's this morning when she was sending wedding invitations. She licked an envelope and cut her tongue. Lloyd probably did the same thing, replying to his fan mail.'

'You have a weird relationship with your ex.'

'I'm not sure I have a relationship with her at all. If I did, I might stand a chance of actually seeing my son.'

Ffion's phone rings and she takes the call gratefully. Relationship angst makes her itch. 'DC Morgan.'

'This is DS Dewing, Soho CID. We've raided Number 36.'

'What did you find?'

'Two bankers, a politician and a somewhat red-faced high court judge. The people running the show will take longer to trace, but a few of the sex workers are singing like canaries.'

'Do any of them know Rhys Lloyd?'

'Why do you think I'm ringing? Your analysts say his membership ended in June, right? Well, the day before, he threw his weight around with his regular girl and left her with a broken jaw and a voicebox too bruised to speak. Turns out Lloyd had a penchant for rough sex – something Number 36 indulged, until he assaulted a woman there so badly she ended up in hospital.'

Ffion feels a rush of nausea. She imagines Rhys's hand around a slim throat. Bruises. Broken bones.

'It seems he had something of an obsession with this particular girl,' DS Dewing says. 'Even gave her his card and suggested they hook up privately – something Number 36 expressly forbids. It wasn't reported at the time, for obvious reasons, but some of the other girls took photographs. I warn you – they're pretty full-on.'

It can't be any worse than anything else she's seen.

'DC Morgan?'

'Can you email what you've got? We have his wife in custody.'

'Will do.'

'Where was this woman on New Year's Eve?' Leo says, once Ffion's filled him in.

'Out of the country. Flew back on the third.' Ffion's head feels light, as though she hasn't slept in days. 'They're looking into her associates, to see if any of them have been in North Wales recently.' She refreshes her inbox, waiting for the email to drop from the Met; for the photos she doesn't want to see. She imagines Rhys coming home after the assault, kissing his wife, his daughters. 'What a bastard,' she says.

'I imagine Yasmin feels the same way,' Leo says. He starts walking back to custody. 'Assuming she knows.'

'I thought he was having an affair,' Yasmin says. She blinks rapidly, her eyes fixed on the table between them. 'I never imagined he was visiting a . . .' She takes a sharp breath. 'A brothel.'

Leo pushes a sheet of paper across the table. 'This is a printout of the malicious communications your husband received on Twitter over the course of the past eighteen months.' Next to the document, he places a plastic bag containing a mobile phone – one of two found in Yasmin's handbag. 'Communications you made from this device.'

163

Yasmin glances at the solicitor, who nods. 'Yes. But I didn't send the first ones.' She points at the first half-dozen tweets, which mock Rhys's diminishing career. 'These ones. I don't know who sent them, but they really upset Rhys.'

'And you wanted to continue upsetting him?' Ffion says flatly. Yasmin Lloyd is a piece of work.

Yasmin lifts her chin, her lips tight. 'I believed Rhys was having an affair. I thought if I made him think the tweets were connected, it might scare him enough to stop.'

'What about the woman who came to your house in London, making threats?' Leo says.

There's a long pause. 'There was no woman. I – I lied to the police.'

Leo notes the time of the admission on his pad. 'I'm further arresting you for giving false information and attempting to pervert the course of justice. You remain under caution.'

'I'm sorry, I truly am.' Yasmin twists her hands in her lap. 'I thought he was having an affair – I wasn't thinking straight.'

'You made your husband think he had a stalker. You gave a false statement to police.' Ffion leans forward, speaking slowly and deliberately. 'You let your teenage daughters believe they were in danger.'

'I—'

The solicitor coughs. There's a brief exchange of glances, then Yasmin rearranges her features into something approximating contrition. 'I've been suffering with anxiety and depression, for which I intend to seek help.'

Intend to avoid a conviction on the grounds of mental health problems, more like, Ffion thinks. 'Gaslighting your husband alleviated your symptoms, did it?'

Yasmin flushes.

'What's the value of your husband's life assurance policy?' Leo says.

The solicitor frowns. 'My client has been arrested for harassment. I'm not sure I see the relevance of—'

'One point five million,' Yasmin says evenly. Everyone stares at her. 'Not that it makes any of this any easier.' She wrings her hands and Ffion narrows her eyes. It'll help, though, right? she thinks. Rhys was worth more dead than he had been alive.

'How do they work that out?' she says.

'Potential earnings, I suppose. Royalties and so on. Rhys took out the policy years ago. We never thought we'd need it.' Yasmin's words become a sob.

The solicitor takes a packet of Kleenex from his briefcase. 'Are you okay to continue?'

Yasmin nods, stemming the tears with a tissue. 'I'm fine.' She looks at Ffion, perhaps noting the scepticism in her expression. 'It's for the girls, of course. The insurance money. Their school fees, their future – it's going to be hard for them, now they only have me.'

When Ffion's dad died, Mam had allowed herself a week to grieve. A week to clutch his old jumpers, to weep until her eyes were raw. Then she packed away his things and pulled herself together. She had a newborn baby to look after; a teenager spiralling out of control. Elen Morgan didn't have time for grief.

'The twins seem to have a good relationship with their grandmother,' Leo says. 'I'm sure that will be a great comfort.'

Yasmin sniffs. 'Glynis thought Rhys could do no wrong. They have that in common, I suppose.'

'Do you and Glynis get on?' Ffion asks.

'Better since my father-in-law passed away. Jac and Rhys locked horns a lot. It caused friction between the four of us.'

165

Leo jots something down. 'When did he die?'

'Two years ago, although he was on his way out for a year before that. Dementia. Not that Glynis ever admitted it. She's very private. Proud, you know?'

'What was your marriage like?' Leo says.

'It was . . . fine.'

'Your husband was paying sex workers,' Ffion says bluntly. 'I wouldn't call that *fine*.' She picks up the plastic evidence bag containing the mobile phone. 'You bought this pay-as-you-go in an attempt to send untraceable tweets to harass your husband, right?'

'My client has already admitted to—'

'But you use this phone for something else, don't you?' Ffion says. She watches the colour drain from Yasmin's face. 'How long have you been having an affair with Jonty Charlton?'

TWENTY

JANUARY 5TH | LEO

The pay-as-you-go phone Yasmin used to send her venomous tweets to Rhys is a flip-style Nokia, slim enough to slip into the lining of her handbag, which was precisely where Leo and Ffion had found it. The phone had no passcode, and there was just one phone number stored in the contacts: Jonty Charlton's.

The string of saved text messages was a mixture of logistics – See you by the generator at 6.30; sentiment – I miss you so much, angel pie; and pure filth – I want to take your throbbing—

'Don't! I can't bear it.' Ffion claps her hands over her ears.

Leo looks up from the list of messages he's been reading, and grins. 'Don't you like my sex talk?'

'Not when I have to picture Jonty Charlton and Yasmin Lloyd doing it behind the bike sheds at The Shore.'

'They actually did do it there.' Leo finds the relevant text message and reads it out. '"You can bend over and I'll park my—"'

'Stop! It makes me want to bleach my ears.'

'I didn't have you down for a prude, Ms Morgan.'

'You *know* I'm not a prude, Mr Brady.'

For a second they lock eyes, and Leo feels that same jolt of electricity he felt on New Year's Eve. Somewhere in the office, the printer whirrs into action. 'So,' Leo says, after a beat, because

167

focusing on work feels like the most straightforward route right now, 'Yasmin inherits her husband's life assurance and Jonty Charlton becomes the controlling partner of The Shore. That's a pretty solid motive for getting shot of Lloyd. I'll tell Crouch we want to nick Yasmin for murder. We can hang fire on Charlton till we hear what she has to say.'

Faced with the revelation that his client had failed to disclose an affair with her husband's business partner, Yasmin's solicitor had stopped the interview for a consultation, which has already gone on for well over an hour. Leo and Ffion wandered back to the office, where Ffion commandeered the desk opposite Leo's and is now doodling on a piece of scrap paper.

Leo opens his laptop to message the DI, who has already left the office for the day. He remembers the door-cam footage Bobby Stafford gave him earlier, and, while he's waiting for a response from Crouch, he inserts the USB and double-clicks on the drive. The Shore's cameras show Lloyd around ten-thirty p.m. on New Year's Eve, staggering across the drive to throw up in the bushes, but once he returns to the footpath he's frustratingly out of shot. Maybe Bobby's camera will show something new. More usefully, it will help fill in the blank space left by the glitch experienced by the resort cameras, earlier that day. Aside from Lloyd, only Jonty Charlton had access to the CCTV. Could he have deliberately messed with the footage, to cover his tracks? Or his lover's?

'Maybe it wasn't premeditated,' Leo says, thinking out loud. 'Several witnesses say the Lloyds had a domestic, before the party started.' The software loads and the screen shows Bobby Stafford's bright yellow McLaren, parked outside his lodge. 'Things get heated, Rhys goes for his wife and she grabs the award to defend herself. He dies, she panics and calls her lover to get rid of the evidence.'

'Mmm.' Ffion is adding whiskers to the cat she's drawn on what Leo now sees is the back of a witness statement. He watches her over his laptop. He must have got his wires crossed over Seren's elimination prints – or Seren really did change her mind. Ffion might sail a bit close to the wind occasionally, but she wouldn't actually lie.

His desk phone rings and he hits the speakerphone, answering with a distracted, 'DC Brady,' as he navigates through the door-cam footage.

'Hi, it's Elijah. Elijah Fox. From the mortuary? Although I'm actually at home, because – well, anyway. Um . . . have you got a minute?'

'Go ahead, Elijah. I'm with Ffion now.'

'The thing with toxicology,' Elijah says, 'is that you have to know what you're testing for. And without an unlimited budget, the lab's never going to speculatively test for hundreds of poisons, just on the off-chance of finding a trace of one.'

'Right.' Leo can just about make out the cars either side of the Staffords' lodge, as well as the visitor bay on the opposite side of the drive. He moves the cursor to two p.m. – roughly when The Shore's camera system went on the blink – and plays the footage at triple time.

'So I took a few samples home.'

'You did what?' Leo looks at Ffion, whose mouth has dropped open.

'It's okay, I don't mind doing stuff like that in my own time. I don't have a girlfriend, or anything like that.'

'I wonder why?' Ffion says, under her breath.

'I thought to myself, *what would be readily available to a murderer in north Wales?* No point testing for batrachotoxin when the nearest golden dart frog's five thousand miles away, right?'

169

He laughs, high-pitched and – to Leo's ears – a little manic. Should a mortuary technician be taking blood samples home? Does Izzy know about this? On his laptop, Caleb mooches down the driveway of The Shore.

'Belladonna, on the other hand . . . aconite, cyanide from fruit stones . . . you'd be amazed how lethal your average garden is. And then I hit on it.' Elijah is triumphant. 'Ricin.'

'*Ricin?*' Leo says. He tries to remember the list of medication seized from the Lloyds' bedroom. It was all over-the-counter stuff – is ricin ever a legitimate ingredient? If Yasmin slipped him something at the party, it would explain her reaction when they showed her the list. 'You mean, poison-tipped umbrella, KGB-operatives sort of ricin?'

'It does rain a lot in North Wales,' Ffion says, laughing. 'They'd fit right in.'

'*Ricinus communis,*' Elijah says. 'That's where it comes from. It's quite popular – Monty Don had it on *Gardener's World.*'

But Leo is no longer listening. He's staring at the screen of his laptop, where the footage from Bobby Stafford's door-cam shows a car parked in the visitors' bay at The Shore for a full thirty minutes on the afternoon of Rhys Lloyd's murder.

Ffion's car.

TWENTY-ONE

JANUARY 5TH | FFION

'Ricin's a bit exotic for Cwm Coed,' Ffion says, once Leo's ended the call. 'We're more your couple-of-joints-after-work-and-a-line-at-the-weekend sort.' She thinks again about Caleb dealing dope to Cwm Coed's teenagers, and wonders if arresting him would put Seren off, or make him more appealing. Never underestimate the allure of a bad boy, she thinks, with a shiver. She looks up to find Leo staring at her. 'What?'

'Has there been much crime at The Shore since it opened?'

'Only the graffiti on the sign.'

'Who dealt with that?'

Ffion shrugs. 'The neighbourhood policing team, I guess. Why?'

'You've not been there on official business, then?'

Leo's staring at her, and the hairs on the back of Ffion's neck start to prickle. She jerks her head in a way that could either be a nod or a shake.

'How about in a personal capacity?' Leo's voice is hard.

Ffion makes herself breathe normally, tracing her pen back over the cat she's doodled, feeling a tremor in her normally steady hand. He doesn't know. He might guess, but he doesn't—

Leo spins his laptop one-eighty degrees and pushes it hard towards her.

He knows.

'Oh, right.' Ffion forces a laugh. 'I was there on New Year's Eve. There was some suggestion of fireworks and the locals were up in arms about it.'

'And that's a CID job, is it?'

'I was in the area. Thought I'd help out.' Ffion looks up, holding his gaze challengingly.

'And you didn't think to mention it?'

'I forgot.'

'You forgot you'd parked outside a murder victim's house, the day he died?'

'I've had a lot on my—'

'For fuck's sake, Ffion!' Leo slams both palms flat on the desk. 'You lied about your sister refusing elims. You lied about going to The Shore on New Year's Eve.'

'I didn't lie—'

'By omission. And please tell me you didn't actually destroy CCTV evidence to hide the fact that you'd been there?'

'I can explain.' She can't, but she needs to buy time, because there has to be a way out of this. She thinks of Yasmin Lloyd, blaming poor mental health for her batshit actions. 'It's been a difficult year. My marriage broke up and Seren took it badly. She got on well with Huw. Saw him as a kind of father figure, I suppose.' As Ffion speaks, she realises it's not far from the truth. Seren had been devastated by the separation, unable to understand why Ffion had walked out.

Leo is frowning, and for a moment Ffion thinks she's successfully distracted him.

'Who?' he says.

'It's pronounced *Huw*. As if there's a "y" after the "h". Move your tongue to—'

'Don't fuck with me, Ffion. Huw what? What's his last name?'

Ffion has underestimated Leo. She looks away. 'Ellis.'

There's a long pause. 'You're married to one of our murder suspects?'

'Separated.'

'I can see why.'

Anger flares inside Ffion. 'Says the man who never sees his son.'

She regrets it the second it's out. The hurt in Leo's eyes turns to anger. 'What did I ever see in you?'

'The feeling is entirely mutual.'

There's a sound from the door. 'Um . . . excuse me.' A custody officer is standing awkwardly in the doorway. 'Yasmin Lloyd's ready for interview.'

If the chairs in the interview room weren't fixed to the floor, Ffion is sure Leo would move his further away. She feels the tension coming off him in waves, as she further arrests Yasmin on suspicion of murder.

'This is ridiculous.' Yasmin looks at Ffion and Leo in turn. 'I didn't kill my husband.'

'How long have you been in a relationship with Jonty Charlton?' Leo says.

There's a long pause, before Yasmin answers. 'Six months. It started in the summer, when The Shore opened. It was only ever meant to be a bit of fun, although Jonty, of course, fell in love with me.' A tiny smile at the corners of her mouth suggests she sees such an occurrence as inevitable.

'That's a classy way to celebrate your husband's success,' Ffion says neutrally.

The solicitor coughs. 'Are you here to interview my client, or to debate her morality?'

Ffion ignores the interruption. 'Who knew you were having an affair?'

'No one. We were very careful.'

'Not even Rhys?'

'Absolutely not.'

'How can you be so certain?' Leo says.

'Because if he'd found out, he'd have—' Yasmin breaks off. An ugly flush moves from her neck to her face like a rising tide.

Leo breaks into the silence. 'Blythe Charlton says you and Rhys were arguing, before the party on New Year's Eve.'

'I was pissed off with him, that's all. He'd been drinking all day. I found him on his knees in the middle of the road at one point – he was totally out of it.' Yasmin shakes her head. 'So embarrassing.'

'Interesting,' Leo says, and Ffion's pulse quickens, but Leo's picking up the pathology report. 'Because toxicology results suggest there was very little alcohol in your husband's bloodstream. Did he take any other substances that day?'

'Rhys didn't do drugs.'

'Let me rephrase that,' Leo says. 'Did you give your husband any substances on the day of the party?

Yasmin's eyes widen. 'What are you suggesting? That I drugged my husband?'

'We showed you a list of medication seized from your bedroom,' Ffion says. 'Your reaction suggested you had something to hide.'

'I don't know what you're talking about.' There it is again: the same panicked look they'd seen at Glynis's house.

Leo leans on the table. 'Did you drug your husband?'

'No!'

'He was killed in his office,' Leo continues. 'Somewhere – by your own admission – you went to several times, during the party.'

'With dozens of guests!' Yasmin gives a humourless laugh. She looks towards the door, as though she's considering walking out – as though she's free to do so. A fine sheen of sweat has broken out across her forehead.

'What do you know about ricin?' Ffion says.

For the first time in the interview, Yasmin seems genuinely confused. 'I don't even know what that is.'

'It's a drug,' Ffion says. 'Prepared from a widely available garden plant and highly toxic. A tiny amount can cause the body to shut down, with death occurring from a few hours to a few days later.' God bless the internet.

'I wouldn't know the first thing about buying drugs, let alone preparing them – I just don't move in those sorts of circles.' Yasmin looks desperately at her solicitor. 'I'm an interior designer; I have respectable friends. I carry a National Trust card.'

'What time did you last see your husband, on the night of the party?' Leo says.

'I'm not certain. I told the twins to give him a sandwich, in an attempt to mop up the booze. I watched him eat it, around nine-thirty or ten, but I'm not sure if I saw him after that.'

'CCTV tells us that Rhys walked from the Charltons' lodge to your own, soon after ten-thirty p.m.' Leo presses play, and four sets of eyes watch Rhys Lloyd stagger down the driveway of The Shore. Ffion lets her own lose focus, until the screen is too pixelated to make out Rhys's figure. 'Did you follow him?'

'Well presumably, *detective*' – Yasmin stresses the title – 'you would see me on camera, if I'd done that. But you won't, because I didn't murder my husband.'

'The cameras are easy to avoid,' Ffion says, 'if you know

they're there.' She doesn't look at Leo. If only she'd thought about CCTV; if only she'd walked along the shore instead of driving, instead of parking in full fucking view of the cameras.

'Tensions between you and your husband pre-date New Year's Eve, don't they?' Leo says.

'I don't know what you mean.' Yasmin blinks rapidly.

'You had an argument on Christmas Eve, didn't you?'

'How do you—'

'What was it about?'

'I don't remember.'

'Oh, I think you do,' Leo says.

'Well, I don't,' Yasmin says firmly, her composure finally under control. 'And I don't see the relevance. Okay, so Rhys and I didn't have a perfect marriage. Who does? As a matter of fact, I was planning to leave him. But that doesn't mean I killed him.'

Yasmin's solicitor interjects. 'According to your disclosure statement, DC Brady, Mr Lloyd's watch shows his heart stopped at 11.38 p.m. My client was at the party until after midnight.'

'She could have slipped out,' Ffion says. 'No one would have noticed.'

'I was singing.' Yasmin widens her eyes suddenly. 'In fact, I can prove it!' She reaches into her pocket, before giving a *tsk* of frustration. 'I need my phone – my main one, I mean. I gave it to someone to record me. I was going to put it on my Instagram Stories this morning, only . . .' She sighs. 'Well, obviously, I didn't. But the video of me singing will be on my phone, along with the time it was recorded.'

'One song isn't an alibi, Mrs Lloyd,' Leo says.

'I did practically all of *Wicked* – Glinda's parts, obviously – and most of *Mamma Mia*. I was asked for several encores – I must have been up there for half an hour.'

'Was Jonty Charlton watching you?' Ffion says.

'I imagine so. The man's besotted.' Yasmin gives a sly smile. 'There's a limit to how much tantric crap a man can take.'

'Is he planning to leave his wife?'

'He would, if I asked him to.'

'Really?' Ffion says, with intentional disbelief.

Yasmin looks affronted. 'Of course he would. Jonty would do anything for me.'

Ffion smiles. 'Is that right?'

Too late, Yasmin realises her mistake. 'Not *anything*, I just mean—'

'The Charltons have a boat, don't they?' Leo says.

'Yes but—'

'Jonty's an experienced sailor. Could easily handle a boat in the dark.'

'I—'

'You're on camera, singing, when your husband died,' Leo says. 'But you could easily have poisoned Rhys earlier that day.'

'This is preposterous!'

'And in fact, no one remembers seeing Jonty between eleven p.m. and the early hours of New Year's Day. I doubt he will be on any footage of your little concert. Where was he?'

'You'll have to ask him.'

'That,' Leo says, 'is an excellent idea.'

Yasmin breathes a sigh of relief. 'Does that mean I can go?'

'You're under arrest for murder,' Ffion says. 'You're not going anywhere.'

TWENTY-TWO

CHRISTMAS DAY | CLEMMIE

Clemmie Northcote can't believe this is now her life. It's nine a.m. on Christmas Day, and instead of staring at the mould in the corner of a kitchen-cum-diner-cum-lounge she is gazing out on a flat, calm lake. Pen y Ddraig mountain is topped with snow, and the forest gleams with frost. Instead of the thud of downstairs's bass, and the rise and fall of upstairs's arguments, she hears . . . nothing.

The lodge is warm and cosy, thanks to the log burner she intends to keep going all Christmas. Unlike the other residents of The Shore, who chipped in for a delivery of kiln-dried logs, sized to fit the grate, Clemmie scoured the forest for free wood, which Caleb chopped and stacked on the deck, beneath a tarpaulin about which the Charltons will undoubtedly complain.

In the fridge is an Aldi turkey, with all the trimmings, and Clemmie has splashed out on a bottle of prosecco for her, and four cans of low-alcohol lager for Caleb. She doesn't want to think about last Christmas, but it is difficult not to make comparisons. With the court case pending, Caleb had gone out on Christmas Eve and not returned until the early hours of the following morning. Clemmie had spent the day on her own, wondering when to put the dinner on. Caleb had emerged from his pit in the evening, his pupils fathomless pools, barely acknowledging the presents Clemmie had saved for months to buy him.

At ten a.m. she decides she can't wait any more. She pushes open Caleb's bedroom door, realising, as she does, that her son even smells different here. She sits on the edge of his bed, watching him sleep. Her beautiful boy. How close she came, to losing him.

The second Clemmie saw the advert for The Shore, she'd felt a physical connection. It called to her. It wasn't just the location, the view, the gorgeous lodges. At The Shore, Caleb would make friends with a different set of people, a different class. Clemmie hates the idea of class, but you can't fight it. Background matters, and Clemmie had known that unless she did something radical, Caleb's was going to drag him further into trouble.

'Mum, stop staring at me,' Caleb mumbles.

Clemmie's brimming over with festive cheer. 'He's been!' she says, with a giggle.

Caleb reluctantly sits up, scrubbing his eyes. 'You're such an idiot,' he says, in that peculiar way boys have of showing affection. He lopes downstairs and Clemmie feels suddenly nervous, worried he'll laugh, or think her stupid, when he sees what she's done.

Clemmie stayed up far too late last night, drinking wine and making paperchains to hang around the room. Caleb's old Christmas stocking – the one he had before he got too old for surprises – is hanging by the log burner, packed with small, silly gifts Clemmie has collected all year. Every one is wrapped. She's 'borrowed' a small tree from the forest, keeping it in a pot and vowing to replant it after Twelfth Night. It's covered with all the decorations she and Caleb made together, before adolescence hit and he morphed into someone she hardly recognised.

'It's silly, I know,' Clemmie says now. 'You're too old—'

She can't finish, because Caleb throws his arms around her, squashing her face with his shoulder. 'It's amazing, Mum. Happy Christmas.'

They have bacon and eggs for breakfast. Clemmie hears voices on one of the decks; the growl of an engine as someone takes a boat up the lake. Late last night, Blythe put a message on The Shore's WhatsApp group to say there'd be a group swim at noon. Clemmie wonders if the enthusiasm on the group will be as apparent this morning – as far as she knows, she's the only resident of The Shore who swims on anything except the sunniest of days – but just before eleven there's laughter outside.

Clemmie steps on to her deck in her wetsuit. 'Merry Christmas!'

There is a chorus in return, 'Merry Christmas!' and as Clemmie crosses to join the gang, she feels that glorious sense of belonging.

The Staffords must have arrived late last night or early this morning. Ashleigh's in a floor-length fur coat, and, unless she's hiding a bikini underneath, she's not planning on joining in. Bobby, on the other hand, is prancing about the deck in a pair of boxers covered with sprigs of holly and drinking a Bloody Mary, celery poking him in the eye every time he takes a sip.

'Stand there a sec,' Ashleigh says.

Bobby puts down his glass. 'Not today, yeah?'

'With the drink.' She lifts her phone, flapping her free hand to get him to move across the deck. 'There. Lean against the railing and—'

'Can we have one day without thinking about bloody Instagram?' Bobby snaps, and there's an awkward silence as Ashleigh stalks back towards their lodge.

'I thought you were going to film the swim.'

'What's the point, if we're not going to put it online?' Ashleigh yells over her shoulder.

The Lloyds are all in dressing gowns. Clemmie catches Caleb checking out the twins, and suppresses a smile. Boys, eh? She can't imagine Caleb is quite what Rhys had in mind for his little princesses, but you never know. Clemmie allows herself a moment to imagine the invitations for the Northcote–Lloyd wedding – or would it be Lloyd–Northcote?

Yasmin is deep in conversation with her husband, and she doesn't look happy. 'No, I can't move on!' Neither of them has realised Clemmie's right behind them.

'This is such an overreaction, Yasmin.'

'You could have killed her!' she hisses, then her eyes widen in horror as she notices Clemmie. She breaks into a wide smile. 'Happy Christmas, Clemmie darling – isn't this wonderful?'

'Wonderful.' Clemmie's heart is racing. She pulls herself together. Caleb's brush with the criminal underworld tends to make her leap to worst-case scenarios.

Jonty Charlton has shrugged off his robe and is talking loudly about how it isn't cold at all really. Rhys's mother, Glynis, has been saddled with young Woody and Hester Charlton, who would launch themselves fearlessly into the water, given half a chance. Clemmie seizes the opportunity to use the festive vocabulary she has specifically learned for today. '*Nadolig Llawen*, Mrs Lloyd!'

The older woman is gazing out to the lake, her eyes shining. 'I spent my first Christmas as a married woman in this very spot, you know.'

'At The Shore?'

Glynis tuts. 'At Tŷ'r Lan. My husband's cabin was right here.' She looks down, as though it might have slipped between the deck's wooden planks.

'Imagine,' Clemmie says, who has run out of Welsh now they've moved beyond small talk. 'If he could see it now, eh?'

'Indeed,' Glynis says tightly.

'Is everyone ready?' Dee Huxley – who, very wisely, is staying on dry land – waves her camera and shoos all the swimmers into a group for a photograph. One by one, they climb down the ladder to the pontoon, the supporters leaning on the balustrade above, ready for the off.

Rhys is down first, then Bobby. Clemmie waits on the top rung for a moment, as Dee takes a photograph.

'Sorry, dear, you blinked. Let's try again.'

Below her, Clemmie is certain she hears angry words, but everyone is urging Dee to hurry up, it's freezing! And, by the time Clemmie is down the ladder, neither Bobby nor Rhys is saying anything. She pushes it from her mind. It's Christmas Day, and she refuses to be anxious. Not this year.

Caleb takes a running jump, bombing into the icy water, and Clemmie's heart freezes until he bursts through the surface again, his mouth an 'O' of shock. He's showing off to the girls, who dip their toes off the edge of the pontoon and squeal. Clemmie slides in, used to the temperature, and swims in circles, all the time wiggling her fingers and toes.

'You're all mad!' shouts Blythe, from above.

'Marvellous!' Dee says. She takes a photograph. Everyone's in the water now, and Clemmie's eyes are shining. What an incredible place. What an amazing Christmas.

Afterwards, when the turkey's in the oven, and Caleb is setting up the new-to-him phone Clemmie bought him for Christmas, Clemmie goes outside to bring in more wood. She's replacing the tarpaulin when Rhys walks across his own deck, jumps on to the Staffords' deck, then crosses to hers. She wonders if he wants to talk to her about what she overheard this morning, if she's about to be brought into the Lloyd circle of trust, and feels a frisson of fear and excitement.

'I need you to pay the full balance on the lodge.'

Clemmie blinks. 'I can't.'

'Things are a bit tight, financially. Sorry about that.'

He doesn't sound remotely sorry.

When Clemmie had enquired about The Shore, she had been firmly informed that there were no payment plans available. Lodges were to be bought in full, upfront. Ever-optimistic, Clemmie had tried another route, contacting Rhys directly and appealing to his good nature. The answer had still been no, but several weeks later Rhys had called her.

'It can't be an official arrangement,' he'd said. 'But if you're happy to keep it to yourself, I'll help you out.'

If Clemmie could stump up a decent deposit, Rhys would allow her to pay off the rest in monthly instalments. It wasn't easy to pull off. Clemmie's south London flat took months to sell, but the equity was just enough for the deposit. The contract for The Shore was unequivocal on the subject of primary residences – *owners will not live at The Shore all year round, and must maintain a principal domicile* – but there appeared to be no process to verify this. As far as Clemmie could tell, none of the other owners intended to stay at The Shore more frequently than a few weeks in every year; how could they possibly know if Clemmie and Caleb never left?

The autumn had been a challenge. The Shore had closed for more building work, after the summer, and Clemmie and Caleb had spent weeks moving from friend to friend, under the guise of catching up. She'd been relieved when the residents' WhatsApp group had announced the work was complete. There would be no more closures. Clemmie and Caleb had moved back and everything had been perfect.

Until now.

'I can't give you the money,' Clemmie says. 'I don't have it.'

There is a long silence. Rhys sighs. 'Then we have a problem, don't we?'

From number five, Yasmin calls for Rhys to carve. Wordlessly he goes back the way he came, leaving Clemmie standing in the cold, the sparkle suddenly gone from her Christmas.

What is she going to do? She doesn't have four hundred grand, and her credit rating won't permit her to borrow it. She's sold her flat. They have nowhere else to live and, besides, Clemmie doesn't *want* to leave. After two years of living every day terrified of what each knock on the door might bring, Caleb has finally come back to her – she will not go back to that.

She will keep her new life.

Whatever it takes.

TWENTY-THREE

JANUARY 6TH | LEO

The following morning, Leo goes straight to Crouch's office. 'Sir, we're going to need an extension on Yasmin Lloyd.'

'You had her in custody all day yesterday – what were you doing? I've been fending off complaints from the community ever since I got in.'

'Because we arrested the wife?'

'Because you haven't charged her.' Crouch scratches his nose. 'Rhys Lloyd is a homegrown hero. When he married an English woman, it seems some of the locals were disappointed. Now they feel they've been proved right – she was always a wrong 'un.'

'Unfortunately Yasmin's alibi checks out,' Leo says. 'We've looked at the videos on her phone, and at the time of Rhys Lloyd's death she was giving an impromptu concert at the party. But if we can nail Jonty Charlton's involvement we could make a case for conspiracy. I'd like to arrest him too.'

'And stir up another hornet's nest? I don't want another English suspect in the traps till you're one hundred per cent certain of a charge.'

'But—'

'Got it?'

'Yes, sir.'

The drive to The Shore feels three times as long, with Ffion at the end of it. A dozen times last night, Leo had composed a text message, only to delete it, not knowing what to say. He's so angry with her, but it's more than that – more complicated. He feels betrayed. They'd had something, hadn't they? A connection.

He'd clearly misread the situation.

For once, Ffion's there before him. She's leaning against the Triumph, a roll-up between her fingers. She gives a curt nod as he arrives.

'Excuse my slippers.' Dee Huxley is pushing neatly folded wrapping paper into a plastic box outside number two. 'I've just remembered the recycling van comes today. How's that murder investigation coming along?'

'We're following several lines of enquiry,' Leo says carefully.

'Terrible business.' Dee goes back inside.

Ffion snorts. 'You really are Mr Corporate Speak, aren't you?'

'Some of us do things by the book.'

'The whole place knows we've nicked Yasmin Lloyd – it's hardly a secret.'

Leo stops walking. *The recycling van comes today.* 'Do you remember there was a ricin assassination attempt at the White House?'

'Vaguely.'

'They sent it in the mail. We know Lloyd was in his office on New Year's Eve, before the party: what if he opened an envelope containing a noxious powder? Yasmin could easily have slipped it into the pile of fan mail.'

Ffion stares at him, and Leo feels stupid. 'I know it's a long shot.'

'No, I . . .' Ffion gives a grudging nod. 'You might be on to something.' She starts walking towards the Lloyds' lodge. 'Although good luck convincing Crouch to spaff his forensics budget on a hunch.' She laughs, and for a second Leo hears Allie in her dismissive tone.

He makes a snap decision. 'I'm not going to tell him. I'll put it through under an existing budget code.'

'Ooh, you rebel.'

Leo can hear the grin in her voice, and he's annoyed to find a smile tugging at his own face. 'Fuck off, Morgan.'

'No chance,' she says. 'You're stuck with me.'

There isn't a lot of post in the Lloyds' recycling box. A few hand-delivered envelopes – Christmas cards, from other residents of The Shore perhaps – but Leo assumes that most of the family's mail goes to their London address. There are two large padded envelopes in the box, and Leo recognises one of them from the fan mail Felicia was responding to when they arrested Yasmin. Each Jiffy bag is labelled with the address for The Shore, and bears a return address for Lloyd's talent agency: Tuttle, Whyte & Associates. There's a stack of torn-open envelopes stuffed into each one. They place all the post in a sealed plastic bag, and Ffion persuades a community support officer to take it straight to the lab.

'They'll test it as soon as they can,' Leo says, coming off the phone.

Ffion looks grudgingly impressed. 'Fair play. I didn't think you'd get that one through.'

Nor did Leo.

'I'd better speak to DI Crouch,' the CSI had said, when Leo gave her the heads-up on the submission. 'It's outside the remit of—'

'He's in meetings today,' Leo said, mentally crossing his fingers. 'Be a bit of a coup if we find ricin, though, right? Front page of the nationals, I reckon.'

There was a long pause before the CSI spoke. 'Okay. Leave it with me.'

'If we don't get a result on it today,' Leo says now, 'we'll have to get authorisation to keep Yasmin another twelve hours. We can't take the risk of witness interference if we bail her.'

'Great,' Ffion says. 'Double time for rest-day working.'

'I'd rather have the weekend off. I've had to cancel seeing my lad.' Leo tries to keep the bitterness out of his voice, but he can feel Ffion's eyes on him. 'My ex is moving to Australia with her new partner,' he says shortly. 'They're taking Harris.'

'They can't.'

'I'd have to take them to court to stop them.'

'So take them to court.'

'I can't.' Leo knows Allie would be on the phone to Social Services in a heartbeat, readying the recording of Harris's cries to be played in court.

'Of course you—'

'It's not that simple.'

'You're the kid's dad – you've got rights.'

'Just forget it. I don't know why I even told you.' Because he hasn't told anyone else, Leo realises. Because he needs to talk.

Jonty Charlton does not want to talk. He takes one look at them and begins to push the door shut. 'If you haven't got a warrant—'

'Yasmin says you'll leave your wife for her,' Ffion says. 'That's sweet.'

Jonty freezes, his mouth slightly open.

'Who is it, darling?' Blythe drifts into the hall. 'Oh, hello, officers!' A band of taut stomach is just visible beneath a cropped T-shirt and baggy cardigan. The crotch of her voluminous purple trousers hangs somewhere around her knees. 'How can we help you?'

Ffion smiles. 'I was just saying to your husband—'

'No!' Jonty's cry is less word and more yelp. 'They hadn't yet – I mean . . .' He clears his throat. 'If there's anything I can help with, I'd be delighted to accompany you to the station.'

'That's very obliging of you,' Leo says. 'But we just wanted to clarify where exactly you were at eleven-thirty p.m. on New Year's Eve. Your statement is a little vague.'

'Where I was?' Jonty swallows and glances at Blythe.

'Yes.' Ffion runs an idle finger along the door frame. 'You see, you aren't in any photos taken then, and you weren't with Yasmin Lloyd, although I understand you do spend a lot of time with—'

'I was doing coke with Ashleigh Stafford.' Jonty's words come out in a rush, too loud and too fast. 'There were too many people coming and going in the lodge, and Ashleigh didn't want to share, so we went to her place. Did a few lines, watched some crap on TV, talked shit.'

Blythe's mouth falls open. 'Cocaine? Oh, Jonty! How could you?'

'We'll need to check that out with Mrs Stafford, of course,' Leo says.

'Of course, of course, but that's where I was.' Jonty looks at Blythe, who is close to tears. 'Lighten up, Blythe, it's hardly heroin.'

'One other thing,' Ffion says. 'Did you take a boat out on New Year's Eve?'

'No.' Here, Jonty seems on firmer ground. 'I told you, *Blythe*

189

Spirit's not in the water over winter. The only boats here were motorboats belonging to some of the guests who came over from the village. I couldn't have taken one out even if I'd wanted to. I happened to take a look at them during the party – I rather fancy getting one – and they all had ignitions with no keys.'

'Thinking about trading Blythe in for something a bit racier?' Ffion says.

'It's *Blythe Spirit*,' Blythe corrects.

'Of course it is. Sorry.'

'There *was* a boat on the lake, though,' Jonty says. 'I remember seeing it. It's quite distinctive: green hull, red sails.' He puts a hand on the door again. 'Will that be all?'

'That's fine,' Leo says. 'We'll chat about your relationship with Yasmin another time,' he adds, just as the door closes.

'What relationship?' they hear, as they walk down the path; Blythe's voice uncharacteristically strident. Leo feels a splinter of guilt, but reasons Blythe's better off knowing the truth.

Ffion says nothing for a while. Then: 'Well, *that* wasn't corporate speak.'

'Maybe I'm not as predictable you as think. Shall we check out Charlton's alibi?'

'Yeah, he burned through my whole stash, as it happens.' Ashleigh Stafford seems to be oblivious to the consequences of admitting to criminal activity. 'One of those guys who only does it "socially", you know?' She wiggles her fingers in the air around the word. 'Which is just another way of saying "I'm gonna sponge off of everyone else when I fancy a hit".'

'How many times did you go off together, during the party?' Leo says.

'God knows. Like, six? Eight? I mean, the last time, we didn't even bother going back between bumps, just hung out here for an hour or so.'

'What time was that?' Ffion says.

'Half-eleven? He was definitely here at midnight, 'cause we had a bit of a snog.' She grins. 'Don't mean nothing, does it? Not on New Year's Eve.'

'Bobby gave us the footage from your door camera,' Leo says. 'So?'

'So you're not on it.'

'We wouldn't be. We went across the decks and came in through the sliding doors.'

'Did anyone see you?' Ffion says. 'Anyone who could confirm your story?'

Ashleigh chews her lip, then brightens. 'Alexa! We were pissing about with her, asking stupid questions.' She gets out her phone and opens an app, tapping deftly across the screen before pressing play. 'See? Eleven fifty-two.'

The recording plays. *Alexa, why is water wet?*

Ashleigh laughs. 'I was so fucked.' She presses the next recording, and Jonty Charlton's voice rings out. *Alexa, what's Welsh for shove a leek up your—* Ashleigh stops the recording. 'He was even more fucked.' She frowns at the memory. 'Two grams of coke gone, just like that. I'll have to get Caleb on the—' She wrinkles her nose. 'Forget I said that.'

Caleb Northcote is Ashleigh's dealer? Leo looks towards Clemmie's lodge and pictures Caleb, chucking stones by the lakeside this morning. Leo had felt sorry for him; he truly believed the lad wanted to go straight.

Is *anyone* at The Shore who they appear to be?

TWENTY-FOUR

CHRISTMAS EVE | BLYTHE

As it's Christmas Eve, Blythe has let Woody and Hester stay up late to eat with the grown-ups. They've been delightful, but it's long past bedtime and Blythe senses Yasmin and Rhys are not entirely charmed by the youngest members of the Charlton family. Apparently it's perfectly acceptable for Felicia and Tabby to be glued to their phones during what was (even if Blythe says so herself) a truly superb meal, but Hester's rendition of 'Jingle Bells' is intolerable.

'If you don't go to sleep,' Yasmin says, 'Father Christmas won't come.'

'Aka *fuck off*,' Rhys says, under his breath, to Jonty, who roars with laughter.

'I'll say!'

Blythe glares at her husband. She used to think Jonty was an excellent father: he plays with the children, takes them to the pantomime and to the zoo, and has even been known to do the nursery run, where he is fawned over by the coven of mothers. At home, they have a live-in nanny, who also accompanies them to their house in the Cotswolds and on holiday to Tuscany.

It has become very apparent to Blythe that Jonty is only an excellent father on his terms. Here at The Shore, where the

192

configuration of rooms doesn't allow for a nanny (there's no second sitting room – where would she go in the evenings?), Jonty has been distinctly reluctant.

'The Shore needs a crèche,' he said, in the summer. They'd been there for three days. 'I'll tell Rhys to factor it into the budget.'

There is, in fact, only one element of parenting in which Jonty excels himself. Blythe supposes she should be grateful for small mercies.

'Jonty, darling,' she says now, 'could you put the children down? You're so much better at it than I am.'

'But we're not tired!' Woody sprints circles around the dining table, and Hester hares after him, tripping on the rug and face-planting the floor. She lets out an air-raid-siren scream.

Jonty gets up. 'Come on, you horrors.'

Bedtime has become Jonty's domain. Woody and Hester, who have always been a nightmare to settle, now go meekly up to bed with a cup of warm milk and a story, and are asleep in ten minutes. Blythe has tried to emulate the same routine, but she lacks Jonty's magic touch.

'Will the children be staying up on New Year's Eve?' Yasmin's seemingly casual tone has a tightness beneath it.

'Don't worry,' Blythe says. 'We're planning a grown-up affair, aren't we, Jonty?'

'Too right. Smalls in bed by seven, and I gather Clemmie's offered her pad for the not-so-smalls.'

'Why can't we be at the party?' Tabby complains.

'I wouldn't have thought you'd want to hang out with us old people.' Jonty grins, and Tabby doesn't contradict him.

'And you're sure you're okay to host it?' Yasmin says.

Blythe smiles sweetly. 'Honestly, we don't mind.' Ever since the party was mooted, Yasmin has angled to host, desperate to showcase her interior design skills, even though the villagers probably think Anthropologie is a BTEC option at the local college.

'It's just, with the children being so young . . .' Yasmin takes a sip of wine.

'They'll be tucked up in bed. You'd never even know we had any.' In their playroom at home, Blythe maintains a strict colour palette of black, white and natural wood, which is much more challenging than Jonty gives her credit for. She allowed Woody and Hester to each choose three toys to keep at The Shore, which she tucks away in the ottoman when they're not needed.

'If Jonty and Blythe are happy to host,' Rhys says, 'I think we should let them.'

'Thank you, Rhys,' Blythe simpers, as is expected, although she knows precisely why Rhys is so keen not to have the party centred around number five: it would mean putting his hand in his pocket. As it is, Jonty – always quick to show off his largesse – has declared the Charlton bar will be bottomless.

'In fact, we should invite some of the locals.' Rhys's lips are stained with port.

'Are there any?' Yasmin laughs.

Blythe is no longer simpering. What a cheek! It's clear Rhys just wants to show off to the village, and on someone else's dime. 'I'm not sure Jonty will want—'

'What won't I want?' Jonty comes back downstairs.

'All and sundry coming across from Cwm Coed,' Yasmin says tartly. 'They're not our sort of people, Rhys – you know that.'

'It's very important to have diverse representation within one's friendship circle.' Blythe read this in the *Guardian*. She isn't entirely sure she wants diverse friends – she's perfectly happy with the ones she has – but it's good to show willing. Do the Welsh count as a minority ethnic group?

194

'It's a ball-ache alright,' Jonty says, 'entertaining the hoi polloi, but we do need to get them on-side. The view's great, but people want more than that from a second home. They want to wander around the shops and chat to the locals. They want *community*.'

'That's settled, then,' Rhys says. 'I'll draw up a list of the right kind of people.'

Yasmin leans towards Blythe. 'Is there anything we can do to help with the party prep? Décor, perhaps?'

Blythe bristles. 'All taken care of, darling. The marquee will go up on the thirtieth, and the deckchairs are coming the same day. I'm still pricing up sand—'

'No bloody sand!' Jonty says.

'And I did wonder about some sort of water feature, to go with the beach theme.'

Jonty puts down his glass with a bang. 'There's a bloody lake out there!' He looks at Rhys. 'Women, eh? All this, *and* we have to make small talk with farmers.'

'Call-me-Clemmie will entertain them.' Rhys chortles, and everyone laughs.

Blythe claps her hands, like a child. 'That reminds me! The locals do a swim on New Year's Day, and I had thought it would be fun to join in, only I asked the girl in the newsagent's about it and . . .' Blythe briefly shuts her eyes, then breathes out. 'Well, let's just say it's a closed shop. *Anyway . . .*' she looks around the table '. . . I thought we'd start our own tradition. The Shore Christmas Day Dip! What do you think, girls? Caleb's doing it. I'll cheer you on from the deck – I mustn't let my meridian lines get cold.'

Felicia doesn't look up from her phone. 'Yeah, whatevs.'

'Tabby?'

'S'pose.'

'Rhys?'

'Can't wait,' he says, with a distinct lack of enthusiasm.

Blythe is delighted. She sends a message to The Shore's WhatsApp group, and fields the thumbs-ups as they come in. Dee Huxley sends a fully punctuated response, complete with a *kind regards* sign-off. Bless her. Blythe hadn't relished the arrival of a septuagenarian as a neighbour, but Dee's young at heart, and very stylish for her age. She also makes a number of barbed comments about Rhys, which Blythe secretly finds delicious.

'Are the Staffords here for Christmas?' Yasmin asks.

'I get the impression that's a bone of contention,' Jonty says. 'Ashleigh fancied Dubai; Bobby wanted to be at The Shore.'

'They've just landed at Gatwick,' Blythe says, holding her phone aloft. She studies Jonty's reaction, but there's not even a flicker. He's not fucking Ashleigh, then. Or he's a better liar than she thinks. She has been through his pockets with forensic detail, and found nothing incriminating, but twice she's caught the drift of a woman's scent on his clothes. In the summer he took the little boat up the lake most days, sometimes disappearing for hours. It isn't *that* big a lake, for heaven's sake.

That night, when Jonty is in the bathroom, Blythe goes through his things again. She feels his jackets, hung in the dressing room, and shakes the trousers he left draped over a chair. She slides a hand under his side of the mattress, and opens the drawers in his bedside cabinet. Just as she is about to give up, she finds something. Not a second phone, or incriminating letters. Nothing to do with an affair at all, in fact.

She finds an envelope, folded into four, containing a crushed, grainy powder.

TWENTY-FIVE

JANUARY 6TH | FFION

After they've left Ashleigh, Ffion rolls a cigarette she doesn't want. 'I know who the boat with the red sails belongs to.'

Leo looks at her. 'Who?'

'Angharad Evans. She lives at the end of the lake. Bit of an oddball.'

'The sort of oddball who offers the use of her boat to dispose of a body?'

Ffion shakes her head. 'It doesn't fit. We think Yasmin poisoned Rhys, and persuaded Jonty Charlton to knock him out then clean up the crime scene, right? But Jonty's the one who told us about seeing a boat with red sails. He'd hardly have done that if he'd used the boat himself.' She lights her cigarette. 'Besides, Angharad hates The Shore. I mean, really hates it.'

Leo shrugs. 'So maybe she's our Plan B. Could she have killed Rhys?'

'Angharad's not a murderer. Although, we did use to call her the witch, when I was growing up, and if you saw her you had to stand on one leg, then touch your left elbow, to break the curse.' Ffion laughs, but Leo isn't smiling.

'We should speak to her.'

'Because I thought she was a witch when I was seven?'

'Because the team's spoken to everyone with a boat permit, and I don't recall Angharad Evans's name coming up.'

'She doesn't need one – her cottage has mooring rights.' Ffion can see Leo's mind working. 'Okay! I'll take you to her. How do you fancy a boat trip?'

'Not remotely.' Leo takes in Ffion's expression. 'My God, you're serious.'

'Her place is awkward to get to by road.'

'Awkward, or impossible?'

'Well, just awk—'

'Then we're driving.'

On the way, Ffion looks out of the window, where glimpses of lake flash between the trees. 'You're not keen on boats, then?'

'I've got nothing against boats; it's water I don't like. Unless it's in a glass, or I'm watching it with my feet on dry land.'

Ffion laughs. 'Noted.'

The road runs alongside Llyn Drych. It's straighter than the serpentine lake, and flashes of silver dip in and out of sight as Leo drives. Ffion sees him glancing at her when he thinks she isn't looking, trying to work her out. If he'd reported her for destroying CCTV evidence, she'd have heard from Professional Standards by now. Does that mean she's in the clear?

She points to a single-track road taking them through the trees. 'Turn off here.' They're at the end of the lake, now, a mile from the village; the forest dense and dark. Half a mile up the track, their path is blocked by a fallen tree. It lies at an angle, caught by the trees on the opposite side, with half its roots still in the ground.

Leo stops the car, and Ffion gets out. 'Come on, it's on foot from here.'

'How long has it been like this?' Leo asks. The forest has grown around the fallen trunk, new branches formed vertically, undaunted by the damage caused beneath them.

'As long as I can remember. It's on Angharad's land, so it's down to her to remove it, but Mam says she likes it this way.'

It's another ten minutes before they reach the clearing in which Angharad's place stands, a thin trail of smoke coming from the chimney. Leo stops walking, taking in the encampment.

'It's quite something, huh?' Ffion says. She shivers and hugs herself, her right hand clutching her opposite elbow. Leo glances down to see Ffion's foot hovering above the other. She catches him looking. 'Old habits.'

'Does she live alone?'

'She does now. Mam says she had her heart broken years ago. She discovered her husband was a bigamist.' Ffion grins. 'It was the talk of the town, as you can imagine.'

Around the small stone cottage are several aviaries, housing birds of different sizes. A run of hutches contains rabbits; another enclosure has small wooden hedgehog shelters. And in one of the large cages beneath the trees is something which looks worryingly like a wolf.

'Silver fox,' Angharad says, when they're sitting in her small kitchen. 'Kept as a pet, then dumped when the owners got bored.'

'I was trying to get my bearings as we were driving here,' Leo says. 'We're at the tip of the lake, right? Does that put this house in Wales, or England?'

'Mostly Wales, although a small part is technically in England.'

'How interesting – which bit?'

'*Tŷ bach*,' Angharad says.

'The loo,' Ffion translates, with a grin.

It's clear Leo isn't sure if they're joking. He looks around Angharad's kitchen, a small room, with dark beams and exposed stone walls. Narrow shelves house dozens of brown apothecary jars, each with a handwritten label. *Rhus tox., Calendula, Podophyllum—*

Leo reads out loud. 'Belladonna?'

'Good for a fever.'

Ffion must have made a sound, because Angharad looks at her wearily.

'Ffion thinks herbal medicine is – what was it you told your mother? – "a load of old bollocks".'

'No offence, Angharad, but if I've got a headache I'd rather pop an ibuprofen than chew on a few petals.'

'I used arnica after I twisted my knee,' Leo says. Angharad looks smug.

Ffion has a thought. 'Do you know anything about ricin?'

'*Ricinus communis*,' Angharad says. 'It's where castor oil comes from. The plant's very popular. There was a spate of cuttings going around after Efan Hughes won first prize at the horticultural show. Pretty shrub. Deadly in the wrong hands, of course.'

Leo's looking at the rows of jars, reading the labels, and Ffion knows what he's thinking. But she's already looked, and there's no neatly labelled *Ricin* on Angharad's shelves.

'I understand you own a boat with red sails,' Leo says. 'Most of the owners we've spoken to take their boats out of the water over winter. You don't do the same?'

'How would I get to the village without the boat?' Angharad speaks as though the answer should have been obvious. 'I don't have a car. My boat's with Steffan at the moment, for repairs, and I've had to stock up in case he has to keep her for a few days.'

'It's damaged?' Leo says.

'My fault. I usually move her to a mooring on the lake when there's bad weather, but a couple of days ago I left her tied to my pontoon and the hull was damaged.'

'Where was she on New Year's Eve?' Ffion says.

'On the lake mooring. I have a small rowing boat I take out to her and tie up in her place.'

Leo looks out of the window, to where the lake can just be seen through the trees. 'Does the boat need keys? I mean – could anyone take it out?'

'If they know how to sail. I lock the cuddy – that's the little cabin – but she's a sailing boat, not a gin palace. There's a small outboard motor I rarely use.'

'Does anyone else sail her?' Ffion asks.

'No one.' Angharad looks as though she's debating whether to share something. Ffion waits. 'Before Christmas, I gave a couple of sailing lessons to a young boy from The Shore. Caleb.' She makes a small *tsk* sound. 'I must be going soft in my old age. I'd sworn not to set foot in the place.'

'So how . . .' Ffion prompts, when it becomes clear Angharad has finished.

'I was out fishing – this would have been some time in October – and saw a swimmer was in trouble. I fished her out and took her back to The Shore.'

'Clemence Northcote,' Leo says.

Angharad nodded. 'She was keen for him to try sailing. I got the impression she was one of those pushy mothers. They came out with me a couple of times, but it was obvious the boy wasn't interested.' Angharad gives a knowing look. 'I've seen him a few times up in the fields by Lowri's farm, picking mushrooms, so I'd say he looks elsewhere for his entertainment.'

Ffion knows exactly what kind of mushrooms grow up by Lowri's farm.

'Has anyone else from The Shore been on your boat?' Leo asks.

'Absolutely not. Have you met them? I've rarely encountered such unpleasant people. The whole place is rotten to its core.'

'I understand some of the locals were opposed to the resort,' Leo says.

'All of them, wouldn't you say, Ffion?'

'People don't like change,' she says diplomatically, although she knows Angharad is right. No one in Cwm Coed wanted The Shore built.

'Careful you don't get splinters sitting on that fence, Ffion Morgan.' Angharad looks at her sharply. 'You know full well what people think about The Shore. *And* about Rhys Lloyd.'

Ffion keeps her mouth shut.

'You didn't like Lloyd?' Leo says.

'I neither liked nor disliked him—'

'Careful of those splinters,' Ffion says quietly.

'—but I know he deliberately went against his father's wishes. I'd never wish ill on another human being, but I will say this.' Angharad leans forward, and Ffion feels a sudden chill. 'Fate has a way of catching up with people.'

TWENTY-SIX

OCTOBER | RHYS

Back in the summer, when Rhys first took his family to The Shore, Tabby and Felicia had spent the long drive finalising plans for their rooms, discussing tanning methods and whispering about the boys they might meet. Yasmin had talked non-stop about what the other owners would be like. The four-hour journey from London to North Wales had been full of excitement, full of the unknown, the sun beating down on the car until it felt as though the heat were running through their veins.

Now, the twins sit sullenly in the back, as Rhys drives the family to The Shore for the October half-term holiday. As they cross the Welsh border, drizzle mists the windscreen, and by the time they reach Cwm Coed the rain is torrential.

At The Shore, the exterior lights haven't come on, and the place looks cold and uninviting. The giant wooden letters at the entrance to the resort have been vandalised again: a red letter 'W' spray-painted on to the 'S', so it reads *The Whore*. Further up the drive the drains are overflowing, and a river rushes down the newly laid tarmac to meet them.

'"Come to Wales", he said!' Sarcasm drips from Tabby's words. '"It'll be fun", he said!' The twins shelter under the overhang as

Yasmin opens up, and Rhys ferries their cases to the lodge, getting steadily wetter with each trip.

Inside, the lodge is cold and unloved. The builder has traipsed mud up the stairs and through the bedrooms, but the windows now seem to be watertight, which is just as well, because the forecast for the week is bleak.

Rhys feels a hard knot of tension in his chest. Jonty has bunged him another few grand, and this time he really has spent it on The Shore. The entrance is now a sleek black driveway, and Rhys is annoyed that Bobby Stafford – who made such a song and dance over the potholes – isn't here to see it.

The Shore's WhatsApp group had fallen silent after the summer, limited to the monthly automated maintenance fee reminder, and the occasional message from Clemmie, with a link to some local news article. In the days leading up to half-term, though, there was a flurry of messages.

Clemmie Northcote: Anyone need me to put milk in the fridge? Caleb and I will be the first ones there, I think! x

Dee Huxley: Dear neighbours, I am very much looking forward to spending a few days at The Shore. Best wishes, Dee Huxley.

Ashleigh Stafford: Me and Bobby are in Barbados for a month – on location for his show! Check out the hashtag and give us some likes ;-) xxx

Jonty Charlton: The engineer will need access to the generator on Tuesday.

The fortnight stretches bleakly in front of Rhys. The Charltons are in Tuscany for half-term, and Rhys would rather chew off his own arm than spend time with Call-me-Clemmie. He bitterly regrets that little arrangement. Jonty had been putting pressure on Rhys to get the first few lodges sold, telling him the financial backers needed to see the project up and running. Clemence Northcote was neither the creative, media-friendly owner Rhys had in mind for The Shore, nor Jonty's preferred cash-rich buyer, but beggars couldn't be choosers.

'Let her have it,' Jonty had said. 'We need to get this first tranche sold – create a buzz about the place.'

But Clemmie couldn't afford it.

'If she wants it badly enough, she'll find the money,' Jonty said, with the confidence of someone who always has something put aside for a rainy day or a likely investment. 'Seal the deal, old man – or maybe you're just not cut out for business?'

Terrified that Jonty would find a way to cut him out of the partnership, Rhys had come up with a plan. He had already ascertained that Clemmie's credit score meant a personal loan wasn't an option, but what if *Rhys* took out a loan? He would pass the money to Clemmie, who would buy the lodge and make monthly payments to Rhys. With a little extra for his trouble, of course.

'You'd really do that for me?' Clemmie had said. They'd met up, to avoid a paper trail. She started crying. 'I can't tell you how much this means to me.'

So Clemmie had her lodge, Rhys had his sale, and Jonty was none the wiser.

But now Rhys has money troubles of his own.

He brings in the last of the luggage and leaves it dripping on the hall floor. Yasmin and the twins slouch glumly on the sofa, faces like the thunder threatened by this week's forecast. The heating is on full blast, but Yasmin shivers in her cashmere cloak.

'I'm going to bed,' she declares.

'Me too,' Tabby says.

'And me.' Felicia gets up. It is nine p.m.

Rhys pours himself a brandy and stands by the sliding doors, looking out on to the blackness of the lake. Maybe they should have waited till the morning to drive up. The girls are tired, the traffic was bad. He opens the bifold doors, stiff from disuse, and steps on to the deck, sheltered by the balcony above. Yasmin is on the phone, her voice low and her tone plaintive. In the dark, the deck disappears into the unseen water, a black wasteland with no beginning and no end. Only the sound of the waves breaking on the rocks tells Rhys the lake is there at all. He drains his drink. Everything will look better in the morning.

If Yasmin and the twins were in a bad mood yesterday, it is nothing to how they are now. Tabby and Felicia stomp around the lodge, opening and closing the fridge, and declaring that they will die if they have to stay here another minute.

Their ill humour rubs off on Rhys.

'Whichever one of you nicked my hairbrush,' he shouts, 'please put it back. And on that note: Yasmin, is it really necessary to leave so much hair in the shower? It's still here from the summer.'

'So get the cleaner in,' Yasmin snaps back. 'She's at the Staffords' now – her car's outside.'

'Bobby and Ashleigh have an outdoor shower at their villa in Barbados,' Tabby says. 'I saw it on Insta yesterday.'

'Maybe we could cut the holiday short?' Yasmin says. 'A long weekend, instead of—'

'It's not a *holiday*,' Rhys roars. 'This is our second home! The plan has always been to spend term-times in London and the rest of the time here.' Hasn't Yasmin been nagging him for years about having another place? Banging on about the Charltons' Cotswolds home till he could have drawn a bloody floorplan in his sleep?

'But look at it, Rhys.' She turns towards the lake. Rain lashes against the windows, flooding the decking faster than it can drain. The sky is dark and moody, the surface of the lake dangerously high. 'It's going to be like this all week.'

'There's no such thing as bad weather.' Rhys isn't sure who he's trying to convince. 'Only the wrong clothing. We'll wrap up and go for a nice bracing—'

'I am *not* going outside in *this*, Dad. And can you *please* do something about the wifi? It's so slow. Ugh. I hate this place.'

Tabby stomps upstairs, Felicia in her wake. Yasmin takes her coffee to the sofa and slumps in front of an Australian reality TV show. Rhys looks around the lodge. If he were in London he might go out for a coffee, but he has no desire to sip Nescafé from chipped crockery at Cwm Coed's only café.

All the lodge-owners were issued with bespoke wellies when they moved in (a nice PR touch, Rhys thought, until he saw the bill) and he pulls on a pair now and fetches his waterproof coat from the hall cupboard. He may as well go for a walk.

When he steps outside, rain instantly finding its way down his neck, he notices a white car with pink lettering parked outside the Staffords' empty lodge. *Sbic & Sban*. Rhys hesitates for a moment, then he steps back into the hall, opens the shallow cupboard by the door and unhooks the bunch of master keys.

Inside the Staffords' lodge, there's music playing from the kitchen. Mia sings above the hum of the vacuum cleaner and Rhys crosses the small hall to stand in the doorway to the main living space.

Mia wiggles her bottom as she sings, thrusting the vacuum cleaner under the dining table. Rhys grins. He wonders if she saw him come in; if this performance is for his benefit. His suspicions are confirmed when she lets out a shriek of *faux* surprise. 'What are you doing here?'

He walks towards her, a flirtatious smile on his lips. 'I was hoping you could *service* my needs.'

Mia turns away to hide her blushes, and Rhys hardens. She's wearing jeans, her feet in pink trainer socks that match her tunic, its pockets stuffed with dusters.

'I'm supposed to be cleaning. Ashleigh's got a thing about moths.'

Rhys is behind her now, his breath on her neck and his fingers running lightly down her arms.

'Don't,' she says softly, quivering beneath his touch.

'It's okay, the coast is clear.'

Mia moans. They can fuck here, Rhys thinks. In the kitchen, in front of the vast expanse of water, the rain lashing against the windows. Then they'll go upstairs and fuck on the Staffords' bed, which he knows will turn her on. He moves a hand to her breasts, then slides it upwards, caressing her neck, slipping his fingers into her mouth so she can suck on them.

'I want you,' Mia moans, through a mouthful of his fingers, and God, does Rhys want her too, but his attention is caught by a movement outside, on the deck. He and Mia spring apart, Rhys's heart beating furiously. Is Yasmin spying on him? Or – God forbid – did one of the twins see him with Mia?

'I should—' Mia breaks off, gesturing to the vacuum cleaner. Rhys knows the moment has passed, and, besides, his cock has been scared into submission, retreating between his legs.

'To be continued!' he says, with more conviction than he feels. He rushes back to number five, where Yasmin's still on the sofa, huddled beneath a blanket. Music comes from upstairs; thuds as Tabby and Felicia practise the latest TikTok dance. Rhys relaxes.

It was a bird he saw, perhaps, or the shadow from a cloud, chasing across the deck. Their secret is safe.

It rains solidly for three days. The lodge, which had seemed so spacious on the plans, is claustrophobically small. The girls spend all day in their rooms; Yasmin huddles in front of the log burner with Rhys's credit card, ordering home accessories which arrive the next day, filling the tiny hall with flattened boxes and bubble wrap.

'I must show you our bedroom,' she says to Glynis, who has come for lunch. 'I've completely restyled it.'

Rhys, who was planning forty winks on the sofa, finds himself chivvied to *help your mother up the stairs*, even though Glynis is fighting fit and manages the stairs in her own house without trouble. Rhys knows this is because he has failed to notice Yasmin's *restyling*, which he now sees consists of adding new cushions and moving a lamp from one side of the room to the other.

'And doesn't Jac's cabinet look lovely in Rhys's office?' Yasmin says, as they walk back through.

'Perfect,' Glynis says, touching a hand to the battered drawers. Rhys escorts his mother downstairs before she can get misty-eyed about Tŷ'r Lan, a glorified shed which Rhys remembers as a storage shack for fishing tackle, and furniture his parents didn't have space for at home. It was a far cry from The Shore, which – even in the dreary October rain – is breathtaking.

The clouds finally clear towards the end of the week. And because they are on holiday, and because The Shore carries the memories of summer, everyone drifts outside, bundled in coats and with blankets over their knees, but nevertheless outside. It's sheltered, by the lodges, but the wind is high and the waves are tipped with white foam. The lake is swollen, the trees around the shoreline seeming to grow directly from the water.

Clemmie, who swims the length of the lake most days, emerges in her wetsuit. If Jonty were here he'd make jokes about Greenpeace, but Rhys keeps his mouth shut. Clemmie spends most days with Dee Huxley, and the more distance Rhys puts between himself and Dee, the better. The older woman hasn't yet said anything to Yasmin, but Rhys knows if he puts a foot out of line, she will.

Clemmie sets off at a surprisingly fast pace, her head low and her arms slicing through the water. Waves break across her, so that there are moments when she's entirely underwater. Yasmin settles into a book, the twins slope off to hang out with Caleb, and Rhys sweeps the deck, finding satisfaction in the pile of green sludge he pushes from the grooves. They have no outside space to speak of, in London, only a basement yard useless for anything but bicycles. He breathes in clean, cold air and thinks of the hours he spent as a child each day, roaming the hillsides around Cwm Coed. He thought coming back would give him that same sense of freedom, so why does he still feel so hemmed in?

There's a sudden commotion behind him; Yasmin is out of her chair, pointing at the lake. 'Clemmie's in trouble.' She's thrashing about in the water, her head dipping beneath the waves, one arm stretched high above her head. Automatically he gets out his phone, then stares at it blankly. Which emergency service covers the lake? He is about to dial 999 when Yasmin puts a hand on his arm.

'I think they're going to help her.' She points to a red-sailed boat, which has changed course and is heading straight for Clemmie. Everyone watches as the little boat comes about, skirting closer to where Clemmie dips in and out of view. The helmsman throws a life ring and Yasmin clasps her hands together as Clemmie grabs it. 'Thank God!'

'Thank God,' echoes Rhys, thinking about all the money Clemmie owes him.

By the time the boat arrives at The Shore, Dee has Clemmie's swimming robe ready to throw around her, Yasmin has a mug of sweet tea, and the twins have their phones out.

Yasmin glares at them. 'That's hardly appropriate.'

'Hashtag dramatic rescue hashtag The Shore, though!' Felicia says, but Yasmin stands firm.

As Clemmie's rescuer helps Clemmie up the ladder, on to the deck, Rhys realises he recognises her. Angharad is his mother's age, although the two women couldn't be more different. The jumper beneath her dungarees is darned in so many places it looks like patchwork. She wears no make-up and her face is mapped with tiny, fine lines. Despite the excitement of everyone around her, there's a stillness about her that Rhys finds unsettling.

'I'm fine, I'm fine!' Clemmie says, her teeth rattling so hard she can hardly get the words out. 'Cramp. So embarrassing. The one time I go without my tow float, too.'

'Cool boat,' Caleb says. Rhys assumes the boy is being sarcastic, then sees him gazing at the long, thin boat with something close to envy. Instead of the fibreglass of modern boats, *Tanwen* has a wooden hull, the varnish thin and chipped. Here and there, sections have been cut out and replaced, the seal around the join still visible. The red sails, now dropped away from the wind, are patched and faded.

'You think?' Angharad eyes Caleb, who reddens.

'I don't really know anything about boats,' he mumbles.

'If you're going to live on the water, you should learn.'

The colour's slowly returning to Clemmie's cheeks. She turns to Caleb. 'Maybe, if you ask Angharad nicely, she might teach you to sail.' Rhys and Yasmin exchange a glance. There she goes again: pushy Clemmie. But Angharad gives a slow nod.

'*Ella.*' Perhaps. 'But for now, you must get warm. Your core temperature will continue to drop for some time.'

Angharad accompanies Clemmie inside her lodge, and the twins and Yasmin drift back to their own lodge. Rhys feels a prickle across his neck and turns to see Dee Huxley watching him.

'Lakes are so dangerous,' she says. 'You think you're in control and then—' She bangs her stick sharply on the deck.

Rhys shivers and follows his family inside.

A bundle of post has arrived from Fleur and Rhys feels a surge of optimism for the future. He imagines recording again, touring proper venues, instead of small-town theatres. He opens the contacts on his phone and sends his new assistant a text message. I've got a couple of hours' work for you, if you can fit it in this week.

Rhys could process the post himself – there's little else to do – but there's something pathetic about licking an envelope in which you have placed your own signed photograph. It hardly says 'Celebrity'. When Rhys's career was at its peak, he had a full-time assistant, working from an office on High Holborn. First the work went, then the office, then the PA. Rhys misses the kudos; likes having an assistant again, even if only for a few hours. A few quid is a small price to pay for self-respect.

She comes the next day, taking over Rhys's desk to sort the mail. She discards the outer envelopes, and paperclips each competition entry to its accompanying stamped addressed envelope, along with a photograph ready for Rhys's autograph.

'This one wants a personal dedication.'

Rhys shakes his head. 'We don't do that – it's in the Ts and Cs.'

'The woman's got terminal cancer, Rhys.' She hands him a photograph and a pen. 'Write a nice message, yeah?'

An hour later, Rhys has written messages on well over half the photographs, including anything which arrived with a note, or appears to be from a child. *You could be inspiring the next generation of singers*, he is told, when he complains.

'Would it inspire you?' he says.

His assistant laughs, standing and gathering the letters to take to the postbox. 'Not really. I can't sing.'

Rhys opens his wallet to pull out a tenner, then recklessly pushes twenty into her palm. 'Everyone can sing.'

She looks up at him through her eyelashes, deliberately provocative. 'Maybe you could teach me some time?' Before Rhys can answer she's halfway down the stairs.

He catches up with her in time to open the front door in an act of chivalry, his free hand resting briefly on her arm. 'It would be a pleasure to teach you,' he murmurs. He feels a stirring in his groin and parks it – parks *her* – for another time. He has never really looked at her before – not like that – but now he lets his eyes run over her curves and wonders what they might look like, out of those jeans.

A white van is coming up the drive, and Rhys is just about to close the door when it stops and Huw Ellis jumps out. 'Still got the use of your hands, then?'

'What?'

'You seem to be having trouble answering your phone, so I thought I'd pop over and check you weren't incapacitated.' Huw walks towards Rhys. 'Where's my money?'

'I'll get it to you. It's just a bit tied up. Offshore accounts, you know?'

'I want it today.'

'I can't get that sort of money today, don't be absurd.'

Huw takes a step forward, and then another, till he's so close Rhys can smell his aftershave. 'Pay me what I'm owed, Lloyd. I've still got the keys to this place, remember.' His eyes rove across the lodges. 'Be a shame if anything happened to it, wouldn't it?'

He gives a slow smile, then turns his gaze back to Rhys.

'Or to you.'

TWENTY-SEVEN

JANUARY 6TH | LEO

'What the fuck,' Crouch says, each word carefully enunciated, 'were you thinking?'

Leo stares at a spot just to the right of the DI's head. 'It's a time-critical situation, sir. Yasmin Lloyd's in custody and we can only hold her for a few more hours. If she planted an envelope with ricin amongst her husband's mail, we—'

'If?' Crouch's face is bright red as he bangs on the desk. 'If, if, if. For fuck's sake, Brady, you're supposed to be a detective. Where was the evidence for spanking my forensics budget?'

'The pathologist said—'

'Ah, but it wasn't the pathologist, was it?' Flecks of white appear at the corners of Crouch's mouth. 'The CSI plays golf with Izzy Weaver, as it happens, and she checked with her after you called. Weaver was somewhat surprised to hear that speculative tests were being run to show any kind of poison in Lloyd's system. Do you know why?'

'No, sir.'

'Because she didn't *order* any speculative tests!'

Leo is relieved that Ffion is with Yasmin in custody, and isn't here to witness his dressing-down from Crouch, who shows no sign of letting Leo off the hook.

'Elijah Fox has been suspended.'

'But he was using his initiative!'

'He's been stealing equipment from the mortuary. Turns out he's set up some hokey lab in his bedsit to test out antidotes to poisons. Cross-contamination all over the place.' Crouch glares at Leo. 'Your ricin theory hasn't only wasted hundreds of pounds of my budget, it's taken up precious hours of Yasmin Lloyd's custody clock. Now get her bailed, before it runs out entirely.'

'But—'

'Now!'

Two hours later, Leo is still smarting from Crouch's words. The worst of it is that Leo *knew* he shouldn't have taken Elijah's theory as gospel; that he should have consulted first with Izzy and then with Crouch. Leo had let himself be goaded into proving to Ffion that he wasn't Crouch's whipping boy. That worked out well, he thinks, as he pulls into The Shore; Ffion beside him and Yasmin Lloyd in the back seat. None of them has spoken a word since leaving custody.

'What will happen now?' Yasmin says, as they pull up at The Shore.

'When you answer bail in three weeks' time,' Ffion says, 'you'll either be charged, released, or re-bailed. In the meantime, don't discuss the case with anyone.'

Yasmin nods and gets out of the car, glancing towards the other lodges to see if anyone is looking. There are dark circles under her eyes, and the pervasive smell of custody has followed her home.

Leo reverses into a visitor bay to turn around. 'Right now,' he says, only half to Ffion, 'I don't know if I'm more of a fuck-up as a cop or as a dad.'

'What are you going to do?'

216

'Get a takeaway, get drunk, and contemplate a change of career?'

'About your son,' Ffion says quietly.

Leo drives slowly away from The Shore. 'If I take Allie to court,' he says eventually, 'she'll report me to Social Services.'

Ffion isn't saying anything. Leo expected her to rip the piss, after he emerged from Crouch's office, but she stayed quiet, and Leo has found her quiet company reassuring.

'I spotted a bloke who'd escaped custody,' he says. 'A paedophile. He was right by a school, so I called it in and waited. It was late – around five – so I figured there wouldn't be kids around, only there must have been an after-school club. A handful of girls came out, and one of them started walking home on her own. She was, like, ten – eleven? Right away, Tackley started following her.'

He turns left out of The Shore, back towards Cheshire.

'I couldn't leave her. I told Harris to stay in the car, I'd be right back, and I went after Tackley. I had my radio and I was updating the control room; I thought I'd only be a few minutes, then back-up would get there. But Tackley saw me, and I don't know if he knew I was job, but he bolted.'

'And you ran after him.'

'He went on for fucking miles. Seemed like it, anyway. And you know the worst of it?' Leo lets out a sharp breath. 'I wasn't even thinking about my son at that point. All I was thinking about was getting hold of Tackley and putting him where he belonged.'

'"For his brave and selfless actions while off-duty",' Ffion recites the words from the certificate on the wall of Major Crime. 'That's what your commendation was for.'

'It was over an hour till I got back to my car. Allie had called my mobile to see where we were, and Harris had answered it. He was terrified – it was dark, and he didn't know where I was.

217

The car was locked. Allie had taken to recording our calls, after I lost my temper with her one time. I'm not proud of it, but I'd just found out she'd cheated on me so . . . Anyway, she taped the whole thing and threatened to take it to Social Services.'

'And she's been holding it over you ever since.'

'I'm only allowed to see him for an hour or so at a time now,' Leo says bitterly. 'And never overnight because "the flat's not suitable".' He gives a hollow laugh. 'I guess I can't argue with that – I hate the place.'

'It's a bit . . .' Ffion hesitates '. . . studenty.'

Leo gives a wry smile. 'Says the woman who lives with her mum.'

'It's a temporary arrangement.'

'It always is, when you separate. Three years later, you're still living next to a woman who burns sage outside her door to ward off evil spirits.'

'Oh, my God, I wondered what that smell was!'

'You didn't think it was down to me, did you?'

'I was more concerned with where my bra was, to be honest.'

Leo clears his throat. 'Um, I found it in the kitchen. I wasn't sure what to do with it. I thought you might be embarrassed if I gave it back.'

'Have you any idea how expensive bras are?'

'Gotcha. I'll bring it in tomorrow.'

'You arrested a dangerous predator,' Ffion says quietly. 'You did a great thing.'

'I put my son at risk.'

'He was shaken up, that's all. No harm done.' Ffion puts a hand on his arm. 'Turn off here.'

'Where are we going?'

'I'm taking you home to meet my mother.'

TWENTY-EIGHT

LATE AUGUST | RHYS

August has been unbearably hot; the air close and heavy, with not a breath of breeze. Rhys stands on the edge of the deck, lethargic yet restless at the same time, and sees his own face staring back at him from water smooth as glass. He hears Dee Huxley laughing at something, and a familiar unease forms in his chest. Her presence – the power she has over him – hangs over him like a noose.

He scrolls through his phone, looking for the #ShoreLife posts and flagging potential opportunities to their PR team. He flicks to Twitter, unable to stop himself from checking his mentions, even though the thought makes his chest feel tight. There are no new tweets, only yesterday's charming direct message.

CUNT.

Closer to the lodges, Yasmin and Blythe are gossiping. Jonty has been perched on the end of his wife's sun lounger, an absent-minded hand stroking her tanned leg. Now, he stands and walks towards Rhys, greeting him with a backslap which sticks Rhys's polo shirt to his back.

Jonty steers Rhys to two chairs, set apart from the others and looking out across the lake. 'The girls are talking babies.' He grimaces.

'Not having another one, are you?'

'Good lord, no! I got the snip the second Hester was home. Not falling for that again.' He guffaws, clinking his beer bottle against Rhys's and settling into one of the chairs. 'I got a phone call today from your builder chap.'

Rhys takes a slow drink.

'I managed four months,' Yasmin is saying, behind them, 'then it was on to formula, so I could get some sleep.'

'Huw Ellis? What did he want?'

'You.' Jonty's gaze burns into Rhys. 'Only apparently you're not picking up, so someone in the office gave him my number.'

'Sleep?' In the background, Blythe gives a hollow laugh. 'Remind me what that is? If Woody's not awake, Hester is – I swear they plan it. I'm exhausted.'

'Tabby was a dream,' Yasmin says. 'But Felicia!'

'I'm supposed to be a silent partner, old man, not dealing with the bloody trade. What's going on?'

'He needs paying.' It's almost a relief to get it out. 'There's not enough money in the business account.' Jonty frowns. 'We had that problem with the electrics, remember? And the bloody rain pushed the schedules out, so . . .' Rhys goes on, knowing it won't be long before Jonty's eyes glaze over, bored with the minutiae.

'How much do you owe him?'

'*We*' – Rhys emphasises the word – 'owe thirty grand.'

Jonty winces. He stares at the lake, flickers of tension crossing his face. Then he gets out his phone. 'Thirty?' He taps at his phone. 'I'll transfer it to you. Get the office to sort the paperwork in the morning. That's it, though, old man – no more wriggle room.'

'Of course.' Rhys is flooded with relief. 'Much appreciated.'

'As for sex,' they hear Blythe say, 'forget it!' The women burst into hysterical laughter.

'Kids not sleeping?' Rhys says. Anything to change the subject.

'Arseholes, the pair of them. Worse than newborns.'

Giddy with relief that his money worries are – for now – solved, Rhys raises his bottle in a self-congratulatory toast. 'You, my friend, are talking to just the person. They call me the Baby Whisperer.'

Later, Rhys calls his agent, Fleur Brockman.

'How's life at The Shore?' she asks.

'It's fabulous – you must come and visit.' The heat in Rhys's study is stifling. He walks through to the bedroom to throw open the French windows, stepping on to the balcony and leaning on the railing. The slim metal pole is fixed to the top of a glass panel, giving an uninterrupted view of the lake from the master bedroom. Beneath the glass on every balcony is a gap.

Blythe had gone ballistic when she saw it. 'The children could slip straight through that!'

'Don't let them on the balcony, then.' It seemed perfectly simple to Rhys.

Down on the deck, the twins get up from their sun loungers and pick up the enormous inflatable flamingos they insisted on. Yasmin and Blythe have gone inside.

'Darling,' Fleur says, 'you know I can't be more than twenty metres from a Pret. Listen, I've had another chase from the branding agency, asking when they can expect the balance for the campaign.'

'Today.' Rhys watches Jonty cross to his own deck. 'I'll pay it now.' Sweat breaks out across Rhys's brow. He's never known

Cwm Coed to be so hot. Beyond the decks, Bobby Stafford is zigzagging across the lake on a jet-ski hired from Steffan Edwards. He's wearing a pair of baggy red shorts, his chest bare and pink from the sun.

'Great.' There's a rustle on the other end of the phone. Rhys pictures Fleur ticking the job off her list. 'The deliverables are looking excellent.' She would say that, given it was her idea to go with the most expensive agency. Bobby's jet-ski loops in front of The Shore, throwing up a spray of water before heading up the lake.

Rhys and Fleur had cooked up the idea over lunch, soon after Christmas, when Rhys had been passed over for a role as a judge on a TV singing show.

'Darling, I hate to be blunt,' Fleur had started, which didn't bode well.

The bottom line was: Rhys was going nowhere. The only auditions in the offing were for panto; Rhys's only income that year was from adverts. If they didn't do something drastic, his career was over. But Fleur had an idea . . .

They had spent weeks looking over presentations from PR firms, committing to an innovative campaign the branding agency called #LoveLloyd. For the price of a stamped addressed envelope, fans receive an autographed photograph of Rhys, which they're encouraged to share on social media for the opportunity to win prizes. The national press covered the launch; regional papers up and down the country feature each excited winner. The campaign has plastered Rhys's face all over the internet and already boosted sales of his last album. Rhys Lloyd was about to be reborn.

'They're absolutely swarming in, darling. I've put another batch in the post to you today.'

222

'I'm supposed to be on holiday, not stuffing envelopes.'

'Hire a PA.'

'I can't afford a PA,' Rhys says, through gritted teeth. 'Maybe if you got me a decent audition—'

'Must dash, darling. Lovely to chat!'

The line goes dead. Rhys stands on the balcony for a while, fighting the cold dread inside him. He starts the breathing exercises he always does before singing, and slowly his heart rate returns to normal. There's only one way out of this: he'll have to use Jonty's money to pay the branding agency. The campaign will be a success, which means Fleur will find him a decent job, and he'll negotiate a good up-front fee so he can pay Huw Ellis's bill. Everything's going to be okay.

Rhys gazes up the lake, towards Pen y Ddraig mountain. Bobby disappeared into a cove a few hundred metres up the lake and hasn't reappeared. Has the jet-ski broken down? Steffan's place is on its knees – it wouldn't surprise Rhys if he was cutting corners.

'Give us a song!' Jonty shouts from his deck, a beer bottle in his hand.

'Oh, yes, do!' Clemmie looks up from her book.

Buoyed up by possibilities, Rhys launches into a single verse of 'One Day More' from *Les Misérables*. His voice is rich and warm, and he imagines it travelling through the still air, across the water, across the village he couldn't wait to leave. He imagines singing this same song, night after night in the Sondheim theatre, amid rapturous applause. A standing ovation. He closes his eyes, letting the final note die before giving the tiniest nod of acknowledgement.

The doorbell goes as Rhys is making his way downstairs.

'Post for you.' Ceri hands him a fat Jiffy bag with his agency name on the return label. She doesn't quite look at him, her eyes sliding away back to her van. She always was weird, even as a kid. 'More autographs, is it?'

'The price of fame,' Rhys says, adding a self-deprecating laugh.

As Rhys on the Charltons' deck, there's a smattering of applause.

'What a voice!' Blythe says.

'*Anhygoel*, Rhys!' Clemmie stands, a solitary ovation which plays painfully into Rhys's insecurities.

Dee raises her glass towards Rhys with a smile that doesn't reach her eyes. 'Not bad, Mr Lloyd.'

Bobby's jet-ski is nowhere to be seen, but coming across the lake is Steffan's motorboat, a small rowing boat bobbing on its tow line. Steffan raises an arm in a wave.

The twins have assumed their usual positions – arms and legs trailing artfully in the water – and are chatting idly with Caleb and a girl from the village. Rhys has seen her tagging after Caleb for the last couple of weeks. With any luck, Caleb will go after her now, instead of panting after the twins. Unlike Tabby and Felicia, who change bikinis as though they're on the catwalk, the local girl's in the same shorts and T-shirt she always wears. No jewellery, no make-up. You'd mistake her for a boy, were it not for the mass of red hair, the colour of autumn leaves.

'Peas in a pod,' Dee says, coming up behind Rhys and making him jump. 'Don't you think?'

Rhys looks at Felicia and Tabby, technically identical, yet so different, in Rhys's eyes. 'If you say so,' he says, churlishly.

Clemmie chimes in. 'And both beautiful.'

'You're a lucky man,' Dee says, and Rhys wonders how it is that only he can hear the hard edge to her voice. He walks back to his own deck on the pretext of helping Steffan, who has killed the engine of his boat, letting the vessel's momentum push him towards the pontoon.

As Rhys crosses the Staffords' deck he hears Ashleigh's loud voice drifting from the kitchen. 'Honestly, babe, it's in the arse-end of nowhere. I can't do it no more. It ain't worth it.'

No loss there. Ashleigh Stafford is easy on the eye, but her voice goes right through Rhys, and she's far too quick to slag off The Shore. Last week, she bitched on Twitter about the lack of hot tub, adding the hashtag #ShitShore. Bobby made her take it down, but the screenshots were everywhere.

Rhys climbs down the ladder to the pontoon between his own lodge and the Staffords', where Steffan stands with his feet planted in the centre of the boat, as easily as if he were on dry land. He throws the painter to Rhys, who catches it and pulls the boat close to the pontoon, squinting into the sun.

Steffan's face and arms are a rich walnut-brown. 'I just finished fixing up this rowing boat. I wondered if your girls might like it.'

The boat's nothing fancy, but it'll do for the kids to mess about in. Tabby's been nagging Rhys to hire a boat since The Shore opened, but one look at Steff's price list was enough to put the kibosh on that.

'Oh, please, Daddy!' Felicia has paddled her flamingo over to the pontoon. Behind her, the local girl and Caleb are diving for stones.

'A boat would be marvellous,' Yasmin says. 'I've seen some cushions which will look simply wonderful in it.'

It seems the decision is made. Rhys turns to Steff. 'How much do you want for it?'

'Nothing. It's yours.'

Rhys isn't one to look a gift horse in the mouth. 'Fair play, Steff, that's very generous of you.'

Steffan hesitates, then he pulls a leaflet from his pocket, and smooths it flat. 'The proper ones'll be glossy, of course, with better photos.' The leaflet is an A4 sheet of paper, folded in three. The front reads: *Boat hire and water sports, exclusively for residents of The Shore.*

Rhys studies it.

'By the spring you'll have another twenty lodges, right? I can give your owners ten per cent off hire, and I've been talking to – is it Blythe? – about stand-up yoga. We can definitely work out a good price for that. Then, look here . . .' Steffan takes the leaflet out of Rhys's hands and flips it over. 'Residents of The Shore can choose a free session when they collect the keys to their lodge. Windsurfing, paddleboarding, sailing . . . whatever they want. See?'

'I see. Great. Thanks for the boat.'

'That's okay.'

'Great job.'

'I appreciate this, Rhys.' Steffan grips his upper arm in an awkward half-hug. 'Between you and me, things have been tough lately. Once The Shore's open all year round – once the rest of the resort's finished – it'll . . .' He stops for a second, as though he needs to compose himself. 'Well, it's going to save my business, mate.'

Tabby and Felicia abandon their flamingos and pile into the boat, spinning in circles as they row in opposite directions. Steffan starts his engine and speeds back towards the boathouse, and Rhys climbs back up to the deck, his mind already back on his career.

The tranquillity of the lake is shattered by a roar from Bobby's jet-ski, slaloming down the centre, with an arc of water in its wake. Where on earth has Bobby Stafford been for – Rhys checks his watch – almost an hour?

Bobby cuts the engine as he comes close to The Shore, drifting towards the landing jetty between his own lodge and Clemmie's, before leaping off and securing the jet-ski. His bare chest is glistening with water, and as he climbs the ladder and emerges on to the deck there's something annoyingly James Bond about the whole thing. Clemmie's gone quite pink, and even Dee is peering over her sunglasses.

Ashleigh emerges from the lodge, wearing a white bikini with six-inch heels. She strides across the deck, before snaking an arm around her husband's head and drawing him in for a kiss.

'Ding dong,' Jonty says.

'Get a room!' Tabby and Felicia shout, in unison.

Bobby and Ashleigh are the focus of everyone's attention, but as Rhys glances up the shore, away from the lodges, he catches a glimpse of a car on the road that runs through the trees. He might have thought nothing of it, were it not for the expression on Bobby's face when he sees what Rhys is looking at. His face darkens, and the 'Jack-the-lad, everyone's mate, diamond geezer' isn't quite so friendly, after all.

Rhys walks to the corner of the deck, keeping his eye on the gap in the trees where he knows he will see a final glimpse of the car before the road snakes out of sight. A second later he sees it: a white Fiat with pink lettering, advertising Mia's *Sbic & Sban* cleaning services, coming from the cove Bobby disappeared into.

'Dad, can I have some money? We're going to row to the other side and buy ice creams,' Tabby yells from the boat, which now contains all four teenagers.

'What happened to the tenner I gave you at the start of the week?' Rhys says, distracted by what he's just seen.

'We spent it,' Felicia says, as though it were obvious.

'I'm not going to dish out cash every time you ask for it. If you want money you'll have to earn it.' Rhys thinks of Fleur's suggestion that he hire an assistant. 'I've got some admin you can do.'

'Can't,' Felicia says instantly. 'I'm busy.'

'I can't either,' Tabby says.

'Why not?'

'Because I don't want to.'

'I'll do it,' the red-headed girl says.

'Seren!' Tabby shoves her. 'You can't work for Dad.'

'Why not?' The girl fixes her gaze on Rhys. 'Six quid an hour.'

He laughs at her audacity. 'I'll give you three.'

'The minimum wage is four sixty-two.'

'Four.' Rhys won't be out-negotiated by a teenager. 'Or I'll do it myself.'

There's a beat, then she nods. 'Deal.'

TWENTY-NINE

JANUARY 6TH | LEO

Elen Morgan doesn't bat an eyelid when her daughter rocks up with Leo in tow. Neither does her expression change when Ffion explains – oblivious to Leo's embarrassment – that Leo's flat is in dire need of a makeover.

'It's really not that—' he starts.

'A woman's touch, you mean?' Elen says.

'Mam, it's not the 1950s.'

Leo tries again. 'I just need to—'

'That toddler bed,' Ffion says. 'The one Seren had.'

'It's in the barn. It'll need a clean.'

'That's fine, he can do that.'

Leo is no match for the pincer movement of the Morgan women. Elen is already striding through the house, pulling things out of cupboards. Leo is soon in possession of Lego, a box of toy cars, a Spiderman duvet cover and a pile of dressing-up clothes.

'Seren used to love that pirate hat, remember? She wore it to bed for six months straight.'

'You're very kind, Mrs Morgan.'

'Nonsense. Better it's used than hanging about here.'

*   *   *

Back home, Leo unloads his car. At Ffion's house he was infected by her enthusiasm, and by Elen's no-nonsense practicality. He imagined himself decorating the box room so that, of all the arguments Allie might throw at him, not having a proper bedroom for Harris wouldn't be one of them. Now he's home, it feels pointless.

He slumps in front of his laptop, his cursor hovering over the Lloyd file. The smell from next door's herbs seeps through the door from the landing, making his head hurt.

Where to start? The investigation is a mess. Rhys Lloyd has been dead for a week, and it still feels as though they're stumbling around in the dark. Elijah's ricin theory is a bust. The trophy used to assault Rhys is still missing, Ffion's mate's drone unable to turn anything up in the dark depths of Mirror Lake. Yasmin was showing off at the piano when her husband was murdered, and Jonty Charlton was taking care of Ashleigh Stafford's coke pile.

Should they look closer at Caleb Northcote? Angharad said he hadn't been interested in learning how to sail, but that could have been an act. Leo pulls up the lad's statement and reads it over. What reason did Caleb have to want Rhys dead?

The smell from next door is intense and cloying. Leo presses the heels of his palms against his eyes. Can a smell send someone mad?

He stands up.

The neighbour's door is turquoise. A garland of strung-together feathers runs from top to bottom, and a handwritten sticker on the doorbell reads *Katchen Grint*. On either side of the doormat are tin cans, the contents of which are smouldering.

Leo rings the bell. He has only seen his neighbour a handful of times in three years – scurrying past him on the stairs with a bag of shopping. The door opens and she eyes him suspiciously.

'Your herbs . . .' Leo starts. Smoke catches the back of his throat, and he coughs.

'You want some? I sell them.'

'No, I—'

'I got sage, for cleansing; juniper for health . . .'

'I don't like them,' Leo says. 'I find the smell really . . .' He wrinkles his nose in lieu of description. 'Sorry,' he adds.

'Oh.' The woman's in her sixties, her face lined but soft. 'The man before you, he was never there, so . . .' She bends down, using the sleeves of her jumper as gloves to pick up the smoking tins. 'I put inside.'

As easy as that, Leo thinks. Why didn't he do that three years ago?

Back in his own flat, he stands for a while at the doorway of the second bedroom. No harm in at least trying to make the place look a bit nicer, and, since Ffion's mum had been good enough to pass on Seren's old bed, he may as well put it together.

By eight p.m., the room is, if not transformed, at least getting there. A lick of paint, and a chest of drawers, and he'll be done. Leo sits on the little bed and imagines reading his son a bedtime story. He thinks about having Harris to stay for the weekend; about decorating a tree next Christmas.

He opens his laptop again. A year ago, he found a solicitor who specialised in custody claims. He was too edgy to take it further, unclear what obligations family lawyers might have. If Leo levelled with them, and admitted leaving Harris on his own in a locked car, would they be duty-bound to report him?

Leo writes an email. *I would like to make an appointment to discuss my ex-wife's decision to move to another country with my son.* He can't live like this any more. He's Harris's dad, and he has a right to be in his life. After he's pressed send, he fetches

231

himself a beer. The data from Lloyd's phone has come back, and he plans to spend the rest of the evening looking over it.

Triangulation has confirmed that Lloyd – or his phone, at least – remained within a fifty-metre radius of The Shore on December 31st, which tallies with the accounts given by Yasmin and the twins.

Call and message data has been retrieved for the twenty-eight days preceding the murder, and the analysts have already identified and traced the most popular numbers. Lloyd's agent features heavily on the incoming calls, as does Yasmin, both daughters – Tabby more than Felicia – and Jonty Charlton. On December 29th the same number rang Lloyd seventeen times; the lines are highlighted in blue and carry a note: *Huw Ellis*. There are pages and pages of text messages, retrieved from Lloyd's iCloud account, including increasingly threatening emails from Ellis, demanding the money Rhys owed him.

Leo scans the texts. Lots from the twins, asking for money or Can we have chips tonight? Mum says it's okay. On New Year's Eve Lloyd had a quick-fire conversation with someone about the party's dress code. It's a bit short, reads the message from an unknown number. Wear the dress, was Lloyd's reply. Leo looks at the list of calls made to and from Lloyd's phone, but the number doesn't appear there.

In fact, Lloyd hardly made calls on his phone at all, and Leo works his way through the list, knowing he'll be able to square away that job, at least, this evening. Then his gaze lands on a number Lloyd called around lunchtime on December 31st. Leo doesn't have a great recall for numbers – he hates parking meters requiring him to enter his car registration – but there's something about this particular number which triggers a memory. He unlocks his phone and scrolls through the contacts, not wanting to be right, yet at the same time knowing he is. He stops and stares at the screen.

The number Rhys Lloyd called on New Year's Eve belongs to Ffion.

THIRTY

MID-AUGUST | SEREN

Seren is definitely getting a tan, even though Cwm Coed is literally the hardest place in the world to get one. It rains for, like, three hundred days a year, and even in the summer – if there's a heatwave, as there is now – you come down to the lake and the beaches are all in shade from the trees. *And* she's a redhead, with the sort of skin which looks like she's actually dead. Except when she goes for a run, when she goes so red she's basically purple.

But her arms are definitely a tiny bit browner than at the start of the summer. She found a sunbathing spot on the other side of the lake, where they've cleared the trees, ready for more lodges, and every chance she's had she's been catching some rays. Let's face it, there's fuck all else to do. Most of her 'friends' – if you can call them that – are away, and Ffion's always working. Seren can't wait till her birthday, when she can learn to drive and get the fuck out of this place. She literally doesn't know how Ffion stands it. The only thing that makes Seren put any effort in at school – and she knows it's uncool to brag, but her grades are shit-hot – is the thought of getting a job far away from Cwm Coed.

The lake's loads nicer on this side. People always go straight to the jetty side, where the loos are, and the van selling cold drinks, but over here you can swim from the coves under the trees and never see another person.

There's laughter coming from the lake. Seren can't see through the trees, but she knows it's the twins. She doesn't know which is which, but she knows they're called Tabby and Felicia, because they shriek it at each other whenever one of them gets splashed.

Right? *Felicia and Tabby.* And people say Welsh names are weird.

Seren pulls her top over her bikini, and skirts through the trees to come out further up the lake. Seren's been at The Shore every day since it opened.

Watching.

It's like something you'd see on Instagram. There are five lodges, and right now they've all got their doors open on to their decks. On the one nearest Seren there's a yoga lesson going on: the instructor's facing the cabin, and the two women she's teaching are looking out on to the lake. One of them's super-skinny and, like, pretzel-bendy, and the other one's Clemmie. Seren is slowly working out who everyone is. Clemmie's been here five minutes and she knows more people in Cwm Coed than Seren does. She's trying to start a book club, and she swims in the lake every day. Mam calls her a 'joiner'.

She watches them for a bit. Clemmie is not bendy. Seren sympathises. They did yoga in PE and Seren spent the whole time trying not to fart.

God, it's hot. She looks longingly at the clear blue lake. It's flat calm, and she can almost feel the cool water on her skin. The lake is always freezing. It could be thirty degrees and the water will still take your breath away. You have to stay in, have to keep swimming, until your arms and legs tingle and then as if by magic it starts to feel warm. When Seren was little Mam used to say that was the *draig*, breathing fire down the mountain, and Ffion used to roar and chase Seren through the water. Seren thought Ffi was the coolest big sister ever. Still thinks that, to be honest, even if she'd never admit it.

Rhys Lloyd is singing. At least, Seren assumes it's him, because who else has the balls to belt out '*Calon Lân*' except at a rugby match? The man's like a God around these parts. The corridor in the music department at school is literally full of photos of him.

Wow. It makes the hair on the back of Seren's neck stand up. She wonders if the twins put him off, shouting to each other from their massive flamingos. They're always either on those things, or on their sun loungers. Seren's never seen them actually *in* the water, and she can tell from the way they've done their hair all swishy, and how their make-up is, that they don't plan on getting wet. One of them shrieks with laughter and tosses her head. She keeps spinning her flamingo back round so she's facing one of the lodges a bit further down, and Seren moves through the trees to see what she's looking at.

It's the boy from number four. Clemmie's son. He's in baggy tracksuit bottoms, as he always is, in spite of the heat, and he's more interested in his phone than in the twins showing off. They're being massive try-hards and he's totally ignoring them. Hilarious.

He stands, chucks his phone on the deck and stretches. His T-shirt rides up a bit, and his stomach's all tanned. He's skinny, rather than toned, and he doesn't seem as if he'd be the twins' type, but then it's not like there's much choice around here. Seren's had a few snogs with boys in her year, but there's no one she'd actually go out with. Shudder.

The boy jumps from his deck to the next, then saunters across number two, where the old lady with the stick lives. When he gets to the other side of the deck he swings himself down the ladder on to the jetty. For a second Seren can't see him, but then she hears running feet and he leaps in the air and tucks himself into a bomb.

He lands smack bang between the twins, sending a massive wave over each flamingo. Seren ducks behind a tree to hide her laughter – not that anyone could hear her over the squawks the twins are making. She walks further down the shore, finding a spot to swim where she won't be seen by the residents of The Shore.

Afterwards, Seren's making her way back through the forest towards town, when she hears a crack behind her, like someone standing on a twig. She carries on walking, then stops short and spins around, and, sure enough, he's there.

'Why are you following me?'

The boy holds up his hands as if Seren's got a gun. 'Why were you watching us?' His clothes are soaked through, dark grey where they had been light.

'I was bored,' Seren says, dismissively.

'Same. I'm Caleb.'

'Seren.'

'Seren?'

'It means star.'

'Nice.' He stares right at Seren, holding her gaze, as though he's sizing her up. So she does the same. They stay like that for ages, and Seren doesn't want to look away first because it feels like losing. Eventually, Caleb speaks. 'You could have come over and said hi, instead of hiding in the trees.'

'I wasn't hiding.'

'Whatever.'

'I'm not—' Seren stops. She can't believe she almost said that: *I'm not allowed*, as though she's still ten and needs Mam's permission to play out. And anyway, Caleb would never understand why everyone in Cwm Coed hates The Shore so much.

'I wouldn't trust them as far as I could spit,' Elen had said, when they'd seen the first signs of life across the lake. 'Arrogant, land-grabbing bunch of . . . You're not to go anywhere near that place, you hear, Seren?'

Caleb gets a baccy tin from his tracksuit bottoms and shakes it. 'Do you wanna go somewhere for a smoke?'

Seren takes Caleb above the forest, and he complains about the hill, about his legs aching. Seren laughs, dizzy with the exhilaration of hanging out with someone new, with the steep climb, with the prospect of getting stoned. 'Just wait!' On and on they climb, until they get to where the forest meets the field, and the waterfall crashes into the stream that winds through the trees back down to the lake.

'Here.' Seren turns him around and they stand next to each other, looking back down the way they came.

'Fucking hell.'

'It's alright, isn't it?'

Cwm Coed isn't the sort of place Seren's ever been proud of living in – not like if you lived in New York, or one of those villages where people have thatched roofs and put their shopping in wicker baskets – but sometimes, like now, she sees it through someone else's eyes, and it looks pretty fucking fantastic.

They collapse on the grass, and Caleb skins up. The first drag is like it always is, so hot and harsh Seren wants to cough, but she swallows it down and closes her eyes, and then it's blissfully sweet, like when the lake is so cold it feels hot. They pass it back and forth, the cigarette paper sticking on Seren's bottom lip and dragging it out as if it doesn't want to leave her mouth.

'Have you always lived around here?'

'Yup.'

'It's amazing.'

Seren sits up. 'Are you taking the piss? It's a shit hole.'

Caleb laughs and sits up too. He has a gap between his front teeth, and when he smiles you can see the tip of his tongue through it. 'All this.' He waves an arm: the lake, the mountains, the forest. 'You can go anywhere.'

'Where? There's nowhere *to* go. The cinema's an hour on the bus.'

'All this, though,' he says again. He gets the tin out of his pocket. 'Can you roll?'

Seren doesn't dignify that with an answer, pulling out two Rizlas and sticking them together to make a joint twice the size of the one they just had. Caleb lies back down and closes his eyes, letting out a loud sigh. The shadows under his eyes look like bruises.

'Stop looking at me.'

'I'm not looking at you.'

Caleb grins, his eyes still shut. 'Your loss, then.'

Seren lights the joint and takes a drag. She exhales slowly, watching the smoke plume in the still, hot air, then she touches the filter to Caleb's lips and holds it there while he does the same, as intimate as a kiss. 'What's it like at The Shore?'

Caleb shrugs, but he opens his eyes and squints up at her. 'S'alright, I guess.'

'Rhys Lloyd went to my school,' Seren says, claiming the bragging rights she usually scoffs at. 'Like, years ago, obv.'

'He's a dick.'

'Is he?' Seren lets go of her knees. 'He seems really nice.'

'He accused me of perving over his daughters.'

'Were you?'

'Was I fuck.'

'What did you say?'

'I told him he was a dick.' Caleb rips a piece of grass out of the ground and shreds it into pieces.

'So, are you, like, really rich?' Seren says, after a bit.

'I wish.'

'You must be, to be at The Shore. And you lived in London – that's like the most expensive city in the world, or something.'

'We used to live on the seventh floor of a tower block in Dagenham. The lift was always broken, and the Babylon might as well have moved in, they were cruising around so often.'

'So . . .' Seren nods towards The Shore.

'Mum wanted to get me away from London.'

'What's so bad about London?'

'If you listen to Mum, it's full of crack dens and gangs who go around knifing people and mugging old ladies.'

'Yeah, but what about the bad stuff?'

Caleb laughs, and Seren feels all warm inside. He's staring at her, as if he's trying to decide something, and then he reaches down and pulls up the leg of his trackpants. Around his ankle is a piece of grey plastic on a black band.

'You're tagged.'

He nods. He's nervous, Seren realises.

'What for?'

'Stuff.'

Stuff could be anything. It could be stealing, or drug-running, or beating people up. Seren's pulse races. It could be taking girls into the middle of nowhere and—

'Mum hates my mates. She reckons they're a bad influence on me. It's just me and her at home, so it's a bit fucking intense, you know?'

'What happened to your dad?'

'He became a woman.'

'I did not expect that.'

Caleb gives a wry laugh. 'Neither did we.'

'Do you still see him?'

'Yeah, of course. I mean, it's a bit weird, but . . . he's still my dad, you know?'

'Mine died.' It comes out a bit fast, and Seren realises she's never needed to tell anyone before. Not in sixteen years. Everyone knows everything in Cwm Coed.

'Fuck.'

'Yeah. I never met him. He had cancer, and then my mum got pregnant. He died two weeks before I was born.' Seren doesn't look at Caleb while she's talking, in case it makes her cry. Seren doesn't miss her dad – how can you miss someone you've never met? – but when she misses the *idea* of him so much it hurts.

'My sister's loads older than me, so I think I was, like, Dad's final present to Mam.' Seren pretends to stick her fingers down her throat, and Caleb laughs.

'How old's your sister?'

'Thirty. She's a p—' Seren remembers Caleb's comment about the Babylon. 'Proper bitch,' she says instead, which is unfair. Ffion's a mardy cow, and she pokes her nose where it's not wanted, but that's just because she's old.

Caleb puts his hand on the grass in front of him, his fingers touching Seren's. 'So it's you and your mum, then? Like me.'

Seren's breathing's gone shallow and her blood feels all fizzy. If he kisses her, she decides, she'll kiss him back. Maybe.

'Come on.' Caleb jumps up and stretches down a hand. 'I'll show you around The Shore. You can hang out with me and the twins.'

Seren feels a buzz of excitement.

Something big is going to happen this year – she can feel it.

THIRTY-ONE

JANUARY 7TH | FFION

As a kid, Ffion went to the lake all the time. What else was there to do, in a town the size of Cwm Coed? She remembers wondering why the grown-ups never swam, then reaching adulthood herself and realising she'd gone weeks without getting her feet wet.

Now, the lake is where she comes to think. Where she comes to de-stress, or untangle a knotty problem; at work, or at home. She has an office – a cupboard-sized room at the top of a community police station – but she rarely uses it. Instead, she works in her car, parked looking down on a valley, or here, by the side of Llyn Drych.

The lake was where Ffion came when she realised she was going to leave Huw. She walked along the water's edge, the pebbles slipping beneath her feet, as she grappled with how to tell her husband their marriage was over.

She needs the lake today.

This morning, Leo had sent her a message.

I know Lloyd called you the day he died.

Ffion had switched off her phone. She'd driven into the mountains, blind with panic and unable to think what to do. All morning

242

she'd fought with her conscience, with the past, with what would happen if she were to tell the truth.

At noon, Ffion drove back down to the lake. Now, she stands next to the Triumph and shrugs off her coat. With the exception of the annual New Year's Day swim – which hardly counts, they're in and out so fast – she hasn't swum in the winter for years. She remembers the sting of the cold, but – more than that – she remembers the high. The sharp mental clarity. That's what she needs.

Ffion leaves her clothes in a neat pile on top of her boots and picks her way across the shore. The sky is white with snow clouds, and the wind whistles down from the mountain to swirl around the valley. Her toes find the water between the stones and curl up in complaint, numb before she's even reached the lake proper. Christ, it's cold. Feet. Ankles. Calves. Knees. Thighs – *God, thighs*! Big breath in, then exhale and—

Fuck fuck fuck fuck fuck.

You have to stay in till it stops hurting. Get out too early and you're just cold. Stay till the endorphins kick in, though, and you get a head-rush like nothing else in the world. Better than booze, better than drugs. Better than the brush with razor blades Ffion had at fifteen, feeling as though the darkness would swallow her whole.

She swims breaststroke, counting the seconds in her head. Five minutes is three hundred seconds; ten minutes is six hundred. Any longer is dangerous – she's not used to swimming in these temperatures.

Is that a hundred and sixty-five, or a hundred and fifty-six? She starts again. Her brain's foggy, but it's beginning to happen; she's feeling the buzz. Her arms and legs tingle, and slowly, where there was cold, there is now warmth. Heat spreads through her body, giving strength to her limbs and making her laugh out loud.

Ffion reaches the first buoy and turns around. As she heads back to shore, her stroke stronger now, and her breathing steady, she sees Leo. He's standing by her car, his hands deep in the pockets of his overcoat, watching her.

She saw a different side to him yesterday. When he'd opened up about his son, about leaving him alone, everything had made sense. The way Leo allows himself to be spoken to; the way he is accepting Harris being taken away. Even the way Leo lives, in that bland, lifeless flat. The man wears his life like a hair shirt.

He waits by the edge of the water. She'll have to stay here until he leaves, she thinks, for one single, absurd moment. Or swim along the shore and get out in the trees, run home . . .

In your swimsuit?

You're a police officer. You work together. Pull yourself together, Ffion Morgan!

Ffion slows down, but the rush is passing and the cold returning, dragging her legs down through the water. There's nowhere else to go.

Getting out is agony. Ffion's feet are blocks of ice, cut to ribbons on the stones and so numb they could belong to someone else. Her teeth chatter violently, her head spinning so fast she has to put out a hand to steady herself.

'Why didn't you tell me the truth?' Leo says, but he's not angry, the way he was when he found out about Huw, about the CCTV.

Ffion rubs at her arms, pink from the cold. She drags the straps of her swimsuit down over her shoulders, her fingers refusing to comply, then pulls her T-shirt over still-damp skin. If Leo gets a

244

flash of breast, he doesn't react to it. Doesn't care, Ffion supposes, now he knows who she is. She puts on her jumper before drying her legs, half sitting, half falling on to the ground, where she tugs her jeans over clumsy feet. She's shaking, but whether from cold or fear she doesn't know.

The truth? The truth has been buried so long ago she sometimes doubts it herself.

'Ffion.' He holds out a hand. Ffion hesitates, then allows him to pull her up. She can't stop shaking, the cold in her bones, in her veins, and she feels the pricking of tears at the backs of her eyes, hot and scared.

Leo takes off his overcoat, wrapping it around her and pulling it tight across her chest. Ffion's legs buckle and she forces herself to stay upright, not to fall against him. She's crying now, ashamed of herself, but then what's new?

'I know, Ffion,' Leo says gently, his eyes locked on hers. He holds her shoulders, firm and solid. 'I know.'

The words hang between them and Ffion begins to weep. She's glad of the cold now; of the numbness she wishes she could have felt all those years ago. She thinks of the way Leo opened up to her yesterday and wonders how it would feel to do the same.

'I gave Elijah a call last night. Figured I owed him an apology.' Leo gives a wry smile. 'Turns out he's not the only student on his course with a home-made lab: a mate of his has a side hustle doing private forensic tests.'

Out on the lake, a bird calls.

'There had to be a reason you stopped your sister from giving an elimination sample, so I took a hair sample from the pirate hat your mum gave me for Harris.'

Ffion holds her breath.

'It's come back as a familial match for Lloyd.' The first flakes

245

of snow begin to fall, softening the pebble shore. 'Your sister is Rhys Lloyd's daughter, isn't she?'

Ffion has nowhere to go now, but the truth. It's always been so frightening, but here in Leo's arms, numbed by the cold, sharing her secret feels more like relief.

'Yes.' The lake shines like polished glass, The Shore reflected so cleanly it's impossible to say where the building ends and the mirror image begins. 'But Seren isn't my sister.' In the centre of the lake, a heron dives for a fish, and the glass shatters. If she tells him, there's no going back.

Ffion takes a breath.

'She's my daughter.'

PART TWO

The sky is a vivid blue. The sun is high above the summit of Pen y Ddraig, the morning mist burned away, and boats tack lazily from one side of the lake to the other. The breeze is light, and when it drops completely the boats drift, their sails empty, waiting for their next chance.

On the edge of the lake – by the jetty, by the ice-cream van – the air is thick with heat and the water peppered with paddleboards and kayaks. Families play in the shallows, beach balls flung high over heads. Day-trippers fling open motor homes, pop van roofs, light fires and leave charred rings on the grass. They look across the lake and wonder who lives in the beautiful log cabins, with their decks above the water and their private jetties. They imagine what it must be like, to be so rich, so lucky, to live in such a place.

The stillness of the air, and the warmth of the shimmering shallows, is deceptive. Beneath the surface, strong currents seize rocks and fallen branches; stir up the lake bed and uncover the dropped watches, the lone shoes. Shoals of minnows dart this way and that, their dance pulling in perch and pike, causing a sudden flurry on the surface, as though rain were falling. Deep in the middle of the lake, the water is still treacherously cold.

The breeze carries the bark of laughter, and the timbre of male voices, although not their words. A sharp pop! cuts through the air. Two men stand on the deck of one of the new lodges. One dangles a champagne bottle carelessly by his side, the cork now bobbing in the water. Rhys Lloyd. He's excited to be here; on the shore of his childhood lake, where it all began. He's proud to call Jonty Charlton his business partner, to carry cards with The Shore's elegant green and off-white logo. He knows that this – the official opening of the resort – is the start of something exciting.

Yasmin and Blythe walk out of the lodge to join their husbands, and the four of them raise their glasses in a toast.

'To The Shore!' Rhys says. 'To where it all begins.'

THIRTY-TWO

LATE JULY | RHYS

Rhys takes a sip of his champagne. The summer heat gives a haze to the water, making the boats indistinct, like mirages in a desert. On the opposite side of the lake, holidaymakers jump off the jetty, diving underwater and surfacing with bursting lungs out by the moored boats. And above it all, reflected in the glistening surface of the lake, is Pen y Ddraig mountain.

'I've got to hand it to you, old man,' Jonty says. 'That's not a bad view. Not bad at all.'

'Who needs the Mediterranean when you've got this?' Blythe tips up her face, eyes closed, toasting the sun. Her glass wobbles, champagne splashing on to her bare arm, and she gives a girlish giggle.

'Steady on,' Rhys says. 'That stuff's not cheap.'

Blythe licks her tanned skin with a pink, pointed tongue.

'Don't get used to it.' Yasmin laughs.

Blythe raises an eyebrow. 'The champagne? Darling, I never drink anything else, you know that.'

'I meant the weather.' Yasmin puts a proprietorial arm through Rhys's, her bracelets pinching his skin. 'When we were first married, Rhys dragged me to North Wales each summer and it rained every bloody time.'

251

'It didn't.'

'It did!'

'Another toast!' Rhys says.

Blythe laughs. 'What's left to toast? We've done The Shore, and "us", and you boys have done each other—'

'God, darling!' Jonty says. 'There must be a better way of putting it than that.'

'We should be toasting too,' Tabby calls. 'It's bad luck otherwise.' The twins are on the sun loungers, their lime-green bikinis contrasting sharply with the tans they presumably stole from Yasmin's bathroom, judging by the shouting match that took place before they left London. Rhys feels the familiar combination of pride and fear peculiar to fathers of teenage girls.

'Nice try, Tabitha Lloyd,' Yasmin says. 'You're not having champagne.'

Next to her, Felicia rolls on to her stomach and props herself on her elbows. 'It's true. Isn't it, Blythe? It's bad juju.'

Rhys clears his throat. 'Please raise your glasses to two people without whom The Shore would never have happened.' Realising they've lost, the twins flop back on to their loungers. 'Our beautiful, talented wives.'

'Oh, now *this* is a toast I fully agree with!' Blythe clinks her glass against Yasmin's. 'To us!' The two women embrace. Yasmin's wearing a floaty wraparound number over her swimsuit, and for a second Blythe all but disappears in it.

'To the little women,' Jonty says.

'I'm owning this one.' Yasmin holds up her glass. 'If I hadn't gone to one of Blythe's yoga sessions—'

'If I'd never mentioned Jonty was looking for investment opportunities—'

'And I'd never told you Rhys was trying to get a development off the ground—'

'We, of course,' Jonty says archly, 'did nothing.' He looks at Rhys for solidarity, his eyes flicking to what he insists on calling Rhys's 'dad shorts'. Despite the heat, Jonty has opted for an open-necked shirt, with washed-out blue jeans and designer flip-flops, and Rhys wonders if he should change before anyone arrives. The new owners are expected at one p.m. and it is already past noon.

'I must show you what I've done in our bedroom,' Yasmin says, draining her champagne.

Jonty gives a dirty laugh. 'Ding dong.'

'The lodges are identical, darling,' Rhys says. 'I hardly think the Charltons need to see—'

'Identical?' Blythe laughs. 'They couldn't be more different!'

Yasmin shakes her head, exasperated. 'We went for Shadow White in our bedroom, darling. Jonty and Blythe have School House White.'

'And our accent colour is lemon,' Blythe says, as though explaining to a small child.

'And ours is citron.'

The men traipse after their wives; through the Charltons' lodge, to admire Blythe's scatter cushions, and down the drive towards the Lloyds'.

'Is that someone arriving already?' Jonty says.

Through the trees, Rhys catches a glimpse of a dirty white Fiat with pink lettering, bouncing across the drive leading up to The Shore. 'It's just Mia, the cleaner.' Once The Shore is finished, it will have its own housekeeping team – smartly dressed and properly trained – but for now they're making do with the local girl. 'I'll have a quick word.'

The others continue walking to number five. Music plays loudly through the open windows of the Fiat, as Mia the cleaner reverses into a visitor space. She waits for the track to finish, before getting out and taking a long, flirtatious look at Rhys. 'Well, well, well. If it isn't Ysgol Crafnant's head boy.'

Rhys was never head boy – he doesn't even think the school went in for that sort of thing – but he dips his head in acknowledgment of what he supposes is a compliment, of sorts. Schools like to claim ownership of alumni successes. One summer, fifteen or sixteen years ago, the teachers had persuaded Rhys back to run a music camp at the school. By that time he already had six albums and a tour under his belt, but the guilt-trip – and the fee from the Welsh Arts Council – had dragged him back.

'And it was thanks to the Urdd Eisteddfod and our very own music teacher, Mrs Hughes, that Rhys Lloyd was discovered!' the headteacher had said, in her introduction. It'd rankled a bit, the suggestion that without the youth competition – without the rehearsals at school – Rhys would be nobody.

'We didn't book you for today, did we?' he says now to Mia. 'You were supposed to do all the lodges before everyone arrived.'

'Chill, they're all done. The Staffords have got a Waitrose shop coming and they want me to unpack.' The list of supermarkets which deliver to The Shore is on the FAQs section of the website, along with whether Deliveroo covers the area (it doesn't) and how far owners are from a Marks & Spencer (an hour and a half). All the essentials.

Mia walks up the path to number three. She's wearing denim shorts and a vest top, under a pink cleaning tabard a centimetre or two longer than the shorts. Long brown legs end in scruffy white trainers. She turns around, catching him looking.

'Was there something else?'

He could suggest a few things, Rhys thinks, with a private smile. He goes to join the others at number one, stopping to take a picture of the row of lodges, the lake glistening behind them, so he can 'check in' to The Shore on Facebook. Almost instantly there are two likes, and Rhys glows inside. He switches to Twitter and posts the same photo. *Arrived at #TheShore for a much-needed break before my next recording session.* There is no recording session, but no one on Twitter knows that. It's all about generating the right impression. *Creating a brand.*

He catches up with the others in his study, where Yasmin is telling Jonty and Blythe what they already know. 'We didn't incorporate office space into the design,' Yasmin says, 'because – well, we're all supposed to be on holiday, right? But by stealing a little from the master bedroom, and the same again from the two back bedrooms, we've ended up with quite a usable space.'

'Where did you find those gorgeous drawers?' Blythe says. 'Is it Perch & Parrow?'

Yasmin runs a playful hand over the filing cabinet. 'How much do you think it was? Go on, guess.' On its corners, and around the handles, the red paint has worn off, exposing bare metal. Dents and scrapes cover the sides. It is the perfect industrial foil for Yasmin's Scandi-themed interior. Rhys knows this because Yasmin has told him. Several times. Never mind that the drawers are locked and the key long lost, as long as it looks good.

'Oh, gosh,' Blythe says. 'Four hundred? Five?'

'It was free!' Yasmin says gleefully. 'Rhys's dad had it in the old shed that was here before The Shore was built. Isn't it fabulous?'

'Fabulous,' agrees Blythe. 'I love how you've used the same red for these shelves.' She admires the awards displayed above Rhys's desk. A bunch of regional trophies, two Echo awards, the Olivier he won for *West Side Story*.

'I wouldn't have brought them,' Rhys says. 'Yasmin insisted.'

'She's proud of you.' Blythe squeezes Rhys's arm. 'And gosh, is this all fan mail?' She looks at the stack of post on the desk. Yasmin opens her mouth, but Rhys jumps in. He doesn't want the Charltons to know he's effectively paying people to like him.

'Total ball-ache, really, but what can you do?'

'I can't imagine having strangers writing to me,' Blythe says. 'It must be extraordinary.'

'Well . . .' Rhys opens his hands, as though shrugging it off.

The sound of a car arriving makes them all look up. As one, they move into one of the two single rooms looking onto the driveway. Yasmin has had Tabby's and Felicia's bedrooms decorated in ice-cream pastels. A black and white photograph of Yasmin, gazing into the camera, adorns the walls in each room. Blythe gets to the window first. She claps her hands excitedly and spins around.

'They're here!'

Rhys feels a bolt of excitement. This is it. The first of The Shore's new residents has arrived.

THIRTY-THREE

LATE JULY | YASMIN

'I wonder who it is!' Yasmin rushes to the stairs, keen to establish her position as The Shore's First Lady.

'Who's next to you and Rhys?' Blythe follows her, breathless with excitement.

'Clemence Northcote.' Yasmin has memorised the list. 'IT professional, teenage son.' Downstairs, she stops to swipe a fresh bottle of champagne from the waiting ice bucket. 'Rhys – glasses.' She clicks her fingers, and he picks up two flutes. 'Gosh, I feel quite nervous!' She has been dreaming of this moment ever since Rhys outlined his visions for The Shore. A haven of well-connected, well-to-do, like-minded people, who will commission Yasmin to design interiors around the world.

'No need for nerves,' Rhys says. 'They'll fall in love with the place the second they see it. The view alone will take their breath away.'

'I agree,' Jonty says. 'It's pretty sensational.' He winks at Yasmin, waiting until Rhys's attention is elsewhere before letting his eyes drop to her cleavage. Yasmin practically purrs. Six weeks ago, the two couples went out for dinner, downing several bottles of wine and splitting an Uber home. Rhys was in the front, boring the driver (who had turned out to be an unlikely fan of classical music) and Blythe was nodding off. Squashed in the middle, Yasmin had felt Jonty's hand stroking her thigh. It was such a thrill, and, although nothing has happened since, Yasmin knows it's only a matter of time.

'Number three's the soap actor, isn't it?' Blythe says.

'Bobby Stafford,' Rhys confirms. 'Middleweight champion years ago, then he started acting and now he's pretty much retired from the ring, as far as I can tell. His wife's the blonde who was in the jungle – the waterfall shower with the see-through bikini?'

'Ding dong,' says Jonty.

'Which just leaves Deirdre Huxley,' Rhys says. 'I don't know anything about her except she's retired.'

'We should have put in an upper age limit,' Jonty says. 'Zimmer frames don't exactly scream The Shore, do they?'

'Luxury lodges,' Yasmin mocks, 'only available to the rich, the aesthetically pleasing, and those in possession of their own teeth.'

They're still laughing as they form a welcoming committee outside the lodges. A grey Tesla is bumping up the drive. Automatically, Yasmin sucks in her stomach and presses her tongue to the roof of her mouth – her latest trick to tighten that annoying saggy bit under her chin – but as the car draws nearer she sees an elderly woman behind the wheel. The sun glints off the windscreen as the Tesla comes to a stop.

Deirdre Huxley emerges with a broad smile. 'Well, isn't this something?'

Jonty steps forward with a glass of bubbly. 'Jonty Charlton, investor. Welcome to The Shore.' Yasmin gives an inward sigh of appreciation. Jonty is so much more refined than her husband. You can take the man out of Cwm Coed, but it seems you can never quite rinse Cwm Coed out of the man.

'Now that's what I call a welcome – thank you, my dear.' She clinks her glass against Jonty's. 'And I'm Dee. Unless I'm in trouble, of course.' Her eyes twinkle. 'Now, who else do we have?'

Rhys sticks out a hand. 'Rhys Lloyd. Creator of The Shore.'

'Indeed.' There's an amused expression on Dee's face as she shakes Rhys's hand. 'How nice to see you here.'

'Will you do the honours, Jonty?' Rhys throws the keys for lodge two at Jonty, who gives Rhys a flash of resentment before turning on the charm.

'My pleasure. Mrs Huxley, won't you come with me?' He offers her an arm, but she declines, reaching for her stick from the back seat of the Tesla.

'Plenty of life in this old dog. Although if you wouldn't mind bringing my bag from the footwell, I'd be ever so grateful. It has all my medication in.'

'Of course.'

Mia comes running out of number three in her cleaning tabard, shouting instructions down the phone. 'Turn around . . . you'll see a farm on your – that's it! The turning's a bit further on the left. I'm outside now.' There's the throaty roar of an engine, and everyone turns, catching a flash of yellow through the trees. 'I see you now! Yes, don't worry, I've got it sorted!' She runs back into the house, as a bright yellow McLaren Spider speeds up the drive and then stops abruptly, with a loud thud.

'Shit,' Rhys says. 'He's hit a pothole.'

The McLaren rocks forward and then back. There's a ghastly grinding sound, and then the car bumps out of the hole and continues towards the lodges, creeping a few feet at a time and snaking around the remaining potholes.

'Good start,' Yasmin mutters. Jonty has taken the champagne, and she's about to fetch more when Mia re-emerges from number three carrying a silver tray. On the tray are two glasses and a bottle of champagne, around which is tied a gold helium balloon in the shape of a heart.

'Special instructions from Bobby,' she says, when she sees the others staring. 'He wanted to surprise Ashleigh.'

Bobby. Ashleigh. Why is the cleaner on first-name terms with these people, when Yasmin hasn't even met them yet? She and Blythe exchange glances.

The man who gets out of the driver's seat is instantly recognisable as Bobby Stafford. He's in his early forties, with a nose so broken it points in three different directions, and teeth too white and straight to be God-given. He's small-framed, and, as he leaps around to the passenger side to open his wife's door, he could still be in the ring from which he retired a decade ago.

Ashleigh must be a foot taller than him. She's in tracksuit bottoms and glaringly white trainers, with a tight band of Lycra passing as a top.

'She's so stunning,' one of the twins murmurs. Yasmin looks at Blythe and flashes her eyes wide for a split-second.

'You wanna sort that driveway out, mate,' Bobby says, striding towards them. He looks at Rhys. 'Lloyd, right? The place looks mint, but that' – he points down the drive – 'is a fucking liability.'

'It's all in hand, I assure you. Welcome to The Shore!' Rhys can't match Jonty's easy confidence, but Bobby shakes his proffered hand, while Ashleigh snatches a glass of champagne from the cleaner's tray. She takes a selfie, the gold heart balloon bobbing behind her as she boomerangs the glass to her lips and down again.

Bobby takes the remaining glass from the silver tray in one hand, and the balloon-festooned bottle in the other, then he plants a kiss – a kiss! – on the cleaner's cheek. 'You're a diamond, Mia, that's what you are. Did the shop arrive?'

'All packed away. I wasn't sure if you'd have eaten, so I did you some sandwiches – they're in the fridge.'

'Star. Okay to do the beds and that when they need doing?'

'Course. Just pop me a text.'

'Legend. Come on, babe, let's take a look round the new gaff.'

'Hopes pinned on the last neighbour for a bit of a class, then,' Yasmin says drily, as they disappear into number three.

'Mum!' Tabby says. 'Did you even *look at* Ashleigh Stafford just now?'

'I tried not to.'

'Omigod I can't *even*!' Felicia rolls her eyes. 'Her eyebrows were on *point* – we should ask her where she gets them done.'

'I think we have different ideas about what constitutes class.' Yasmin pours herself and Blythe more champagne.

'I'm with the twins on this one,' Rhys says. 'I thought she was very nicely put together.' He's staring at Dee Huxley's lodge, his brows knitted together.

'She's not made of Lego, Rhys.'

Everyone looks up at the sound of another car, and, as an ancient BMW barrels over the potholes, Yasmin feels her dreams slipping away.

If Ashleigh Stafford really were made of Lego, Clemence Northcote would be built from Duplo. Short and dumpy, she has multicoloured hair and the dress sense of a toddler at a birthday party.

'Call me Clemmie,' she says, when she's been introduced. 'Everybody does!' She nudges her son forward. '*A dyma Caleb.*'

'Mum, give it a rest, will you?'

'You speak Welsh?' Blythe says. 'Gosh, how terribly impressive.'

The woman flushes. 'I'm learning. Introductions, hobbies, that sort of thing. I can work from anywhere, and Caleb's college course is online, so we're planning on spending a lot of time here. I want to try wild swimming, and of course learn the language and—' She looks at Rhys, apparently seized by an idea. 'Maybe you could run a conversation class here at The Shore? I read in the papers that Bobby Stafford's bought a lodge, and you know he has Welsh roots? We could make it a regular thing!'

Rhys looks utterly horrified by the idea. 'Shall I show you around your lodge?'

'So lovely to meet you!' Yasmin lies, giving Blythe *the look* which means she's to follow her for a debrief, *stat*.

The two women are about to disappear when Dee Huxley's door opens.

'Any problems at all,' Jonty's saying, 'just call.'

'Thank you so much, dear. Now, I think I'm going to put my feet up and have a snooze. That was quite a drive.'

Next door, at number four, Rhys is opening the front door for Clemmie and Caleb. She's talking to him in Welsh, and he's faffing with the suitcases and clearly trying to get in and out as quickly as he can, which means he doesn't see what Yasmin sees.

Dee Huxley, standing in her open doorway, staring at Rhys as if she knows him. *Really* knows him.

Staring at him, Yasmin realises, with a shiver, as if she hates him.

THIRTY-FOUR

JANUARY 7TH | LEO

Leo doesn't know what to do with Ffion, except keep his arms around her. Her whole body shakes with silent sobs, and he holds her until she's still. 'Shhh,' he says. 'It's okay.'

Is it?

He's struggling to process what she's just told him. Around them, dark clouds bunch above the mountain range. *Draig* means dragon, Leo knows, and for the first time he sees the shape in the rocky outline, its tail stretching into the water. He leads Ffion to his car and opens the door, lifting in her legs as though she's frail, instead of simply cold. He starts the engine and cranks up the heater, and wonders where to start.

'You can't tell anyone,' Ffion says fiercely. 'No one knows. I told Mam it was a lad from the summer party – she and Dad were raging over whoever it was not facing up to his responsibilities, but I wouldn't give them a name. I couldn't bear anyone to know what I'd done.'

'What *he'd* done,' Leo says gently.

'It wasn't rape, if that's what you're thinking.' Ffion wipes her face on the sleeve of Leo's coat. 'He wasn't – he wasn't violent.' She swallows. 'Not in that way.'

'You were fourteen.' Lloyd had been forty-six when he died;

he'd have been thirty when he . . . Leo looks at Ffion, huddled in the passenger seat, and nausea swells in his stomach. Fourteen is statutory rape. Fourteen is a *child*.

'People called me Ffion *Wyllt*.' She pulls her knees to her chest. 'It means "wild Ffion". I bunked off school, answered back, nicked stuff from the shops. I played up to it a bit, I suppose. Told the teachers I'd been up late drinking and partying, when all I'd done was watch TV with Mam and Dad. Told my mates I'd got off with this lad and that lad, when I hadn't got off with anyone at all.'

'When did you meet Lloyd?'

'The school persuaded him to come back one summer to run a camp for a few kids who were good at music.' Outside, a handful of snowflakes spin this way and that. 'I haven't sung a note since,' she says quietly.

'You don't have to do this. Not now. Not unless you want to.'

'He was good-looking. Smooth. Kind of charming, I guess. Older, but not old like parents. Some of the others told him how crazy I was – how I drank and slept around, and all the rest of the crap I'd made up for them. And I played along, because, once you've got a reputation, that's who you are.' Ffion's jaw wobbles, and she pulls her mouth into a grimace. 'Anyway, we had a summer party. Rhys's idea. Celebrate the end of the project.' Ffion speaks fast, her face screwed up as though she's in pain. 'He took me outside. Said he had a bottle of champagne just for the two of us to share. My dad had been diagnosed with cancer – it was a really shitty, shitty time, you know? I wanted to be somewhere else – be some*one* else.'

'Where did he take you?' Leo's interviewed dozens of rape victims in his career, but he's never found it so hard to force out the questions.

'To his studio, in his mum's back yard.' Ffion gives a hollow laugh. 'I didn't want to go, but I didn't know how to say no, and all we were doing was talking and drinking so . . .' She trails off, staring at the windscreen. The snow's settling, covering the rocky shore with a dusting of white. 'I started to feel nervous – out of my depth – and I remember seeing her at her kitchen window on the first floor, hoping she'd look down and see me, that she'd somehow know I wanted to go home.'

'And did she?'

Ffion's face is deathly white. 'The light went out. I guess she went to bed. And I always wondered if she knew what her son was like. What he might do.' She starts crying again, slow, mournful sobs which make Leo's heart hurt. He can't bear to hear any more, but, more than that, he can't bear Ffion to have to say it. He reaches for her and holds her until her breathing steadies.

Leo leans his head against Ffion's, and watches the wind chase waves across the lake. Rhys Lloyd raped Ffion and fathered a child she had to give up. Little wonder she hated the man. Slowly, he lets himself acknowledge what he's been thinking ever since he found out the truth.

Had she hated him enough to kill him?

THIRTY-FIVE

LATE JULY | DEE

Dee Huxley's faculties are still in full working order, thank you very much, but soon after her seventieth birthday she had finally conceded it was time to slow down a little.

'This house is too much for you to manage, Mum.' Her son had come for one of his six-monthly visits. 'There are some lovely warden-controlled flats overlooking the river.' He had slid a brochure across the coffee table. A born salesman.

Dee was blowed if she was leaving her five-bedroomed Victorian rectory, with its sweeping lawns and walled orchard, to live in a beige box, with bingo on a Wednesday evening and the smell of cabbage seeping through the walls. She'd flicked through the pages. 'There's no room for an office. Where would I keep my paperwork?' Dee's study at the rectory was lined with bookshelves, neat handwriting labelling each year's meetings and accounts.

'So step down from the board! Come on, Mum – you should have retired years ago.'

'I wonder if you would say the same if I were a man?' Dee had no wish to retire, and, although the business ticked over perfectly well without her input, she liked to keep an eye on things from a distance.

Nevertheless, she'd had to agree the house was getting on top of her. It wasn't so much that she *couldn't* prune the fruit trees, or shin a ladder to clear the gutters, it was more that she no longer *wanted* to.

Dee's son had been delighted when she put the rectory on the market. He was less delighted when, instead of the retirement apartment and cash-in-the-bank option, Dee had bought a two-bedroom flat in King's Cross – and number two, The Shore, north Wales.

'You haven't even seen it!'

'I've seen the plans,' Dee had said calmly. 'And, thanks to Google Earth, I've had a lovely wander through Cwm Coed. I think I'll be very happy there, and I'll have my *pied-à-terre* for business meetings and seeing friends.'

As Dee turns into The Shore, she knows she made the right decision. The drive sweeps in a semi-circle from the main road to the lodges, allowing teasing glimpses of glistening water and wood-clad lodges between the trees. The surface of the drive, however, is pitted with holes, and Dee navigates carefully around them in her new car.

A small throng of people stands outside the lodges and, as Dee parks in the bay allocated to number two, she recognises Rhys Lloyd.

The question is, will he recognise her?

A handsome man in blue jeans and an open-neck shirt shakes her hand. He has an excellent grip – Dee notices these sorts of things – and he's either genuinely delighted by her presence, or he's very good at faking it.

'Well, isn't this something?' Dee says.

'Jonty Charlton, investor. Welcome to The Shore, Mrs Huxley.'

Ah, an investor. Well, that explains the handshake and the crocodile smile. Dee clinks her glass against Jonty's. 'Now that's what I call a welcome – thank you, my dear. And I'm Dee. Unless I'm in trouble, of course. Now, who else do we have?' She sees Rhys Lloyd staring at her, a frown creasing his forehead in confusion. The penny hasn't dropped yet, clearly.

'Rhys Lloyd,' he says, when Dee reaches him. 'Creator of The Shore.'

'Indeed.' It does not surprise her that Rhys would describe himself as the Creator. She has deduced enough about him to know he is arrogant. Most men are, in Dee's experience – and she has plenty of experience. 'How nice to see you here.' Rhys's frown deepens.

'Lovely to meet you, Mrs Huxley.' Rhys's wife offers a slim, tanned hand. Dee eyes her with interest.

'Mrs Huxley.' Jonty proffers an arm. 'Won't you come with me?'

As they make their way towards the lodge, Jonty carrying Dee's capacious handbag, a garish yellow sports car comes up the drive with a throaty roar. Dee catches the look on Jonty's face. 'I'm afraid you've been landed with the old banger, dear.'

'A classic model never goes out of style, Mrs Huxley.'

Smooth, Dee thinks. Perhaps a little *too* smooth.

She walks through the ground floor of her new lodge, taking in the clean, Nordic-style lines and the carefully chosen furnishings. The steel outline of the vast doors frames the lake like a painting, a hot haze softening the view. She tries the handle, and the doors slide open with a satisfying swoosh.

Turning, she eyes the layout of the open-plan kitchen, dining and sitting rooms, then looks at Jonty. 'I wonder if I could borrow those muscles of yours . . .'

Fifteen minutes later, Jonty's shirt is circled with sweat. 'Anything else?' he asks, his earlier enthusiasm distinctly lacking.

'That's perfect.' Dee beams. They – or rather Jonty, with Dee waving her stick to direct proceedings – have switched around the furniture so the table is on the opposite side of the room; the L-shaped sofa in the kitchen area, by the glass doors.

'I never eat at a table,' Dee says. 'I'd rather be on the sofa with a tray on my lap and this view, wouldn't you?' She walks across the room and waves towards the lake, the inky blue water contrasting with the line of green along its shore. 'This is what we're all paying for, isn't it?'

Outside, the sports car is parked in front of the middle lodge, and a bashed-up BMW has taken the final spot, by number four. A teenage boy is unloading cases from the boot, and a woman with rainbow hair is talking to Rhys Lloyd.

Dee watches him for a moment. Even as she drove here, she didn't know if she'd confront him, but now that she's seen him – now that she's seen his family – she knows that it's inevitable.

As it turns out, it's Rhys who confronts her. He rings her doorbell an hour or two later, just as Dee's about to settle down with a book. She has said hello to her neighbours, who seem perfectly pleasant; although Dee – more than most – knows that looks can be deceiving.

Rhys looks uneasy, his eyes darting from Dee's face, to the stick in her hand, to his own feet. 'I came to see if you'd settled in okay.'

'It's all wonderful, thank you. You must be delighted with the place.'

'Yes, I'm very—' He breaks off, his face creased in confusion. 'Look – have we met before?'

'I think you'd better come in.'

Dee walks back into the lodge. She doesn't wait to see if Rhys follows her, but she hears the click of the front door closing and the rubber soles of his deck shoes, squeaking on the tiled floor. She sits and extends the same invitation to Rhys. He stands for a moment, then reluctantly perches at the opposite end of the sofa.

Dee makes a final decision. What she knows about Rhys is very powerful indeed: the sort of information his wife – and indeed the police – would be very interested in. The sort of information she could use as collateral; perhaps in exchange for shares in The Shore, which she can see has the potential to be an excellent investment.

More than anything else, Dee wants Rhys to know that he hasn't got away with it.

'Number 36,' she says, eventually.

Rhys stares at her, his face slowly paling beneath its sheen of perspiration.

'I own it.'

'But—' Rhys looks as if he's struggling to breathe. 'But you're—' He stops, his gaze falling on Dee's stick, on the crêped skin on the back of the hand holding it.

'Old?'

Rhys flushes.

Dee had opened Number 36 in the early eighties, after a brief stint as a call girl. The industry had been almost entirely led by men, when it should surely be dominated by women? Moreover, the brothels in which so many of these women worked seemed to be dark and dingy places, making the whole affair – pun entirely intended – rather sordid.

Number 36 itself was a tall, thin townhouse in Soho, bought when it was still possible to snap up a bargain. Dee had renovated the ground floor and two bedrooms, and gone into business. Over the years, as Number 36 became more successful, she'd completed the work on the rest of the building. The result was a stylish, aspirational club, with roaring fires and cocktail cabinets, staffed by elegant, intelligent women working on an excellent commission rate.

'God.' Rhys croaks out the word. He's sweating profusely, now, a streak of damp down each side of his face.

His membership had been revoked, of course, after the assault. Dee was out of town when it happened; the woman concerned in hospital by the time she'd rushed back.

'You can press charges,' Dee had said. Number 36 – and Dee's involvement – was protected by a series of Russian-doll holding companies, and the welfare of her staff had always come first. But the woman had shaken her head.

'I want to forget it ever happened.'

Afterwards, Dee had sat in her office for a long time. Incidents like this were rare, but they left her shaken and angry. She had enough information on enough high-profile men in London to bring down the government, scandalise churchgoers and collapse what was left of public confidence in the police, but, if those men were doing nothing wrong, why would she? As long as they were polite and respectful, as long as her staff were happy and in control . . . where was the harm?

'What do you want?' Rhys says. He's thinking of the headlines, Dee knows: the tabloid exposé of his fall from grace.

'I don't want anything.' *Yet*, she adds privately. Dee has expensive tastes, and isn't above the occasional bit of blackmail.

'Why are you here?'

Dee looks around, taking in the polished floor, the big windows, the view. 'For this.' Dee has always been able to separate business from pleasure, and she's always had an eye for investment. The first row of lodges at The Shore will always attract a premium, and, if Dee ever chooses not to use the property herself, she knows she'll get an excellent return. In the meantime, what's not to like about a lakeside cabin?

'If my wife ever finds out—'

'Oh, there's no one better at keeping secrets than Dee Huxley. Although . . .' She keeps her gaze on him, enjoying seeing him squirm. 'Now I've seen that lovely wife of yours and your two beautiful daughters, I'll be keeping a close eye on you.' She leans closer to him, lowering her voice even though no one's here to listen. 'And you'd better treat them better than you treated my staff, or I might forget how to keep a secret.'

THIRTY-SIX

JANUARY 7TH | FFION

Ffion's heart hurts as much as her head. She's raw. Exposed. Ripped open before this man she hardly knows and yet who knows more about her than every one of her friends. Her eyes are pressed against Leo's shoulder, but she can't shut down the images in her head.

They had gone outside for the champagne Rhys brought *especially for you*, and for a while it had been fun. Ffion had laughed as the bubbles went to her already light head, and stumbled when they wobbled her legs. She could still hear the voices of the others at the party, still see the light from the school hall windows. She was still safe.

Then Rhys offered his arm – extravagantly, with a little bow, as though they were in a costume drama – and suggested they finish the bottle *somewhere more comfortable*. Ffion knew what that meant, and she knew, too, she didn't want to be *more comfortable*. But, in making a joke of the escort, he had unseated her. A part of every girl is poised to defend herself, long before she knows why she might need to. If Rhys had grabbed her, or dragged her from the hall, Ffion would have known what to do. She would have fought him. Kicked and bitten and screamed her way out.

Instead, she—

'Curtsied.' She turns her head to speak, shame falling out of her in choking sobs. 'I bloody curtsied.'

She had dropped her head and pulled wide an imaginary skirt, grateful for the excuse to stare at the grass and blink away her fear. *I want to go home now.* She'd stared at the toes of her trainers, at the mud Mam would go mad about. *I want to go home*, she said silently, as she straightened and heard herself laugh even though nothing was funny.

'Is Madame ready?'

He was wearing a jacket – smarter than the occasion merited – and the cuffs of his shirt pushed out from beneath the navy sleeves. Ffion stared at a gold cufflink and felt the ground shift beneath her, felt her hand reach out and slip into its expected place, felt her feet move *right left right left*. She felt her heart pound with fear.

'I've had enough of being with all those kids, haven't you?'

'Yeah.' They walked through the back streets to the Lloyds' family home, and each step was heavier and more hopeless. Ffion was so much more mature than the others, he told her – so why did she feel so much younger?

'We can make our own fun, can't we?'

'Yeah.'

Ffion feels Leo's breath against the top of her head, warm and reassuring, urging her to speak as much of her truth as she feels able to share. What happened that night has existed only in pictures – haunting and terrifying, keeping her awake and driving her to places which scare her, even now. Now she's trying to shape it with words that hurt to handle.

'I said yes.' Ffion clasps her hands together, the tips of her fingers still white with cold. 'I said yes to everything.'

It had felt impossible to say anything else. This was what she had pretended to want, after all. What she'd *thought* she wanted, even. She had flirted and pouted, and spoken loudly of clandestine meetings with older boys from out of town. She had asked for this. It was unstoppable.

'No!' Fleetingly, Leo tightens his grip on her, only to release her instantly, as though scared she might break. He moves her gently away from him, holding her shoulders so she's facing him. He wants her to look at him, but her head is heavy and her shame heavier still. She stares into the footwell and wishes she could stop her tears.

'Ffion, this wasn't your fault,' Leo says, insistent yet patient, telling Ffion what she can't yet believe. 'You didn't ask – you *couldn't* ask for it. Fourteen, Ffion. Fourteen!'

He takes a breath. He rubs his hands up and down Ffion's arms, and she isn't sure if he's trying to calm her, or himself, but it does both. Slowly, she lifts her head, chin wobbling, and looks at him. She swallows.

'If you dealt with this at work,' Leo says gently. 'A fourteen-year-old who'd been raped—'

'He didn't rape me.' But she remembers the torn button on her jeans; the bruises on her shoulders, her thighs.

'—what would you say to her?'

Leo waits, keeping his eyes locked on Ffion's as she shakes her head, remembering how still and quiet she was on Rhys's sofa, how she didn't move away, or say no, or fight back.

Rhys had whispered in her ear, hot and damp as the pain tore through her. 'You've wanted this all summer, haven't you?'

'Yes,' she heard herself say.

'*What would you say to her?*' Leo repeats. His eyes are urging her onwards, and she knows, she knows what she's supposed to say, but she was Ffion *Wyllt*, Rhys knew that and so she had to expect—

'I'd say it wasn't her fault,' Ffion whispers. Her voice cracks, and she's crying again. 'It wasn't my fault. It wasn't my fault.'

THIRTY-SEVEN

MID-AUGUST | CALEB

By rights, Caleb should be bored out of his skull. His mum says by next year The Shore will have a games room, with a bar and coffee shop, and a crazy-golf course in among the trees. Right now, there's none of that, just the deck and the lake and the shadow of the mountain. Cwm Coed village is less than a mile away, but there's nothing to do there either.

There are hardly any people around. The morning after they'd arrived at The Shore, Caleb had taken one of the resort's forest-green bikes and cycled around the lake without seeing a single car. He had felt his shoulders, usually hunched up to his ears, slowly returning to their correct position. He'd pedalled faster, the wind whipping a grin on his face. He felt *alive*.

'I know you'll be missing your mates,' Mum said, but all Caleb felt was relief. Relief that when his phone beeped with a message from the lads he could ignore it, knowing that when they came looking for him, they wouldn't find him.

It had started when Caleb moved schools halfway through the first year at secondary. Everyone already had friendship groups, and Caleb was grateful to be taken under the wings of Brett and Jamil. It was fun at first – even the shoplifting was a laugh – but then people started getting hurt, and Caleb got scared. He took it out on his mum, knowing he was being unfair, but at the same time unable to stop himself lashing out.

'They're a bad influence,' she'd say, and Caleb would slam his bedroom door and hide from the truth.

Now, Caleb stares at his phone. Two doors down, Rhys Lloyd is singing, and even though Caleb hates classical music it sounds right for this place, with the sun sparkling on the water. Tabby and Felicia are messing about on pink flamingos.

'Caleb!' one of them shouts. 'Are you coming in?'

He ignores them. He's scrolling through his contacts, systematically blocking each number in turn. Brett, Daz, Jamil. With each one, he feels as though he's shedding a skin.

'Oh, my God, Tabs, you just flashed a nipple, I swear!' Felicia's voice carries through the still air. Caleb looks – he's fifteen, after all – but sees nothing.

'Shit, do you think there are fish in here?' Tabby says. She pulls her feet on to the flamingo. 'Like, actual fish?'

Caleb catches Bobby Stafford's eye. He's on the neighbouring deck, stretched on a sun lounger with a beer in his hand.

'D'you reckon twins can share a brain cell?' Bobby says. Caleb laughs and Bobby points his beer can at him. 'East London, right?'

'Dagenham.'

'What d'ya do for kicks around there?'

Caleb shrugs, unwilling to let himself be dragged back to Brett and his crew.

'Play any sport?'

'Bit of footie.'

'Ever tried boxing?'

'Not really.'

Bobby points up at the overhang from the upstairs balcony.

'I'm putting a punchbag there. I'll give you a few pointers, if you like.'

Caleb feels a glow inside. 'Yeah, alright.' He throws his phone on to the deck. 'Might go and check out the water.'

Bobby winks. 'And the rest, right?'

Caleb stretches. He jumps to the next deck, climbs down to the pontoon and takes a running jump, landing in a perfect bomb between Felicia and Tabby. The lake is ice cold and dark, and Caleb opens his eyes and takes long, strong strokes through the clear water. He bursts into the sunlight, laughing at the outrage on the twins' bedraggled faces, then hauls himself out.

There's a movement, further down the shore, and Caleb sees the red-haired girl hiding behind a tree. She's been there for a few days, spying on them, thinking she can't be seen. For want of anything better to do, he heads after her, but as he rounds the side of the lodges, a hand grips his shoulder and spins him around, then pushes him roughly against the wood cladding.

'Perve at my girls again and I'll cut your balls off.' Rhys's hand is locked around Caleb's throat, pressing against his windpipe. Caleb can hear the twins laughing on the lake; his mum's voice, talking to Mrs Huxley at number two. Sweat trickles down his spine.

'I wasn't—' Caleb tries, but Rhys's fist tightens on his throat and he can't speak.

'They're out of your league.'

'I—' Beneath the humiliation and the fear, white-hot rage is building inside Caleb, pushing its way to the surface.

'Got it?' Rhys says.

Caleb's fist readies itself, but never has a chance to act.

Rhys brings up his knee and Caleb's vision swims black.

THIRTY-EIGHT

JANUARY 7TH | LEO

'He walked me home afterwards.'

Leo's turned the car's heater on full blast, and the colour is slowly returning to Ffion's cheeks. She huddles beneath her own coat and Leo's, steam rising from her still-wet hair. Outside, the snow has blown itself out, the few flakes which had settled already whipped away. The lake is grey, violent waves thrashing against the shore, and Leo shivers at the memory of Ffion in the water.

'I remember him kissing me goodnight. I said thank you,' she says wretchedly, her eyes pressed shut against the memory. On the other side of the lake, The Shore seems to taunt them, and Leo tries to focus on the lake, the mountains, the trees. A couple of hundred metres along the shoreline, two lads are messing about with fishing tackle. Leo tries to imagine Harris at that age.

'I had a bath every day for weeks and weeks,' Ffion says. 'I never felt clean. One day I realised my body felt different. And I knew I was pregnant.'

'Did you tell your parents right away?'

'Mam guessed. By then, it was too late to do anything about it.'

'What did they do?'

'They shouted. A lot. Demanded to know who I'd slept with,

but I refused. Mam listed every lad on that summer camp – *was it him? Or him?* Dad was disappointed, that was the worst of it. He called me *gwyllt*; said he was disappointed to discover that all the rumours about me had been true.' Ffion lets out a shaky breath. 'He'd already been diagnosed with terminal cancer – we knew he had less than a year left. I hate that I let him down before he died.'

'So he never got to meet Seren.' It means *star*, Leo remembers. A bright light in the darkness. He looks out of the window and frowns. The lads with the fishing rod are causing a commotion, one of them running up to the boathouse, the other on his knees, bending over something.

'It was Mam's idea to make her my sister. They'd wanted more children after me, but Mam had six miscarriages, and eventually they stopped trying. She said they'd bring Seren up as theirs. I don't know what Dad really thought about it – he and Mam spent a lot of time talking about it behind closed doors – but he agreed. He said it would give me a chance to straighten myself out. To—' Ffion chokes back a sob. 'To make him proud.'

'And look at you.' Leo squeezes her hand. 'A detective. Wouldn't he be proud of that?'

Ffion laughs – a messy, hiccupy laugh, but nevertheless a laugh. 'Maybe underneath. He used to say the police were a "waste of bloody taxpayers' money".' She makes her voice a growl, then gives the same sad little laugh. Tears streak her face, and she scrubs at her cheeks with her hands. 'Mind you, there's a few would agree with him if they saw me bawling my eyes out when there's a murder to solve.' Ffion takes a long, deep breath and looks at Leo with resolve. 'Which we should probably get back to.'

'There's no rush,' Leo says, but now there's a patrol car pulling into the lake, heading for the boathouse, and Ffion sees it too and she's searching for her radio. Leo bumps the car along the foreshore, meeting the police car as it slows to a halt between the boathouse and where the two lads were fishing.

'DC Brady.' Leo shows his warrant card to the uniformed officers. 'I'm working on the Rhys Lloyd incident room.'

'Good timing.' The officer nods to the two lads, who are wide-eyed with excitement. 'I believe these young fishermen have caught your murder weapon.'

THIRTY-NINE

LATE AUGUST | STEFFAN

Steffan Edwards is in the pub. There was a time when this would have sent digital smoke signals around the village, until someone's husband was despatched to persuade Steff out of the danger zone and back home; or, at the very least, to drink with him and keep him out of harm's way.

But Steffan has been sober for two years, nine months and six days, and after the first eighteen months – when he couldn't even trust himself to walk past Y Llew Coch, let alone set foot inside – he'd returned to his habitual spot at the bar.

He takes a sip of his coffee – black, two sugars – and stares morosely at the boathouse accounts. He deserves some kind of medal, doesn't he, for staying sober in the face of these figures? You wouldn't blame a man for having a drink, when his business was going down the pan.

He won't have a drink, though. He isn't even contemplating it. Some blokes could do that: have a pint or a quick voddy, just to take the edge off, not give it a second thought. Not Steffan. Steffan would have the second ordered before he'd finished the first; be three sheets to the wind before you could say *last orders*. Steffan is all or nothing.

At the end of every week, he tots up the takings and enters the amount in his ledger, along with the running total for the season, compared to the previous year. Every year he works a little bit harder; every year, he takes a little less money. He can fix boats all year round, but eighty per cent of his income comes in the holidays, when families fill the campsites and head to the lake every morning. Years ago, when his dad ran the business, it was all pedalos and pleasure cruises; now it's kayaks and wind-surfing. Steff's got the right gear – that's not the problem. The problem is China. Or Japan, or wherever they make those bloody inflatables. Time was, you'd hire a boat on holiday, because of course you couldn't *buy* one – where would you put it? Now, you shove it under the stairs, or in the loft, packed up all small in a rucksack. Steffan's heart sinks every time he sees the camper vans rock up, spilling their contents on to the grass. He adds up the hire fees: two paddleboards, a kayak, a crappy yellow boat for the kids. Another hundred quid lost.

Sometimes, they don't even take them home. The plastic bursts, or they're late and the boat isn't dry. What arrived folded into a tiny cube is now far too big for the bag. It was only thirty quid in Aldi – they'll get another one, next summer. They stuff them into already-full bins, or leave them on the shore for Steffan to tidy away before the lake takes them.

Steff's no quitter, though. He's always moved with the times, always looked for opportunities. He turns over the piece of paper he was using for his rough figures, and sketches a boat at the top. Below, he makes a list of all his hire services – kayaks, paddle-boards, dinghies – and taps the end of the pen against his teeth, as he contemplates what he can add.

Huw Ellis brings his empty glass to the bar and nods to Steff. '*Iawn?*' His eyes flick automatically downwards, checking what

Steffan's drinking. It's humiliating, but Steff can't complain – Huw's picked him off the floor more than once.

'Yeah, not bad.' Steffan's doodling on the hull of the boat he's sketched, his mind still on his list of hires, when something suddenly occurs to him. 'What colour's that green they use, over at The Shore?'

'No idea. I've got the name somewhere.'

Steff looks at him.

'You want me to find it now?'

'Cheers.'

Huw gives a small shake of his head, but gets out his phone. 'It's on my invoice, which – by the way – is still outstanding, so if you're thinking of doing any work for them, get the cash up front.' He zooms into the document on his screen. 'It's called Hunter.'

Steffan scribbles it down. 'And white, yeah?'

Huw snorts. 'You think Lord and Lady Lloyd would go for something as bog-standard as white? That's Timid Mist, I'll have you know.'

'He's done alright for himself, hasn't he?' Steffan says. 'Rhys, I mean. And, fair play, he's brought his money back home. There's a lot who wouldn't.'

'Do you see them in the shops?' Huw interrupts. 'There's an Ocado van there most days, and Ewan says he's not sold as much as a rasher of bacon to them since the place opened. Bloody English.'

'Not Rhys – he's as Welsh as you or—'

'You reckon?' Huw laughs. 'He couldn't wait to get out of here.'

Steffan stays quiet. Rhys owes Huw money, and where there's money, there's trouble.

*　　*　　*

Tucked away inside the boathouse is a wooden rowing boat Steffan built by hand and was planning to sell. Over the next five days he ignores his paid jobs and instead works on the boat, sanding and priming and making her watertight, before giving her two coats of Hunter. He finishes the detail in Timid Mist, and stencils letters on the stern, faithfully replicating the type he's seen online. *It's a Shore thing!* Smaller letters say *Tabby* and *Felicia* – one name on each oar. Finally, Steffan applies a coat of varnish, and the hull gleams.

There's been hardly any wind for days. The only sailors on the lake are those skilled enough to read the ripples; patient enough to wait for the pockets of breeze which will take them another hundred metres. Steffan fires up his RIB and heads towards The Shore, the newly painted boat bobbing behind. He has a handful of paddleboards out on hire, dotted around the lake, and further towards the mountain he can see Angharad, fishing from her red-sailed lugger. Earlier, Bobby Stafford – who, fair play, didn't once haggle over the price of a summer's rental – took Steff's jet-ski into the cove up the lake. Steffan sees him from the boathouse: noon every day, regular as clockwork.

The teenagers are in the water in front of The Shore, and Steffan pulls back the throttle to slow the boat. He spots Elen's youngest, Seren, and Rhys's twins on pink flamingos.

Rhys himself is on the deck of number four, talking to two women – one plump, with mad hair; the other grey-haired and leaning on a stick. Rhys looks up as Steffan approaches, and starts walking towards his own lodge. A few metres from the pontoon, Steff cuts the engine completely, his speed and direction perfectly judged. He's been bringing boats in since he was eight or nine – he could do it blindfolded.

Steffan throws the painter to Rhys, jumping out as soon as the

RIB is close enough. 'I just finished fixing up this rowing boat. I wondered if your girls might like it.' He's so nervous he's just dived right in, and he could kick himself. Rhys looks like he's been ambushed – Steff should have thought up some small talk, maybe asked after the family. But the rowing boat looks good, its green and white livery gleaming in the sun. It looks as if it belongs.

One of the twins sculls her flamingo over to inspect the boat. Steffan wants her to find her name on the oar, but she's looking at Rhys, her hands clasped in front of her. 'Oh, please, Daddy!'

'A boat would be marvellous,' Rhys's wife says. 'I've seen some cushions which will look simply wonderful in it.'

'How much do you want for it?' Rhys says.

'Nothing. It's yours.'

'Fair play, Steff, that's very generous of you.'

Steffan takes a deep breath, then he hands Rhys his mock-up leaflet. It's taken him every hour he wasn't finishing off the boat; working out his prices, and finding quotes for printing. 'The proper ones'll be glossy, of course, with better photos.' He explains his plan for a partnership between the boathouse and The Shore, and Rhys studies the leaflet as he listens.

'I see. Great! Thanks for the boat.'

Steffan's flooded with relief. Rhys likes his plans. Now Steff can order the boats he's reserved and buy more paint. He'll need more paddleboards, too, and buoyancy aids – maybe green ones, with The Shore's logo. 'That's okay.'

'Great job,' Rhys says, and Steffan's so fired up with relief and excitement that he grips Rhys in the sort of hug usually reserved for after rugby matches and drunken renditions of 'Land of my Fathers'. As he speeds back across the lake to the boathouse, ready for this new chapter in his business, he feels a buzz he never got from booze. There are people in Cwm Coed who won't give Rhys the time of day since he built The Shore, but Steffan won't hear a bad word against the man.

Rhys Lloyd is going to save Steff's business.

FORTY

JANUARY 7TH | FFION

Osian Wynne is thirteen and dangerously overexcited. When Ffion and Leo reach the jetty, he and his mate are standing several metres away from Rhys Lloyd's trophy, as though they've dug up an unexploded bomb.

'I said it would be a crime scene.' His mam, Donna, arrived seconds after the patrol car. 'Didn't I say it would be a crime scene?' She looks at the crowd of twenty or so locals, summoned by the power of Facebook.

'She did,' offers Osian. 'Will you be putting up some of that blue and white tape, Ffion?'

'Do you need some chalk?' someone asks.

Dear God. Ffion blames the government's rural broadband grants for Cwm Coed's relatively newfound love of Scandi dramas. Armchair detectives, the lot of them. She turns to the rubberneckers. 'Has anyone got a carrier bag?'

'Will there be a reward?' Osian says. 'I'm saving for a new rod.'

'Your reward is the warm glow that comes with assisting a murder investigation,' Ffion says, picking up the trophy, which weighs more than she expected. Strands of weed cling to the golden spikes.

'Great.' Osian is clearly unimpressed.

'This could be the key to the whole job, mate,' Leo says. He fishes a tenner from his pocket and hands it to Osian, with a wink. 'Good work.'

'You're too nice,' Ffion says, as they head back to the car, the crowd behind them dispersing, disappointed with the lack of spectacle.

'I always think niceness is underrated,' Leo says mildly.

It certainly isn't something they find when they get to Chester, where Crouch rolls his eyes dramatically at the evidence bag Leo brings into his office. 'What have you got there? More wild geese?'

Leo puts it on the DI's desk. 'The murder weapon. Retrieved from Mirror Lake earlier today.'

Ffion watches conflicting emotions cross Crouch's face. This was a great result – surely the guy would muster a *well done*?

'About fucking time you earned your keep.' Crouch gives a bark of laughter. He does that, Ffion's noticed: dilutes his obnoxious remarks with grins and guffaws, as though everyone's in on the joke.

'We're on our way to the lab with it now,' Leo says. 'If you're happy to authorise it, of course.'

'Of course the water will have destroyed any useful evidence,' Crouch says, as though it's Leo's fault.

'Well, actually,' Ffion says loudly, 'latent prints have been recovered from items submerged in standing water for several weeks. Studies were carried out on firearms thrown into freshwater lakes and the results showed very little degradation.' She holds Crouch's gaze. 'So we could be in luck.'

The DI leans back in his chair. 'I'm coming to the conclusion you might be wasted in north Wales, DC Morgan.'

'Only on my days off, sir,' Ffion says. 'They're lethal with the measures in my local.'

'Ha!' Crouch swivels to his computer and jabs, one-fingered, at the keys. Ffion and Leo wait. 'They'll be expecting you at the lab.' Crouch looks up, as though surprised to still see them there. 'Well, go on, then!'

'Thanks, boss,' Leo says.

'You want to take a leaf out of that one's book.' Crouch gestures towards Ffion, already half out of the office. 'Your ball-sacks empty, are they?'

'No, sir.'

'Then show a bit of spunk, for Christ's sake.'

Ffion turns. If Leo won't tell him, then she bloody well—

But she feels Leo's hands on the backs of her arms, propelling her gently but firmly out of Crouch's office.

'He needs telling,' she says, when they're on their way to Forensics.

'It's just the way he is. He's a dinosaur.'

'He only gets away with it because you don't challenge him.'

'It doesn't bother me.'

Ffion gives a burst of laughter. 'Yeah, right.'

'Even if it does, it's my life, isn't it? Nothing to do with you, or anyone else.'

Anger swells inside Ffion. 'Wrong.' She stops dead, forcing Leo to do the same. 'Men like that keep going until they're stopped. Even if it doesn't bother you – which, by the way, is the biggest crock of shit I've heard since Yasmin Lloyd claimed to be grief-stricken – what about the next person he picks on? A waitress, a bus driver, an officer who *is* bothered by it.' Her eyes flash. 'Don't you get it? It's not about how *you* feel. Every time Crouch goes unchallenged, you're letting some other schmuck down.'

Ffion flings opens the door to Forensics, letting it swing shut in Leo's stunned face. Her heart's thumping, and she doesn't need a psychologist to tell her she's projecting. Still, she's surprised to discover there's something on which she and Crouch are in complete agreement.

Leo Brady needs to grow a pair.

FORTY-ONE

OCTOBER | MIA

Mia's back is killing her. She cleans for Glynis Lloyd once a fortnight and always dreads it: the woman's hoover weighs a bloody ton. The flat above the shop has two sets of stairs and Mia's lugged the vacuum cleaner to the top floor to finish off there.

'Do you want me to move these boxes, or work around them?' Mia calls. Glynis is never far away. Mia's never sure whether the older woman likes to check up on her, or whether she wants the company. Sure enough, Glynis is in the spare room in seconds.

'It's a bit of a mess, I know – just do what you can.'

'Having a clear-out?' Mia eyes the files, which cover the bed and most of the floor.

'I was trying to find some paperwork of Jac's but, as you can see, it's like looking for a needle in a haystack.' In amongst the files are bunches of keys, piles of bank statements, letters and articles torn from magazines. Mia picks up a newspaper clipping, yellowed with age. A teenage Rhys smiles awkwardly for the camera, holding a trophy.

Rhys Lloyd, Enillydd, Eisteddfod yr Urdd.

'That's from when he won best solo. There's another one, somewhere, with a picture of him with Lesley Garrett.' Glynis sits on the bed, leafing through a pile of newspapers. 'I don't even know why I kept this lot. I suppose there must be a mention of Rhys in there somewhere, and I never got around to cutting it out.'

The newspapers are all regional, a mix of Welsh and English. One of them has been folded open, and Mia sees the name of the local school in the headline. She pulls it out and smiles at the familiar faces. 'Is that Hari Roberts?' She points to a boy in the front row. 'And there's Ffion, and I think that's Mari Alys Pugh, from Fronbach.' The kids are in the music room at the secondary school, the picture taken at the end of a summer school *led by special guest and former student Rhys Lloyd.*

Glynis puts on her glasses and takes the article. 'I never liked that photo of him. He was exhausted all the time in his late twenties – it was all that touring, you know.' She stands. 'Are you not in that photo? You did the camp, didn't you?'

'I was in the loo when the photographer came.' Mia grins. 'Mam gave me such a row for it.'

Glynis bends down, dragging another box from under the bed. 'There's a whole pack of photos somewhere.'

'Oh, Glynis, don't worry on my account.'

'I've got young Caleb coming tomorrow to put up some shelves – he'll put them all back for me.' She opens the books and starts looking through the contents.

'Caleb from The Shore?' Mia's surprised. The Shore might as well be a hundred miles away, for all the mixing there is with Cwm Coed. Present company excepted, she thinks, with a private smirk.

'He's a lovely lad. He's done a fair few odd jobs for me recently – for pocket money, you know. Here you are.' Glynis hands her a pile of photographs.

'Oh, my God, why have I never seen these?' Mia bursts out laughing. 'Look at my hair!' She flicks through the photos, remembering clear as day the freedom of being sixteen, of having nothing to care about but what you looked like and who you were going to hang out with that day.

'Take some,' Glynis says. 'They'll only go back in the box.'

'If you're sure?' Mia pulls out three or four, still laughing. She's off to clean Elen's holiday let later today – she'll have to show Ffion. 'That make-up! We thought we were so cool.' She looks around the room. 'Now, can I help you find the file you're after?'

'Thank you, but I'll put the radio on later and work through it. It must be here somewhere. If you could hoover the bits you can see, I'd be grateful.'

Later, after she's finished at Elen's, her phone rings. She smiles at the screen. 'Hello, you.'

'Alright, gorgeous?' Bobby's voice is low and gentle, and it flips Mia's stomach.

'What are you up to?'

'I'm on set. I've just been reunited with my love child, but I've got another two scenes before I find out he needs a kidney transplant and I'm the only match. How about you?'

'Same.' She hears him laugh and she misses him so badly she could cry.

Mia hadn't believed in love at first sight until she'd met Bobby. It's something they talk about a lot, because Bobby didn't believe in it either, yet when they remember that first meeting, it was as though the world had stopped.

'Nothing else mattered,' Bobby always says.

'Like a bomb going off, in a film,' Mia adds. 'Everyone's running around screaming, but you're in slow motion, and all you can hear is your own heartbeat.'

She had been intrigued to meet the Staffords. The Shore's first celebrity guests – if you didn't count Rhys Lloyd – and even though Mia didn't watch *Carlton Sands*, the soap is famous for its controversial storylines, and Bobby Stafford is often in the gossip mags. His new wife, Ashleigh, is never out of them. Moving from one reality TV show to the next, if she's not pimping her appearances she's being papped in nightclubs, always with someone slightly more famous than her.

Mia had given Rhys permission to pass her number on to the lodge-owners, in case any of them wanted to hire her directly. She had been surprised when Bobby had called her personally. She'd assumed people like the Staffords had staff for that sort of thing. Bobby had laughed when she said that.

'Only wankers have people to book their cleaner.' He was coming up to look over the lodge, wondered if Mia would give him a bit of a tour. 'I don't know anyone else in the area.'

'You don't know me.'

'I will once you've shown me around,' Bobby had said, with a grin Mia could hear down the phone line. The cheek of him.

He had come up a week later, and the second he stepped out of his car, she'd felt as if something had exploded.

'Fireworks,' she said, afterwards.

'Like I'd stuck a knife in the toaster,' Bobby said.

Mia had taken him for a walk up Pen y Ddraig mountain.

'My grandmother was Welsh,' Bobby said. 'I've always loved the place.' They were standing at the summit, Llyn Drych snaking along the valley below them. 'It feels like coming home,' he sighed, and he wasn't looking at the lake, but at Mia, her cheeks flushed and her eyes shining.

He'd called that evening, on his way home. Mia could hardly hear him over the sound of the McLaren.

'This is going to sound crazy . . .' he'd said.

It was all crazy. From the way it began, and the way it is now, to the way it will be, as soon as they're able to be together.

'Not much longer,' Bobby says now. Mia trusts him, and she can wait – she feels as though she's already waited a lifetime for him – but he feels so far away, right now.

'I wish you were coming next week.'

'Me too. But I've got a break in filming in a couple of weeks. We'll go somewhere, yeah? Just me and you.' There's a pause, then Bobby clears his throat. 'Look, I hate to ask, but . . .'

'Ashleigh wants the lodge cleaning?'

'It's too weird, isn't it? I'll tell her you can't do it.'

'And have her pay someone else to do it? So not only do I have to spend the next week on my own, I can't pay the rent—'

Mia's teasing, but Bobby cuts in, horrified. 'You can't pay your rent? Why didn't you say, babe? I'll send you the cash.'

'Don't you bloody dare. I'm not taking your money. Course I'll clean the lodge.'

'Can you get the key from Rhys or Jonty? They're going up next week, right?'

'I can, but I'm fully booked next week – it's half-term, and the holiday lets are mental. I've got a couple of hours tomorrow, though, I'll sort something out, don't worry.'

'Thanks, babe. I love you, you know.'

'I know.'

Huw Ellis is wearing pyjama bottoms and slippers in the shape of Shrek's head. He opens the door with a piece of cheese on toast in one hand, crumbs sticking to his T-shirt. On the floor in the hall, his work clothes are in a pile around his boots.

'Does Ffion know what she's missing out on?' Mia says, taking in the scene.

297

'She collected more of her stuff today.' Huw ignores the jibe. 'Waited till I was at work, of course.' He takes a bite of toast, talking through a mouthful of cheese. 'Will you talk to her again?'

'Yeah, because that went well, didn't it?'

A few weeks after Ffion and Huw split up, Mia – against her better judgement – had attempted to reconcile the couple. The result was her friend refusing to speak to Mia unless she promised to never again bring up the subject of Ffion's love life.

'I came to blag the keys to The Shore off you,' she says, before Huw can ask again. 'I've got to clean number three.'

Huw eyes her suspiciously. 'How do you know I've got a set of keys?'

'Rumour has it you're refusing to give them back till you're paid.' Mia leans against the porch door. 'Come on, Huw, I need to get my bunions into salt water.'

'I did not need that image in my head.' He leaves the front door open and walks through the hall to the kitchen. Mia follows, watching as Huw rummages in a drawer. Dirty dishes are piled in the sink, and the worktop is smeared with the traces of what might be bolognese sauce.

'You should get a cleaner.'

'You offering?' He opens another drawer.

'Nope.'

'Some women would consider it an honour to pick my pants off the bathroom floor, you know.'

'I think that's unlikely. Bloody hell, Huw, how many keys have you got?'

'I'm a builder. Buildings have keys.' He scratches his ear. 'I swear they were here last time I looked.'

Mia's feet are killing her. She walks towards the front door. 'I'll have to wait till Rhys gets here, and fit it in next week. But honestly, Huw, sort this place out – it's a shit pit.'

Later, with a glass of wine in her hand and her feet in a bowl of hot water, she re-jigs next week's diary, then messages Rhys and arranges for him to leave number three open for her. In a fit of pure masochism, she finds an old episode of *Carlton Sands* and fast-forwards between Bobby's scenes. Their daily rendezvous in the cove over the summer seem light years ago, and she aches with longing.

It's pouring with rain when Mia gets to The Shore. She's worked all weekend, getting holiday lets ready for half-term visitors, and she's got Airbnbs on one-night turnovers all week. She sends Bobby a photo of his bedroom.

Wish you were here.

Ditto. He sends a photo back: dazzling white sands and turquoise sea.

She sends one of the loo brush and receives a string of laughing emojis, followed by dozens of hearts. *Love you, my Mia.*

Downstairs, Mia cracks open the sliding doors to let in some air, and puts on music while she works. She turns up the volume, singing as she pushes the vacuum cleaner under the table. Bobby has come good on his pledge of time away together, booking a suite and promising to spoil her rotten.

She catches a movement and looks up, screaming when she realises it's the reflection in the glass doors. She spins around, one hand on her chest as she gets her breathing back under control.

'What are you doing here?'

Rhys walks towards her, his face twisted in a sleazy leer. 'I was hoping you could *service* my needs.'

Mia turns away. She has encountered this sort of thing before. Clients – or clients' husbands – making suggestive comments as she vacuums their offices. Once, she turned up at a new customer's house to find him in a bathrobe, the belt 'accidentally' falling open once the door was closed. She has a one-strike rule, which is easy to do when you work for yourself and it's a single client. But Rhys owns The Shore. If she tells him to fuck off, he won't hire her again, and when the rest of the lodges are built that's a lot of money.

'I'm supposed to be cleaning,' she says. She moves away, her eyes on the vacuum cleaner. 'Ashleigh's got a thing about moths.' If she ignores him, he'll go away. He's trying it on, is all.

But now he's behind her, and she can feel heat on her neck, and she's so scared she can't move. He runs his hand down her arms.

'Don't—' she starts, but she's shaking from fear and she bites down to stop her teeth from rattling.

'It's okay, the coast is clear.'

Mia lets out a whimper of terror. She tries to tell herself he won't do anything, not here on his doorstep, with his family two doors down, but now he has a hand on her breast and she tries to move but he's pressing her against him and the hardness in his trousers is a threat not a promise. He touches her lips and she turns her face, but he forces his fingers into her mouth.

'Please. I want you to stop.' The plea is pitifully small, smothered by his fingers. She's crying, now, so scared and feeling so stupid for letting this happen. Her head is telling her to use her elbows, to smash her head back against his, to twist away, to scream . . .

But her body won't comply. It won't do anything. It stays frozen, letting this man's hands control it, cover it, take what they want.

Mia feels as though she's watching from above, screaming at herself to wake up, to do something, do *anything*, but—

There's a sudden jolt. Space, clean air. His hands, leaving her body, and she feels as though she's breaking through waves, pulled to the surface just as she was drowning. She doesn't know why he's stopped, but she isn't questioning it – she just wants him to go, and for the buzzing in her ears to subside.

'I should—' Mia grips the hoover, trying to stop her limbs from shaking. She hears him walk away, saying something under his breath, and then the front door slams, and relief floods out of her in hot, noisy tears.

'My dear, are you alright?' Dee's on the deck, pulling open the doors and picking Mia off the floor with an embrace so tight and safe it makes Mia cry more.

'Rhys—'

'I saw.' Dee's voice is soothing. 'He thought he could take what he wanted. But you're safe now. It's all okay.'

'Bastard,' Mia says. She is slowly feeling normal again, fear morphing to anger. Bobby will go ballistic when he finds out.

'He certainly is,' Dee says. She strokes Mia's hair, like she's a child. 'And he'll get his come-uppance, never fear.'

Mia hopes she's right. Rhys can't be allowed to get away with it, and, if he's done it to her, who knows who else he's tried it on with?

'Oh, yes,' Dee says, a hard edge to her voice. 'Men like that always get what's coming to them.'

FORTY-TWO

JANUARY 8TH | LEO

As Leo walks down the corridor towards the briefing room, his stomach tightens. Working with Ffion and spending so much time in and around The Shore has provided Leo with the perfect excuse to miss briefings, and it's only now he's back in the office that he realises how much he dreads seeing his DI.

'You're early.' Crouch looks at his watch. 'Shit the bed, did you?'

Leo sits down. He can feel Ffion's eyes on him, but really – what can Leo do about it? *Sir, sir, I don't like the way you speak to me*. Leo would be laughed out of the job. You don't hear anyone else complaining. It's just Crouch's way. Blunt, coarse. Nothing personal.

'You know,' Crouch is saying to the DC nearest to him, 'I hear Liverpool's the only place you can be called a paedophile for shagging someone's mum.'

Except it *is* personal, isn't it?

Is he like that to everyone? Ffion had asked, the first time she'd met Crouch, and Leo was forced to admit the truth. No one else in the office bears the brunt of Crouch's special brand of humour. Even if the jibes are childish – the sort of shit joke Leo heard time and time again when he was growing up – Crouch only makes them to Leo. It *is* personal.

'What do you call a Liverpudlian in a suit?' the DI says now, to no one in particular. Leo hears Ffion's words in his head. *What about the next person he picks on?* He thinks about everything she's been through. She looked so broken yesterday, yet here she is. Still standing.

'The defendant,' Leo says, before Crouch can give the punchline. The DI blinks, then opens his mouth to impart yet another 'joke'. 'I don't think you've done the one about the Scouser who won't accept a blow job in case it stops his benefits. Or there's the one about holding a shell suit to your ear, to hear a Liverpool accent.' Leo fixes his eyes on Crouch. 'Shall we just get them all out of the way now, sir?'

Silence falls heavily across the room, as the two men look at each other. The DI's face is a ruddy red, his jowls wobbling as he moves his mouth to formulate a response. 'What's the matter, Brady?' he says finally. 'Everyone else finds it funny – what's wrong with you? Don't you know how to take a joke?'

Leo's gaze doesn't waver. 'I don't know, sir. Try me with one that isn't offensive or discriminatory, and let's see if I laugh.'

Somewhere in the room, someone moves a chair, the leg scraping against the floor. Crouch clears his throat. Leo is stifled by the silence, by the eyes of more than a dozen officers, not a single one of whom gives enough of a shit to raise a hand and—

'I don't find it funny, sir.' DC Clements speaks quietly but clearly, her unwavering gaze taking in first Leo, then Crouch.

'Me neither.' A DC by the window speaks up.

'Nor me.' Another.

'Or me.' Ffion. And of all the voices, Leo realises it's hers he wanted to hear.

Crouch looks around the room. 'Bloody snowflakes, the lot of you,' he blusters, but there's an ugly flush across his neck. 'Who's got the update on Number 36?'

'MetPol are still looking into the assault.' As DC Clements starts talking, Leo's pulse begins to slow. All around the room, he sees nods of support, eye-rolls aimed towards the DI. Whatever Crouch does next, Leo won't be on his own. 'The victim's associates have been alibied, but they're still working on tracing the owner of the club. The accounts are all offshore – the directors well hidden.'

'And in the meantime,' Crouch says, 'DCs Brady and Morgan have a new theory.' He looks at Leo, and it's so obvious he wants to have another go at him, to remind him of the hours spent interviewing Yasmin, and chasing after dead ends. But all he says is, 'And *this* one might actually hold water.'

'I think so, sir.' Leo coughs, self-conscious at once again being the centre of attention. 'We've had a good result on the trophy found in the lake. The fleck of glitter retrieved from Lloyd's facial injuries is a match, so we're confident this is the weapon used in the assault.'

'The award's been in the water for a week,' Ffion says, 'but CSI have been able to recover several sets of prints. Both the Lloyds' prints are there, as you'd expect, but they also found a partial belonging to the postwoman, Ceri Jones.'

'She had a long-standing grudge against Rhys Lloyd,' Leo says, when Ffion doesn't elaborate. He glances at her, but her face gives nothing away. 'She's on her postal round till midday. We'll be waiting for her when she finishes.'

'She didn't do it,' Ffion says, when they're on their way to Cwm Coed. Other members of the team have been tasked with establishing a timeline for Ceri Jones on the night of the party, piecing together the information they have from witness statements and photographs.

'Her prints are on the weapon.'

'It's not technically the murder weapon, though, is it? Izzy Weaver said the injuries were superficial. The assault brought on a heart attack – that's what she thinks.'

Leo looks at Ffion. She's zipped into her enormous coat, and, with her hair tucked under a bobble hat, only her face is visible. 'So what are you saying? Ceri Jones didn't hit Lloyd with the trophy? Or she did, but she didn't kill him?'

'I'm saying there's an innocent explanation. I know Ceri. She's not a violent person.'

'She was bullied by Rhys Lloyd so badly she left school a year earlier than planned, and never did the art degree she'd dreamed of. Her fingerprints are on a weapon known to have been instrumental in his death.'

'It wasn't her.'

'What makes you so sure?' Leo waits, but she doesn't answer. 'Ffion, you being on this case is already a terrible idea. If arresting Ceri is too great a conflict of interest, then you should—'

'I'm staying on the job.'

Leo glances at her. Four days ago, Ffion had been told she could go back to her own force.

'Apparently she begged her DI to let her stay,' Crouch told Leo. 'I'd assume it was because you were knobbing her, only she's not blind.'

Had Ffion stayed on the case so she could interfere with evidence? Leo tugs at his seatbelt, suddenly too tight across his chest. Is that why she's so insistent about staying on it now?

They're waiting for Ceri when she pulls up outside her house. In spite of the cold, she wears shorts beneath her uniform fleece. She eyes Ffion and Leo with resignation.

'Please tell me you don't need another statement. I've had a shocker of a day – you'd think I was personally responsible for missing Christmas presents, the way people go on. Like it's my fault they—'

'Ceri.' Ffion interjects. 'We need to talk to you about something else.'

Leo waits for Ffion to make the arrest – it's her patch, her community. But when the hesitation begins to hint of reluctance he steps forward. 'Ceri Jones, you're under arrest on suspicion of murder. You do not have to say anything, but it may harm your defence if you do not mention, when questioned, something which you later rely on in court. Anything you do say may be given in evidence.'

'What?' Ceri gives a burst of laughter. 'Is this some kind of joke?' She looks at Ffion. 'Ffi?'

'No joke, Ceri,' Ffion says shortly.

They travel to custody in silence, Ceri white and shaken in the back seat. A good actor? Leo thinks. Or simply shocked to have been caught? Ffion stares out of the window, her entire body radiating *fuck off* vibes. There are so many different women there, Leo thinks. The caustic, spiky Ffion, making him laugh with one-liners and piss-taking. Yesterday's open, raw Ffion, in so much pain it made Leo's heart hurt. Today's shut down, don't-talk-to-me Ffion. And, of course, the Ffion he'd met on New Year's Eve. The caution-to-the-winds, don't-care-who's-watching woman, who had kissed him as though they were the last two people standing, and curled into his outstretched arm when they finally fell asleep.

Leo likes them all.

He looks out at the road ahead, the snow becoming lighter as they leave Wales. Maybe when they aren't working together. Maybe they could have a drink, or something.

Maybe.

Because Ffion has a stronger motive for killing Rhys Lloyd than anyone else in Cwm Coed, and, for all that Leo wants to spend time with her, the detective in him can't rule out the possibility that she was involved. Ffion was in a bar with Leo at the time of Lloyd's death, but she'd been with the man just hours before. Had she set something in motion that resulted in his death?

If she had, it makes Leo her alibi.

In custody, Ceri listens to her legal rights in silence, the only sign of stress two vertical lines in the centre of her brow, then she asks for a solicitor. It's late when they finally get into interview.

'Tell me about your relationship with Rhys Lloyd,' Leo starts.

Ceri shrugs. 'We went to the same school. Like everyone did.' She looks at Ffion. 'You know all this – this is such bullshit.'

'Were you friends?'

Ceri exhales noisily. 'You know we weren't.' She places her hands flat on the table, as though bracing herself, then looks up. 'He bullied me, alright? No doubt you've heard it from various people in the village, so you might as well hear it from me too. From the minute I started at secondary school he made my life a living hell. He wrote *dyke* on my locker. He sent notes to girls in my year, with my name at the bottom. He stuck a picture of my head on to porn. He and his mates threatened to rape me to "turn me straight".' Ceri's voice is flat and hard.

'That must have been awful.' Ffion puts a hand on the table then pulls back, as though she'd been about to reach across, before realising where they were.

'There was this girl I fancied.' Ceri stares at the table. 'I don't know how he knew, but he did. He sent me a message, making out it was her, and she wanted to meet up.' She breaks off, shaking her head at her naïvety.

'In Rhys's music studio,' Ffion says flatly, but Ceri frowns.

'I'd never have gone there. She said she'd meet me at the park, by the kids' play area. She told me things she . . .' Ceri flushes. 'Things she wanted to do with me.'

'Rhys was waiting for you, wasn't he?' Ffion says. Her voice is cold and Leo shifts in his seat. She shouldn't be here. If they charge Ceri with Lloyd's murder, the defence will look for every possible chink in the prosecution's armour. Even if what Lloyd did to Ffion never comes to light – even if she has nothing to do with his death – she's just too close to the case. How can she possibly be objective?

'Him and a bunch of his mates. I was all dressed up and . . .' Ceri brushes angry tears from her eyes. 'So yeah. I hated him. Wouldn't you?'

'How did you feel about Rhys when he returned to Cwm Coed? When he built The Shore?'

'I hated him even more.'

Ceri's solicitor coughs. She looks at him, then shrugs. 'I'm not going to lie. Yes, it was a long time ago; yes, he was a kid, but he made my life a misery. I lost all my confidence – I wouldn't even go to the shops, in the end, in case I saw him. I didn't have any friends, I didn't go to art college . . . he ruined my life, and there he was, waltzing back into the village with all the trappings of success. I hated him for it.'

'Enough to kill him?' Leo says.

Ceri meets his gaze. 'No.'

'Do you know what this is?' Ffion lifts the Rising Star award from the floor and places it on the table. It's in a clear evidence bag, sealed with a red plastic tag.

'It's a trophy.'

'Have you ever seen it before?'

'No.' Ceri's eyes flick to the side. 'Maybe. I don't know.'

'Which is it?' Leo says. 'No, maybe, or you don't know?'

'I don't know!' She blinks rapidly, pressing her hands against her thighs.

'It has your fingerprints on it.'

'I didn't kill him.'

'The thing is, Ceri,' Ffion says, 'Yasmin Lloyd gave tours to almost everyone at the party. No one remembers seeing you on one of them. So if you weren't given a tour, why are your fingerprints on this award?'

There's a long silence.

'Okay.' Ceri lets out a long breath. 'I went up to Rhys's office to deliver his post.'

'Funny place to put a letterbox,' Ffion says.

Ceri ignores the sarcasm. 'If you must know, he tricked me. Again. He made me think he was out – talking to me on the phone, through the intercom. I put the parcel in his office and then I saw – I realised he—' She swallows and looks at the table. 'He was in the bedroom. Pretty much naked, watching me walk around his office.'

Next to him, Leo feels Ffion tense. 'What did you do?'

'Got the fuck out of there, of course.'

'That must have been upsetting,' Ffion says, her voice level. 'It must have brought everything back: all the bullying at school, all that emotion, all that anger.'

Ceri holds Ffion's gaze. 'I didn't kill him.'

'Who did, then?' Ffion says.

The solicitor interjects. 'Officer, you're not seriously asking my client to do your job for you?'

But Ceri shrugs. 'Spoiled for choice, aren't you? Yasmin's a money-grabbing bitch, for a start. It wouldn't surprise me if she killed him for his money. Do you know what she gave me as a Christmas tip? A used Primark card with three pounds forty-nine left on it.'

'If bad tipping makes you a murderer, half the population would be in prison,' Leo says, earning himself a frown from Ceri's solicitor.

'Chuck a stone in the lake,' Ceri says, 'and the splash'll hit someone who's glad Rhys Lloyd is dead. I don't care what they said when he was alive. Even Steffan was mouthing off about him, and he was sucking up to Rhys something chronic all last year.'

'Mouthing off?' Ffion says. 'When was this?'

'It was the day Rhys gave me the party invites to hand out – like I was his personal butler, for fuck's sake.' She screws up her face. 'Day after Boxing Day, I think. I left them in the pub and Steff was off on one about Rhys.'

Leo leans forward. 'Saying what?'

'He was talking to Huw. Ellis. Ffi's—'

'Huw Ellis,' Leo says quickly. 'The builder, right?'

'They were saying something about instructors, and boat hire. I wasn't really listening, I just wanted to get home and start painting, but I remember thinking Steff sounded really pissed off.' Ceri leans back in her chair. 'You want my advice? You need to look closer at Steffan Edwards.'

FORTY-THREE

CHRISTMAS EVE | FELICIA

This is going to be the worst Christmas ever. Last year Mum said they were too young to go to the pub with their mates, even though everyone was going, and Barnaby in Year Eleven had sorted them all out with fake IDs.

'Next year,' Yasmin said. 'Sixteen isn't so bad.'

But where are they? At the bloody Shore. A fat lot of good Barnaby's ID is now.

'Seren says we could go to the pub in the village.' Tabby looks at the message on her phone, sounding out the Welsh. 'Y Llew . . . how do you say the double "l" again?'

'Who the fuck cares?' Felicia thumps her pillow. 'Esme's dad's put five hundred quid behind the bar in a private room at the Frog & Hammer, and the whole of Year Eleven's going.'

'You hate Esme.'

'That's not the point!'

Yasmin pops her head around the door. 'Darling, where's that Primark card Auntie Laura sent you for your birthday? The post lady's here.'

Felicia picks it out of the mess on her bedside table. 'Here. Why?'

'Can I have it? I'll pay you back.'

'I don't know what's left on it.'

'It'll do.' Yasmin grabs the card and runs downstairs.

'Let's hang out with Seren,' Tabby says. 'We can ask Caleb too.'

Felicia gives her sister a sly grin. 'That's literally the only reason you want to go, isn't it? Because you want to shag Caleb.'

'I do not want to shag Caleb.'

'You do.'

Tabby grins. 'Well, maybe a bit. Come on, let's get ready. We can flirt with the Young Farmers.' They shriek with laughter at the idea. There's less talent in Cwm Coed than there is in their school, and that's saying something. 'I'll tell Seren she has to dress up.' Tabby's fingers fly over the keyboard.

'You know she won't.' Seren spent the whole summer in the same pair of shorts, and half-term in the same pair of jeans. 'She only puts make-up on when she's working for Dad.' Felicia flutters her eyelashes and Tabby screams.

'Rank! God, I feel sick, now.'

Two hours later, they're ready and they look fucking fantastic. They've straightened their hair, so it falls in shiny curtains either side of their contoured cheeks, and outlined their lips into perfect pouts. They've posted a million selfies on Instagram and muted Esme's Story tagging the Frog & Hammer.

'Bit much for a kitchen supper, isn't it?' Rhys says, when they trip downstairs. Literally, in the case of Felicia, who's borrowed Yasmin's heels.

'We're going out,' Tabby says.

'No, you're not.' Yasmin's in tight black jeans and sneakers, her sparkly top the only festive concession. 'We're having supper with the Charltons.'

'But—'

'No buts. It'll be nice.'

It isn't fucking nice. Neither Felicia nor Tabby are the sort to throw tantrums – they know exactly how many presents are under the tree right now, and they also know their parents aren't above removing a few to teach them a lesson – but both girls are expert sulkers. They give monosyllabic answers until the adults give up.

Felicia messages Tabby. Pub afterwards? Seren says there's always a lock-in. Her sister nods furiously. Woody and Hester are being brattish, as usual. Blythe got them to sing 'Jingle Bells' and they literally did it ten times without stopping. Now they're chasing each other around the table.

'If you don't go to sleep,' Yasmin says, 'Father Christmas won't come.'

Felicia and Tabby exchange glances. Mum's not taking any shit tonight, they can tell from her voice.

Blythe puts a hand on her husband's arm. 'Jonty, darling, could you put the children down? You're so much better at it than I am.'

Jonty swoops down on the brats, who could be crying or laughing, Felicia can't tell. 'Come on, you horrors.'

Mum's gazing at Jonty as if he's the fucking Messiah. It's still going on, then. She wants to cry, or hit something, or run around screaming, like Woody and Hester.

Felicia had found a text from Jonty on her mum's phone, back in the summer. I can't wait to fuck you. She'd deleted it, then dropped the phone as if it had bitten her, shaking with fear and confusion. What had she just read? She'd wanted to tell Tabby, but talking about it would make it real, and Felicia didn't want it to be real. Maybe it was a mistake. Maybe Jonty thought he was texting someone else.

Felicia had watched her parents closely over the next few days, but they seemed the same as they'd always been. Not lovey-dovey – which would be gross – but they didn't seem to hate each other, either. Mum wasn't acting as if she was having an affair. Three days later Felicia snuck Yasmin's phone out of the bedroom, when her mum was in the shower.

You taste as good as I imagined.

Felicia thought she was going to be sick. Jonty Charlton and Mum. Mum and Jonty Charlton. It was disgusting. And poor Dad! He'd be devastated if he knew – he mustn't ever, ever find out. Felicia had clung to the thought that it was a one-off, or that her mum had gone temporarily insane – some sort of menopausal crisis – and that everything would go back to normal soon. In the meantime, she'd stuck to Yasmin like glue, doing her best to make sure she was never on her own with Jonty.

There were no more texts on Yasmin's phone, after The Shore closed at the end of the summer, and Felicia could have cried with relief. But the look in Yasmin's eyes just now . . . if there isn't still something going on between them, it's obvious she wants there to be.

'Why can't we be at the party?' Tabby is saying. They're talking about New Year's Eve. Felicia's torn between not wanting to be anywhere near the Charltons, and knowing it's going to be an awesome party. Like, an Instagram *gold* kind of party.

'I wouldn't have thought you'd want to hang out with us old people,' Jonty says. Felicia glowers at him. He's not wrong there. She imagines the vibe, right now, at the Frog & Hammer, and wants to be there so badly she can almost taste the Porn Star martinis she'd be ordering with Esme's dad's money. Her mum starts arguing with Blythe about who's hosting the party, and Felicia just can't be fucked with any of it.

'We should invite some of the locals,' her dad is saying, and now Jonty's back from putting his kids to bed and rubbing Blythe's shoulder like he's not fucking someone else's wife. God, she doesn't know how Mum can sit there next to Dad as if nothing's wrong.

Blythe says something about having diverse representation within your friendship circle, and Felicia gives her a supportive look. Like, that's a bit of a wanky thing to say, especially when Felicia knows for a fact the only ethnic minority in Blythe's circle is her Korean masseuse, but the woman's married to a shit, so.

Felicia goes back to her phone, till Blythe claps her hands and announces some mad plan for a Christmas Day swim. 'What do you think, girls? Caleb's doing it.' Like that makes a difference.

'Yeah, whatevs,' Felicia says, as rudely as she dares.

It takes forever till Yasmin says they're allowed to leave – *and no more than half a cider!* – and it's pissing with rain as they totter the mile to the village on their stupid shoes. Seren's already in the pub, a round of Cheeky Vimtos squashed on the window-sill, where she's carved out a space. Felicia's coat steams in the warmth of the pub.

'Happy Christmas!' Seren's eyes are shining. 'How is everyone? How's your dad?'

God. Felicia can't even. She downs her drink and slams it down on the windowsill. 'Catch up, lightweights. I want to get fucked.'

They can't get fucked, because the barman lets them have two drinks each, then leans over and says, *Don't push your luck, kids.* Seren shrugs and says she's knackered anyway, so Tabby and Felicia wind up walking home even before last orders.

'What a shit Christmas,' Felicia says, as they reach the drive leading to The Shore.

Tabby takes off her shoes and walks barefoot on the icy tarmac. 'I tore a corner of wrapping paper off those square boxes under the tree – they've got us AirPods.'

'Cool.' Felicia sighs.

As they reach the front door of number five, they hear raised voices. Felicia feels her stomach pitch. *Dad's found out.* She opens the front door and, in tacit agreement, they creep into the hall and listen.

'I can't believe you would do that!' Yasmin is saying. Felicia frowns. This is all wrong. Dad's the one who should be saying that. 'And to *brag* about it to me, as though I'd be impressed!'

'You were impressed enough when you thought Jonty had "the magic touch".'

Felicia thinks she might be sick.

'Because I had no idea what he was really doing – what *you've* been doing. It's – it's criminal!'

'You're overreacting,' Rhys snaps. 'It didn't do her any harm.'

'How do you know? It could be in her system – a build-up, over the years, and one day it'll come out—'

Rhys gives a bark of laughter. 'Sixteen years later?'

Felicia claps her hand over her mouth, her eyes wide.

'They're talking about us,' Tabby whispers.

'One of us,' Felicia adds, darkly.

'And now you're risking the life of those two precious babies – it's beyond awful. I shall tell Blythe, I can't keep it from her.'

Felicia is lost. What has Dad done, and what does it have to do with Woody and Hester?

'Oh, no – you're not pinning that on me,' Rhys says. 'That's all Jonty's doing.'

'You gave him the sleeping pills! You gave him the idea!'

'I simply told him it had worked for us when Felicia was a nightmare going down—'

'For *you*, Rhys! You drugged my baby for three years without my knowledge. You could have killed her!'

Tabby turns to Felicia in horror, but Felicia's eyes have filled with tears and she runs up the stairs. Her mother's affair with Jonty is the least of her worries, now that she knows what Rhys has done. It's child abuse, that's what it is.

Her dad is a monster.

FORTY-FOUR

JANUARY 8TH | FFION

'Still think she did it?' Ffion turns to Leo as they pull out of Ceri's street.

'I don't know what to think any more.' Leo manoeuvres slowly through the snow. The weather's worsening, and, as they drove into Cwm Coed earlier, flurries of white had whirled against the windscreen, bright white against the darkening sky.

Burned from Yasmin Lloyd's fruitless hours in custody, Crouch had refused to allow them to hold Ceri a minute longer than they had to.

'Stick bail conditions on her and let her go,' he said, and Leo and Ffion had had no choice but to comply. Ceri had arrived at the party at eight and was gone at ten-thirty, when – she said – she'd *had enough of all the bullshit*. They'd bailed her for two weeks; enough time to seek advice from the Crown Prosecution Service, and to follow up the lines of enquiry generated by Ceri's interview – including the conversation she'd overheard between Huw and Steffan.

'She could have gone back to the party,' Leo says now. 'She says she was tucked up in bed by eleven, but there's no partner to corroborate that.'

'She's never—' Ffion stops herself. She was going to say that

318

Ceri had never had a girlfriend; thoughtlessly repeating what she'd heard others say. But isn't that precisely what Ffion hates about Cwm Coed? The gossip that becomes folklore, the cap made to fit you so well you wear it your whole life.

Ffion *Wyllt*.

Rhys Lloyd turned an entire generation against Ceri. Was it any wonder she felt she had to keep her love life private?

Ffion's phone rings and she frowns at the screen. She can count on one hand the number of times Seren has rung her. The younger girl prefers to WhatsApp and, even then, only ever when she wants something. A late pass, when Mam's said home by nine. A lend of Ffion's jeans.

Ffion answers. '*Ti'n iawn?*'

There's no reply. Ffion moves the phone away from her ear, checking the line hasn't dropped.

'Seren?'

She hears a jagged intake of breath; a rough, angry sob. And then, finally, Seren speaks.

'Tell me it's not true.'

Ffion's heart splinters. Her whole world crashes about her feet. 'What?' she whispers, even though what else could it be?

Seren's voice rises, hysterical, pleading. 'Tell me it isn't true!'

'What?' Ffion says desperately, because if there's a chance Seren hasn't worked it out, Ffion won't be the one to—

'You're my mam, aren't you?'

Years ago, Ffion had sometimes allowed herself to imagine what it would feel like to be called *Mam*. She would slip into a parallel world – one in which Ffion had been older, able to keep her baby – and she would picture them at the park, or walking to school, Seren's hand in Ffion's.

Mam.

She'd never once imagined it sounding like this.

'Seren, where are you? We need to talk.' Ffion tries to stay calm, knowing Seren feels out of control; hoping she sounds like the mam she's never had the chance to be.

'You've had sixteen years to talk, and instead you've lied to me!'

Leo puts a hand on Ffion's arm, but she shrugs him off, fighting to focus.

'You had me, and you gave me to Mam like I was *nothing!*'

Ffion stares out at the whirling snow. 'How did you find out?'

'Caleb nicked a photo from Glynis. He thought it was funny – said the girl in it looked like me.'

Ffion closes her eyes. She wants to press pause; to rewind. She wants to find Caleb and shake him, ask what the fuck he thinks he's doing, interfering in something he knows nothing about.

'It's you. With Rhys.' Seren's crying. 'And I kept thinking about something Mrs Huxley said, that Felicia and Tabby and me, we could be sisters, and—' Her voice rises to a shout, hysterical and pleading. 'He's got his arm around you in the photo, Ffi. And you're looking up at him like—' Noisy sobs fill the phone.

Ffion remembers that photo. One of the photography GCSE students had covered the camp as part of their coursework; taken a load of pictures of the workshops, the show, the party. There'd been some piss-taking afterwards, about how, wherever Rhys was, Ffion wouldn't be far away. Ffion had wanted to cry. *It was the other way around*, she'd wanted to say. *Everywhere I went, there he was.*

Did any of the teachers see the photos of the party? Or were they too concerned with the workshop, the performances? They didn't look beneath the surface, to where Ffion was gasping for breath.

'It's all true, what everyone says, then.' Seren's suddenly harsh. 'Ffion *Wyllt*.'

'Please—'

'And with—' Seren falters, sobs slicing into her words. 'With *him*!'

'Seren, let me explain.'

'I can't believe Rhys Lloyd is my dad.' She's crying so hard Ffion can hardly make out what she's saying. *Disgusting . . . Old . . . How could you . . .*

'*Wear the dress*, he said!' She's getting hysterical, dragging gulps of air between each word screamed down the phone. Ffion's trying to speak, but everything she says prompts another volley of abuse from Seren. Leo's pulled over, and now he's reaching into the back seat, unzipping his folder and rifling through papers, and Ffion glares at him. Can he not just sit still for two minutes? Surely he can see how important this is?

'I hate you.'

'Seren, please—'

'And I hate him!'

'Where are you? I'll come to—'

'I wish I was dead.'

'Don't say—' But the line's quiet. Seren has gone.

Ffion drops the phone in her lap and screws her fists into her hair, pulling her head on to her knees and pressing a moan into her jeans. She feels Leo rub her back, and this time she doesn't shrug him off. She makes herself breathe – in and out, in and out – and then she releases her grip on her hair and sits up.

'She knows.'

'I heard. Sorry,' Leo adds, apologetically.

'It'll be okay.' Ffion gives herself a pep talk she doesn't believe. 'Seren's got my temper – she'll calm down.'

'Ffion.'

'It's a huge shock, but I'll call Mam, and—'

'Ffi.'

She looks at Leo. His face is creased in concern, and he's still looking in that bloody folder. 'What?'

'"Wear the dress",' Leo says.

'You what?'

'That's what Seren said, right? "Wear the dress". Ffion, I think—' He breaks off, taking his pen from his jacket pocket and marking several lines on the page he was looking at. He hands it wordlessly to Ffion.

It's a printout of text messages, sent to and from Rhys Lloyd's mobile phone in the week before he died. Ffion reads the first line Leo has marked.

I can't stop thinking about you.

She reads down the page.

You'll look amazing, whatever you wear.

The final text was sent on New Year's Eve.

Wear the dress.

The phone number Rhys was texting is Seren's.

FORTY-FIVE

CHRISTMAS EVE | BOBBY

The airport was rammed, but now they've left London the roads are empty and the McLaren gobbles up the miles. For once, Bobby and Ashleigh flew home first class. Business class is more than comfortable enough for Bobby, but Ashleigh begged, and Bobby's a soft touch. It would at least give him some decent kip before the long drive to The Shore, he reasoned, handing over his credit card.

He had reckoned without Ashleigh, who insisted on 'banking' images for her social media channels, requiring several changes of outfits so she could make out they take even more luxury trips than they already do.

'Can I borrow your seat?' Ashleigh said, to a bemused man in the middle row.

'Ash!' Bobby was appalled. 'You stay where you are, mate.'

'It'll look well dodge, if I'm always in the same seat.'

The whole thing is *well dodge*, if you ask Bobby. He's not daft – he knows social media isn't real life, and he's not averse to sharing shots of his car from time to time – but Ashleigh's dedication to her craft is at once impressive and terrifying. Every meal is 'styled up' before they can touch it; every hotel room shot from a dozen different angles before Bobby's allowed to unpack.

As he trotted after Ashleigh to the aeroplane bathroom to take a photo of her in the shower, he thought he might just as well unzip his balls and pop them in her washbag.

Bobby has been a celebrity, of sorts, for most of his adult life. Soon after he retired from the ring he was booked to do a walk-on in *Carlton Sands*, and he proved such a hit with the viewers that they wrote him into the series. But celeb life has never sat comfortably with a man who would rather have a pint in a spit-and-sawdust pub than drink mojitos in whatever trendy bar the Instagrammers have deemed worthy of their grids.

As they leave the motorway and head for north Wales, Bobby feels the pressure peeling off him. He loves being at The Shore. He loves messing about on the lake, and climbing mountains, and exploring the forest trails with a backpack of snacks and a cheeky beer. He loves mooching into the village, where the only cameras are the kids with iPhones, more interested in his car than in him. The place reminds him of childhood holidays, when his nan packed him and his brother off with sandwiches and a bucket and spade, and instructions not to come back till tea.

With nothing to photograph, Ashleigh has pushed back her seat and is lying with her mouth open, a thin strand of drool reaching to her shoulder. Bobby imagines posting it to her grid. *Hashtag no filter*. Brilliant.

It's the early hours of Christmas Day when they arrive at The Shore. Ashleigh peers blearily through the windscreen. 'It looks even shittier than I remembered.'

'You didn't have to come. You could have gone to your parents.'

Ashleigh pulls on her trainers. 'And mess up the plan?'

The plan. Bobby is sick to the back teeth of the fucking plan. For a simple man, who likes simple pleasures, Bobby's life has got a bit too complicated for his liking. Behind the row of lodges the lake is as black as the sky. A single light is still on at the Lloyds' place. 'I don't think I can go through with this,' he says, surprising himself with his sudden honesty.

There's a beat, then Ashleigh gets out of the car. 'You don't have a choice.'

On Christmas Day, Bobby wakes up early. He pads downstairs, makes himself a coffee and pulls on his coat, then walks into the woods to call Mia. Mia is the best thing ever to have happened to him. Better than boxing, better than acting, and better – so, so much better – than Ashleigh. He would feel bad for cheating on his wife, if it weren't for her habit of shagging Premier League footballers whenever she could get away with it.

'Merry Christmas, gorgeous.' Out on the lake a bird dives for a fish, emerging with a flash of silver in its beak.

'Did Santa come?' Mia sounds sleepy.

Bobby gives a dirty laugh. 'He will later.'

'I can't wait.'

They'd been careful, in the summer, meeting outside, or in pubs miles from anywhere. Mia's neighbours were the net-curtain-twitching type, and all it would take would be an anonymous tip-off to the papers for Bobby's extramarital affair to be common knowledge. Bobby doesn't give a fuck, but Ashleigh would go apeshit. *What about the plan?*

Meeting outside was all well and good in the summer, but December, in north Wales? He'd be lucky to coax Little Bobby out from his boxers. Tonight, Mia will leave her front door on the latch and Bobby will slip in, and then – well. Slip in.

Just before eleven, the Christmas Day swimmers start to congregate. Bobby and Ashleigh have put their differences aside, helped in no small part by the Gucci handbag Bobby wrapped up for Ashleigh.

'Oh, bae, I love it!' She threw her arms around him. A second later, he heard the *click* of her camera phone, and knew the moment would be online within minutes. *When your man knows exactly how to make you happy . . .*

Now, the air is clear and fresh, the deck glistening with frost. Bobby puts a steadying arm on Dee's elbow as her stick slips on the wood.

'Don't you worry about me, dear,' she tells him. 'I'm tough as old boots.' She's carrying a proper camera. Discounting the paps, Bobby can't remember the last time he saw one – it's practically vintage. He poses for her, a cheesy circus strongman pose which makes her laugh.

'Now mine, bae.' Ashleigh's in the fur coat Bobby gave her for her birthday. It's fake, of course, although it cost as much as a real one. She's just spent an hour doing her hair, so Bobby knows there's no chance of getting her in the water.

'Merry Christmas!' Clemmie's in her wetsuit, looking as if she means business. Bobby probably looks a right dick in his festive boxers, but he never minds playing for laughs. He takes a slurp of his Bloody Mary.

'Stand there a sec.' Ashleigh waves her phone at him.

'Not today, yeah?' He puts down his glass, but she frowns.

'With the drink. There. Lean against the railing and—'

'Can we have one day without thinking about bloody Instagram?'

Ashleigh glares at him, then walks away. Bobby calls after her. 'I thought you were going to film the swim?'

'What's the point, if we're not going to put it online?'

Plan or no plan, Bobby isn't sure how much more of this he can take.

The Lloyds have dressing gowns over their swimsuits. It's the first time Bobby's seen Rhys since Mia told him what the bastard did in October, and his jaw tightens. Yasmin's muttering something at Rhys, who glowers. Has Yasmin found out her husband made a pass at Mia? Even the twins seem subdued – red-eyed and sullen. Something's definitely up with the whole family.

Mia had made Bobby promise not to touch Rhys. 'I can't have him badmouthing me around town,' she said. 'I need the work.'

Bobby wanted to tell her to send her bills to him, but he knew exactly what she'd say. Mia's no freeloader – not like Ashleigh – and he loves her even more for it.

Dee's getting all the swimmers together. 'Is everyone ready? Say cheese!' Bobby sees Yasmin lean into her husband for the photo, then practically push him away the second the shutter has clicked. Maybe Bobby can keep his promise to Mia after all – it looks as if Yasmin's got it covered.

Bobby climbs down the ladder to the pontoon between the decks. For a few seconds it's just him and Rhys, and although Bobby's fists are bunched tight, he's thinking, *Just leave it, Stafford. He's not worth it.* But then Rhys leans in, a sly smile on his face, and says, 'Shame I got interrupted – she was well up for it,' and Bobby has him by the throat before he knows what he's doing.

'I'm going to fucking kill you.'

'What a start to Christmas Day!' Clemmie's arse appears above them, and Bobby releases his grip. Rhys rubs at his throat. Clemmie looks nervously at each of them, and, just when Bobby thinks she's about to confront them, Caleb jumps down and runs along the pontoon, and the others are crowding around them, and it's time to get in the water.

Bobby jokes around with the others, as he splashes about in the icy water, but he never once takes his eyes off Rhys.

One way or another, he's going to make him pay.

FORTY-SIX

JANUARY 8TH | LEO

'I have to find her.' Ffion grapples for the door handle, but Leo's already started the engine again. It'll be quicker in the car. Ffion's dialling Seren's number, over and over, the tinny sound ringing out until Seren's voicemail kicks in. It's impossible to see through the snow now, the windscreen wipers working uselessly against the blizzard.

'Call me back. Please, Seren. It's important.' Ffion's dry-eyed, wrung out by emotion but back in control. She ends the call, spinning her contacts to land on *Home*. 'Pick up, pick up,' she mutters. Leo puts the car in gear and begins moving slowly towards the centre of the village. If Seren's at home, Ffion will want to go to her, and if she isn't . . . well, they won't find her here. 'Mam? It's me. Is Seren there?'

Ffion's long exhalation is all the answer Leo needs.

'Do you know where she is?' Leo hears the rise and fall of Elen's voice at the other end of the phone as he drives through Cwm Coed, crawling in second gear to scan the doorways, the side streets. Dusk is falling – the shops closed – and few people are braving the weather. Snow has swallowed the pavements, the high street a sheet of white from one row of shops to the opposite one. The air is a blur of furious white.

'She knows, Mam.'

Leo brings the car to a standstill, half wondering if he should get out and leave Ffion and Elen to talk. Ffion closes her eyes, but the pain on her face is still evident, and Leo feels like an intruder. The silence stretches out, and Leo unclips his seatbelt, but, before he can move, Ffion grips his hand.

'Yup. I'll look there. I know.' Ffion's opened her eyes, her answers now clipped and curt. 'It's fine. I know. Okay, then.' This is Ffion Morgan, police officer, not Ffion, the daughter. Ffion, the mother. The only indication of her distress is the pain in Leo's hand, as Ffion squeezes it.

Ffion takes the phone from her ear, releasing his hand at the same time. Leo surreptitiously flexes his knuckles. 'Mam hasn't seen her since lunchtime. Seren isn't answering calls from her, either.' She lets out a shaky breath. 'I can't tell Mam about the texts, about Rhys being the one who . . . Not over the phone.'

'What about friends?'

'I only know where two of them live – Siân and Efa – and I don't even know if they hang out much any more.'

'It's worth a shot.'

Neither girl has seen Seren since before Christmas, and when Ffion asks Efa to call Seren's mobile, hoping she'll at least accept a call from a friend, it's switched off.

'Do you want to call it in?' Leo says, when Ffion has battled her way back to the car.

'She's sixteen, she's been missing for – what – less than an hour? You know as well as I do how that'll be graded.'

'Any history of mental health problems?' Leo hates asking, but Ffion shakes her head. 'Self-harm?'

'Not that she's disclosed to me.' Ffion frowns, scrolling through her contacts again in search of someone – anyone – to try. No one looking at Ffion now, Leo thinks, would know Seren was her daughter. It's as though there's a series of doors inside her head, each one locking away one part of her life and enabling her to function in another.

They loop back on to the high street, their previous tyre tracks already consumed by the storm. Ffion's window is open and she calls uselessly into the flurry of snow that enters the car. 'Seren!'

A movement catches Leo's eye – someone standing in an open doorway, one arm up against the blizzard. Glynis Lloyd.

He pulls up by the hardware shop; winds down his own window. Glynis is in her shop coat, a thick cardigan pulled hastily around her shoulders, slippers on her feet. Her face is etched with worry.

'Is everything alright?' Leo says. She shakes her head, pointing to her ear, and he shouts it again, above the noise of the blizzard.

'I saw your car from upstairs. I thought . . .' Glynis seems to run out of strength, leaning against the doorpost.

'We haven't charged anyone with Rhys's murder yet,' Leo says, 'if that's what you were hoping.'

Glynis gives a small nod, her lips tight. 'People are saying you arrested Ceri.'

'A woman is helping us with our enq—' Leo stops. What is it Ffion calls him? *Mr Corporate Speak*. 'She's been bailed,' he tells Glynis.

'I think . . .' Glynis looks close to tears. 'I think you've got the wrong person. I know what Rhys did to her, but that was years ago, they were just kids.'

'Have you seen Seren?' Ffion leans across Leo.

At the sight of her, something crosses Glynis's face, and Leo wonders if Ffion was right. Had Glynis known, deep down, what her son was like? Had she turned a blind eye to what lay beneath her son's talents and success?

'Not me,' Glynis says. 'But I was just on the phone to Llinos. She saw Seren walking towards the boathouse an hour or so ago. Said she had a bottle of vodka with her. Is everything—'

But Leo is already driving away, too fast for the snow, his tyres losing traction as they turn the corner at the end of the high street.

The boathouse is in darkness, bar a single light in the office, and Leo shines a torch around the yard, checking for movement. There are several boats on trailers, some with cabins they should check. At least Seren would be warm and dry, if she's climbed into one of them.

'Seren!' Ffion hammers on the door to the boathouse. There's no sound from within, but, when she pulls on the huge sliding door, it's unlocked. She drags it open and Leo brings up the lights with a flicker that feels like lightning.

'Seren?' Leo walks through the boathouse. The office is in the corner of the vast space, a light showing through the obscured glass pane in the door. Inside, Steffan's slumped at his desk. Leo shakes his shoulder and the man groans.

'Has Seren been here?' Ffion says. There's no response from Steffan. Leo shakes him again.

'Gerroff!' Steffan pushes himself upright, blinking at the intruders in his office. He scowls at Leo, then slowly focuses on Ffion. He jabs a finger towards her. 'Where's my boat?'

'He's out of it,' Leo says.

'What boat?'

'You took my boat!' Steffan gets unsteadily to his feet then frowns again. 'No, not my boat. Fixing a boat. You stole it!' The words slide into each other, making no sense, except Steffan seems quite certain Ffion has—

Leo looks at Ffion, as realisation dawns on them simultaneously. 'Steffan.' Ffion speaks slowly. 'Did Seren take a boat out?'

The boatman peers at her then nods gracelessly. 'Not you. The other one.'

Leo looks out towards the lake. The blizzard's too dense to see the water, but the sound of the waves makes him shiver. 'She wouldn't have tried to go out in this, would she?'

Ffion's mouth is set tight. 'She'll be okay.' Leo isn't sure who she's trying to convince. 'She's been sailing since she was six. She knows the lake like the back of her hand, even in bad weather. She'll have got off the water when she realised how bad it was getting.'

Steffan bangs a hand down on the desk. He's swaying, leaning on the desk and waving his free arm around as though conducting the words he's now trying to force from his mouth. 'Angharad,' he manages. 'Angharad's boat.'

'That's okay,' Ffion says. 'She knows her way around a lugger.'

'No!' Steffan shouts. He bangs the desk again. 'Not fixed yet.'

The colour drains from Ffion's face.

'Boat broken.' Steffan sways. 'No time to fix it. Not been well.' He slumps back into his chair and shrugs. 'S'got a hole in the hull.'

FORTY-SEVEN

DECEMBER 27TH | STEFFAN

As the year draws to an end, Steffan Edwards is feeling optimistic. He's spent much of the past month putting together a business plan for the boathouse, in order to apply for a bank loan. No sooner does the money hit his account than it's out again, paying for much needed repairs on the boathouse, as well as the additional kit needed to accommodate The Shore's owners.

The second round of building is due to start at the end of January, with another ten lodges built by Easter, and the whole resort finished in time for next summer. Steffan's head is buzzing with possibilities. He's bought a giant Zorbing ball for the kids, and paid a deposit on a water trampoline. He wonders about more jet-skis. Bobby Stafford rented one for the entire summer this year, and other owners might do the same. Steffan hovers over a listing on eBay: would an inflatable obstacle course be too much? He has already spent such a lot of money, but you have to speculate to accumulate.

Steffan's even given the boathouse a lick of paint. He always touches up the woodwork each winter, but this year he's transformed the place. Instead of the usual reddish brown wood stain, he's painted the boards a deep blue, the window and door frames a buttery cream. If you stand by the jetty now, and look across the water, the boathouse and The Shore balance each other perfectly.

The final touch is Steff's new website. He's never felt the need for a website before, but even he can see that his Facebook page – where posts about kayaking are interspersed with football predictions and ice bucket challenges – is a far cry from what the residents of The Shore are used to. So he's paid a company in Manchester an obscene amount of money for a slick, mobile-responsive website, which is so beautiful he keeps looking at it.

'What do you think?' Steff shows his phone to Huw. He popped into the pub, ostensibly to have a celebratory sandwich, but mostly to show off his website to anyone who stands still long enough.

Huw looks at the screen. 'Fair play, Steff, that's a good job, that is.'

Steffan shows him the gallery of images: a mosaic of happy holidaymakers wakeboarding, kayaking, picnicking on paddle-boards. On Steffan's website the sun is always shining, the lake always sparkling.

'You're getting ready, then?' Huw says.

Steffan, who has a mouthful of cheese and pickle, nods with vigour. He has never felt readier. There will be people viewing The Shore from early in the New Year, he's heard, seduced into buying off-plan by the flagship lodges already in place. When they look across the lake, the newly smartened boathouse will be the first thing they see. Steff pictures them – wealthy, successful, influential – picking up his leaflet with their new owner pack, making plans for their year.

Oh, do let's hire kayaks – what fun!
I've always fancied windsurfing.
The children absolutely must *have sailing lessons.*

Huw's still talking. 'Sometimes you've got to fight fire with fire, right?'

Steffan tears himself away from his imagination. 'What do you mean?'

'You don't want to be on the back foot when the water sports centre opens.'

Slowly, Steff puts down his sandwich. What water sports centre? He feels cold inside, like he's coming down with something, and now Huw's face has changed to something which looks a lot like pity.

'You didn't know.'

'Water sports centre?' A piece of bread is stuck in Steff's throat, his mouth suddenly devoid of saliva. The pub door opens, and Ceri comes in, still in her Royal Mail uniform.

'At The Shore. Discounts for lodge-owners, day memberships for visitors.' Huw picks at a beer mat, his eyes sliding away from Steffan. 'I only know because I quoted on the job. He turned me down, of course. He'll bus in a load of Eastern Europeans on the cheap.' He snorts. 'Not that I'd lay another brick till he pays me what I'm owed.'

'*Iawn?*' Ceri says.

Huw nods a greeting. 'Alright, Ceri?'

Steffan says nothing. He's thinking of his expensive website; the Zorbing ball and the trampoline. He's thinking of the hours spent refurbishing the boathouse and painting a fleet of dinghies in the colours of The Shore. 'Offering what, exactly?' His voice is strangled.

'Can I nab a bit of paper?' Ceri is saying. Behind the bar, Alun pulls a page from his order pad.

'And you've got your local trade.' Huw drains his coffee. Reaches out and claps a hand on Steff's shoulder. 'You'll be alright, mate.'

But Steffan knows it's over. How many of the Shore owners will walk to the other side of the lake to hire a boat, when it can be delivered to their deck? How many of them will care about Steff's years of sailing experience – that he knows every eddy and curve of Llyn Drych – when they can have some buff guy in a branded polo shirt sucking up to them? The locals are loyal, but they're a fraction of his business.

'With instructors?' He blinks rapidly, focusing on Ceri's pen as she scribbles on a piece of paper, because he can't trust his eyes not to water. 'Are you sure?'

'That's what Rhys said.'

'I don't understand.' Steffan's voice rises. 'I went there at the end of summer, I gave his daughters a rowing boat, for fuck's sake!' The door bangs as Ceri leaves the pub, an icy blast reaching the bar. 'Why didn't he say anything?'

Huw raises his hands, flat palms fending off Steffan's words. 'Listen, I've got to get back to work. Don't let the bastards get you down.'

How is Steffan going to pay back the bank loan? Even if he hadn't borrowed the money, invested in the promise of what he thought The Shore could offer, how can he survive another season? He's barely been able to pay his bills this year; once The Shore opens a water sports centre, Steffan's business is over. He's ruined.

He stares morosely at the bar. Ceri's left a pile of cards behind, her scribbled note on top, and he leans over to read it. *Open invitation. Free bar.* Curious, Steffan takes a card, and rage floods through him.

The residents of The Shore warmly invite the neighbours for drinks and canapés.

Drinks and fucking canapés. Rhys Lloyd will drink champagne

while he pisses on Steff's business – on the business that his father built up, that his grandfather founded. The invitation shakes in Steff's hand, the black words swirling before him. It's not enough for Lloyd to take the trade Steff could have got from The Shore; they're inviting the locals to ooh and ahh over the lodges. No doubt Lloyd'll tell them all about the water sports centre, offer them taster membership, discounts, freebies . . .

Steffan tears the invite in half, then in half again. He tears and tears until in front of him is a pile of confetti. Then he looks up. 'Pint of Purple Moose,' he says.

Alun speaks levelly. 'I think that's a bad idea, don't you?'

Steff's teeth clench hard, his fists itching for the feel of a glass, his tongue already working, waiting for the bitter taste of beer. 'A. Pint. Of. Purple. Moose,' he repeats, each word a separate sentence.

'I'll make you a coffee.'

'I don't want a fucking coffee!'

A chair scrapes behind him and Steff turns around. They're all looking at him. All of them. Gruffydd Lewis, Euros Morgan Davies. Idris fucking Evans, who gets so pissed after darts, his wife makes him sleep with the dog. All staring at him, judging him, just because he wants one fucking pint.

'Fuck you.' Steffan slams out of the pub. There are plenty of places to buy alcohol. One beer, that's all he wants.

Then he'll work out what to do about Rhys.

FORTY-EIGHT

JANUARY 8TH | FFION

Ffion slaps Steffan's face. The boatman groans, but doesn't open his eyes, and she shakes him hard by the shoulders, shouting his name.

Leo pulls her gently back. 'He's out cold.' He's holding his radio to his ear, and, as the operator responds, he walks away from the office. 'DC Leo Brady, Cheshire Major Crime. I need to report a MisPer.'

Ffion picks up Steffan's log book. The man's off his face; maybe he's confused – forgotten he's already fixed Angharad's boat. She runs her finger across the line logged against Angharad's name. *Taking on water. Damage around centreboard.* The column headed *Completion* is empty.

'Sixteen,' Leo is saying. 'Very upset. We believe she's out on Mirror Lake in a boat which may not be structurally sound.' Ffion pushes past him, looking around the boathouse, and beyond, to the yard, where boats list on stilts, waiting for repairs. Is Steffan mistaken? Could Seren have taken out a different boat? But Angharad's lugger, with its distinctive green hull and red sails, is nowhere to be seen.

'The helicopter can't take off while the weather's so bad,' Leo tells Ffion, when he's off the phone. 'Control room's contacting

Search and Rescue, but the nearest team with a boat is twenty miles away.'

Ffion's back in the office, rifling through the drawers in Steffan's desk, scanning the boards on the wall, where a handful of keys hang, each with a brown label bearing a customer's name. She shakes Steffan again – 'Where the fuck are your keys?' – but there's no response. Ffion checks his pockets.

'Does Steffan work with anyone?' Leo says. 'Maybe they could—' His radio crackles, the operator giving his call sign. Ffion finds what she was looking for: a single key attached to a large cork fob. She grabs a searchlight from the rack on the wall and runs.

'The fire service has a water rescue capability,' Leo shouts, running after her. 'They'll be here in ten minutes.'

'We don't have ten minutes!' Outside, snow as hard as hail stings Ffion's face as she runs towards the jetty. Steffan's motorboat jerks against the fenders as though the engine's already running. It's senseless calling Seren's name, but she does it anyway, the wind hurling it into the blizzard.

She'll be fine, she keeps telling herself. She'll have moored up somewhere. She might even be off the boat by now, sheltering in the woods.

Leo catches up with her on the jetty. A fierce gust almost throws him off balance, and he braces himself – knees bent – against another attempt. 'This is crazy – we have to wait for a specialist team.'

'She might die!' Ffion jumps into the motorboat, and it rocks precariously. The cockpit's open, a low windscreen the only protection from the elements, and water sloshes around the bottom of the boat. A wave breaks over the bow, crashing inside. Leo is ashen, his feet still stubbornly planted on the jetty.

'I can't . . .' His eyes close briefly, a look of intense shame on his face. 'I can't swim.'

Ffion thinks of Seren, out there in the blizzard, in an unsafe boat. She looks at Leo, fear and panic combusting into anger. 'Then don't fucking fall in.'

Leo doesn't move.

When they find Angharad's dinghy they'll need one of them in Steffan's motorboat, while the other gets Seren to safety. Ffion can't do this on her own.

She might have to.

She starts the engine, and the boat fights against the mooring lines.

Leo takes a step forward, then two back. 'I – I don't think I can.'

Just then, a sound rings out: the *pop* of a firework, audible even over the wind. Above the water, shooting high and bright into the whiteout, comes a streak of vibrant red.

Not a firework.

A distress flare.

FORTY-NINE

NEW YEAR'S EVE | 11.45 A.M. | RHYS

'I want a divorce.' Yasmin says this as she's making the bed, as casually as though she's asking for a cup of tea. Rhys looks at her in the reflection of the dressing table mirror, where he's assessing the level of grey in his hair. *Divorce?* He knew this wasn't going to blow over as easily as their usual spats – they've barely spoken since Christmas Eve – but *divorce?*

'Don't you think that's a little extreme?'

'No, Rhys.' Yasmin pummels a pillow with unnecessary force, before placing it on the bed. 'Poisoning our daughter is extreme.'

'For the hundredth time, I did not poison her!' There is an art to shouting in a whisper, and Rhys and Yasmin are experts at it. They might not agree on many things, but they have always tried to keep their arguments from the twins.

'You will agree to a divorce,' Yasmin says. 'You'll give me the house – it wouldn't be fair to expect the girls to move – and fifty per cent of your share of The Shore. Plus maintenance, of course.'

'And if I don't?'

Yasmin smooths the bedspread and contemplates it as she answers. 'I'll tell the papers what you did.' She turns to leave the room. 'I imagine that would rather undermine the good work your expensive publicity campaign's been doing.'

342

'Over my dead body,' Rhys hisses.

'Don't tempt me.'

When she's left the room, Rhys looks at himself in the mirror. If Yasmin goes to the papers, just as he's starting to claw back a profile, it'll finish him. He's done two adverts in the last three months, and there are murmurings of a West End audition. Things are finally on the up.

And what does Yasmin expect him to live on? Rhys owns fifty-one per cent of The Shore; Jonty the remaining forty-nine per cent. If Rhys signs half over to Yasmin, Jonty will become the controlling partner and Rhys'll be left with just twenty-five and a half per cent.

Over my dead body, he thinks again.

His phone pings with a message – another chivvy from Blythe on The Shore's message group. Lots to do, chaps!!!! Last night, she had sent a spreadsheet with everyone's allocated jobs, from sweeping the decks and putting up decorations, to unloading the wine and laying out the canapés. Disaster! she'd messaged, at gone midnight. The ice sculptor has let me down. Is there someone local we could use?

Rhys walks from the bedroom on to the balcony. Beneath him, the row of decking ends abruptly at the Charltons' lodge, where a vast marquee hides the organised chaos Blythe is orchestrating within.

Rhys should show his face before Corporal Blythe comes looking for him. He's had another text from Seren, and he feels the heady rush which accompanies the promise of something exciting. Their flirting's been careful. Contained. The sort of flirting you can explain away as a joke – to yourself, as much as to anyone else. The sort of flirting which could be nothing, or could be something.

Tried on the one I told you about but it's really short . . .

343

Rhys smiles at the ellipsis, inciting the response he knows she wants.

Wear the dress, he types.

Tonight could be interesting after all.

Outside, the air is crisp; the sky a bright winter's blue. A Fortnum & Mason driver's talking to Dee, who leans both hands on her stick. As Rhys approaches, the van moves away and Rhys has no choice but to walk past his neighbour.

'Good morning, Rhys.'

'Mrs Huxley.' He still finds it hard to look her in the eye; still gets the jitters at the thought of what she knows. Recently, he's found himself thinking about the girl at Number 36 – and not in the way he once thought of her. He's found himself wondering if the girl (what was her name?) really had enjoyed herself as much as he once believed she did. He's been thinking of that night – of her big eyes and her silent resistance – and he's felt something akin to contrition.

'I've just passed the triplets down by the lake,' Dee says, pleasantly enough.

Rhys frowns. 'Triplets?'

She laughs, brushing away the joke. 'Your girls, and their friend, from the village. Seren, is it? Like peas in a pod. Except for the hair, of course.' She eyes Rhys's dark hair with a pseudo-critical eye. 'No sign of red there – you're in the clear!'

She laughs again, but Rhys is only half listening. He's thinking about another redhead he once knew – a local girl, years ago. Fox-red, with curls just as wild as Seren's. He's thinking that the last time he saw her was at a party, how they'd got together and . . .

As Dee says goodbye – *time to report to Blythe for my next task!* – Rhys is doing sums in his head.

Triplets. Peas in a pod.

Blood buzzes in his ears. He stumbles away from the lodges, down to the water's edge. For a moment, he can't remember her surname – she was only ever Ffion *Wyllt* – then it comes to him. He gets out his phone, searches *Ffion Morgan*, scanning the hundreds of hits in vain. He adds *Cwm Coed* and gets a dozen hits for the local police force. He's about to try a different search term when he sees a photo attached to one of the articles. He opens it and zooms in.

Ffion Morgan is a police officer.

Rhys dimly recalls knowing this – a snippet of information shared by Glynis in her weekly round-up of *News from home*, as though Rhys really cared that Mrs Roberts, three doors down, had had a cataract op, or that the old surgery was being turned into flats. *The Morgan girl's joined the police, can you believe?*

A moment of recognition, that's all: the memory of that night as brief and as careless as a shrug. Ffion *Wyllt*. She'd been maybe seventeen or eighteen? Something like that. Older than the others, certainly. Rhys has had many comparable encounters over the years, and he assumes the women he meets are similarly promiscuous. Why else would they be so flirtatious, so willing?

Rhys looks across the water to where Cwm Coed lies, behind the band of trees. He hasn't thought about that summer for years, but slowly the memories are filtering back. Those God-awful workshops at the school, made bearable only by the flirting of half a dozen girls, competing for his attention. The celebratory party, all kids and cola, till Rhys and Ffion made an after-party of their own.

He feels a kernel of disquiet, like a fruit seed lodged in a tooth. He works at it, wanting to be free of it. He thinks of the girl at Number 36, who said yes to everything until she said no, only by then Rhys wasn't listening. He thinks of Mia, so provocative, so teasing, and yet oddly unyielding beneath his touch. Despite the cold of the day, heat spreads throughout his body, the seeping, uncomfortable sweat of a fever, of sickness, of shame.

Google only gives a switchboard number for North Wales Police, but as Rhys searches further he finds Ffion's details on an old community Facebook group. He calls the mobile before he can change his mind. He has to know.

'Detective Constable Ffion Morgan.'

Rhys hasn't planned what to say. His words dry up, his mouth working uselessly, and she speaks again, irritation in her voice.

'Hello? Who is this?'

'It's Rhys,' he manages. 'Lloyd.'

There's a tiny sound on the other end of the phone. A silence, then: 'What do you want?'

Rhys can hardly hear her. He searches for the right words. 'Did we – were you . . .' *Peas in a pod*, Dee said. But she couldn't – it couldn't . . . He takes a deep breath and tries again. 'This is crazy, but is Seren—'

Ffion hangs up.

Rhys feels a pain in his chest so violent he wonders if he's having a heart attack. Nausea rises in his gullet, acrid and intense, and he lurches to the edge of the lake, hands on his knees, face reflected in the glassy water. He thinks of the flirting in his study, as Seren helped with his post. He thinks of the text messages they've batted back and forth.

Wear the dress.

Rhys vomits into the water, acrid bile stinging his throat. He wipes his mouth with the back of his hand, takes out his phone and swipes blurrily at the screen, deleting the messages and wishing he could delete his thoughts as easily.

He half walks, half runs back home, skirting the Charltons' lodge, where the front door is wide open. He can see Yasmin, and a pile of balloons; Blythe with a clipboard.

Bobby's carrying boxes of wine up the path. 'There are more in the car if—'

Rhys doesn't stop. He gets to his study and sits heavily in his chair, fighting his breathing under control. His phone pings with a text from Seren, and Rhys lets out a low moan. She's sent a photo, and he catches a glimpse of smooth thigh before he deletes the message. *Oh God oh God oh God make it stop.* He deletes her contact then blocks her number, his breath coming in painful lumps, as though he's been running.

He doesn't know how long he spends there, slumped at his desk, but it's gone two when Yasmin sends Tabby looking for him, telling him there are too many jobs to do and not enough people.

Rhys snaps at her. 'Can't you see I'm working?'

'You don't look like you're working.'

Rhys snatches up the latest padded envelope from his agent and rips it open, mail spilling out across the desk. 'Happy now?' He hears the door slam and knows she'll be running straight back to Yasmin, but he doesn't care. His world is on fire and he doesn't know which blaze to tackle first. He starts opening his mail, stuffing the waste paper back in the padded envelope and laying out the entry forms; slotting signed photographs into the waiting SAEs. He winces as he cuts his tongue on an envelope, pressing angrily on the seal then pushing it into the post bag. Over and over: slot, seal, push. Slot, seal, push. And breathe. The repetitive action quietens his mind and blocks out the thoughts, and slowly he begins to calm.

An exhaust backfires outside, angry and loud in the crisp air. Rhys stands and looks out of the window to see a rusty Triumph Stag jerking to a stop in the space outside their lodge. The driver's door opens, and Rhys's chest tightens.

Ffion.

He can't let her get anywhere near Yasmin or the girls, not when he doesn't know what she might say – doesn't even know the facts himself. He races downstairs, tripping on the last step and hurtling into the hall so fast he smashes into the door before he can open it. Black blurs the edges of his vision as he lurches down the path towards Ffion.

She hasn't changed. Still small, still with a groove between her eyebrows, as though she spends more time scowling than laughing. Her hair's lighter than Seren's – Rhys doesn't remember if it's always been that way or if it's mellowing with age – and scraped into a bun, so what's on show is straight.

'Am I right?' Rhys says. 'Is Seren . . .' He still can't say it, is still horrified by the very thought. But Ffion's eyes are flashing. It's true.

'How did you find out?' She spits it out, as though it's Rhys's fault this happened. 'Nobody knows. Nobody!'

'I – I guessed.' Rhys looks towards the lodges, anxious this conversation should finish before Yasmin comes looking for him. She's going to be furious. Does that matter? Rhys wonders. She's furious anyway – she wants a divorce.

Ffion takes two steps one way, then the other. She stops and looks at Rhys. 'Have you said anything to Seren?'

'No.'

'You promise?' Ffion's voice cracks, and tears spill over her lower lashes.

'I promise.' Rhys feels a sudden need to atone – for the girl at Number 36, for the nameless, faceless women he's cast aside, over the years. 'But I have two daughters – two other daughters. They should know – in time – that they have a half . . .' Hunger gnaws at his insides, sweat breaks out across his brow. When did he last eat anything?

Ffion stares at him. 'No fucking way.'

'Not now, but . . . when you've told her. Once she's got used to the idea.'

'Tell her? I'm not telling her anything.'

'She has a right to know who her father is.'

Ffion walks slowly towards him, her eyes never leaving his. Rhys blinks nervously, his stomach twisting. She's close enough to touch him – he can smell shampoo and cigarettes in her hair.

'You go anywhere near my daughter . . .' Ffion spits out the words '. . . you *dare* tell her *anything* – and I swear to God, Rhys Lloyd, I will kill you.' In a move too sudden for Rhys to step back from, she brings her knee sharply up into his groin.

As Ffion disappears down the drive, the Triumph backfiring into a cloud of dust, Rhys sinks slowly to his knees.

FIFTY

JANUARY 8TH | LEO

Leo grips the top of the windscreen and lifts one foot to step into the boat. Lightning flashes bright white, and a gust of wind lurches the vessel to one side. Leo has no choice but to fall into the cockpit, scrambling on to the seat next to Ffion, who's wasted no time in releasing the moorings. By the time thunder cracks overhead they've left the jetty behind, and now Ffion releases the throttle, and the motorboat bounds forward, throwing Leo into the hull of the boat.

He can't see the water, and he doesn't know if that helps, or makes it worse. He knows there are trees within striking distance, but the snowstorm hides them, consuming everything, until it seems there's nothing for miles. The boathouse light is lost in the first curve of the lake, and now they've passed The Shore, are already beyond the parts of the lake which could be seen from the jetty. He clutches the side of the boat as it crashes through the water, every wave lifting him from the base of the boat. His heart hammers against his ribcage and he doesn't dare crawl back on to the exposed, narrow seat.

As a new police officer, catapulted into Liverpool city centre, Leo found himself in risky situations all the time – any number of which could have ended badly. The brawl outside All Bar One;

the nunchuck nutter fighting anyone who came near. The guy on the bridge who threatened to take Leo down with him if he didn't let him jump. None of those jobs scared Leo.

But now?

Now, Leo is terrified. Growing up, there was never spare money for extra-curricular activity, and when you live on an estate, miles from natural water, swimming lessons aren't a priority. Leo reached a moment, somewhere in his teens, where it was too late – too humiliating – to learn, and so he never did.

In the dim light from the dashboard Ffion's jaw is rigid, eyes set on the red haze in the sky, fading even as Leo looks at it. He takes a deep breath. Somewhere beneath that mark, lost in the blizzard, is sixteen-year-old Seren, alone and in danger, and way more frightened than Leo has any right to be. He can't imagine being any colder than he is now, yet every wave which crashes over the windscreen reminds him of the bitter depths of the lake.

Gingerly, Leo inches his way on to the seat next to Ffion. The windscreen offers a little protection, and he tries to find the rhythm of the boat, softening his body so it absorbs the impact instead of flying into the air. The lake seems at once liquid and solid, each wave a brick wall against the hull. Ffion doesn't waver, her knuckles white on the steering wheel, snow swirling about her.

Leo feels a quiet strength begin to build, somewhere between the rough water and the storm raging overhead. He grabs the searchlight from between Ffion's feet and switches it on, sweeping it across the water. Ffion's doing whatever it takes to get her daughter back, and Leo can't let her down. Then, once Seren is safe, he'll do whatever it takes to get his own kid back.

FIFTY-ONE

NEW YEAR'S EVE | SEREN

Wear the dress.

Seren's stomach gives a little flip as she looks at the message again. This is it. She's been wondering if it's all been in her head, thinking he might fancy her, even *notice* her in that way. She even wanted to ask him, like some stupid kid. *Do you like me? Is something happening between us?*

Wear the dress is her answer.

She's giddy with excitement as she gets ready. She washed her hair this morning, and now she straightens out the frizz, before using the irons to tease each section into soft, loose waves that ripple over her shoulders. She smudges her eyes with golds and browns, coats her lashes with mascara and shapes her brows the way she's learned online. With every layer of make-up she looks older. By the time she's finished, she feels nothing like Seren Morgan. She's glad of it because, right at the back of her mind, a tiny warning is trying to make itself heard. She pushes it away. She's sixteen. She could leave school. Get married. Drive a moped.

Have sex.

Seren's eyes are wide in the mirror. She isn't going to have sex. She doesn't want to – not yet. But she knows she could. She knows she's reached that age where she has power over men, and the feeling is intoxicating.

Wear the dress.

She's wearing it. It has long sleeves and a neck so high the dress appears boring – chaste, even – until you see how short it is. If the fabric were loose it would be impossible to wear without showing her knickers, but it clings to her bum like a swimsuit, skimming her buttocks and coming to a stop just above her thigh gap. It is an amazing dress, and Seren is a queen in it.

'You look lovely,' Elen says. She takes in the black leggings Seren is currently wearing between her Doc Marten boots and her dress. The boots will stay on; the leggings will not. 'Although I wish you wouldn't wear so much make-up.'

Seren has not yet put on the blood-red lipstick she bought especially for tonight.

'Have fun with Efa and Siân.'

Seren's heart is thumping as she gives Elen a hug and says *Blwyddyn Newydd Dda*, because Mam will be at Angharad's at midnight, where there's no reception. Mam made Seren promise not to go to The Shore. She says she's heard there's a bunch of idiots planning to crash the party, and she's worried there'll be trouble, but Seren knows that's not the problem. Angharad let slip to Elen that Seren's been hanging out with Caleb, and she must know about his police record because Mam's been funny about it ever since.

'He's a city lad,' she said to Seren. 'He's a bad influence.'

If only she knew. Elen and Ffion have no idea that Seren hasn't seen Efa and Siân outside school for months; that her pocket money comes, not from babysitting, but from helping Rhys with his fan mail.

Eventually, Mam will find out that Seren went to the party. She

353

might even hear it tonight, through her network of spies, the way she found out that time Seren bunked off school to go shopping in Wrexham. Seren will deal with that if it happens; for now, she's living in the moment.

She's at the lake when she sees Huw, a smart shirt poking out from beneath his coat. He takes in her outfit. 'Off to the party? Me too.'

'You're shitting me.' Everyone in the village knows Huw's raging with The Shore over money they owe him.

'Does your mam know you talk like that?' Huw spins a key in the air, catching it with the same hand. 'Come on, I'll give you a lift.'

Huw's boat is fast and powerful, leaping across the surface of the lake. Seren ducks behind the shelter of the curved windscreen, the hood of her coat pulled up to protect her hair.

'Caleb, is it?' Huw shouts.

Seren shrugs. Points to her ear and pretends she can't hear him. Wind whips at their faces.

'—with Rhys, I hear.'

Seren reddens. What did Huw say? But then she catches something about *working* and *bloody fan mail*, and she breathes out.

'Saving for uni,' she shouts back.

They're within spitting distance of The Shore now, and he pushes in the throttle so the engine's just turning over. The sudden silence is almost painful. 'You want to be careful around that man,' Huw says. He hands her the painter and she stands on the edge of the boat, one hand on the windscreen. Glad of the excuse to look away. 'He'll fuck you over soon as look at you, that one.'

As soon as they're close enough, Seren jumps lightly on to the pontoon and ties up the boat. 'Thanks for the lift!' she says, running to the ladder and leaving Huw behind.

A string of lights surrounds the deck outside the Charltons' lodge, the windows of the marquee already steamed up. Inside, the sliding doors to the lodge are open. Seren steps inside, suddenly shy, and looks around to see who's there. The room's full and noisy, cheesy music pumping from the speakers in the wall. Old Mrs Huxley is sitting on the sofa with Caleb's mum, Clemmie, and two women from the village. The Staffords are here, laughing at something Blythe's saying. Yasmin's over there, talking to Mia, but there's no sign of Rhys, and Seren feels suddenly anxious; overdressed and out of place. Some of the women are in posh dresses, and a few of the men are in dinner jackets, but most people are dressed as if they're going to the pub.

'Hey.'

Seren feels a hand on her shoulder. She spins around, but her face falls when she sees who it is.

'You look good.' Caleb looks her up and down. 'You look fucking amazing, actually. Listen, I was going to say this anyway, it's not because you look – I mean, you really do look great—'

Seren's still scanning the room. Where is he? Her chest is tight, from nerves and excitement, and Caleb's talking at her but she isn't listening. She's imagining the way Rhys will look when he sees her, how he'll know she's dressed up just for him.

'—if you're not seeing anyone else. Maybe,' Caleb finishes uncertainly. He waits for her to say something.

Seren stares at him, then finally catches up. 'Did you just ask me out?'

Caleb chews his lip. 'Sort of.'

There he is! Wearing a black dinner jacket and a red bow tie, a matching handkerchief folded in his top pocket. He looks the way she's seen him dress for concerts on TV.

'What do you reckon?' Caleb waits, then he follows her gaze

and lands on Rhys. He looks back at Seren. 'Jesus, Seren. Really?'

'What?' Seren feels herself getting hot. Caleb's staring at Rhys as if he'd like to punch him, and she turns her back on them both and goes to find the bathroom. Mam was right: there's a group of lads who drink in Y Llew Coch here, leaning against the wall like they're waiting for something. Steffan Edwards is drinking, which even Seren knows is going to end badly.

On her way back from the loo she picks up a glass of champagne and downs it in one, then takes another. It settles her nerves and makes her head buzz, but she's still not ready to speak to Rhys. She wants him to come and find her, she's too anxious to make the first move – already feels out of her depth. She gets out her phone to send him a message.

Great party!

That should do it. Casual. Not needy.

Seren frowns at the screen. The message hasn't been delivered. That's never happened before. Next to her, Clemmie bangs Seren's elbow, shouting, 'Sorry!' as she whirls about, doing some kind of Irish dancing.

'Amazing party, right?' Mia says, leaning into her to be heard.

Automatically, Seren conceals her champagne glass behind her back. 'It's okay.'

'Is your mam here?' Mia asks.

'Mam, at The Shore?'

Yasmin appears, her perfume sickeningly sweet. 'Seren! Have you seen Tabby and Felicia? I've been looking everywhere for them.'

'I think they're watching Netflix at Caleb's.' That's where the

356

twins are, Seren knows – they messaged her to tell her to come over.

'Tell them I need them to make their father eat something.'

'Um. Okay.' Seren doesn't want to go to number four. She wants to stay here, where Rhys can find her. Her face is aching from the effort of smiling and laughing, so that when he notices her, she looks like she's having a good time, that she isn't waiting for him.

'I put a sandwich under clingfilm in the fridge,' Yasmin is saying. 'They can give him that. He's completely off his face, it's mortifying.'

Seren sighs in resigned acceptance. She walks towards the door, then peels off and fetches herself another drink, then another. Only when Yasmin glares at her across the room does she reluctantly do her bidding.

Tabby and Felicia are sprawled on the sofa in Clemmie's lodge; Caleb is on the floor, leaning against the coffee table. The TV is on mute and the music is up loud, and all three are on their phones. Empty pizza boxes litter the floor, grease pockmarking the cardboard.

'Alright?' Seren says. Tabby and Felicia exchange glances, before fake-smiling hello. They've been talking about her. Fuck them, then. Caleb is frowning at his phone, as if he's in the middle of something important and can't be interrupted, but Seren knows it's because of what he said earlier. The stupid thing is, she really likes Caleb. It's just that he's still a boy. Girls mature faster than boys, everyone knows that, so it's not weird to fancy someone older. Not really.

Seren delivers Yasmin's message.

'Fuck that.' Felicia doesn't hesitate.

'He has to eat.' Tabby looks torn. 'Mum says he's wrecked, it's going to be really embarrassing if he, like, voms everywhere, or something.'

'Not after what he did,' Felicia says.

Seren's confused. 'What did he do?'

The girls look at each other. Felicia shrugs an *if you want*.

'He drugged Felicia,' Tabby says, eventually. Seren blinks. She looks at Caleb, to see if he's as shocked as she is, but it's clear this isn't news to him. 'She didn't sleep when she was a baby, so Dad drugged her every night and didn't tell Mum, and now she's found out and she's gone batshit crazy.'

Seren shakes her head. 'That's insane.'

'Right?' Tabby says.

'I don't believe it.'

Felicia stares at her. 'Are you saying we're lying?'

'No, but—'

'Wait.' Tabby pretends to gag. 'This is because you've got the hots for him, isn't it?'

'What?' Seren tries to force a laugh, but it sounds fake, even to her. 'God, no. Look, I only came to give you Yasmin's message. I don't give a shit about any of this. I'll give him the sandwich myself if you—'

'Er, I don't *think* so.' Tabby stands up and extends a hand to pull a reluctant Felicia up, too. 'We'll do it.'

The girls leave, and Seren wants to die. Everyone knows she's dressed up for Rhys, and he hasn't even noticed her and *God*, why did she even come? She's standing awkwardly in Clemmie's house, and Caleb isn't even looking at her, just pretending to watch something on his phone.

'So . . .' she says, hoping he'll say something. He doesn't. 'Um. What you said earlier. When you . . .' Her face is on fire and she finishes quickly. 'Asking me out, I mean. Like, we could. You know,

358

if you want to. Some time.' It's pathetic, she knows. Like a dog begging to be stroked.

Caleb stares at her. There's the briefest flash of something soft, before his face hardens. 'What are you on about? I didn't ask you out.' He gives a short laugh, then goes back to his phone.

Seren can't get out of there fast enough. She's breathing fast, close to tears and suddenly aware of how drunk she already is. She stands in the dark, listening to the sounds of the party coming from the Charltons' lodge. She could walk home now. She could have one of Mam's hot chocolates and watch shit on TV till midnight.

She chews her lip miserably. There's shouting coming from further up the drive – *Fuck off, you piece of shit* – and a burst of laughter and noise as a door opens then closes. Seren pulls herself together and walks back to the party. She jumps as she passes Steffan Edwards, off his face and muttering to himself in the shadows. Everyone's drunk, now, the party full of sweaty, swaying bodies, pressed tight and shouting above the music. Seren watches from the sidelines, steeling herself.

Mia's abandoned her trays and is talking to Bobby Stafford; she breaks off when she sees Seren. 'You alright, chick?' She looks down, checking to see what Seren's drinking, and Seren's sick of being treated like a kid, so she takes the half-drunk champagne from Mia's hand and knocks it back.

'Cheers,' she says, handing it back.

'Is Huw taking you home later, love?' Mia's face is full of concern.

'I'm paying you to waitress, not socialise.' Jonty pushes into their space.

'Technically, you're paying me to hand canapés around,' Mia says. 'And they're all gone, so . . .' She turns back to Seren. 'Don't

359

walk home on your own, will you? I know you girls think you can handle anything, but . . .' She doesn't finish, but she doesn't need to; Seren's heard it all before. *Don't walk home on your own, stick to main roads, don't wear short skirts . . .* Old people – Mia, Ffion, Mam – don't get that things are different now. They've spent their whole lives covering up and changing their routes, but women are reclaiming the streets. Wearing what they want, doing what they please.

Seren pulls herself tall. The drink is blurring her edges; she walks away from Mia with a careful steadiness, the movement feeling as though it belongs to someone else. Rhys is in the kitchen. He's eating a sandwich and talking to Jonty, and Seren hovers, wanting Rhys on his own before she loses her nerve. Jonty leans close to say something over the music, clapping Rhys on the back before walking away.

Now.

Seren's heart races. Rhys is walking through the party now. In a minute she'll lose him to someone else, and then it might be ages till he's on his own again.

'Hey.' She goes for soft and casual. Still sexy, she hopes, although her make-up's rubbed off, and the heat of the room has flattened her hair. She pushes her lips into a pout and looks up at him from beneath her lashes.

Rhys stops. He stares at her, but it's not the way she imagined him looking. He's frowning, his eyes taking in her dress, her boots, her make-up; his mouth turning down in what looks like disgust. He finds her revolting. She teeters on the edge of tears, drunk and emotional.

Rhys pushes past her and goes in search of someone different, someone less repulsive. Tears roll down Seren's cheeks.

Wear the dress, he said. And she did, but now . . .

Seren takes a deep breath and scrubs angrily at her face. She will not cry over a man; will not let him make her feel so humiliated, so worthless. Anger starts to simmer inside her, and it hurts less than the alternative, so she lets it swell until it's boiling. She stares after Rhys as he leaves the party. Bastard, she thinks. It makes her feel better, so she says it out loud. 'Bastard, bastard, bastard.' She stands tall. Rhys Lloyd doesn't deserve her.

He doesn't deserve anyone.

FIFTY-TWO

JANUARY 8TH | FFION

For months into her pregnancy, Ffion didn't look at her stomach. She closed her eyes in the shower, pulling baggy clothes over still-damp skin to avoid catching sight of herself in the mirror. The waistband of her school skirt was forced a little higher each day, until the hem was indecent enough for her form teacher to pass comment. After that, Ffion left the zip undone, extending the button with a hairband and letting her oversized jumper fall over the top.

Dad didn't look at her stomach, either. In fact, he rarely looked at Ffion at all, and her heart ached with unhappiness. She wished they could talk about it, but she'd agreed with Dad's insistence that if the baby was to be brought up as his and Elen's, it would be best for them all to behave from the outset as if that really were the case. The three of them moved around the house in an uneasy silence, Ffion's belly the elephant in the room. As Ffion's clothes grew baggier, so did Elen's, hidden beneath big coats on her rare forays to the shops.

'We're just spending time as a family,' she said, explaining away her sudden retreat from village life. No one questioned it. Her husband was dying – why wouldn't they hide themselves away?

When Ffion was twenty weeks pregnant, she felt a tremor

beneath her jumper, like a moth trapped between cupped fingers. She gasped, instinctively putting her hands to her stomach, and Elen looked up in alarm. 'Do you have a pain?'

'No, I . . .' It happened again. Like the flip of your tummy on a rollercoaster. Realisation spread a smile across Elen's face. 'The baby's moving, isn't it?'

Ffion's eyes were wide with wonder, her hands creeping across her bump. She splayed her fingers wide, realising for the first time how taut her skin was, how heavy and solid the bump was beneath. 'Shhh,' she murmured, and the moth fell quiet. Elen crouched beside her, slotting her own hands around Ffion's, and the two of them waited for more signs of life.

'Does it really hurt?' Ffion asked her mam. She'd read the books Elen had bought, even watched that awful video in school, but she still found it hard to comprehend that – in a matter of weeks – there would be an actual baby coming out of her. 'Like, *really*?'

Elen stood, kissing her daughter fiercely on the forehead. 'You know the best antidote to pain?'

Ffion remembered the woman on the video. 'Is it an epidural?'

Elen laughed. 'It's love, Ffion Morgan. Love is the answer to everything.'

Ffion keeps the throttle on full, the motorboat bounding forward to meet each wave. *Seren, where are you?* Leo swings the torch from left to right, the snow like shoals of fish in the beam, twisting in the wind.

Love is the answer to everything.

More than sixteen years ago, Mam had taken Ffion's hand – just when Ffion was thinking *No more, I can't take any more* – and placed it between Ffion's own legs, and amazement had won over revulsion, when she had felt her baby crowning.

'One more push,' Mam said. The pain tore Ffion in two, but the house was still full of condolence cards, and she felt the love come off them in waves. People loved Dad – loved them all – enough to send flowers, send cards. And love was the antidote to pain.

Seren slipped out, and into Mam's hands, and in a single heart-beat she was lying on Ffion's chest, her mouth open in a cartoon wail. There was a moment when Ffion wanted to say *I'm keeping her*, and she could have sworn the same thought passed across Mam's eyes too. But they had made a plan, and besides, the thought of being a mother was too terrifying, too impossible to comprehend. It would be better for the baby to hand her over, wouldn't it? It would be easier.

Wouldn't it?

'Do you want to try to feed her?' Mam was gentle, encouraging, but Ffion turned away.

'Take her.'

'You can—'

'Take her!'

When Ffion's milk came in, it felt like a betrayal. She sat hunched in the bath, her breasts throbbing and the taps running to block out the sound of her baby – no, her *sister* – crying downstairs, taking the bottle from Mam. It was better this way.

Wasn't it?

A flash of lightning illuminates the sky.

'There!' Leo points. The silhouette has already vanished, back into the swirling white of the snowstorm, but not before Ffion saw it too. A boat. Buffeted first one way, then the other, wrenching and fighting, its mast snapped in two. She yanks on the wheel, turning west and willing the motorboat to go faster, Leo training the torch on the water.

Slowly, the anchored dinghy takes shape, five hundred metres up ahead.

'Seren!' Ffion shouts. She can barely hear it herself above the clap of thunder, telling them the storm is right overhead.

Four hundred metres.

And now Ffion can see a figure on the boat, clinging to what's left of the mast.

Seren.

They're going to make it. Ffion lets out a sob of relief. But the wind isn't done. It swirls around Pen y Ddraig mountain, and roars down the dragon's back, gathering momentum as it travels across the lake, each wave bigger than the one before. Angharad's boat tips, teetering on its side as if deciding which way to fall, and Ffion screams at the rescue boat to go faster, but it's too late.

Angharad's boat is capsizing.

FIFTY-THREE

JANUARY 8TH | LEO

As they draw closer to the wreckage of Angharad's boat, Leo sweeps the torch in an arc, searching for a glimpse of Seren. The light bounces back at him, the white of the snow almost blinding. Debris floats in the water: plastic containers, rope, pieces of canvas, ripped from the hold.

'Take the wheel,' Ffion shouts.

Take the—?

But Ffion is on her feet, up on the seat with her arms raised, her coat shrugged on to the floor. One moment she's there, the next she's gone, entering the water in a shallow dive.

'Ffion!' The motorboat lurches to one side, and Leo clutches the wheel, fighting it back to face the spot where he last saw Ffion. Have they drifted already? Angharad's boat has turned over, her dark red hull the only part visible.

Leo stares at the controls. No different from a car, right? He steers one-handed, trying to circle, all the time knowing the wind is throwing him off course, that he risks losing track of where Ffion went in. The torch light flickers and he shakes it hard – 'Not now, not now!' – pointing it at the water.

'Ffion!' he calls again, consumed with fear, with anger that he can't swim, can't save her. There's a life ring on the back of the

366

boat, but what good's that when he can't see the people who need it? He circles again – and again and again – and thank God the thunder has stopped, and is the snow slowing? His fingers are numb with cold, adrenaline making the beam of the torch shake, casting shadows on the waves, playing tricks with his mind.

Ffion.

Leo stares. Ffion? He slides up the throttle, as carefully as he can, and the boat pitches forward. And there she is, kicking furiously and slicing through the water with one free arm; the other gripping a white lifejacket wrapped around a motionless Seren.

FIFTY-FOUR

JANUARY 8TH | FFION

For a man who's never been on a powerboat before, let alone driven one, Leo is doing a surprisingly good job. Ffion stays low in the boat, water swilling about her knees as she holds on to her daughter's inert body. Seren's barely conscious, her eyes closed and her limbs loose, but she's breathing. Ffion feels for her pulse, but her own hands are clumsy with cold and what she finds is dangerously slow. Is that Seren's pulse, or her own?

How long was Seren in the water? Her core temperature will keep dropping; they have nothing to warm her with. Leo's thrown his sodden coat over her, and Ffion's, too, and Ffion's rubbing Seren's arms hard, trying to get the circulation going.

'Come on, baby, come on,' Ffion says, quiet and urgent. Seren was unresponsive when Ffion reached her, the younger girl's head flopped back against the lifejacket she'd had the presence of mind to put on. Could she have hit her head? Ffion bends over and presses a kiss to Seren's forehead, a sob rising up from nowhere. Seren was a toddler when she last kissed her like this. Stolen moments when Mam wasn't around; moments when Ffion allowed herself – just for a second – to acknowledge the tightening around her heart.

'What do I do?' Leo shouts. There's panic in his voice, and

Ffion looks up, realising they're approaching the jetty. Leo drops their speed.

'Kill the engine!' Ffion doesn't want to leave Seren. The sudden silence is a relief, but they're still coming in too fast. Wind and waves shove them towards the shore, and they overshoot the end of the jetty, where they found the boat. 'Brace yourself!' Ffion shouts. The lake bed doesn't slope gently away from the shore – something which regularly catches out day-trippers, paddling with their trousers rolled up. Instead, the bed falls away, the water depth dropping from knee-height to chest-depth in a single step. The lake has risen, and it's hard to know exactly where the shelf is, but it must be about—

There's a violent *thud*, and Leo lurches forward on to the steering wheel, swearing loudly.

—there.

The boat grinds on to gravel. Leo leaps out, up to his knees in the icy water, dragging the boat until it's high on the foreshore.

'She's not moving.' Ffion's trying to be calm, trying to be professional, trying trying trying but— 'She's not moving!' The wind howls, snow snapping at her face, covering Seren in icy flakes as fast as Ffion can wipe them away.

At Dad's memorial service, Mam soothed a fretful Seren with a bottle.

'I've got no milk,' she said, truthfully, to friends with shining eyes. Ffion's breasts ached. She stared at Dad's photo on the order of service, feeling guilty that the tears she shed were as much for Seren as for him.

'Be strong, *cariad*,' people murmured. 'Your mam's going to need help with your baby sister.'

Ffion has been strong for sixteen years. She's exhausted.

Leo hauls Seren up and over his shoulder as though she weighs nothing. He runs towards the boathouse, looking back to check on Ffion, who is barely able to support her own body, let alone carry another. She stumbles behind Leo, not taking her eyes off the limp girl over his shoulder.

As Seren grew from baby to toddler, Ffion trained herself to forget. She made herself think *sister*, not *daughter*. She forced herself to forget the birth, to pretend her belly had never been full, and, slowly, she began to believe it. She pushed Seren away. Told herself Seren was too small, too needy, too immature. Too irritating.

Ffion chokes back a sob. It was survival, that was all. Grief for a baby lost, even though Seren had lived.

At the boathouse, everything is as they left it. Steffan's comatose at his desk, and Ffion ransacks the cupboards, pulling out fleeces and spare socks, while Leo calls for an ambulance. Swiftly, Ffion removes Seren's wet clothes, enveloping her in the dry ones she's found and ignoring her own chattering teeth. Seren murmurs, drifting in and out of consciousness.

Ffion pulls a hat over Seren's sodden hair. The shock of cold water makes you hyperventilate, reducing the flow of blood to the brain. That's what makes your head fill with fog; what causes you to pass out. Seren is not out of danger – not by a long way.

'Did you check for injuries?' Leo's examining the drenched lifejacket Seren was wearing. 'Cuts?'

'Yes, of course.'

He runs his fingers over the jacket. 'Check again.' Panic rises in Ffion's chest. Has she missed something, in her haste to get Seren warm and dry? She traces a path around Seren's head, feeling for bumps, checking for blood. Seren moans, and Ffion cups her face, reassuring her help is on its way. She moves her hands down each of Seren's arms, and around her torso, but there are no marks. If Seren has injuries, they're hidden. In the distance, Ffion hears the wail of an ambulance siren.

'I don't understand.' Leo frowns, passing the lifejacket to Ffion. It would have been white at some stage, now a dirty grey. An old-fashioned jacket, bulky and square. 'This is definitely blood on the side, at the back.'

The stain is brown and earthy, ingrained in the fabric, despite immersion in water. Ffion stares at it. If it isn't Seren's blood, whose is it?

FIFTY-FIVE

JANUARY 9TH | LEO

Ffion's waiting for Leo at the lake the next morning, her hands pushed deep into her huge coat and the toes of her boots dark with lake water. Leo gets out of the car and walks towards her, feeling suddenly awkward. Last night was more intense – more intimate, even – than the time he and Ffion had spent together on New Year's Eve, and everything Leo wants to say seems inadequate.

He stands a few steps behind her. 'Big night,' he says quietly. The lake is flat calm, the surface so glassy Leo feels he could step right on to it. Trees stretch their reflections on to the water, without so much as a ripple to shatter the illusion. Overnight the storm has cleared, leaving snow-covered mountains beneath a bright blue sky.

Ffion says nothing. She moves backwards, just a step, and Leo moves forward, so that when she tips her head back to lean against him, he's already there. They stand watching the lake, Leo's chin grazing Ffion's hair, and after a moment he slides his arms around hers. He thinks of her at the wheel of Steffan's boat, fear channelled into grit, and knows he'll never meet another woman quite like her.

'Pretty big,' Ffion says eventually.

'You take me to all the best places.'

Ffion laughs and turns around, and for a second they're so close it feels as though they might—

'Don't suppose you stopped for coffee?' Ffion walks towards the car, the moment lost.

'Flat white, one sugar.'

'You're going to make someone a lovely wife.'

As they drive towards Angharad's, Leo casts surreptitious glances at Ffion, whose eyes are swollen and bloodshot. She cradles her coffee in both hands, steam warming her face.

'Did you get any sleep at all?'

'Not really.'

'You should be at the hospital, with Seren.'

'She doesn't want to see me.' Ffion turns away, the subject closed.

Angharad stands in the centre of the clearing, as though she knew they were coming. As though she was alerted by the wind, by the animals in the forest, Leo thinks, then chides himself for the sentimentality. In rapid Welsh, Ffion arrests Angharad, who wears the same dark overalls she had on when Leo first met her; laced boots and a blood-red scarf holding back her hair.

Later, when they're sitting in an interview room, Angharad having declined the offer of legal representation, Leo repeats the caution in English. He turns his notepad to a fresh page.

'How did you know Rhys Lloyd?'

'The same way everyone in Wales did. The *child star*.' Angharad's tone is mocking.

'You didn't like him?'

'I didn't like what he did to the lake. To the shore. All those trees, ripped up to give the English more holiday homes.'

'Ah, you don't like the English?'

'You're putting words in my mouth, detective. I have no objections to English people—'

'I'm glad to hear it.'

'—when they're in England.' Angharad's expression is misleadingly neutral. 'But when a young family in our community can't afford a two-bedroom house and across the lake Londoners think nothing of spending half a million pounds on a holiday home . . .' She pauses. 'Then, yes. I object to English people.'

'You don't mix with the residents of The Shore, then?' Leo says.

'No one does. They keep to their side of the lake; we keep to ours.' Angharad looks at Ffion. 'I didn't see you in the water on New Year's Day morning.'

'I was busy.' Ffion gives a tight smile. 'But we're here to talk about your movements, not mine.'

'It's not like you to miss the swim.'

'I hear there were a lot of people there,' Leo says, realising Ffion would have been leaving his flat just as the village was congregating on the lakeshore.

'Almost everyone. It's been that way since I was a girl. Not everyone swims, of course.'

'Did many come across from The Shore?' Leo says.

Angharad narrows her eyes. 'No one. As I said: they have their side, we have ours. They wouldn't have been welcome.'

'Yet there was an open invitation issued to The Shore's New Year's Eve party. Dozens of people from the village went.' Leo tries to keep his focus on the interview. Something Angharad just said has triggered a memory – something which feels significant, if he could only grasp hold of it.

'More fool them.' Angharad looks at Ffion. 'You know the strength of feeling there is. You know how the Welsh feel about the English.'

'*Some* Welsh people,' Ffion says.

'England has always viewed Wales as a colony. Theirs to be controlled. They stole our coal, our water, our steel. They try to take our language.'

'The Shore is built on the English side of the lake.' Leo is trying very hard not to take this personally.

'Only because the English took the land.'

'Shall we move on?' Leo has lost patience. 'This isn't about relations between England and Wales.'

'Oh, but it is,' Angharad says darkly. 'It always is, under the surface.'

Ffion leans forward. 'How well do you know Ceri Jones?'

'I've known her all her life. She has great talent as an artist – such a shame she never pursued it.'

'Did you know she was bullied by Rhys Lloyd?' Ffion says.

'We talked about it. He was unbearably cruel to her.'

'Did she ever say she wanted to pay Rhys back for what he'd done to her?' Leo is working on a theory. Ceri and Angharad are both women living in the margins of their community, scarred by events in their past. What if their mutual hatred of Lloyd drew them together? Ceri had left The Shore before Lloyd died, and they know from the cameras on the driveway that she didn't return on foot, but could she have come back by boat?

Ffion reaches behind her chair and pulls up an evidence bag. 'Do you recognise this?'

'It's my lifejacket. I keep it in a locker on the lugger.' Angharad gives a sad sigh. 'Kept.'

Shortly after arresting Angharad, this morning, Ffion had broken the news that the red-sailed lugger was at the bottom of the lake.

Angharad had wept. 'She's been with me for forty years.'

'I'm so sorry.' Ffion had looked as though she might cry too, and Angharad had put a hand on her arm.

'Seren is safe. And that is all that matters.'

Leo indicates the rusty stain on the grubby lifejacket. 'How can you explain the fact that it has Rhys Lloyd's blood on it?'

Angharad frowns. 'I can't.'

'And that divers have retrieved rope from your boat which matches fibre patterns found on his body?'

'I have no idea.'

'Where were you on New Year's Eve?' Ffion says.

'I was at home all evening.'

Ffion makes a note in her book. 'Can anyone corroborate that?'

'Of course.' Angharad smiles at Ffion. 'Your mother.'

'My—'

'Elen came to me around eight-thirty, I think. I'd prepared supper, although we ended up eating it outside, with the animals. Bloody fireworks – they should be banned.'

Leo can feel a headache brewing. Is there anyone Ffion and her family aren't tangled up with? 'Your boat went in to Steffan Edwards for repair on January second, correct?'

'Yes. It had been out on its mooring for a few days, and when I rowed out on the second I noticed a hairline crack on the central buttress. I must have forgotten to pull up the centreboard, and the lake had been choppy, so . . .' She catches Leo's blank expression. 'Bigger boats have keels below the waterline, to stop them tipping over. In smaller boats, like mine, the bottom of the boat is flatter. The stability comes from the centreboard.'

'Is that something you've done before?' Ffion says. 'Left the centreboard down?'

'I can't recall ever doing it.'

'Apart from the centreboard,' Leo says, 'was anything else out of place?'

Angharad's gaze drifts to the wall as she thinks. From the corridor, Leo can hear footsteps; one officer briefing another. 'The locker.' Angharad snaps her attention back, her eyes wide. 'I didn't think anything of it at the time, but . . . I never wear a lifejacket, you see – I know I should, but old habits die hard – so it's always at the bottom, under the spare rope and the diesel can.' She grips the side of her chair, animated for the first time since the interview began. 'But when I rowed out on the second – when I found the damage to the buttress – the lifejacket was on top.'

'You're sure?' Ffion says.

'A hundred per cent.' She sits up straight. 'Someone had been on my boat.'

Leo thinks through the possibilities. If it was Ceri who used Angharad's boat to dump Lloyd's body, how had she got out to the mooring? Did someone take her? And in what? Leo runs through the guests who arrived at The Shore's party by boat. Any one of them could have slipped away from the party, but only one of them had a grudge against Lloyd.

Huw Ellis.

Was he working with Ceri? If so, why go to all the trouble of taking Angharad's boat, when they could have taken Lloyd's body on Huw's motorboat? It doesn't make sense.

And then, suddenly, it does.

There's more than one way to travel through water. Leo thinks about Angharad's assertion that no one from The Shore was at the Cwm Coed swim on New Year's Day, and he knows with absolute certainty that he's been lied to.

He knows who dumped Rhys Lloyd's body in the lake.

FIFTY-SIX

NEW YEAR'S EVE | GLYNIS

Glynis Lloyd is not enjoying the party. Parties are for young people, and Glynis is feeling her age. There is nowhere to sit down, and, even though she is surrounded by familiar faces, she feels lonely.

It was Yasmin who persuaded her to come.

'You'll have a nice time,' she said, before following it up with: 'And what will people think, if Rhys's own mother isn't there?' which was so obviously the primary motive that Glynis almost refused on the spot. Her daughter-in-law cares a great deal about appearances.

'I tried to get *OK!* to cover it,' Yasmin went on. 'But they said it wasn't the "right fit" for them.' She tutted. 'Heaven knows what would fit better. The Staffords alone are surely a draw, even if Rhys is no longer—' She swallowed her words, remembering who she was talking to.

Glynis is under no illusions about her son's failing career. Oh, he has talent, no one ever doubted that, but she – more than anyone – knows how duplicitous this business is. On the surface, all success and smiles, but dip below and the truth is a murky affair.

She feels a pang of guilt whenever she thinks about Rhys's career. About the favour she'd done one of the Eisteddfod judges, which meant they owed *her* a little favour, and it wasn't all the world to mark Rhys the tiniest bit higher, was it? So, there he was, on the main National stage, in the right place at the right time to be spotted for success.

Glynis looks for Steffan Edwards – a far cry, now, from the boy-next-door runner-up who should, by rights, have won that competition. He's gone home already, or perhaps someone has had the sense to throw him out, before he disgraces himself any more.

'There aren't any male, working-class Welsh singers out there right now,' Fleur Brockman – Rhys's newly acquired agent – had said, all those years ago. 'It's rich territory.'

Glynis had found this casual branding of their family abhorrent, but she'd bitten her tongue, for Rhys's sake. 'You really think he's got the talent to make it?' she said, wanting more of the flattery which justified her cheating.

'Talent?' Fleur shrugged. 'Sure, he's talented. But what it's really about is building a brand.' She winked. 'Put the right marketing in place and I could send a guinea pig to number one.'

Rhys had had the right marketing, for a long time, but over the years the budget was slowly cut, and the team changed, until it was unrecognisable. Now, despite all the money her son is throwing at a publicity campaign, Glynis knows it's only a matter of time before his career is over. She wonders if Yasmin knows it, too.

Her daughter-in-law was in the middle of one of her tours when Glynis arrived at the party. Yasmin kissed her on both cheeks and introduced her as *the twins' granny*. Glynis winced. She was *Nain* to Tabby and Felicia, despite Yasmin's reticence when they were born.

'No one will know what it means,' Yasmin had complained.

Glynis had stood firm. If Tabby's and Felicia's NCT contemporaries could have grandparents called Oompa, Glammy, Loli and Pop, Glynis could be Nain.

The noise at the party is giving her a headache. All around her, people are shouting, the decibels slowly increasing, as everyone fights to be heard. She hears snatches of conversation, almost all English, even though half the room is Welsh. Rhys's father would have been devastated.

Jac Lloyd had been a staunch nationalist. A railwayman by profession, he could turn his hand to most trades, fitting out the hardware shop which had once belonged to Glynis's parents. The wooden cabin on this side of the lake was set back to allow for the rise of the water, a tall row of pine trees just hiding it from view. Glynis and Jac would meet at Tŷ'r Lan cabin when they were courting, away from village gossip. Jac would fish, and Glynis would read her book, and then . . . Glynis smiles at the memory.

The plot itself extended to less than an acre, part of the woodland which had once been Welsh. In 1972, the Local Government Act had defined the UK's counties, and the strip of land to the east of Llyn Drych had become English.

Glynis had never seen her husband so enraged. The very idea of owning a property on English soil was unthinkable – the butt of so many jokes at Y Llew Coch that Jac took to drinking elsewhere – until a journalist planted a seed which changed Jac's outlook.

Wales's Last Bastion, read the headline, above a photograph of Tŷ'r Lan, its red dragon flag flying. The article had presented Jac as a warrior, protector of his language and culture, guarding the soil which remained morally – if not legally – Welsh.

'*Cymru am byth*,' Jac had said proudly, showing Glynis the article. *Wales forever*.

380

How he would despair at what his son has done. Glynis feels a pain in her chest as she imagines the emotion in her late husband's eyes. No longer Tŷ'r Lan, but The Shore. No longer a bastion for the Welsh but a playground for the English, running roughshod over traditions, and not as much as a *diolch* from any of them except that Clemmie, who – Glynis had to concede – makes an attempt to fit in.

When Jac died, Glynis had spoken to their solicitor. 'I've got his will somewhere,' she'd told him. Jac had organised it a few years before – one of those kits you could buy from the newsagent. Properly witnessed, all legal and proper. Jac was the belt-and-braces sort – at least, he had been, before the dementia set in. Tŷ'r Lan would pass to Glynis, who would keep the Welsh flag flying, in honour of her husband.

Only then Glynis had received a call from a different solicitor. One in the next town, who didn't know the Lloyd family from Adam, and whose brusque tone made Glynis want to cry.

'I'm sorry for your loss,' the woman said. Glynis heard the snap of a rubber band. 'Now, your late husband came in six months ago with your son. I have a copy of his will here—'

'I think there's been some mistake,' Glynis said.

But there was no mistake.

Jac Lloyd – who, in the year before his death, all too often tipped orange juice on his cereal and put his shoes in the fridge – had made a replacement will, leaving Tŷ'r Lan and its surrounding land to Rhys.

'This can't be right,' Glynis said. For years, Rhys had been trying to persuade his father to develop the land, and Jac had always said the same thing. *Over my dead body.* Tŷ'r Lan was a Welshman's cabin; it was part of the landscape. The land might be English, but those trees were as Welsh as Jac.

381

'It's all watertight, I assure you,' the solicitor said. 'Although if you bring me your late husband's DIY will, I'll double-check the dates.'

But the original will was nowhere to be found.

Glynis stands by the window in the Charltons' lodge and looks at the view that hasn't changed in the seventy-odd years she's known it.

Doesn't Jac's cabinet look lovely in Rhys's office? Yasmin had said, when she was showing off the lodge to her mother-in-law for the umpteenth time. Glynis touched the bashed metal, remembering it in Tŷ'r Lan, thinking of the mess of papers inside it.

'Safe and sound,' Jac used to say, as he locked the drawers and pulled his mother's tablecloth back over it.

Jac had wanted Glynis to have Tŷ'r Lan and the land around it; wanted her to continue protecting it. What if the original will he made is in Rhys's filing cabinet? Finding it would prove Jac's intentions for the land.

Glynis has spent weeks hunting for the key, turning her spare room upside down as she trawled through old photographs and papers. She found it in an old tackle tin, along with a handful of floats and some rusted fishhooks.

Now, it hangs on a long chain around Glynis's neck.

She looks around the room. Rhys is in the kitchen, talking to Jonty, the twins offering him a sandwich. Yasmin is pouring champagne in the corner. There will be no one at the Lloyds' lodge.

Nobody notices Glynis as she slips outside: one of the few perks of old age. She walks along the lodges, perfectly calm, because what is she doing wrong? She's Rhys's mother and the girls' *nain* – why shouldn't she nip out of a party to rest at their place for a while?

The front door is unlocked. Inside, the lights are low, and Glynis goes straight upstairs to the study to open the filing cabinet, the key turning as easily as if it had been used yesterday. Inside, manila folders form a muted rainbow, packed tightly together, Jac's loopy handwriting on the flap of each one. She pulls out each in turn, flicking through the papers with a practised eye, knowing Jac's filing system as well as her own. Not alphabetical, not grouped by subject, or correspondent's name. Electricity bills were always filed under *Gethin Jones*, because old Gethin had done the original wiring job in the cabin. Maps of footpaths in the area weren't filed together but under the names of farms they passed through. Jac had his quirks, Glynis thinks fondly, even before he lost his marbles.

She pulls out a folder marked *Anti Nesta*, and her heart skips a beat. Nesta – not a real aunt, but a much-loved friend of Jac's mother – had worked in a funeral parlour. Glynis opens the folder, and knows instantly that if Jac's will is anywhere, it will be here. There are leaflets for headstones, careful notes considering the merits of various coffins.

And the will.

Glynis feels grief swelling inside her all over again, so many years after she lost Jac. She reads his writing, the clear capitals spelling out what should happen to the shop, the flat, the land on the lakeshore. Rhys had known that was what his dad had wanted, yet he had taken advantage of Jac's illness – and his refusal to see a doctor about it – and deliberately gone against his wishes. Jac would be devastated.

There's a sound downstairs.

Someone bangs the door, then thuds against the stairs. It sounds violent, out of control. Glynis is panicking. What if it's a burglar, here to take advantage of an empty house? What if he attacks her? She looks wildly around for some kind of weapon, as the intruder's steps come heavily up the stairs. Putting down the folder, she takes a trophy from the shelf above the desk. It's so heavy she almost drops it, but she grips it tightly, so far out of her depth she can hardly breathe.

And then the door opens and Rhys comes in, and the rush of relief is overwhelmed by anger, the way a mother snatches at a child's arm when she had thought him lost. He staggers against the wall, too drunk to notice his own mother – although would he even care, she thinks, if he did? Rhys has always done exactly what he wanted. *Taken* exactly what he wanted. She pictures Rhys telling Jac what to say, where to sign – convincing him he was doing the right thing – and before she knows what she's doing she's using all her strength to lift the trophy and hurl it at her son.

Only when he falls to the floor like an axed tree does Glynis come to her senses.

She claps her hand over a scream, every limb trembling.

What has she done?

FIFTY-SEVEN

NEW YEAR'S EVE | CLEMMIE

Clemmie Northcote is having a wonderful evening. She has tried her Welsh on all the local guests (and a few of the English ones), has drunk way more than she should have done, and doesn't give two figs because it's New Year's Eve! It's a party! Hurrah for free champagne and stunning surroundings!

Clemmie does some more Irish dancing, which she's discovered she's amazingly good at, for someone who has never tried it before. Everyone is cheering, or possibly laughing, it's hard to tell, but Clemmie doesn't care either way – it's all such a hoot.

She takes a breather, bequeathing the dance floor to some of the youngsters, who don't dance at all, really, just shift their weight from side to side and shout at each other over their drinks. On the other side of the room, Bobby Stafford has his hand on the cleaner's bottom.

'Doing his bit for cross-border relations,' Clemmie says, giggling to herself. Ashleigh's seen too, and is glaring at Bobby from the sofa so hard he must feel her eyes on him, because he turns around. Clemmie mentally reaches for the popcorn, but Bobby gives a sort of shrug and doesn't take so much as a finger off Mia. Mind you, Clemmie's seen Ashleigh coming out of the loo with Jonty twice tonight, so maybe they're both at it. People have the oddest relationships; Yasmin and Rhys haven't said a word to each other all night – those poor twins, having parents argue like that, so publicly.

She looks around, but Tabby and Felicia must have gone back to Clemmie's place. Clemmie hasn't given up hope of one of them falling madly in love with Caleb, and spends a fair proportion of her lake swims contemplating a Northcote–Lloyd wedding. Sadly, Caleb seems to be more interested in Seren, who is a very sweet girl but who has turned up to tonight's party dressed – there's no way to put this nicely – like a prostitute. If Clemmie gets a chance, she'll have a word with the girl. Woman to woman. Vet her for Caleb, at the same time, just in case the Tabby-or-Felicia thing doesn't come off.

Any one of those girls would be lucky to have her son, Clemmie thinks, as she wanders off in search of a drink she really shouldn't have but who's counting? Caleb's slowly growing back into the sweet, thoughtful boy he used to be, and it's all thanks to The Shore. Clemmie's quite evangelical about the changes in Caleb since they left London, and she feels a bolt of fear as she remembers Rhys's insistence that she pay back the money he borrowed on her behalf. It's so unfair – they had an agreement. Maybe not a legal one, but a – what's it called? Clemmie hiccups. A gentleman's agreement, that's it.

'Gentlewoman's agreement,' Clemmie says out loud. She snorts, somewhat louder than she'd intended. Rhys has finished his conversation with Jonty and is walking towards the main living area. Seren puts out a hand to speak to him, but he just stares at her – probably wondering what her parents were thinking, letting her out like that – and carries on. He looks a little worse for wear – too much of the old vino, Clemmie thinks, imagining it in Jonty's voice, which makes her laugh and then hiccup again.

386

Champagne has made her bold. What if she talks to Rhys now, when he's softened by alcohol? She's not asking to be let off the loan – although obviously she wouldn't say no. Imagine! She's simply asking to stick to their original agreement. Their gentleman's agreement.

'Gentlewoman's agree—' Clemmie frowns. Has she made that joke already? She weaves unsteadily through the party. Rhys went out of the front door. This is good: they can talk in private. No one else knows about the loan, and Clemmie's keen to keep it that way.

As she leaves the Charltons' lodge, she sees Rhys at the other end of the drive. He bends over and throws up into the flower-beds, then opens his front door. He's clearly decided to call it a night. Clemmie scurries after him. He's left the door open, and she doesn't knock, just steps inside and calls, 'Hello? Rhys?' There's no sign of him downstairs, so she pops up the stairs, tripping over her own toes in her effort to get upstairs before Rhys starts getting into his pyjamas. She hears a small sound – like someone swallowing – and she calls out again as she rounds the corner and takes the last few steps into the study.

'It's only me. Clemmie. I was hoping we could—'

Clemmie wonders momentarily if she's hallucinating. She has drunk an awful lot. But then Glynis makes that sound again – a sort of strangled gurgle – and the blood rushes to Clemmie's head. Rhys is lying face-down, a smear of blood on the wooden floor beneath his face. Next to him lies a golden trophy, its base a block of marble.

'Oh, my God,' Clemmie says. She drops to her knees beside Rhys, rolling him over and checking frantically for a pulse. A deep gash runs down the middle of his face, blood filling his mouth. He isn't moving.

387

'He made my husband write a will.' Glynis speaks so quietly Clemmie can hardly hear her. She feels a strong pulse, beating fast and furious, then realises it's her own and changes position. 'Jac would never have left the land to Rhys if he'd been well.'

Clemmie doesn't know what Glynis is talking about, but she has a terrible feeling she knows what it implies. She sits back on her heels for a second and stares at the older woman. 'Did you do this deliberately?'

'No!'

'Well, thank goodness for—' Clemmie resumes her search for a pulse.

'I mean, not entirely.'

Clemmie looks at her, appalled by what she's hearing.

'I just saw red. I was so angry and . . .' Glynis covers her face. 'Oh, my God, what have I done?'

Clemmie's heart is pounding. She fights to keep her breathing in check, trying to speak calmly. 'We have to get rid of him.'

'Rid of – what do you mean? We need to call an ambulance. Do you have a mobile? I don't have one and there's no landline here, I don't know why they don't—'

'Glynis!'

She stops talking, her face ashen and her lips pinched with panic.

Clemmie speaks slowly. 'They'll arrest you, Glynis. You'll go to prison.'

'No, no, no. He'll be okay, we just need to get him to a hospital.'

'I'll help you.' Clemmie sounds stronger than she feels. 'Protect you.'

'I don't understand.' Glynis is crying.

'It's too late, Glynis.' Clemmie's fingers are slippery with blood. She presses them to Rhys's neck again, even though she knows what she'll find. 'A doctor won't be able to help him.'

Clemmie's head is spinning. She came to Rhys's lodge to talk to him about their loan agreement. An agreement no one else knows about. She knows this is awful, that Glynis is in shock – may never recover – but, inside, Clemmie's heart is leaping. She thinks of the money she won't have to pay back, and the future she can promise her son.

'Are you—' Glynis chokes back a sob. 'Are you sure?'

Clemmie leans over Rhys, shielding Glynis from the terrible sight of her son, lying motionless on the floor. 'Quite sure.' She feels once more for a pulse, willing things to be different, but nothing has changed. Nausea rises in her throat, but Clemmie thinks of the freedom she can have, now she doesn't have to pay Rhys back. Everything happens for a reason, she tells herself.

'I'm afraid you've killed him,' she tells Glynis.

As Glynis collapses into a chair, sobbing, Clemmie remains motionless, her fingers on Rhys's pulse. Slow and weak, but unmistakably present.

For now.

FIFTY-EIGHT

JANUARY 9TH | FFION

Before a decision can be made to release Angharad, Ffion and Leo have to check out her alibi, and Ffion's mam is delighted to finally be allowed to stick her nose in. She confirms that she did indeed spend New Year's Eve with Angharad. 'Now, will you stop for a *paned*?'

'Mam, we're in the middle of a murder investigation. Leo's waiting outside.'

'I'll give you some space,' he'd said, when they arrived at the Morgans' house, and Ffion had been grateful for his understanding.

'I wish you'd mentioned you were with Angharad,' she says to Elen now. 'We might not have nicked her.'

'You refused to discuss the case.'

'Mam, that's diff—'

'I believe your words were: "especially not to my mother". Because presumably I'm going to shoot my mouth off around the village, am I? Never mind that I've got more on half of them than you'll ever know.'

'I'm not interested in tittle-tattle, Mam.'

'It's not tittle-tattle if Jos Carter's run off with his driving instructor, is it?'

390

Ffion rolls her eyes. 'I mean, Mam, it literally is—'

'Or if Glynis Lloyd is disputing Jac's will?'

'What?'

'She's found his original will, leaving Tŷ'r Lan to her. She's going to take legal action.'

'Oh, my God, Mam, I don't care!' Ffion should know better than to get sucked into Mam's gossip. She glances upstairs. 'How's Seren?'

'Sleeping.'

The hospital had discharged Seren after the morning rounds and, once they were home, Mam packed her off to bed with a hot water bottle and a mug of tomato soup. The consultant confirmed there'd been no ill-effects from her terrifying ordeal, but they all know how lucky she was.

'She hasn't answered my texts.'

When the ambulance had reached the boathouse, Ffion had gone with Seren to hospital, Leo following in the car. Ffion had squeezed Seren's cold hand and prayed she would be okay. Seren was so angry with her, but Ffion had saved her life – that would count for something, surely? But the moment Seren came round, she pushed Ffion away, making such a commotion that the nurses came to see what was happening. 'Get away from me!'

Ffion's texted her all morning, in between briefings and interviewing Angharad, but even though every message has been marked as *read*, there's been no reply.

'Give her time,' Elen says.

'She hates me.'

'All daughters hate their mothers at some stage. It's a rite of passage.'

Ffion opens her mouth to disagree, then catches Mam's eye and gives a wry smile. They stand in silence for a while, each

391

lost in their own thoughts, and then Elen gently touches Ffion's arm, her face darkening.

'Rhys, then.'

Whatever Seren has told Mam can only be half of the truth, and now she waits for Ffion to tell the rest of the story. For sixteen years Elen has raised Ffion's daughter as her own. She encouraged Ffion to leave Cwm Coed, to find her own way in life, unhindered by a baby. Ffion knows Mam deserves the truth, but all she can say is, 'I didn't want it, Mam. I didn't want him,' before she's sobbing again.

Elen's own face crumples in pain and she holds Ffion so tight she can hardly breathe.

'I'm so sorry, Ffi, so sorry for everything that's happened.'

Back in the car, Ffion calls the incident room to confirm Angharad can be released. If Leo notices her red eyes, he doesn't mention it. There is a comfort, she realises, in being with someone who knows everything about you.

There were several times over the course of her relationship with Huw when she wanted to tell him the truth. Not about Seren – she'd sworn blind never to breathe a word about that – but about the rape.

Rape.

It's the first time she's used the word, even to herself, and yet it's the only word for it. Rhys raped her.

Ffion had dealt with a job at work once: a girl in her twenties who'd had too much to drink and woken up with no memory of what her body told her had happened. Ffion had driven home on autopilot, then walked through the front door and fallen apart. Huw poured her a glass of wine and said all the right things. That Ffion was amazing to do the job she did; that the stress was bound to come out from time to time. And Ffion took a breath and thought, Now. I'll tell him now.

'Silly girl, getting so plastered,' Huw said then. 'You see it all the time, don't you? They get the beer goggles on, then the next day they regret it.'

Not now, Ffion thought. I won't tell him now.

Not ever, as it turned out. And without knowing she'd been raped, without knowing about Seren, was it any wonder Huw couldn't understand why Ffion wouldn't start a family? She didn't deserve a baby, not when she'd given her first away.

Leo knows all of this, now. And more. He knows what Ffion is afraid of, and what she loves. How she feels about the lake, and the mountains, and the village she once couldn't wait to leave.

'I suppose—' she says.

'Maybe we—' Leo starts speaking at the same time. 'You first.'

'No, you go.'

Leo takes a breath. 'I was thinking about when we met.'

'Right.'

'Seeing you at the mortuary. It was . . .'

'Awkward?'

'Very.' Leo says. 'But then . . . Well, I just wanted to say it's been great working with you. And not awkward.' He stares over the steering wheel, suddenly quiet, as though he's run out of steam.

It's a goodbye, Ffion knows. Her secondment to Cheshire Major Crime will be over soon and she'll return to her own patch. She and Leo might exchange a few emails, perhaps see each other at court in a few months' time, but that will be it.

She mirrors Leo's brusque tone. 'You too.'

'What were you going to say?'

Ffion had been going to suggest they gave it a shot. She wanted to say she'd never felt so comfortable with someone, and that when he'd put his arms around her and they'd stood looking out over the lake, she'd never felt so safe.

'Same.'

Something has happened to The Shore. It isn't just that the twinkly lights are no longer lit, or the champagne isn't flowing. The resort seems somehow tarnished, a place no longer coveted, but feared. Avoided. Even the sky seems a little darker on this side of the lake, the clouds a little greyer.

As they get out of the car, the door of the Staffords' lodge opens and a couple appear, their arms so entwined they have to walk sideways, crab-like.

'That's not Ashleigh Stafford,' Leo says.

'Your powers of observation are remarkable.' Ffion watches as the couple stop to kiss, Bobby cupping the woman's face and then picking her up and whirling her around. 'Get a room,' she mutters.

'Alright?' Bobby says, when he realises they have an audience. His grin's so wide it makes Ffion's cheeks hurt. 'This is the future Mrs Stafford.' The woman blushes.

'S'mae, Mia,' Ffion says. 'Fancy seeing you here.'

'No need for introductions, then, eh?' Bobby pulls Mia to him. 'She's a cracker, isn't she?'

'Is that why you pulled me?' Mia nudges him and they kiss again. Leo and Ffion exchange glances.

'What happened to Ashleigh?' Leo says.

'Not under the patio, if that's what you're wondering.' Bobby laughs, then stops. 'Sorry. Bit close to the knuckle given the current sitch, right?'

'Just a bit.' Ffion can't stop looking at Mia. She's still dressed in her usual jeans and fleece, a pair of ratty old trainers on her feet, but her skin is glowing and she looks . . . *radiant*. There's no other word for it.

'Ashleigh left me,' Bobby says.

'I'm sorry,' Leo says.

Bobby winks at him. 'I'm not. The whole thing was a sham.'

'We've all been there, mate,' Leo says.

'No, I mean it was an actual sham. Turns out Ashleigh wanted the headlines more than she wanted me. Once I realised, I said we should jack the whole thing in, but she said she'd get more coverage if we kept it going a bit longer. She had this big plan to leak some stories to the tabloids – arguments over having a baby, that sort of thing.' He grimaces. 'I should never have gone along with it. I just want a quiet life, you know?'

Next door, at number four, Clemmie Northcote's door opens. Ffion gives Bobby a tight smile. 'I'm not entirely sure you chose the best place for that.'

They wait until they're inside before they arrest Clemmie. Out on the deck, a pair of wellies lies next to a chair over which a wetsuit drips on to the deck.

'You told me you'd been to the village swim,' Leo says later, the interview tapes rolling. 'But that was a lie, wasn't it?'

Clemmie nods silently, tugging nervously at her dress.

'For the tape, please.'

'Yes.'

'So why was your wetsuit wet when my colleague spoke to you on New Year's Day?' Ffion says.

Clemmie blinks rapidly. 'I went for a dip before the party.'

'Really?' Ffion checks her notes. 'Because, from what we understand, you were quite the busy bee, helping with the preparations.'

Clemmie chews her bottom lip, and Ffion keeps a level gaze on her.

'Tell us what happened.'

'I don't know what you mean.'

'Did you follow Rhys to his office?' Leo asks.

'No.'

'Jonty Charlton says lodges at The Shore have to be bought outright,' Leo says. 'Yet you told me you bought yours on a payment plan. Which is it?'

Clemmie swallows, but doesn't answer.

'Rhys Lloyd's bank records show regular cash deposits,' Ffion says. 'Were they from you? Did you have a financial arrangement with him?'

Clemmie shifts in her seat, her expression miserable. She lets out a breath, like a balloon deflating, then she nods.

'How much did you owe?'

There's a long pause. 'Four hundred thousand pounds.'

Leo whistles. 'That's a lot of money. Who else knew about the loan?'

'No one.'

'How convenient,' Ffion says, 'for the only person who knew about the loan to die.'

'I didn't kill him!' Clemmie bursts into tears.

Ffion puts a series of images on the table. 'These photos were all posted on Instagram during or soon after the party.' She points to where Clemmie appears in each one: laughing, dancing, drinking. 'We've pulled the metadata from these images, and you know what's interesting? In this picture' – Ffion indicates an image of Clemmie doing some kind of jig – 'which was taken at ten p.m., you have dry hair. Yet in this one, taken at one a.m. on New Year's Day, your hair is wet.' Clemmie stares at the photo.

In it, she stands in the Charltons' kitchen, staring into her glass, while the party continues around her.

'Why is your hair wet, Clemmie?' Ffion says.

'I washed it.'

'Halfway through a party?'

Leo leans his elbows on the desk. 'You swam out to Angharad Evans's boat, didn't you? So you could use it to dispose of Rhys Lloyd's body. Which suggests to me that you killed him.'

Clemmie's shaking, her face ashen. 'I think,' she says finally, 'I think I'd like to speak to a solicitor.'

FIFTY-NINE

NEW YEAR'S EVE | CLEMMIE

Is it murder, Clemmie thinks, as she hauls Rhys's unmoving body through the master bedroom, if someone dies because you didn't save them? She doesn't let herself listen to the answer. She thinks instead of Caleb, of the downward spiral he was trapped in, back home, and of his transformation at The Shore. The lodge can be theirs. No loan hanging over their heads, no paperwork, no threats. Gone.

Clemmie grunts as she pulls Rhys on to the balcony, a blast of fresh air chasing away the last vestiges of drunkenness. He's heavy, but she told Glynis to stay in the study in case someone comes. Clemmie is pretty certain Rhys is too far gone to cause any trouble, but what if he suddenly groans, or moves?

At the far end of The Shore, the party marquee pulsates with music, lights criss-crossing the steamed-up windows. Clemmie's chest is tight. She waits so long she risks losing her nerve entirely, she has to pull herself together. There's nobody outside, nobody can see.

The glass surrounding the balcony stops a foot from the floor. Clemmie pushes Rhys under it, sickened by her own actions but in too deep to stop. There's an awful moment when she thinks his stomach is wedged, and Rhys is hanging off the balcony, but Clemmie puts her foot against him and pushes and—

Thud.

Clemmie gasps. Doesn't dare look down. The sound was so loud she imagines Rhys splattered across the decking, body parts strewn like the aftermath of a train wreck. But when she peers gingerly over the balustrade he's lying intact, as though he's asleep.

Clemmie takes several deep breaths, then returns to the study. Glynis hasn't moved from the spot in which Clemmie found her. She's stopped crying, but her face is drained of blood and her jaw trembles.

'If we put him in the water too close to the shore he'll be found.' Clemmie doesn't recognise herself; the words she's using. 'Clean up here – there's bleach in the bathroom, use lots – and meet me on the pontoon in fifteen minutes. And bring that with you.' Clemmie points to the trophy, still lying on the floor.

Glynis lets out a sob. 'I can't—'

'You have to.' Clemmie speaks harshly, but she has no choice. They have to get rid of Rhys, and they have to act fast. Who knows if Yasmin will come back to freshen up, or the twins will tire of hanging out with Caleb. At the thought of her son her heart clenches. *I'm doing this for you*, she tells him.

Down on the Lloyds' deck, she doesn't stop long enough to let the doubts creep in. She drags Lloyd's body across the wood, grateful for the muscles she's built up swimming, and lets it fall down the ladder on to the pontoon between the Lloyds' deck and her own. Only once it's out of sight of the lodges does she breathe; only then does she stoop to check again for Rhys's pulse. She thinks at first he's dead, but there's a faint flutter against her fingertips – a barely there reminder that she hasn't – yet – gone too far. His skin looks waxy in the thin moonlight, a dark tinge around his lips. Even if she called an ambulance now, would they be able to save him? And what would happen to her? The police would be called, for certain, and how would she explain how Rhys got outside, what she was doing with him? Clemmie is committed. She hasn't yet gone too far, but she has gone far enough.

Several guests arrived at the party in motorboats. Clemmie crosses to the next pontoon, but all three of the boats bobbing in the water need keys. 'Fuck!' She's close to tears. Above her, a shadow crosses the Lloyds' bedroom window and she hopes to God it's Glynis, that the woman's doing what Clemmie told her to do. She looks frantically around, as though a boat might materialise from the depths of the lake. Moonlight glints on the water, and, as the dark clouds scud across the mountain, Clemmie has an idea. She shivers.

She couldn't.

Could she?

Clemmie's wetsuit is hanging over a chair outside her lodge. She skulks in the shadows, her breath catching when she sees Caleb and the twins inside. The table's littered with bottles of beer and wine, and the mother in Clemmie wants to rap on the window and lecture them. Instead, she grabs her swimming things and returns to the pontoon.

She's swum at night before, a torch in her tow-float like a firefly on the water, but never alone, never with her blood fizzing with alcohol and fear. Her breathing's already too fast, too shallow, and when she slips silently into the water it abandons her entirely. She keeps moving, trusting her body, fighting the side of her brain which tells her she's drowning. She surfaces, and slowly her lungs expand, and she can breathe again.

Clemmie swims breaststroke so she can better keep watch, although she knows she's hidden in the darkness. The water is inky black, its choppy surface accustomed to hiding what lies beneath. Ahead of her, the mast on Angharad's boat glints in the moonlight. The water plays tricks on her sense of distance. The boat seems to stay out of reach until suddenly it's just thirty metres away, and then twenty . . . ten.

Clemmie hauls herself up, her limbs like jelly. She's praying there's fuel in the outboard motor, because in spite of the lessons Angharad gave her and Caleb, she isn't capable of sailing – especially not in the dark. She remembers to push the centreboard down through the slot in the bottom of the boat, locking it into place, then she releases the hinge on the motor and drops it into the water. She turns it on, grips the starter rope and tugs it hard.

There's a splutter and a cough, then silence.

'Oh, come on, come on . . .' Clemmie tries again, and again. Tears of frustration spring to her eyes, her teeth chattering as the cold seeps into her bones. She pulls again, and the splutter becomes a roar. She fiddles with the choke, finds the tiller, and points the boat towards The Shore.

As Clemmie draws near to the lodges she kills the engine, slotting the oars into their housings and rowing silently through the water towards the pontoons. She makes out the lumpen outline of Rhys's body and for a second she thinks he's alone. She curses Glynis, but then she realises there are two shapes, one cradling the other. Clemmie is at once torn apart by Glynis's grief, and terrified Rhys has made a recovery – is, even now, telling his mother what Clemmie has done. But as she brings the boat inexpertly alongside the pontoon she sees that he's in the same position she left him in, his mouth open and blood obscuring his features. Foam flecks his mouth. She reaches for his wrist, ostensibly to pull him closer to the boat, but really to see if—

Clemmie lets out a breath. He's dead. And she can't let herself wonder whether she killed him, or Glynis did, and, now that it's done, does it even matter? Rhys is dead.

'Help me get him in the boat,' Clemmie says. 'I can't manage on my own.' She's struggling to make her limbs comply, the cold enveloping her so completely she can't remember what it is to feel warm. Together, the two women heave Rhys into the hull of the boat.

As they leave The Shore behind, Clemmie rummages in the locker beside her and throws a lifejacket to Glynis. 'Put that on.' She doesn't know if Glynis can swim, and she can't risk the woman falling in. There's a short length of rope in the locker, and she throws that too. 'Tie the trophy to his ankle.'

'This is wrong. We have to go to the police. I'll explain—'

'They'll put you in prison, Glynis!' Clemmie shouts, the wind whipping the words from her mouth. She holds Glynis's gaze until the older woman looks away, defeated, and begins knotting the rope.

If there's no body, thinks Clemmie, trying to still her whirring mind, there's no evidence. She doesn't know how much they've already left – fingerprints, fibres, DNA – and how much of that will be washed away, and she's panicking, now, about what they've left at the Lloyds' lodge. Has Glynis done enough? Did Clemmie leave anything incriminating at the scene, anything which can't be explained away?

'It's done.' Glynis's voice breaks. She cradles her son's head against her chest.

Clemmie kills the engine. She nods. Moves to Rhys's body and grips both his wrists. 'Take his feet.'

Glynis looks at her, her eyes pleading.

'Prison,' Clemmie says. 'A life sentence – you'll die behind bars. Is that what you want?'

'I could explain, tell them it was an accident.'

'And what about me? I didn't ask to be dragged into this – I'm here to protect you.'

'I know and I'm grateful, I really am, but—'

'What will happen to Caleb, when they lock me up? I got him back on the right side of the tracks, but do you think he'll stay there, with a mother in prison? If you won't do this for me, do it for Caleb.'

The clouds shift and, for a second, moonlight illuminates the boat. Glynis looks at Rhys's corpse. She takes his legs. Clemmie has a sudden, incongruous memory of giving Caleb the bumps at a birthday party, flinging him into the air once for each year he'd been alive. *Three, four, five.*

'After three,' Clemmie says. 'One, two, three—'

Above the village, the sky lights up in reds and blues, electric rain pouring down on to the water. A rocket shoots for the moon, exploding in a cascade of silver.

And Rhys Lloyd plunges into the lake.

SIXTY

JANUARY 9TH | FFION

'I need to go and check something out,' Ffion says, after they've returned Clemmie to her cell to wait for the duty solicitor.

'Check what out?' Leo holds open the door, and they leave the custody block.

'Just stuff.'

'I'll come with you.'

'One of us needs to be here when Clemmie's ready to go back into interview.' She flashes a smile. 'Anyway, I'm the Lone Ranger, remember?'

For once, the Triumph eats up the miles between Chester and Cwm Coed all too quickly. Soon, Ffion is dropping down towards the serpentine glimmer of silver in the valley. She pauses by the turn-off for The Shore, the huge letters seeming more of a warning, now, than an invitation. What will become of them all? Of the five owners, only Dee Huxley's life is unchanged by what's happened, and Ffion wonders what the old lady has made of it all.

But Ffion isn't going to The Shore today. She drives on, into Cwm Coed and down the high street, where last night's blizzard has left sludgy snow on the sides of the road. She parks the car and feels the familiar sense of dread as she walks towards Glynis Lloyd's shop.

It takes a while for Glynis to open the door. When she does, she steps back in silent invitation, and Ffion doesn't want to go inside, but they can't have this conversation on the doorstep.

'Go on up,' Glynis says, when they're standing in the narrow hallway. She gestures to the stairs which lead up to the flat, but Ffion walks straight on, towards the back door. Blood sings in her ears and she sees it all over again, that summer's evening walk, her hand in Rhys's. She feels it all again.

Glynis follows her into the back garden. Ffion looks at the summer house, now full of junk and stock for the shop. She remembers the sofabed, the piano, the music stand. She remembers the feel of the woollen blanket, scratchy against her bare skin.

'Ffion.'

She will not cry. Not here, not in front of Glynis. 'You knew, didn't you?' She turns to the older woman. 'You said this was where Rhys had bullied Ceri, but you got that wrong.'

'I knew something bad had happened here. When Jac told me what Rhys had done to that poor girl – Rhys had bragged to his dad, like it was all a big joke – I thought that must have been what I saw that night.'

Ffion looks up at the first-floor window. She's breathing too fast, feeling dizzy and scared, even though it's only Glynis. She centres herself. Not Rhys. It isn't Rhys. 'You knew. You were watching.' For years, Ffion has assumed she couldn't hate anyone more than Rhys Lloyd, but right now, she thinks she hates Glynis more. To stand by and let him . . . She can't let the thought take shape.

Glynis is crying. 'Jac tried to warn me about what sort of man Rhys had become – what sort of boy he'd been – but I wouldn't listen. I didn't want to hear it. He was my only child, my special—'

Ffion can't hear any more. 'You. Saw. Me.'

'I thought I was mistaken,' Glynis pleads. 'I wasn't sure. I just knew—' She takes a big breath, covering her face with her hands as the rest of her words fall out in a sob. 'I just knew they were too young.' Ffion moves backwards, knocking into a bird table, which judders precariously on its stand. She thinks she might be sick.

'For years, Jac had worried about Rhys, told me there was a bad seed in him. Towards the end, he said Rhys was trying to take Tŷ'r Lan, that he'd destroy the one thing that mattered to his father. I told him he was crazy, but he was right. I'd been blind.'

She's found his original will, Elen had told Ffion. *She's going to take legal action.*

'That's why you killed him,' Ffion says.

Glynis doesn't move.

'We've arrested Clemmie. She's in the cells, right now.'

'She mustn't go to prison!' It explodes from Glynis as though she hadn't planned to say it, and she claps her hand over her mouth. But it's too late, and slowly she lets her hand fall. 'I – I made her help me.'

'You *made* her?' Ffion doesn't believe Glynis for a second.

'Her son needs her. Boys need their mothers. They need strong mothers, to keep them on the right track, otherwise they . . .' She trails off, but Ffion doesn't need her to finish. *Otherwise they turn out like Rhys.* Glynis Lloyd is atoning for the sins of her son.

Ffion takes a step towards her. 'Glynis Lloyd, I'm arresting you on suspicion of murder . . .'

This is where it ends.

SIXTY-ONE

JANUARY 10TH | LEO

Leo's desk phone flashes with the number for the front desk.

'Someone here to see you. Says she knows you.'

There's still half an hour until morning meeting, so Leo makes his way downstairs.

At the front desk, Nellie is dunking a Hobnob into a cup of tea. 'I put her in the side room. Didn't get a name, sorry – it's been manic.'

Leo looks around the empty office. 'Looks like it.' He raps twice on the door of the small room used for witness interviews, and walks in.

'What the fuck are you playing at, Leo?'

Leo looks at his ex-wife and feels none of the anxiety she usually instils in him. She's brandishing a letter, the contents of which Leo is familiar with, as his solicitor shared a copy for approval before serving it.

'I'm taking you to court,' Leo says calmly.

'You're not having joint access, and you're not stopping us from moving.' Unusually, as Allie rarely sets foot outside the house without make-up, her face is bare. Her skin is threaded with tiny red veins, and last night's wine stains the inside of her lips.

407

'I am, and I will.' It is something of a revelation to Leo, to discover that the calmer he remains, the more irate Allie becomes.

'It's all going to come out in court, you know. What you did.'

Leo nods. 'Okay.' He could tell her, he supposes, that he finally summoned the courage to speak to colleagues in Child Protective Services, who, in turn, spoke to Social Services. He could tell her that no one has identified a concern over Harris's welfare from what was a highly unexpected and isolated incident. Leo's solicitor is a glass-half-empty woman, so when she said she was confident of winning joint custody, Leo felt a surge of optimism.

'Harris doesn't want to see you. He doesn't want to stay in your shitty flat. He said the other day, "Don't make me go to Daddy's".'

There was a time when Leo might have believed Allie; when her words would have corresponded so perfectly with his own thoughts, he would have slunk away like a wounded animal. Leo opens the door. 'Goodbye, Allie.'

'I'm not finished!'

'I am.'

The briefing room carries the hum of anticipation which accompanies the prospect of good news. Crouch stands by the smartboard, chest puffed with proxy pride. 'You will no doubt have seen the headlines this morning.' An array of newspapers is spread across the desks, their headlines variations on the same theme: *Rhys Lloyd murdered by his own mother*.

Under caution, Glynis Lloyd gave a full and frank confession to her son's murder. 'I just lashed out,' she said, between tears. 'I didn't think I'd hit him that hard, but he went down like he'd run into a wall.'

Leo and Ffion spent an hour on the phone to the Crown Prosecution Service, outlining the case against Glynis. Izzy Weaver remained adamant that the injuries Lloyd sustained from the trophy could not have killed him, but it was clear from Lloyd's demeanour at the party – and the data from his watch – that his health had been compromised at the time of the assault.

'The straw that broke the camel's back,' Izzy said. 'Or, in this case, your chap's face.'

The case against Clemence Northcote was more straight-forward. She hadn't been present at time of the assault, and there was no suggestion that she and Glynis Lloyd had conspired to bring about Rhys's death – the two women had barely spoken before the night in question. Clemmie would be prosecuted for assisting an offender and concealing a crime, as well as the unlawful disposal of a dead body.

'You will make it clear?' Glynis said, in her interview. 'That she had no choice but to help me?'

'I was scared,' Clemmie confirmed.

'Of Glynis Lloyd?' Leo was sceptical.

'She said she'd tell the police it was me. I knew you'd find out about the money I owed Rhys – I knew it would look bad for me.'

There was, Leo thought, something not quite right about this case.

'You think too much,' Ffion said, when both women had been charged. 'They've both coughed to it.'

'And they're obviously both guilty; it's just . . .' Leo shakes his head. 'I don't know. I'm not sure we'll ever know exactly what happened that night.'

Maybe it doesn't matter, he thinks now, as everyone's sitting around the briefing table, Crouch in self-congratulation mode.

'Our department has been in the nation's spotlight,' he finishes, after what seems like an hour. 'We have not let the public down!'

If he's hoping for applause, he's disappointed. With the exception of a handful of keen-and-green officers borrowed from shift, the detectives in the room are far too jaded and cynical to be roused by a Churchillian speech. Nevertheless, there is an audible buzz of satisfaction.

'A fine day indeed,' Crouch goes on, 'for Cheshire Constabulary.'

'And North Wales Police,' Ffion says. 'Sir.'

'Ah. Yes, of course. And North Wales.' Crouch turns to the pair of them. 'Perhaps you'd like to fill everyone in on the loose ends?'

'We're anticipating guilty pleas from both,' Ffion says. 'But obviously we'll ensure everything's in place, should that change. Meanwhile, the Met are charging Yasmin Lloyd with wasting police time, and Jonty Charlton's under investigation for drugging his kids with sleeping pills he got from Rhys Lloyd.'

No wonder Yasmin had been nervous when she was presented with the list of medication seized from the Lloyds' bedroom: it included the sleeping tablets Rhys had used for years – the same ones he'd used to drug their own daughter when she was a toddler.

Crouch runs through the tasks for the day – the tedious but necessary post-charge investigative work – then raises a hand to summon the team's attention for a final time.

'Some of you may not be aware that, in the course of the murder investigation, DC Brady and DC Morgan responded to an emergency situation on Mirror Lake.'

Beside him, Leo feels Ffion tense. Leo had glossed over their exploits when briefing the DI, telling him only that a local girl had got into difficulties. Ffion's story is her own to tell. Hers and Seren's.

'The conditions on the lake were treacherous,' Crouch says. 'Yet these officers went on to the water with no consideration for their own welfare, and brought a young girl to safety.' He smiles at Ffion, then his eyes rest on Leo. 'Great work, you two. Really great work.'

This time, even the oldest and most jaded members of the team are stirred into a response. Leo tries to stay nonchalant, but he can't stop the swelling in his chest as his colleagues give him and Ffion a round of applause. He takes in the admiration on their faces, and the curt but genuine nod of respect from Crouch, and he grins.

He won't ask for a transfer back to Liverpool. He'll stay on Major Crime, and maybe he'll look again at promotion. And in among all of that, once he and Ffion are no longer working together, maybe he'll pluck up enough courage to ask her out for that drink.

SIXTY-TWO

JUNE | FFION

The summer brings with it the sort of heat that makes Ffion long for rain. She's spent the day in a stuffy courtroom with a lad from down south, who came to North Wales on a climbing holiday and went home on bail. The hearing over, Ffion drives across the mountains to the small village of Bethfelin, not far from home, to tell Mr and Mrs Roberts that the man who put their son in hospital has been found guilty.

'I know it doesn't change anything,' Ffion says. Twenty-six-year-old Bryn Roberts was an instructor. His group had been boisterous and arrogant, reluctant to listen to the leaders. What began as messing around had ended in permanent brain damage for one man, and a GBH conviction for the other.

'*Diolch*, Ffion,' Mrs Roberts says. 'For keeping us updated . . . for everything.'

Her husband shows her out. 'I knew your dad, you know,' he says gruffly. 'He'd be proud of you.'

Ffion's eyes sting as she drives the Triumph back towards Cwm Coed. She remembers the disappointment on her dad's face when he'd learned she was pregnant. 'For God's sake, Ffi, sort yourself out.'

Ffion had tried. She'd tried relationships, jobs, friendships . . .

they'd all seemed to end in chaos, and Ffion had begun to think that was just *her*. Just the way she is.

But now she thinks that perhaps Dad *would* be proud of her.

And maybe – just maybe – she's beginning to sort herself out.

The sun's still warm when Ffion draws level with Llyn Drych, and the Triumph turns towards the lake almost of its own accord. She has no swimming things, but her underwear is serviceable, and she'll use her jumper to dry off.

Two minutes later she's in the water, gasping as the cold tickles her stomach. Ffion holds her breath and plunges under the surface, the grime of the day gone in a second, pulling herself through the water in long, even strokes. Beneath her, she sees the silver dart of a fish, before it's lost in the murky weeds far below. Every third stroke, Ffion takes a breath, and the shore passes in a series of snapshots, a flipbook of trees and birds and boats. High above her, Pen y Ddraig mountain keeps watch.

As Ffion swims back towards the jetty, she sees a figure standing next to the Triumph.

Seren.

Ffion makes herself carry on at the same steady rate. Every time she lifts her head, she expects the shore to be empty, and she wills Seren to stay. *Give her time*, Elen keeps saying. But how much time?

'Has she said anything to you, Mam?' Ffion asked recently, and Elen sighed.

'I'm sorry, *cariad*. It's a lot to take in. She needs someone to blame, and . . .' Hesitation hid Rhys's name. '*He's* not here, so I'm afraid you're taking the brunt.'

Ffion faltered before saying what was in her head, and, when she spoke, she couldn't look at Elen. 'It wasn't my idea to say Seren was my sister.'

There was a heavy silence.

'No.' Elen turned away, staring out of the window, her voice small and uncertain. 'And every day I've wondered, did we do the right thing?'

Did they?

It's felt right, Ffion supposes, for much of the past sixteen years, when Seren was free from the stigma attached to the children of young single mothers. It felt right when Ffion was able to stay on at school, get A-levels, go to university. Seren was happy, well-adjusted – until she learned the truth.

Ffion senses, rather than feels, the moment the lake meets the shore. She takes a final dip beneath the surface, her eyes wide in the clear, cold water, then surfaces and wades the few metres to dry land. Seren looks on the verge of flight, and Ffion's pulse races. She mustn't mess this up.

'Hey.' Ffion towels herself off with her jumper and tugs on her trousers. She pulls her buttoned shirt over her head, taking off her wet bra and dropping it on the floor in one fluid movement.

'Hi.'

Early evening has brought a chill to the air. Ffion sits on the bonnet of the car, deliberately leaving room beside her. On the lake, Angharad's new boat tacks back towards the boathouse. Out of the corner of her eye, Ffion sees Seren shuffle into the space next to her. They sit side by side, watching a windsurfer make his way from one side of the lake to the other. Ffion waits.

'I don't know how to *be*,' Seren says eventually. 'Like, you were my sister, and I knew how to be around you. But now . . .'

'I'm still the same—'

'No, you're not! You're my – you're my – God, I can't even say it!'

'You don't have to say it. You don't have to do anything, *be* anything. I'm not going anywhere, okay? When you're ready, we can hang out. Maybe.' Ffion grits her teeth. God, this is hard.

'I hate it here.' Seren kicks one foot against the other. 'It's so, fucking, *in your face*. Like, you can't go anywhere without seeing someone you know. I feel like I can't breathe.'

'I know.'

Seren scoffs. 'You don't.'

'I was exactly the same. Desperate to escape, to see the world, to find – oh, I don't know – something *real*.'

'Yes!' Seren turns to her, her eyes flashing with enthusiasm, before she remembers who Ffion is. What she's done. 'And then you came back! Like, what the fuck for?'

'I came back for you,' Ffion says simply.

Seren's bluster vanishes. 'Oh.' There's a beat, before she frowns.

'That's not why I stayed, though.' Ffion grins at the mock indignation on her daughter's face. 'Well, not entirely.' She sweeps an arm in the direction of the lake. 'I stayed for this.'

'Llyn Drych?'

'All of it. The lake. The mountains. The stupid stories about throwing rocks and waking the dragon by hitting its tail. It's in my blood.' Hesitantly, she puts an arm around Seren's shoulders. 'It's in yours,' she says quietly.

They stay on the bonnet of the Triumph, silently watching the lake. A minute or two passes, and then Seren slowly drops her head on to Ffion's shoulder, and Ffion holds her breath and digs her nails into her palm to stop herself crying. All these years she's told herself she isn't a mother, won't ever be a mother, doesn't want to be a mother. She's emptied her heart without even realising, and now it is full – so very full.

'I can't call you Mam,' Seren says, breaking the silence.

'You can call me whatever you want.'

'Shit-for-brains?'

'You're not funny, you know,' says Ffion, smiling.

'I get my sense of humour from my mother.' Seren moves, and Ffion feels bereft for a moment, but Seren turns and throws her arms around her, squeezing so hard it takes Ffion's breath away. No sooner is she there than she pulls away. 'I'd better go. I said I'd meet Caleb.'

'Things still going well between you, then?'

Seren shrugs, but her face is lit up. 'S'pose.'

'That's good.' Ffion keeps her voice neutral. She is keeping an eye on Caleb Northcote. Clemmie narrowly escaped a custodial sentence for her part in a crime the judge described as *abhorrent*. She has her son to thank for that, as well as Dee Huxley, whose character reference spoke glowingly of Clemmie as a friend, neighbour and mother. Ironically, it is now Clemmie, not Caleb, who is under supervision, who must sign on at a police station and fulfil her community service obligations.

That evening, Ffion meets Huw in the pub. It's the third time she and Huw have gone out in the past few months. Back in April Ffion had opened the door to find Huw standing there with a bunch of flowers.

Ffion eyed them suspiciously. 'What are those for?'

'Well, they're not for me.'

They were proper flowers, not supermarket ones, wrapped in brown paper and tied with raffia. 'Do you want to come in?' Ffion knew she sounded ungracious.

'You're alright.' Huw scuffed the toe of his boot against the doorstep. 'So, you said you might come for a drink. When you'd finished that job.'

416

'I did.' Ffion counted the petals on something that looked like a daisy but probably wasn't. *He loves me, he loves me not . . .*

'And the job's finished. Isn't it?'

'It is.' *He loves me.*

'Ah, come on! Will you have a drink with me, or not?'

Ffion looked at Huw's furrowed brow, and thought about what it must take to keep asking.

'I miss you.'

Everything was there, waiting for her. A husband. A house. Even children, if she ever decided she could; and for the first time in sixteen years she wasn't ruling it out. All she had to do was take a step.

'It's just a drink, Ffi. Yes or no?'

'Oh, go on, then.'

She worried it would be awkward – how did you date someone you'd already married? – but she'd forgotten what easy company Huw was. He talked about the lads at work, his jokes familiar and new at the same time; and she traded the guy who'd been caught dogging in a layby between Llanwys and Brynafon.

'Whereabouts, exactly?' Huw had pretended to make a note of it, and Ffion had grinned, feeling the warmth of familiarity, security.

'I've got something for you,' she says now. She pushes an envelope across the table. Huw frowns as he opens it, his eyes widening as he pulls out a cheque for thirty thousand pounds. 'The prison finally gave Glynis authorisation to access her bank accounts.'

'I'll get the pork scratchings in.' Huw taps the cheque. 'Make it a real celebration.'

'Proper class, you are.' Ffion grins. 'How's your mam doing?'

Ffion's mother-in-law had taken their separation badly, asking

417

Ffion what was wrong with her for not wanting a baby *like a normal woman.*

Huw grimaces. 'Same old. Yours?'

'Driving me nuts. She treats me like I'm still a teenager.'

'You know . . .' Huw stares into his pint '. . . you could always come home.'

Home. The three-bedroomed house Huw built with his own hands, with its open-plan kitchen-diner and neat garden. The little box room, painted nursery-yellow by Huw, one Sunday, as though seeing the space would change Ffion's mind about wanting to fill it.

'I don't mind being at Mam's.' Ffion tries to gloss over the offer. 'I'm mostly at work, so—'

'I decorated the bedrooms,' Huw says suddenly, and Ffion realises he's read her thoughts. 'Ours is blue, now, and the . . .' He stumbles. 'The box room's grey. I've got the computer in there, so it's just an office, not . . .' He looks at her. 'Come home, Ffi.'

Ffion's breath catches. *Home.*

SIXTY-THREE

JUNE | LEO

'Bedtime,' Leo calls.

'Come see!'

Leo dries his hands on a tea towel and walks to his son's bedroom. On the floor, by the bed that Elen Morgan gave them, is a rug Leo bought online, with a race track printed on the weave. Harris has made a series of buildings out of Lego, placing each one carefully around the track.

'Hey, good construction skills, mate!'

'This one is our house.' Harris holds up one made from yellow bricks, with a red roof.

'Fingers crossed, yeah?' The offer was accepted a month ago, and there's no chain, so with any luck they'll be in by the end of the summer.

Leo sits on the carpet next to Harris, picking a car from his son's vast collection and idly pushing it along the track. The new house is nothing special – a two-up, two-down in a quiet street – but it has a garage and a garden, and neighbours with kids who play out while it's light. It's the sort of house Leo wishes he'd grown up in; the sort of house he wants Harris to grow up in.

'It's miles away,' Allie had said, when he'd told her the address.

'Half an hour. With school slap bang in the middle.'

419

They have reached a truce, of sorts. It turned out Dominic had never been keen on the idea of Australia; Allie was the one pushing for the glistening water of the Sunshine Coast. Faced with a potentially expensive legal battle, Dominic became an unexpected ally, and he and Allie had decided to stay put. Harris now spends every Wednesday and every other weekend with Leo, his bedroom stuffed with so many clothes and toys that Leo wonders how they'll get it all in the moving van.

Harris's room isn't the only part of the flat to have had a makeover. Leo's no Yasmin Lloyd, but it's amazing what a lick of paint and a few prints can do. Ffion would hardly recognise the place.

Leo leans against Harris's bed and fishes his phone out of his back pocket to text her. How's the sheep rustling?

The reply comes almost instantly. Fuck off, Brady.

Leo grins. That's Detective SERGEANT Brady to you . . .

You got a promotion? You NEVER MENTIONED IT. This is followed by three eye-rolling emojis, a capital W and a picture of an anchor. Leo frowns at the screen, then bursts out laughing when the penny drops.

'Let me see!' Harris jumps on him, expecting another of the funny animal videos Leo often finds online for him.

'Not this time, mate. Come on, into bed.' He tucks Harris in, and finds the book they're reading, ignoring the flashing screen which tells him Ffion has sent another text.

Clemmie and Glynis entered guilty pleas at their first hearings.

'No trial, then,' Leo said, for something to say. He and Ffion were standing outside court, Ffion having a cigarette before driving home. She gave a lopsided grin, the roll-up still in her mouth.

'I won't need to look at your ugly mug for weeks on end, then.'

'Right back atcha.'

There'd been radio silence, after that, and Leo ached with the absence of her. Ffion hadn't called, and Leo was glad he hadn't humiliated himself by asking her out for a drink. He thought about messaging to say he'd be at the sentencing, but whichever way he put it, it sounded as though he was fishing to see if she'd be there. Which, of course, he would have been.

'Fancy seeing you here.' Ffion had snuck up on him, standing on the concourse waiting for the ushers to open court, catching Leo's broad smile before he had a chance to make himself look more chilled about it. 'You look great.'

'Thanks. You, too.'

Once Harris is asleep, the Lego town moved carefully to one side to avoid either of them treading on it in the night, Leo sits with his feet up in front of the TV, scrolling mindlessly through his newsfeed. He catches sight of a name unusual enough for him to remember. *Elijah Fox is the youngest person ever to secure a post-doctoral research fellowship at Liverpool University. Professor Benjamin Milne said, 'I have rarely encountered someone with Dr Fox's level of knowledge and natural ability.'*

Leo raises his beer in a toast. 'Good on you, mate.' He remembered how sorry he'd felt for the hapless Elijah, stuck working with someone who gave Crouch a run for his money in the bad boss stakes. And now look at them both: Elijah with his – what even was a *post-doctoral research fellowship?* – and Leo with his sergeant's stripes. In fact, there was only one thing left for Leo to summon up the courage to do.

Ffion's last message is still on the screen of his phone: Pretty boring here without you, tbh, Brady.

Leo taps a response. Remember that time you said we should forget the way we met?

Ffion's response comes straight away: Er . . . yes.

He takes a deep breath and a swig of his beer.

I can't. Will you have dinner with me?

SIXTY-FOUR

JUNE | FFION

Ffion takes a box of books from Huw's van and carries them up the drive. There are another three boxes by the front door.

'That's everything.' Ffion feels light-headed, impetuous. She has questioned her decision over and over, and she still doesn't know if she's doing the right thing. She laces her fingers through Huw's, and leans into him, feeling his strong arm pull her close. 'I'm so sorry,' she says.

'Yeah. Me too.' It's curt enough to make Ffion wince, but still kinder than she deserves. 'See you around.'

Ffion waits on the drive as Huw drives away, then puts the box of books in the hall with the others, despite Mam's protests. 'I'll put it away later,' she promises, although where, God only knows. Mam's house is bursting at the seams.

'That's what you said when you moved the first lot of boxes back,' Elen says. 'Three months later, and we were still stepping over bin bags of clothes to get to the loo.' She pulls a towel from the kitchen airer. 'I'm going for a swim – I don't want to see those boxes when I get back.'

'Sir, yes sir,' Ffion mutters, because even when you're thirty, mams make you feel thirteen again.

423

Elen scrutinises her daughter's face. 'I hope you know what you're doing.'

'Don't start, Mam.'

'He's a good man.'

'Too good.'

'Oh, Ffi.' Elen sighs, then she puts her hands either side of Ffion's face and drops a kiss on her forehead. 'Now' – she stuffs her towel into a tote bag – 'move those bloody boxes.'

Once the front door is closed, Ffion gets out her phone and looks at the message from Leo.

Will you have dinner with me?

She stares at the screen for the longest time, then puts the phone back in her pocket. Later. When she's worked out what to say.

The house is quiet without Mam and Seren, who is almost certainly at The Shore with Caleb. Ffion wanders upstairs to find somewhere to store her books, but she's already used every cupboard in the house. From her bedroom window, you can just see the lake – a shimmer of silver beyond the treetops – and Ffion stands and watches the sun dip towards the mountain range. A scattering of fairy lights, like fallen stars, marks out the decks of The Shore.

Dee Huxley is sticking around, and Bobby Stafford is still smitten enough by Mia to do the same, but Yasmin Lloyd has accepted an offer on what the papers are calling *the murder lodge*. The Charltons have separated, Blythe keeping number one as a holiday let and yoga retreat, and the second phase of the development is now under way, with lodges springing up seemingly overnight. Ffion wonders who will buy them; how the new owners will fit in with the people of Cwm Coed.

Back downstairs, Ffion eyes up the boxes. They'll have to go in the shed. She'll need to move them before the winter, or the damp will get them, but at least it'll get them out of Mam's way. Elen Morgan might be houseproud, but she's not green-fingered. Since Ffion's dad died, the Morgans' overgrown garden has been loved more by wildlife than by the neighbours on either side, who each boast neat strips of begonia-edged lawn.

Ffion pushes through swathes of ox-eye daisies, sticky goosegrass clinging to her shorts. The shed is side-on to the house, the door warped so badly it only closes with a kick. Ffion puts down the box and yanks it open. Inside is a muddle of tools and bags of dried-up compost; of stacked plastic pots and fertiliser long past its use-by date. She begins moving everything to one side, to make space for the boxes.

A moment later, Ffion is wishing she'd never started. She contemplates how, if she had said yes to Huw, she would never have needed to set foot in this shed. That, really, she's only here, among the rusty tools and the bags of compost, because she can't stop thinking about Leo. She pulls out a bag and the contents spill on to the floor in front of her. 'This is all your bloody fault, Leo Brady,' she mutters. But, as she bends down to pick them up, she realises what she's seeing. She sits down among the dirt and the spiders, suddenly light-headed.

This changes everything.

SIXTY-FIVE

JUNE | FFION

Pen y Ddraig mountain looms high above Llyn Drych, the water shimmering in the last of the evening light. A tiny boat tacks slowly from one side of the lake to the other. On the shore, a handful of day-trippers are barbecuing on piled stones; smoke, and the smell of sausages, drifting hazily into the warm air. Ffion looks for her mother.

Across the water, The Shore has doubled in size since last summer. The slope of the forest means the second row of lodges is higher than the first, although nothing could match the panoramic views of the front five properties. There are people on the middle deck – too small to make out – and, as Ffion watches, someone dives from the pontoon, shallow and long.

Elen Morgan never swims with a float, and she shuns the brightly coloured swim hats advised by the lake wardens. Like Angharad, she swims barefoot, seemingly unaffected by the sharp stones around the water's edge.

Ffion scans the lake until she catches movement, travelling from one buoy to another. Elen swims breaststroke; unhurried, but faster than most. No splashy showmanship, just smooth, even strokes, low in the water. She is as much a part of the lake as the reeds which edge the coves; as the buoys which spend all year in the water, weeds clinging to their chains.

Ffion sits on the end of the jetty, letting her feet dangle in the cool water. Beside her is the black bin bag from the shed, and as Elen swims closer to the jetty Ffion carefully arranges the contents of the bag. There's a handful of photographs taken at the summer camp party, a note from Mia slipped into the envelope. *Thought you and Ffion might like to see these. Trip down memory lane!* Elen had not shared the photos with Ffion and, as Ffion looks through them now, she can see why. In every photo, Rhys is looking at Ffion, or Ffion is looking at him.

Elen Morgan knew Seren's father had been at that party. These photographs had been enough to send her in search of proof.

Elen had sent for a DNA test. Wrapped in a carrier bag is a an ebony hairbrush, the letters *RL* etched on the back, and a folded piece of paper.

Rhys Lloyd is not excluded as the biological father of Seren Morgan. The probability of paternity is over 99 per cent.

Even though it could be no other way, Ffion catches a sob in her throat. The paperwork is dated November last year. Elen had known Rhys was Seren's father months before Ffion told her. Before Seren discovered the truth.

Ffion's pulse is a drum in her ears, as she watches Elen pierce the mirrored surface of the lake. She feels the beat in her toes, as the water ebbs against her sun-baked skin. She pictures Rhys's corpse on its stainless-steel bed.

In the bin bag from the shed is a smoky brown apothecary jar, identical to those on Angharad's kitchen shelves, and Ffion thinks of poor Elijah and the ease with which his theories had been dismissed.

A few metres from the jetty, Elen stands, shaking water from her hair and tipping her head to catch the last of the sun. She smiles.

'Oh, Mam,' Ffion says quietly. 'What have you done?'

Elen takes in the objects lined up on the jetty. Tiny fish dart around her, glinting in the light.

'You were fourteen.'

'God, Mam.' Ffion's way out of her depth. 'How did you get his hairbrush?'

'I used your key to get into Huw's house when he was at work. I took the keys to The Shore and went to Rhys's lodge when the place was closed for building work.'

'Does Angharad know you took the ricin from her house?' Ffion remembers Angharad's description of *Ricinus communis*; the ease with which she sailed past the truth.

'No!' Elen starts walking out of the water. 'She had nothing to do with it, Ffi. She uses it in a homeopathic remedy, but not in its purest form – not like that.' She indicates the jar, and Ffion shivers. You only need a tiny amount to kill someone, Elijah said. A poison so deadly, it hardly leaves a trace.

'You sent it to him, didn't you?' Ffion picks up the pack of envelopes she found in the bag. The cellophane is torn, an envelope missing. *It's a paper cut*, Leo said, of the tiny cut on Rhys's tongue. He and Ffion had been so close – so damn close. The ricin hadn't been at the crime scene for them to discover.

'I mixed the ricin into a paste.' Elen wraps a towel around her, walking towards Ffion at the end of the jetty. 'I brushed it on to the seal of a stamped addressed envelope and sent it with a request for a signed photograph.'

428

Ffion scrambles to her feet. Poison applied to the seal of a stamped addressed envelope, the evidence sent away from the crime scene by the victim himself. It was the perfect murder. Around them, crickets pulse in the long grass. Ffion thinks of the witness accounts from the night of the party; the way Rhys appeared blind drunk. She thinks of his erratic heart-rate, the ease with which Glynis's attack ended his life.

'You killed him.'

Elen says nothing.

'Mam . . .' Ffion gathers up the evidence, throwing it back into the black plastic bag. She thinks of how she told Leo she was related to half the village, and how a criminal's a criminal, no matter which branch of your family tree they sit on. 'This is – I'm a police officer, Mam. I've got a duty to—' She breaks off, rubbing her head, unable to process what's happening. 'You let Glynis think she'd killed her own son!'

'I know.' Elen is calm. It's Ffion who's crying. 'It's okay, Ffi. I did what I had to do, *cariad*. Now you do what you have to do.'

No one in Cwm Coed can remember what year the swim began, but they know they wouldn't welcome the new year in any other way. They don't remember which year it was that Dafydd Lewis went in wearing nothing but a Santa hat, or when the rugby lads bombed off the jetty and drenched poor Mrs Williams.

But everyone remembers last year's swim.

'No dead bodies this year, hopefully!' someone shouts. Everyone laughs, but it's an uneasy, uncomfortable laugh. It will take longer than twelve months for the people of Cwm Coed to forget that one of them is a murderer.

'Bloody freezing, it is,' Ceri says. 'I hope you know what you're letting yourself in for.' She's brought someone with her – a woman with laughter lines and a silver chain around her neck, who touches Ceri's arm when she talks and makes her eyes light up.

'I know a good way to warm up.' Bobby winks at Mia, and the pair of them giggle like kids.

The first klaxon sounds, and there's a collective cry of excitement. Everyone races for the water, squealing and hopping from the sharp stones. Steffan – sober nine months and counting – stands up in the safety boat, siren at the ready.

'Five!' he shouts, and the crowd picks up the countdown. 'Four! Three!'

'Ready?' Ffion says. She looks down the shore, to where Seren and Caleb are bunched with the other teenagers.

'Two! One!'

'Ready,' Elen says. They run, eyes bright with cold, with adrenaline. They wade into the lake, and, when they're deep enough, they plunge, mind over matter through the low-lying mist. Cold clamps a vice around their chests, mouths opening in shock as their breath is wrenched away. Keep moving, keep moving! Ripples become waves, the movement of people this way and that, as the wind picks up and sends shivers across shoulders.

Out in the centre of the lake, far below the kicking legs of Cwm Coed's New Year's Day swimmers, is Angharad's red-sailed boat. Every few months, a piece of it will wash up in one of the many coves around Llyn Drych, but – for now – the hull lies wedged between the rocks at the bottom of the lake.

Close to the boat, a black plastic bag is tied tightly to a heavy weight. It lies half-buried in silt, the rope so tightly knotted, it could never come free. Weed has grown around the rope and tiny fish flick round it, biting, nibbling.

One day, the rope will fray, and the bag will begin to move through the water.

One day.

But not yet.

ACKNOWLEDGEMENTS

As always, I owe a great debt to many people, without whom this novel would not have been written. My thanks go to Anna Morgan, who endured endless discussions over lunch and while we swam in the very lake which inspired the story; to Emma Norrey, who offered invaluable thoughts on character; to Simon Thirsk, for talking to me about palindromic poetry and mirror structure; to the artist Sarah Wimperis, whose paintings influenced much of the imagery in this book; to Nia Roberts, for checking my Welsh (and more); and to Colin Scott, for more than I have room to mention.

Forensic pathologist Amanda Jeffery was kind enough to discuss poisons, head injuries and post-mortem findings. All departures from reality are down to me, made for the purposes of plot and entertainment. To that end, I'd like to thank Lisa Jewell for her advice on research, which has transformed my writing process.

I have been out of the police service for almost as many years as I was in it, so I'm indebted to my 'crew in blue' for their patience, when I ask yet another question to which I should know the answer. Huge thanks to Katy Barrow-Grint, Katie Clements, Jennifer Fox, Claire Thorngate, Kelly Tuttle, Sarah Thirkell, Beth Walton and Fran Whyte, for the virtual incident room. Yes, I know that's not how it would happen in real life . . .

433

Cwm Coed and The Shore are fictional, but the beautiful lakes and mountains of North Wales are very real and I feel incredibly lucky to now call them home. Thank you to the friends and neighbours who have been so welcoming. *Diolch chi i gyd.*

Each of my books is the product of hard work and passion from my publishing teams around the world. Thank you to Cath Burke; to my editors, Lucy Malagoni, Tilda McDonald and Rosanna Forte; to publicists Kirsteen Astor, Millie Seaward and Emma Finnigan; and marketing team extraordinaire Gemma Shelley and Brionee Fenlon. Thank you to Hannah Methuen and her sales team; to Andy Hine, Kate Hibbert, Helena Doree and Sarah Birdsey in rights; to cover designer Hannah Wood; the queen of copy-editors, Linda McQueen; to brilliant editorial manager Thalia Proctor; and to all the unsung heroes in contracts, accounts, distribution and more. I know how hard you all work to put my books into the hands of readers.

I'm grateful to Shana Drehs and Molly Waxman at Sourcebooks Landmark, in the US, and to all my overseas editors, who publish me with such care and enthusiasm.

The Clare Mackintosh Book Club continues to grow, and I love reading all your posts and emails. Thank you to Ella Chapman and Sam Suthurst for making my newsletters sparkle; to Lynda Tunnicliffe and Sarah Clayton for keeping the Facebook group under control; and to my book club community for all the recommendations, laughs and reviews. If you haven't yet joined, you'll find details at claremackintosh.com – I'd love to see you there.

Thank you to my agent at Curtis Brown, Sheila Crowley, and to Emily Harris and Sabhbh Curran; you're truly the best in the business. Thank you to my family, who let me escape to Lake Vyrnwy for a week between lockdowns, when I temporarily lost the ability to write; and to Ann-Marie and Rob for sharing the tranquillity of Glan-y-Gro.

And finally, thank you for reading this book. If you enjoyed it, I hope you'll leave a review, choose it for your book club, or recommend it to a friend. Word of mouth remains the best possible way to share stories, and I'd love you to share this one.